Synchronic

Edited by David Gatewood (www.lonetrout.com)
Cover art and design by Jason Gurley (www.jasongurley.com)
Print and ebook formatting by Polgarus Studio (www.polgarusstudio.com)

To those who live in the present
But wouldn't mind an escape now and then

STORY SYNOPSES

The Santa Anna Gold *(Michael Bunker)*
A father tries to help his son—the only family member he has left—pursue his interest in finding the legendary Santa Anna Gold. The only problem is: the boy wants to go back in time in order to locate it. Sometimes the things a father will do for an only child are limitless.

Corrections *(Susan Kaye Quinn)*
Time traveling through murderers' minds to prevent the crimes that landed them on Death Row? This is what psychologist Ian Webb lives for. But his training with the Department of Corrections, along with fifteen successfully resolved cases, is of little help when the original timeline proves to be nothing like the court records show. The past can only be changed so much, and pushing it too far won't just fail to prevent a murder—it might erase his patient from the timeline altogether.

Hereafter *(Samuel Peralta)*
Cpl. Caitlyn McAdams returns home from war, back to her family and the life she knew—but she doesn't return whole. How can she forget the man she left behind—a man she'd met only once before—a casualty of a roadside bomb, dying in front of her? And then, one day, he comes back.

Reentry Window *(Eric Tozzi)*
Space exploration is dead and buried. But a strange atmospheric anomaly on Mars single-handedly resurrects the program, giving birth to the first manned mission to the Red Planet. For astronaut Brett Lockwood it's a dream come true. A chance to make history. But what he discovers is a window through time that will change the entire course of space exploration—decades before he was ever born.

The Swimming Pool of the Universe *(Nick Cole)*
War, remembrance and a grenade play havoc with the time machine we all carry inside ourselves as Private Dexter Keith battles alien spiders on the surface of a spinning asteroid beyond the edge of the solar system.

The River *(Jennifer Ellis)*
Destroyed by guilt and sorrow over a childhood mistake, Sarah Williams lives alone and buries her grief in long-distance running and triathlons. But when Sarah's running partner invents a time travel device, Sarah is determined to change her past, even if it means living twice—and betraying the man she loves.

A Word in Pompey's Ear *(Christopher G. Nuttall)*
To Julia, a young student of the Roman Empire, the past seems a realm of missed opportunities. But when she is sent back in time to meet Pompey the Great, she discovers that changing history may not be as easy as it seems.

Rock or Shell *(Ann Christy)*
Everyone wishes they could change something in their past. Whether it's taking back that embarrassing comment at an office party, or going back to save a life lost too soon, we all wish for the impossible at least once. But when too many people are given that power—and no ability to control their fleeting thoughts of change—what happens is more than chaos. It could be the end.

The Mirror *(Irving Belateche)*
Peter Cooper sells the past for a living. He started out as a poor boy from Indiana and now he's a successful antique dealer in Manhattan. But he's about to find out that there's more to the past than inanimate objects. Sometimes the past refuses to die.

Reset *(MeiLin Miranda)*
Sandy's best friend Catherine changed when she turned sixteen. She withdrew from life, and spent all her time drawing pictures of seven children she said would never exist. Thirty-four years later, Sandy finds out why.

The Laurasians *(Isaac Hooke)*
Horatio Horace, paleontologist extraordinaire, discovers that time travel isn't all it's cracked up to be—when he comes face to face with the living and breathing versions of the fossils he has studied his entire life. And they are hungry.

The First Cut *(Edward W. Robertson)*
In the future, there are many parallel Earths. Only one of them has time travel. Known as Primetime, its criminals break into the pasts of other worlds, far beyond the reach of conventional police. Blake Din is the newest graduate of the agency tasked with stopping them, but he's already on the verge of washing out. And now, one of his fellow recruits has just gone rogue.

The Dark Age *(Jason Gurley)*
On the day she was born, he left for the stars. He watches her grow up on screens. Misses her first words, her first steps. She's never kissed his scratchy cheek, or fallen asleep on his shoulder. He's never wiped away her tears, or sung her to sleep. Now she's a toddler, and the crew of the *Arecibo* is about to enter hibernation sleep for one hundred and fifty years. And when he wakes, his family will be gone.

CONTENTS

Foreword
by Nick Cole

Time.

The great human enemy. Maybe the greatest. It's beaten everyone so far. The scoreboard doesn't lie:

Time: an immense, incalculable number
Us: 0

Forget Caesar and Alexander the Great, and while you're at it, name any empire: time's beaten them all. It's beating us every day. That thing we meant to do goes undone again, and we tell ourselves, "Tomorrow. Tomorrow I'll get it done. Tomorrow I'll do that thing I've always meant to do. Tomorrow I'll live my life, but right now I've got something more important to do." Don't we always find ourselves there, undone and too late? Our chance has slipped away, again, and eventually it's forever and we've never managed to do all the things we meant to do. What did Shakespeare's Macbeth say about time? I think it was something like:

> To-morrow, and to-morrow, and to-morrow,
> Creeps in this petty pace from day to day,
> To the last syllable of recorded time;
> And all our yesterdays have lighted fools
> The way to dusty death. Out, out, brief candle!
> Life's but a walking shadow, a poor player,
> That struts and frets his hour upon the stage,
> And then is heard no more. It is a tale
> Told by an idiot, full of sound and fury,
> Signifying nothing.
>
> — *Macbeth*, Act 5, Scene 5

Rough stuff. Time and consequences are inevitable.

But wait…

Along come a bunch of crazy science fiction writers saying, "Wait a minute. Not so fast." Scribbling, they cry their warnings, out of both sides of their mouths (or on the same sheets of paper, to be more precise): "Maybe we can conquer time."

Crazy, huh?

They said that about the bottom of the sea—and, oh yeah, the moon also. They said we could go there if first we dreamed. But c'mon, we've never been to those places.

So why the time travel fantasy? I think it has something to do with our desire to get it right, our very human desire to avoid the critical mistakes. To take a vacation in the mysterious kingdom of WhatMightHaveBeen. We all do it. We do it on Mondays as we drive to work. We ask ourselves what that other road, the road less traveled (we say, as we turn into the place we'll be going to for the foreseeable future) might have looked like. What if we'd done this, or what if we'd said that other thing?

That's a very human question. If you ever feel all alone in the world and much different than the company you find yourself in, simply remember that everyone in the room has felt that way and asked those questions of themselves at some point in their lives. Every so often you meet the guy who worked at Google way back when and quit because it seemed like they were wasting time cataloguing this thing called the Internet. Besides, they weren't paying much at the time. Who knew?

If not Google, then it's the someone who claims to have invented the hula hoop or male hairspray. The millions almost made—if only.

What we're saying is that, if we could master time, why, things might be quite different. Very different indeed. We'd probably be a lot more successful and much happier. That's what we like to tell ourselves. Sadly, that doesn't make for good science fiction. No. Those same writers who've promised us it might be possible to leap around in time like Golden Retrievers down at the lake haven't done much to ensure us that we'll be happier in doing so. In fact, more often than not they warn us that we'll make things much, much worse. Far worse. We'll step on a butterfly and wipe out Van Gogh or some such.

Who knows?

But there's a time machine inside all of us. In fact, maybe we *are* that time machine. Moving forward, exploring the future. Able to go back and relive the good moments—and even sometimes make peace with the bad. Perhaps, in some very safe way (compared to actual time travel and all its quantum trap doors), we're just trying to *get it right*. And maybe we should just leave it at that. Maybe memory is enough of a time machine.

So we've written these stories about Time Travel. I've read them, and I want to warn you about some of them first. I want to warn you that you're not going to like some of them. These stories won't encourage you to finish your degree in physics and get cracking on that time machine you'd like to build out in the garage. They won't inspire you to return to the past and confess that unconfessed love to the someone that got away. To bet big on Google, or Secretariat, or even George Lucas. No, these stories more often than not are going to break your heart and leave a giant gaping hole in your dreams of going back and learning to play the guitar—of touring with Zeppelin.

Time's a dangerous place. Always has been. Remember when I said it was undefeated? So far, it still is. You'll find out when you read "Hereafter" by Samuel Peralta. I just wept when I put that one down. He's captured the heartbreak of humanity and time travel, and unlocked why it might not be a good thing to go messing around back there. And then again, maybe love hurts no matter what. And maybe, Samuel reminds us, maybe it's also worth it, too.

"Reset" by MeiLin Miranda deftly dispels the illusion of the time travel fantasy of youth, wisdom, and the chance to do it all again and again until you get it right. She, too, breaks your heart with a beautiful take on the saddest words of all: "what might have been."

"The Dark Age" is a very personal gift from Jason Gurley. It's about him and his daughter. Someone once posited intelligent space travel and the ability to know it when we see it out there in the big dark that is the Universe, by the phrase, "you shall know us by our velocity." Jason Gurley shows us that time, speed and distance, even on a galactic scale, are insignificant compared to love and its power to reach out into the unknown.

In "Rock or Shell" by the talented Ann Christy, we tackle the philosophical mindtrap that emerges when the genie in the bottle—the wish-fulfillment ability that mastery of time travel would enable—is potentially extended to all of us. Except, as she wickedly points out, not everyone wants to erase the mistakes they've made. And some might want to just go ahead and erase everything.

Michael Bunker tells us that time travel's all in your head in "The Santa Anna Gold," his brilliant and classic homage to the time-looting adventure (and a clever and perception-bending tale). The problem with metaphysical time travel, as he points out, is you might get trapped there. The exact meaning of "there" being up for debate and for you, the reader, to decide.

Jennifer Ellis's "The River" takes us on a clever, complex, and desperate journey down time's flow as she steers this tale of fractured lives like a master guide shooting the rapids of quantum theory and boldly confronting the terminal waterfall that is the "should we?" of time travel.

"The First Cut" by Edward W. Robertson is a gritty time-cop drama with all the taut tension of a great Saturday night noir. I can easily see this as the beginning of a series, and there isn't a publisher who should pass up a chance to lock down a six-book deal on this fully realized and interesting milieu of crime and time.

Christopher Nuttall, in "A Word in Pompey's Ear," displays an awesome grasp of history and shows us that despite hindsight, victory is not assured, even if you know how all the cards are dealt. Rich history and theoretical musings offer a well-crafted romp through the birth of imperial Rome, guided by a gifted author.

If you liked *Jurassic Park*, then you're going to love Isaac Hooke's dash through the prehistoric in "The Laurasians." It's a feat he pulls off quite capably with both wit and terror, all of it based on a *Choose Your Own Adventure* he read as a boy. I'd love to see what he might do with *The Mystery of Chimney Rock* or *Deadwood City* or even *The Third Planet from Altair.*

In Susan Kaye Quinn's "Corrections" we find out that time travel and therapy might just be the answer to society's problems. If only someone were there to help you, way back when, to make the right choice, why, everything might be just as awful. This is an excellent short story that almost feels like a procedural, and I can easily see this as a full-length, genre-spanning novel for a very damaged main character.

In "Reentry Window" by Eric Tozzi we find—and I'm just going to be vague here because the story is sublimely brilliant; you'll see in the last moments—that the best explorers are truly intrepid, even understanding the potential of discovery to revolutionize cultural zeitgeist.

"The Mirror" is one of those stories that feels like a classic. I think Irving Belateche has pulled the ultimate time travel stunt right here in front of us all by writing tomorrow's classic time-travel/cursed-bauble tale for today's anthology. I think you'll enjoy it, unless you're afraid of antiques, and then, well, you might really enjoy it.

So there we have it, twelve tales of time travel. Oh, and I wrote a little something too. A military sci-fi time travel story that I'm hoping you'll like as much as the others.

Should we? Shouldn't we? These masterful stories might just help you make up your mind, so when that dark stranger steps out of the alley and offers you the chance to go back…

To make things right…

To find the gold and get rich quick…

Well, I don't know what you'll do. Just be very careful. Time's a tough opponent.

> *For all sad words of tongue or pen,*
> *The saddest are these: "It might have been!"*
> — John Greenleaf Whittier

The Santa Anna Gold
by Michael Bunker

I REALLY DID HAVE A SON. No matter what they tell you today, him gone and them all acting like he never did exist. My daughters died young. Car wreck, back before all this happened, and not long after their momma went away and then got the cancer and died. But, like I said, that was before I got put in here. The way it is now, it's like I never had any children at all.

My boy was named Richard. Richard Henry Smalton. He was named after his great-uncle on his mother's side. He was born in early 1997, right on our big bed in the cottage down by the creek. We lived off the grid just north of the Santa Anna Mountains. *Completely* off the grid. No electricity or conveniences at all. Say that too loud now'days and they'll lock you right up and throw away the key. Had our babies at home, too. We didn't get birth certificates or vaccinations or social security numbers because we don't believe in those things. That's our right, and we didn't feel like we needed to burden our children with government before they could make up their own minds what contracts they wanted to enter into and such. I didn't want my boy drafted into Uncle Sam's wars, so he grew up and lived the pure and good life like we all did, and no one was the wiser.

I can tell you exactly when the story started too, or when things changed, back before all this went sideways and I got put in here forever—or until I change my mind (at least that's what they say). It started when my boy—We called him Rick—got interested in the legend of the Santa Anna Gold. But first I have to tell you the story of the gold, or else none of the rest of this'll make sense.

To most people the gold was only a legend, and the stories had been told and re-told to anyone who ever did move to Coleman County. Not that many people move to Coleman County, though. Most folks just die off or move away. High schools in this county pump out graduates who leave skid marks gettin' out of here. Population of the county has dropped precipitously since the early 1930's or so. But when folks do move here—usually ranchers or city-dwelling cattlemen, but sometimes homesteaders like ourselves—someone eventually gets around to telling them all about the Santa Anna Gold.

The great historian J. Frank Dobie wrote about it, and we found bits and pieces of the story, sometimes with all the elements changed about all scattershot-like, in lots of different histories of the area. We bought books written by locals that couldn't be bought or had anywhere else unless you knew who to go to in order to get them. Dobie shared a story from a man by the name of J. Leeper Gay, who shared the legend as it was told to him by a Mexican, who claimed it was told to him by his grandfather down in Sonora, Mexico. But just because a story has a long and twisty path don't make it not true.

I'll try to make the story short, because before long they'll be by here to make me take pills, hoping I'll forget my own flesh-n-blood boy or change my mind that I ever had one in the first place. No pill I ever took could do that, but they give 'em to me anyway. Even after I showed 'em the picture that proved me right. That's what tells me they're probably with the government. They took the picture away too, but I kept an extra that they don't know nothin' about. They go to great lengths to convince me I'm nuts. Sometimes I laugh at what they come up with.

Anyway, there are lots of different stories of where the gold came from. Some say it was gold brought down from Colorado, or even the Seven Cities of Cibola or some nonsense like that. Others say it was gold carried along with the Spanish military—used to pay the soldiers as they tried to tame Texas during the time of the Spanish colonization.

Most of the stories agree that the gold came out of the San Saba mines, and that a large load of it was stolen from the Spanish miners by an Indian raid. In turn—the best stories say—the Spanish outfitted a cavalry unit and sent them far up north—maybe as far as Colorado—to search for the stolen gold. This particular cavalry unit raided an Indian village and killed almost everyone there, and in the ashes and ruin of the camp (the story goes), the Spanish found a large sack full of gold dust and coins (although some say it was up to a wagonload of gold ore) in one of the teepees.

11

Having gained the prize, the unit was pulling back with the bounty and heading south, when the surrounding Indian forces counterattacked. The Spanish cavalry fought bravely and continued to retreat, taking losses, slowly making for their forts and bases to the south, fighting their way along as they were constantly harassed and attacked from the rear. The attacks became fiercer and more violent, and it came to pass that the Spanish got to thinkin' they'd never make it back to Mexico at all. The Rio Grande might as well have been the river Jordan or heaven's own pearly gates as far as they were concerned.

Nearly a month had passed since the Spanish had stolen the gold back, and the raiders were making very slow progress down southward. At last they came to the twin mesas of the "Santa Anna Mountains" in an area that is now called Coleman County, in central Texas. My home. These mesas I can see from my window today, they're not named after the Mexican emperor, but instead after an Indian war chief named Santana who ruled from here. Santana sure 'nuff met future president James Polk one time, but that's a whole 'nother story.

Well, when the Spanish came near to the Santa Anna Mountains, they made camp at a creek not far from the twin mesas. I make that creek out to be Mud Creek to the north, or maybe Home Creek to the south. Coulda been any number of other creeks though, since many were runnin' back then and most of 'em are dried up now. That evening, they received word that a large force of Indians was bearin' down on 'em. A scout was sent to spy out the enemy from the peak of one of the twin mesas, but he'd not returned by darkfall, so the commander of the cavalry ordered his men to douse their fires, entrench themselves, and prepare for battle.

Around midnight or thereabouts, the scout finally returned with the report that the attack was coming—he knew not how soon—and that the opposing force was so large that all was expected to be lost. That's a mighty scary story right there—in and of itself—but then to lose the gold again after all that'd already been lost... well, for the Spanish officers, it was too much to stomach.

Now, traveling with this Spanish force was a black man—a slave brought up from deep in Mexico to serve the Spanish cavalry. He was a strong man, and he'd become a handy guide for the Spanish officers on their way around Texas. The Spanish commander ordered the black man and two weary soldiers to carry away the gold in secret—"half a day's ride," it's said—and to bury it so the Indians could never reclaim it.

According to the legend—and in this one detail it seems that all the old legends agree—the gold was buried on top of a hill, under a large flat rock. On the rock, the men inscribed three M's, so that it could be located again when necessary.

The three men returned to their unit just as the Indians made their final attack. In that battle, every member of the Spanish force was killed or captured, and the prisoners were— each and every one of 'em—put to death by burning... all except for the black guide, who alone was left alive and kept as a slave by the Indians.

After many years of torture and mistreatment at the hands of the Indians, the black man escaped his tormentors and fled back into Mexico. He was the lone survivor of the Spanish raiders, and the only one—it is believed—who held the secret in his bosom as to the whereabouts of the Santa Anna Gold.

Deep in Mexico, the man was shunned by the superstitious Mexicans as cursed, except for the many sojourners who would travel there to attempt to coax from him the location of the buried gold. He, however, believed that it was the *gold* that was cursed and not himself, and refused to disclose its exact whereabouts, other than in the very general sense I have related to you here in this story.

According to legend, the gold has never been found.

But legend has a way of not always being the whole truth. I know, because my son, Richard Henry Smalton, musta found that gold—even if he didn't go dig it out—and because of this, he's no longer with me. He's gone over... or gone back... and I'm here alone with the tale. I didn't believe in time travel then, no sir, but I do now.

In a way, I'm brother to this brave black man who buried the gold at the first. We two keep the secret, but for different reasons. He kept it by not tellin' it, because he believed the gold was accursed. I don't share that opinion, since "luck" or "curses" don't have legs or eyes or any science to them. *I* hold the secret by tellin' it, and tellin' guarantees it'll *stay* secret, because no one will believe it. All told, the end's the same. We both hold gold in our bosom as a secret no one knows in our lives but us.

Now I'm going to tell the rest of the story, but since I can't be believed (on account of them sayin' I'm crazy), it'll be just like I told no one.

* * *

My son got on to the story of the gold and he couldn't let go of it. He wasn't a covetous boy—actually a young man of fifteen years when this happened—but he was a curious one and smart as can be. "If no one found the gold," he said, "then it has to still be out there."

Believe me, I argued with him. "If I found it, I wouldn't tell no one," I said. "And I'm probably not the only one thinks that announcing I found millions in gold to the whole wide world is a bad idea."

"Don't mean it was found," he'd say.

"What would you do with it if you found it?" I asked.

"Don't know that I'd do anything with it," he said. "I may not even dig it up at all. I'd just know the story was true."

I argued again, because I don't see sense in findin' gold you're just plannin' to leave there, but he said, "History's about finding out what happened and what's true," and that was that as far as he was concerned.

So he went about trying to verify the story. On his own time. He'd search the Internet and he'd go to libraries, and eventually his interest got me hip-deep involved too. He and I would go to book and estate sales—especially those held to sell off the goods of folks who've lived in this county a long time. Young folks don't want books, so they sell 'em off for pennies as soon as their folk die off. Now I say readin' books is the best form of time travel, but that's an argument for another day.

Then one day Rick came upon a mention in a small Internet forum posting about the Santa Anna Mountains. He came to me and we tried to reason it out.

He said this to me—

"An old man, close to dying up in Canada, has posted his story on the Internet, and I think it may be of importance."

"What'd he say?" I asked.

"Old man was a retired U.S. Marine, name of Joe Paul Scotland. He said he was born in Santa Anna, in the old Sealy Hospital back in 1933."

"I remember that hospital," I said. "I don't remember it personal-like because it was gone before we got here, but I remember pictures of it. It was built right up against the west mesa, and a lot of babies were born in that hospital."

So Rick tells me to hush for a minute while he keeps tellin' ol' man Scotland's tale.

It seems Mr. Scotland said he played on the twin mesas almost every day of his life, right up until he left Santa Anna when he was twenty years old. Knew them like the back of his own hand. He said that sometime around 1946 a company began mining the east end of the western mesa for silica sand, and in the process, likely ruined many priceless cave and wall paintings that existed in that area.

I quote here directly from the Internet posting of Mr. Joe Paul Scotland, Retired U.S.M.C. (from memory, of course):

On the North face of the caprock at approx 31 deg, 44 min, 50.08 sec North and 99 deg, 44 min, 20.97 sec west (An area

referred to as an Indian holy place and/or Lover's Leap) were more
relief carvings:

    a) A stylized Indian Swastika approx 18" x 18" (No
    wording)
    b) What appeared to be a "Bag" gathered and tied at
    the top approx 14" high and 10" wide (No wording)
    c) Several "Doves Flying" (No wording)

The local legend intimated that the "Bag" represented treasure
and the direction of the flight of the doves represented the location
of the treasure. (I never did find it!)

So my boy becomes convinced that the gold was still in its
place back in 1946 when the silica company destroyed the cave
paintings (despite the fact that I told him that his story was not
necessarily true) and that the paintings were a clue as to the
whereabouts of the gold. Rick said that the "bag gathered and
tied at the top" musta been the gold. He then determined that
the "doves flying" represented the distance and direction one
must go to find the gold.

I asked Rick what the Indian swastika could have meant,
and he said he didn't rightly know. Said it sometimes
represented legend or mysteries for the Navajo, and that for
some others it was a sign of spirit healing. In order to blend it
into his theory though, Rick assumed that the swastika was a
sign that a mystery was being revealed in these paintings.

Now, none of that followed for me. What I mean to say is
that logic didn't demand any of it, and I told Rick so, but he
became convinced. Beyond convinced. Further, he was certain
that the gold would only be found in one of two ways. First,

by accident. Someone would be digging or excavating and would come upon the gold by pure luck alone. Second, by miraculous find or else by time travel. Someone would have to either go back in time and read those wall paintings and then see the direction of the doves flyin' and figure it out from there... or... perhaps miraculously find more clues in another as-yet-undiscovered book or letter from the time, tellin' more about the cave paintings and the evidence.

I told Rick that time travelin' was a fantasy (and back then I believed that), so he could just knock that option out right from the get-go, but he disagreed. Told me Einstein proved that time travel was possible. Had me read some books by Mr. Jack Finney that were fiction, but that talked about how Einstein conceived that time travel might happen in a very weird concurrence of events. So I read the Finney books, and here is the gist of what they say...

So, according to Einstein (Finney says), time is more like a river that flows along, and the only reason we sense it passing is because we're like bein' on a boat on that river. So you pass a tree and then it's behind you, and unless you get off the boat or find some other method to do so, you can't go back to that tree you saw awhile ago. But (and this is the trick) everything you've passed in time is still back there. Still just like it was. That tree is still back there and always will be. So just by gettin' off the boat, you think you've traveled in time, when in reality you just got off and stayed in one moment of it. None of it makes sense to me, I'm just tellin' you the way it was explained in the books.

Finney went on to describe a method of time travel that he believed would actually work. First, you have to disconnect yourself from the millions of little threads of reality that grasp you and hold you in your boat (in your present time, moving forward). These threads are all realities in the time you belong in, not in the time way back before they existed. And get this (since we were talkin' about trees): when you see a tree every day, its growth and passage through the seasons is part of it bein' in the boat of time with you. You're movin' together to the future. But say you wanted to see that tree when it was still a sapling! You'd have to get off the boat of time and go visit it back where it was, and not where it is in the mobile now ("mobile now" is my phrase, not Finney's). In a tree's growth and maturity, it's a thread holding you into the mobile now too.

So the threads belong to a point in time (or to the mobile now), and you have to sever all those, even in your brain, so's you can go back to another time. Next, you got to immerse yourself in the time you want to be in. Everything has to be perfect. You have to have the right dress, the right money, the right environment. It all has to be just right. Now, even if you can do these two things, and even if you can get your mind convinced completely, only a tiny percentage of the population could ever do it. If the person's mind isn't suggestible enough to make the leap, they won't ever go. The tiny threads of the mobile now in their minds will hold them in the boat, so to speak.

But... if someone can do these things... if someone can totally immerse themselves in the time they want to visit, and they can really believe they are sometime else… then they can do it. So let's say you wanted to visit the Alamo back in the day of the great fight there. You'd have to go down to San Antonio, be in the proper garb, sneak into the building (maybe at night), block out any sound at all that ain't right for the time (traffic, radios, et cetera), and totally immerse yourself to the point that you really, actually believe you're in the Alamo. Then, if everything goes right and you're one of the people that can do it, you can just step out into that world and be in that time, because all the threads that hold you into your place in the universe are from that period. Now, you might step out of the Alamo in the middle of the battle, or maybe you're a few weeks, months, or years too early or late. But the theory is that you can do it, and Rick firmly believed this theory to be true.

"You gotta have the right kind of mind to go back," Rick said. "The reading kind of mind. Able to get into the story."

Which is why he set his mind to going back to 1910 or so, when Santa Anna was first being founded as a full-fledged town. He wanted to go back so he could climb that mesa, find those cave drawings, and figure out where to go hunt for that Santa Anna Gold.

* * *

The first thing he did was gather up the right clothing and other paraphernalia he thought he'd need. He studied the time like he was lookin' at something in a microscope. He went to museums and talked to experts. We cashed in a bunch of our savings (I wasn't a believer in time travel then, but I wanted to encourage my boy to take risks and be interested in something other than his own self all the time), then we bought clothes for both of us: shoes, the right woolen pants, everything with period buttons and thread. Nothing could be amiss. They couldn't be replicas—they had to be the real thing. We even bought money for our pockets, and wind-up watches and combs for our hair, all what belonged to the era.

Next, we found a cabin down on Home Creek that was there in 1910 and hasn't changed since then. It was kept up for most of the last thirty years by the local high school history department working with the historical society, but when the economy collapsed in '08 the thing got shuttered and mostly abandoned. Weren't enough money to keep it up right.

We cased the place for weeks, makin' sure it wasn't just boarded up temporary-like, and once we were convinced it was abandoned, we moved in. We opened the place up, then set ourselves to making it all perfect. We removed any locks, hinges, knobs, and what-not that weren't from the right period. Fixed the place up right—basically refurbished it using all original materials. We switched out the beds that were in the place (they were replicas, put there by students in order to impress tourists who never showed up) with right proper beds from the first decade of the twentieth century. We even filled the cottage with food that was preserved and stored up just right. We took the period food out of its packages and stored it in old tin and copper cans we bought at auction from the right time period. We had old, cured bacon, and jars of oil and flour for biscuits too. We had access to a water pump or water from the creek, but we found out they had powdered milk back in that day, so we bought up some o' that and put it in glass jars up in the cabinets.

There was one problem with this plan, and I guess I should mention it now. If the plan worked (and I had no reason to believe that it would), then we might wake up in the cabin back in 1910, and there would likely be people livin' there. Rick and I discussed this, but he said, "I don't know what to do about that except worry about it when it happens." And since I figured it would never work anyways, I just said, "Okay, then."

Once we knew the place was perfect, that's when the experiment started. For weeks we tried our best to sever all our ties to our old world. During the day we'd immerse ourselves in period books and magazines. We'd play games from the time, and read old newspapers and magazines we'd bought online. We made sure it was all just right. No modern staples or stickers or any repairs made from the twenty-first century. We tried to govern our talk so that we didn't even use modern colloquialisms at all. But… I got to tell you that, all told, none of it seemed to work. We'd wake up and go outside in the early morning dew, and we'd see an airplane contrail in the sky, or hear the truck traffic way up on the highway, and we'd know we failed.

Truth be told, I think it was all startin' to affect me a little in the head. Not that I'm crazy like they say, because that's all a scam by the government (I propose). But it was gettin' to me. I was having very realistic dreams of being in the past. In one of those dreams, I was up at the old Sealy Hospital (which I'd never seen with my own eyes), and it was as real as real can be. I walked in the place after midnight and just looked around. I had to hide from a few of the night nurses doin' rounds, but except for a locked-up part way in the back they used for crazy folk, I could see everything. The moonlight and the windows were all just right, and I could open up cabinets and look at the medicine bottles, and I ain't never had any other dreams so perfect as those in all my life.

I know it might be getting things out of order and the cart before the horse and all that, but I have to say here that I think the government is behind all this. I think either they took the gold back in 1946, or they've been lookin' for it ever since. I think with all their NSA email spying and their scanning our search terms and following our every move, they figured out that Rick and I were gettin' close to figuring out what happened to that gold. Maybe they thought the Spanish government or the Indians would be wantin' that gold back. I don't know the reasons, but it's important that you have in the back of your mind that I think the government was watchin' us and plannin' things all along. Of course, the doctors here will tell you, "That's exactly what a crazy person would say." But I didn't know they'd be watchin' us during that whole time when Rick and I were doing our best to make everything in our lives lined up perfect with the year 1910.

And this is how it went for weeks. Rick never did get tired of it all, but sometimes I did. The night dreams of being in the past were gettin' more intense, and during the day sometimes my mind would go the other way and flash forward to things like hamburgers and hot showers, but I was usually able to subdue those thoughts and get back into character.

Then one day it happened. Not for me, though. It happened for Rick. I woke up and he was gone. And that was the day everything changed.

* * *

I knew Rick wasn't kidnapped and that he hadn't run back to the modern times. Not unless the government got him. But if they did, there'd be no sense in making me think he never existed. No, I don't believe they got him, or that he quit neither. He was too in love with this idea, and he was really convinced it was going to work. That's what convinced me it *did* work, because he believed in it so much, it had to have worked for him.

One day, before we started the experiment, Rick told me that there was no difference between what he wanted to try, and getting really deeply into a good book or story. He said, "The better you can get into it as a reader, the more real it becomes." I said, "Yes, I'll have to agree with that." So he says, "Well then, logically—there has to be a point where you get *so* into it, that it *does* become real. That's a logical conclusion from what you say you agreed to."

"I don't know about that," I said. And I really didn't.

And now I have to tell you about my dream that night. The night before Rick went back to the past.

I dreamed (for some reason) that I was up near the Sealy Hospital. That was usually where my dreams took me. It was 1933 and that old man, Joe Paul Scotland, was just days born (in the dream) up in the hospital. I went in just after midnight,

24

like usual, and I went to see where the baby was sleepin' in his crib in the nursery. There was a sign on the end of the wrought-iron crib that said "newborn male," and some instructions about feeding him. There was no name, and he was the only baby in the nursery, but somehow I just know it had to be Joe Paul Scotland since he's the only child I ever read about being born in that hospital. After I saw the baby, I was hoping I'd wake up and be back in my bed in the cabin down by Home Creek, but I didn't wake for a long time. So I ended up walking all the way back. *Real* walkin', not dream walkin'. My feet started hurting, and I was pourin' out sweat after a while.

It was the most realistic dream I can ever remember. In the dream, I was really back in 1933. But then it got weird. In my walk home, I wasn't in 1933, but in 1910. At some point, the dream switched (like dreams do), and when I actually got into the heart of town, it had to be 1910 that I was seein'.

It was dark out, and I walked through the town and saw some of it like it must have been back then. It looked like it was still horse-and-buggy days, for the most part, and the main street through town was still dirt. I saw the Stockard building (which we today call the "Opry House") and from what I could tell it was still the W. R. Kelly building because there was a "Dry Goods" sign pretty prominent on the face of it. A new-looking Ford automobile was parked next to the building, but the ruts and horse manure in the road told me that most folks were getting around by horse and wagon.

I walked right in front of the S. H. Phillips Drug Store and the S. J. Pieratt's Quality Store right next to it (they were housed in the same building, and Pieratt was Santa Anna's first mayor). I remembered these places somewhat from pictures Rick and I studied from 1910 out of Ralph Terry's book, *Looking Backwards*, that had a lot of pictures from the time. That's how I figure the images got in my mind. But what I saw in this dream was so real that it scared me. I could even look in the window of Pieratt's and see clothing on wooden hangers and pink and yellow ladies' dresses readied up for Easter.

It was a strange dream, me switching times from the 30's and then back to the 1910's. But I can't explain it any other way. Of course, I never saw the outside of the hospital. The Sealy Hospital that got built in the 1920's was the only one I knew about. And the dreams started once I was inside, so I understand now that I can't be sure of the "when" of all of it..Anyway, I headed south and walked right by the Meador and Erwin Transfer business, which (from what I can tell) must have been like a moving company is today. There were five heavy-duty horse-drawn wagons lined up next to the business office, all with hanging signs that said "for hire" on them.

Before long I was out of town, and I walked for hours until I came to Home Creek, then made my way down until I came upon the little cottage we'd borrowed. In the dream I went inside and collapsed onto the bed, and was so tired I thought I might sleep for days.

Anyway, I awoke that next mornin' before dawn. Early it was—musta been near four or five in the morning. It was quite dark, and I had to pee, so I stumbled outside to do my business. When I was finished, I went back in and tried to find

Rick, but that's when I realized he was gone. His bed was empty, and it was like he'd slept pretty roughly that night—the blankets all thrown about and hanging on the floor. The sun hadn't come up full yet, so I couldn't see much, but it wasn't long before sunrise and I could see the pink-orange glow off to the east, just coming through the trees here and there.

But here I was, walking around the whole area, lookin' for my boy... and he was sure enough gone. Gone as can be. And now I was stuck waiting and hoping he'd be able to come back once he figured out where the gold was buried. So I sat on the step and waited and waited, hoping he'd make his way back.

As I said before, I never believed he would make it, so I went along with his plan even though I didn't expect it would come to much. And the plan was this. He was going to go see if he could find the gold, and if he could, then *where* he found it would determine what he did next. If it was in a location where he thought it would remain unmolested until the future (our time), he'd just remember the place and come on back home to get me (our real home, up north of Santa Anna, not our temporary and borrowed cottage on Home Creek). He should be able to do this at any time, and from any location, by merely grasping hold of the modern times in his mind... reattaching those silken threads of the mobile now, until he could open his eyes and be back in the real time. We never even asked ourselves if this plan would work. We just assumed that it would. That just goes to show you that we weren't thinking things through completely.

If it turned out that the gold was someplace where it obviously was going to be found (like buried right up there in the caves on the Santa Anna Mountains where the silica company was digging as early as 1917), then he'd find a way to remove the gold and bury it somewhere else.

Rick kept reminding me that he wasn't interested in getting the gold for himself, but I have to admit that I was interested even if he wasn't.

I never went back inside the cabin. I would have, but I never made it back in there. I didn't figure Rick would go back there anyway, since it was very probable that people lived in that place in 1910, but my intentions became immaterial pretty soon after the sun came up. I was gettin' up from the step and thinkin' about walking back up to Santa Anna just as the light of day started illuminating my surroundings, and that's when a couple of men rushed at me and knocked me down. They were screamin' at me this and that but I couldn't make out what they were sayin' on account of their accents were so thick and they were so plumb angry. They beat me godawful bad and then tied me up and dragged me over to a flat-bed. When they threw me into the back of it I hit my head and went unconscious.

I figure this is when the government took over. It was on the day when Rick went back in time. They'd been watchin' the place, no doubt, and when they saw me lookin' for Rick I figure they knew the jig was up. So they grabbed me and locked me up in this place.

The rest of the story you know. Though I suspect I can fill in some of the gray places if I have enough time.

They'll tell you that the building I'm in is the old, wooden hospital in Santa Anna, and that the concrete and steel Sealy Hospital is just in the planning stages. They'll tell you that the nurses at first thought this old hospital was haunted because they'd seen a man walking pretty-as-you-please around the place after midnight some nights—but then they got worried and reported it to the constable after the man was seen in the nursery, looking down at a newborn baby boy someone dropped off there for adoption.

They'll say that I broke into the Walkers' cabin down by Home Creek while the Walker sons were off one morning fishing, and that I'm a drifter and I talk about crazy things like airplanes and the Internet and fast-food joints and rocket ships going to the moon and computers that you can hold in your hand and talk with anyone else in the world. They'll say to me that these things haven't been invented, and that I'm a danger to society.

They've gone to great lengths to shut me up. Using old-timey syringes to give me shots, and lighting oil lanterns when it's dark or gray outside. Them all wearing period clothes and making me write with a pen that has to be filled with ink from a bottle. Mocking me while I stare out this back window full of bars at the west mesa of the Santa Anna Mountains. They even muted the walls with insulation or some such thing so I never do hear the airplanes fly over or the trucks rumbling up Highway 84 all day and night.

Nah, they'll just say I'm crazy. That's why I have to take my pills, and why they try to convince me I never did have a boy named Richard Henry Smalton who went back in time and musta found the Santa Anna Gold.

A Word from Michael Bunker

Time travel has long been one of my favorite genres. I suppose I love the concept of time travel because, as a writer, the conceit of traveling through time is one of the greatest tools ever invented for portraying vivid portraits in the mind of the reader. It allows us to show the reader that ideas have consequences, to emphasize the necessity of thinking generationally, and to reinforce the very real fact that history (and the future) are not only different epochs, but different worlds altogether.

Ever since I first stumbled upon a Jack Finney story, I've loved a well-told time-travel tale. The best stories are those that cause us to travel along with the protagonist, to see the story as if we are in it. When I read Jack Finney's *Time and Again* for the first time, I picked up on the subtext of what Finney was doing in the story. He constantly reiterated that "not everyone can do it." Time travel, that is. You have to be really willing to give yourself over to the process in order to travel. And this is true of Finney's books, too. Not everyone will "get" them. But if you can give yourself over wholly to the journey, you really can travel in time with an author.

That is what I want to accomplish when I write a story. I'm not there yet, and maybe I'll never get there, but I know that the best in literature—no matter the genre—accomplishes this one thing for those readers who give themselves over to it. It takes them on a journey through time and space and includes them in the story. It changes them, and through words alone grants them the ability to experience other worlds, other times, other lives.

I am so pleased to be involved in this anthology, and to be included in it with so many writers whom I know and admire. My closest friends know that I keep stacks of books next to my easy chair. In that stack *always* are all the books in my Jack Finney collection. I read and re-read them because they are all so good. I know that this anthology will be joining my Finney stack, and I'm so pleased to have been involved in the making of it. And I thank you all for reading!

Corrections
by Susan Kaye Quinn

Chapter One

MY PATIENT TWITCHES as he settles into his chair. They're always anxious, but the final session is especially difficult. Completely understandable, given it may result in his death. Or possibly his extinction, which may or may not be worse. But an overly nervous patient is twice as likely to fail to enter the procedure, and neither of us wants that. So I lead with something that will jar him from his anticipatory fears and focus him on the task at hand.

"So you've only committed the one murder, is that right, Owen?" I ask.

His twitches coalesce into a single jolt, like my therapy chair is wired for electroconvulsive treatments. But my question focuses those darting eyes on my face, just as I'd intended.

"I ain't killed no one, Dr. Webb."

Not the response I expected. And a bigger problem than I'd hoped for.

I give a calculated sigh. "Owen, you know the rules here. If you don't admit the crime, if there's no remorse, you're not eligible for the Shift."

I study him for a moment: the twitch is back, taking up residence in his hands. Owen's tall and lanky, with nervous-mouse eyes and a sprawl of prison tattoos up his pale arm. He's not as heavily inked as some who come through my door, probably because his time has been mostly on the Row. He hunches over, shoulders caving forward. He's protecting something—a secret—afraid I'll discover it when I travel back through his memories and step into his life at the exact moment a dozen years ago when he brutally murdered his friend. Like many inmates on Death Row, Owen maintained his innocence from the start... right up until he qualified for the Shift in lieu of the needle.

It pains me to see him regress back into denial.

I unfold my legs and straighten in my chair, opening my own posture in hopes that he'll mirror it. "Owen." I wait for him to look me in the eyes. It takes him a long moment, but he gets there. "You've been a model prisoner from the day you walked through the doors at San Quentin. You've admitted to the murder already. Even over our three sessions, I've seen you make progress in owning your responsibility for it. I know you wish it never happened. I know you want to fix this. Patients like you are the reason I'm in Corrections."

Which is only a half-truth: the full story is far more complicated and not something I would share with a patient.

But it *is* true that traveling back in time to stop these murders is almost the only thing I live for. My earnestness in wanting this to work is entirely genuine. "You want this, Owen, I know you do. And I want it for you. It's entirely normal to feel some last minute jitters, but we need you to set that aside in order for the procedure to work."

He takes a calming breath, like I taught him in the first session, in preparation for this one. It's a very good sign. "Okay, Dr. Webb."

"Please, call me Ian. Dr. Webb makes me feel like my father." It doesn't—my father is dead, and I don't feel like that, most of the time—but I'm hoping the familiarity and humor will help Owen relax.

"Ian, huh? What's that, like Irish?" He scratches the back of his neck, a self-soothing motion that seems to work. His shoulders relax a little.

"Scottish. Means pain in the arse. My mother gave it to me."

Owen snorts a laugh. His shoulders fall the rest of the way, and I allow myself an internal sigh of relief that wars a bit with the guilt that that particular lie raises up. *Iain is a lovely name. Why would you want to change it? If it was good enough for your grandfather, it's good enough for you.* My mother's voice rises from the grave to dig the knife of guilt a little deeper.

Owen's face holds the humor only for a moment, then falls back into seriousness. "It's just that... if you had a guy who *was* innocent... would that mess up the procedure? I mean, would that guy just... you know... disappear?"

35

Extinction. Not simply changing the man Owen was in the past, but erasing him altogether from that moment forward. It can happen: a possible price for traveling through time with the intent of changing its course. It's what keeps inmates from signing up for travel unless their lives are at stake.

As for Corrections, they only approve the Shift for capital crimes where the probability of recidivism is low. Serial killers don't qualify—they'll just kill again, so it's the needle for them. But even if they did qualify, they generally lack remorse, and it's already hard enough to land in the right memory even when the patient cooperates. Forcing travel simply doesn't work, no matter how much enhancer you pump through a murderer's body.

I've been quiet too long. "Extinction *can* happen, and you know the stats. But to answer your question, I've never traveled with an innocent man before. I honestly can't tell you what might happen, but I don't think the odds of extinction would go down. It could be the opposite."

Has Owen convinced himself he's innocent? His defense of being unconscious during the crime is consistent with extreme denial of a heinous event. There's even the possibility that he dissociated during the time of the murder, but I've seen no indication of dissociative tendencies during our sessions, and all of his workups have cleared him of any of the varieties of Dissociative Identity Disorder. Besides, those kinds of murderers usually get treatment. And don't land in my office.

Owen frowned. "But what do you think, doc? Would this innocent guy still get the tag?"

I decide to humor this fantasy a little longer, if it will keep him calm and ready him for the procedure. "Tagging is the first thing I do, once I'm back to the time of crime, so yes. One of the reasons you qualify for the Shift, Owen, is because there's a tattoo shop licensed for tag work near where your crime was committed. I'll go there first. If anything in the Shift sticks and actually changes the timeline, you'll have the tag."

He nods, like he expects this, and I'm glad he's accepting of at least this much. Even if we're successful, even if we can warp the timeline just enough to prevent the murder, but not enough to snap him out of it and send him to wherever inmates go when they extinguish... even then, he'll wear the seventeen-digit tag for the rest of his life. It will forever mark him as a would-be murderer: for society's protection, and as a condition of living a relatively free life.

"That's kind of a bum rap for that innocent guy," Owen says, but there's not too much grumble in his voice. "But life isn't fair, is it, doc?"

No. Life isn't even close to fair. Even though I spend all my time, energy, and a substantial risk to my mental health to nudge it just a little closer to fair each day.

But that's my issue, not Owen's.

"We can only play the cards we're dealt."

Owen nods, like this is some profound truth and not a platitude.

"How about we play the cards we have now?" I ask. "Are you ready to go back and fix the one thing you can actually change?" Technically, he won't be going back at all. Both our bodies will remain in my office, inert while I mentally travel back through his memories to try to change reality. His mind will remain in the present, asleep, just like during our practice sessions.

Owen takes a deep breath and lets it out slow. "Yeah. I think I'm ready."

I take a breath as well, calming my own jitters, a mixture of anxiety and that peculiar adrenaline surge that comes just before traveling through a murderer's mind. The dose of enhancer is already approved and prepared—I don't do that part, and that's probably for the best. Only the tight regulatory controls, the severe penalties for misuse, and the extreme probability that I would be caught before I could finish traveling actually keep me from making off with Owen's dose. The Department of Corrections does an extremely thorough job of screening psychologists who apply for the traveler program, but the temptation will always be there. Which is why a traveler never gets to touch the enhancer: a sort of check that keeps things in balance.

I tap on the datapad built into my chair to message the Corrections-trained nurse who has chain of custody over the enhancer. Owen and I are both quiet as the nurse steals into the room with quiet shoes and administers the injection. It takes several minutes for the enhancer to make Owen suggestible as well as pump up the reality-changing potential of his memories. It always strikes me as ironic that the drug was discovered during experiments to treat posttraumatic stress disorder. In that rogue scientist's quest to tame the flashbacks—those intense re-experiences of the past—with mind-altering chemicals, she actually did the reverse and allowed others, therapists like myself, to travel back and relive them for real.

Once the nurse leaves, I get up and stroll over to Owen's seat. He's already leaning back, easing into the body-conforming cushions as the enhancer starts to relax him.

"How are you doing, Owen?" I ask as I reach past him to activate the neural-link hologram in the headrest of his chair.

"Yeah, I'm okay, doc."

The blue spider-web hologram springs to life, surrounding Owen's head with a neural net. It's the final piece in the technology puzzle, the part that allows me access to Owen's mind, once he relaxes enough to let me in. The connection nodes buzz around in a constantly shifting pattern, matching up with the activity in his mind. I run a quick diagnostic using the control panel in the back of the seat, but all seems in order.

I return to my own chair, lean back, and activate my own neural net with the controller built into the armrest. Owen's net is just a reader, but mine is the kind that links up to the implant in my brain. Getting the implant was the first step in joining the Department of Corrections as a traveler. The thousand tiny neural filaments are delicate and don't always take—and even then, training the implant to work with the net to transmit the neural impulses of another person can be difficult. Not everyone makes it through the program, but people with high empathy factors and motivation, like me, have a higher success rate.

Owen has already closed his eyes. I take another calming breath, but it's really pointless. I'm already swimming in his anxiety.

"Whenever you're ready, Owen," I say, because I know he's waiting to hear it.

"Ready." His voice has a looseness to it, like his mouth isn't working quite right, and I can feel the relaxants taking hold.

"All right." My own heart rate picks up and wars with the artificial calm in Owen's. "We're going back to before you came to the office today. Before you woke up this morning. It's easy. Simple. A walk back through the days. Most of them are the same. Repetitious. We skip over those. We're floating back, seeing all of them flip by, days on a calendar, months at a time... and now years..."

The script is the same as our practice session, only then we were half-dosage on the enhancer and traveling on a strictly *look but don't touch* basis. Landing at a specific memory is a tricky business. It helps when the event stands out—like Owen's first day in court, or the day of the conviction—but memories aren't linear things, and pinning one down isn't as simple as looking up the address or traveling backward through a film of your life. Memories are patterns imprinted in the recognition centers of the brain, and convincing the brain to cooperate in resurrecting those patterns is essential in evoking an exact time and place from the patient's past.

Today we're traveling to the event that changed Owen's life. It's heavily imprinted, but recalling it isn't exactly a pleasant experience. I feel the resistance building as we get closer.

"We're going back to that day, Owen. The one when the murder happened." I use a passive construction to reduce his resistance. I'll be fighting that the whole way, but it helps to ease into it.

His breathing slows as the enhancer kicks in, but his mind is flying with mine.

I close my eyes, letting go of the verbal directives and giving my own mind over to sync with Owen's. My breathing evens out.

The day of the murder, I direct. *We need to go there.*

Resistance. Owen is still in control, still driving where we land.

I try a little misdirection. *That day when someone knocked us out.* Owen's mind telescopes down. A single moment slams into my mind. Owen stands on a bare concrete floor, looking down on... *no, the blood, no, no.* His horror and mine commingle: his at reliving the event, mine from panicking that we've landed *after* the murder.

I hoist his mind away from that moment, but his resistance is even greater now than it was when we arrived. He's transfixed. *Look away!* I command, even though that's a dangerous thing to do. It could kick us out of the sync altogether, and we only get one shot at this: one bite at the apple, because traveling to the same spot twice distorts the timeline too much. It's virtually a guarantee of extinction. But Owen *wants* to look away: suddenly we're pulled back into a gray haze of timelessness. I scramble for some anchor to keep us close to the time of the murder. I grasp onto his fantasy and work with that. *Earlier. Someone knocked us out before the murder. How did that happen? When?*

That does it. Owen's mind snaps us back into another memory. It's crystal clear. Spring. Warm on our face. A background smell like ancient campfires. My sense of the chair, my office, the tiny whir of the neural net all fade. I open my eyes, and the glare of the hazed sun burns them. I squint against it, and the first thing I see is a giant, faded billboard for *Harmony*, the no-drowsy sleep aid. A faded image of a pill bottle sits next to a beautiful woman, blissfully curled up, asleep. A scroll of disclaimers slides by at the bottom of the ad, ending in a message with the time and date. We're a couple of hours before the crime.

Okay, Owen. Close enough.

I take in the rest of the detritus of a decaying LA neighborhood all around me: pawn shops holding forgotten dreams behind bars, old men with nothing better to do than haunt porches of rotting wood, and street junkies teetering out into broad daylight to find their fix.

I'm taller in Owen's body. Lankier. I look down at my long-fingered hand and an arm with only one tattoo: a skull wrapped in red ribbons, as if you can tie up death with a bow.

I've traveled.

Chapter Two

Time travel is a funny thing.

On the one hand, you've got your mind controlling someone else's body. On the other, you've got someone else's body dousing your mind with chemicals and sensations unique to their fairly horrific life experience. Not to mention that the murderer's mind isn't entirely detached: I might be driving the car, but it still has coke hidden in the glove compartment and a .38 caliber under the seat. A whole host of stressors ensures you're basically simmering in a stew of rage hormones and bad situations. Keeping on track can be tricky.

So far, Owen's ride is pretty even.

I hold my arm still as the tattoo artist burns in the tag. Owen's body pumps anxiety and adrenaline through me, but my own memories and some steady breathing exercises keep the pain under control and my arm from twitching too much. Owen's street-fashion-ready shirt, with its buttoned-down, overly long sleeves, would only trap the stress heat reaction to the tattoo, so I took it off.

Oddly enough, I've experienced more tattoos than Owen. Seventeen tags... although only fifteen have stuck. I filed the other two with Corrections anyway, even though no one would ever know I'd failed. After extinction, my patient simply becomes an unsolved missing person case, assuming anyone actually bothered to report them missing. Sometimes the murder will still occur, sometimes not. I had one of each. Either way, the only evidence of the travel is my own memories and the tag—and the tattoo disappears along with the patient. Technically, I could pretend it never happened, but I suppose it's the principle of the thing. That, and I don't want Corrections to flag me as a traveler with a too-perfect record.

The department can get paranoid about that sort of thing.

The tattoo artist is more nervous than I am. No one gets a Death Row tag for fun, so he knows I'm the real deal. He keeps peering over his wireless, fish-eye glasses to check a tiny digital clock propped on his cart. Thankfully, his hands are steadier than the intermittent tremble in his lips, but I understand the tension. Having a potential murderer sit in your chair isn't the most comfortable experience. Some conversation might ease his anxiety.

"Business good?" I start.

He makes a noncommittal snort.

Or perhaps not.

He bends over my hand, closer than necessary to properly see the numbers. The needle buzzes. I take his body language cue and affect the tough exterior expected of someone like Owen. I casually sip the sugary drink I picked up before coming in.

Just doing the tattoo warps the timeline a little. I can feel it, like a second skin I wear on top of Owen's. The contours of it stretch as I move through this time, each action pushing against that invisible boundary, like I'm an artifact that doesn't belong. A warthog slowly stretching the snake as I pass through the digestive system of the universe. Time travel is tough to wrap your head around. Sometimes I think *I'm* the timeline— a thin stretch of consciousness between this past time and my current time, back in the office. Focusing on that tenuous connection to the future is how I'll return when I'm done.

This sense of the timeline helps me follow Owen's script as much as possible, right up to the murder. Landing too far out from the crime can cause a lot of problems—not least that the probability of extinction goes way up. The universe can tolerate a small change, a life here and there, but if anything deviates too much, the universe pushes back. *Hard.* Sometimes, it's difficult to know which things will cause the universe to resist—a seemingly small change can have a big impact later on—but I can always feel it starting to happen. Making the wrong move at the wrong time can send me hurtling back into my own head and make my patient disappear like he was never there. All because I stretched that skin just a little too far, and it snapped.

It's like walking through a field of time bombs.

The tattoo artist dabs at the snaking outline of the numbers with his gloved hands and a sterile cloth. At least I hope it's sterile, for Owen's sake. While the tattooist swaps his outline needle for the thicker shading needles, I go over the known details of the crime in my head.

Owen Henry Thompson murdered James Skeely on April tenth. Cause of death was a point-blank gunshot wound to the stomach, but the body was also mutilated in some pretty gruesome ways: disembowelment, facial disfigurement, severed genitalia. Basically, Owen hacked the shit out of his friend, and he didn't much wait until James was dead. Autopsy showed most of the torture was inflicted post-gunshot, but before James had died. So he was tormented while he lay with a baseball-sized hole in his gut, because simply bleeding out wasn't enough to satisfy the rage of his murderer. There was some post-mortem mutilation as well, so the rage must have continued for some time after death. And all of it was committed within the next few hours by the hand that just held a fizzy drink to my lips.

Revulsion wells up in me. I acknowledge it, just like I acknowledge the pain of the needles shoving ink under my skin. Understanding the grisly and brutal nature of the deaths I'm trying to prevent is the most difficult part of my work. Yet I don't want, nor can I afford, to diminish my own empathy in the face of that. Having that empathy is essential to my ability to travel.

But I sure as hell don't enjoy the process.

I let the sickness sit at the back of my throat until I'm sure I've given it its due, then I swallow it back down. It's the brutality of the deaths that brings men like Owen to the Row in the first place... and eventually to my office. It's what we're both trying to change, and why I'm here, rather than treating someone whose biggest problem is that they can't get along with their spouse.

I review the case again, focusing on the parts of the timeline I can change, not on the horror of what will happen if I don't. Evidence at trial included DNA at the crime scene and on Owen's clothes, his prints on the gun and knife, and a damning surveillance video where James and Owen fought over a woman.

I've watched the video at least two dozen times. The first half of their fight is unintelligible, as they keep it to the back of the dingy convenience store. Then Owen marches to the front, and James rushes up, into camera range, to stop him.

"You can't have *her!*" That's James shoving his finger in Owen's face. James is a shorter and stringier version of Owen. They've supposedly known each other all their lives.

"You can't stop me." That's a younger Owen, full of menace and danger. He's got a can of beef stew in his hand and looks like he wants to bash in James's head with it. Young Owen is a completely different person than the nervous-mouse man who sits unconscious in my office.

"Do what you want," James says, "but if you take her out, you're gonna die, man." I trip over that part of the video each and every time. James is making the threat, but it's clear that Owen is the one ready to beat him bloody. And that phrase: *if you take her out.* As if they're going to kill each other over who gets to take the girl to dinner.

There's something off about it. Unfortunately, there was never any girlfriend found to explain it.

The prosecutor constructed a timeline as part of the investigation, and Corrections fleshed it out further with as much detail as possible before approving Owen's Shift, but Owen himself was little help. Claimed he couldn't remember the events surrounding the murder, even as he finally flipped to remorseful guilt in time for the final Shift hearing. Once Owen was in my office, he still stuck to his story about not remembering the events leading up to the crime. So, all I've got is the official court records, which say Owen had his encounter with James at the convenience store approximately two hours before James's death in the basement of the rental house they shared on LA's East Side. The events of those two hours are unaccounted for, but forensics showed some kind of struggle in the basement prior to James being shot. Then the torture and mutilation, which soaked Owen's clothes in James's blood. And after that, Owen abandoned the body and went on the run…

I realize we must have stepped into that moment earlier, when we were looking down on James's mutilated body. Owen's horror was probably the same emotion he felt at the time, as the rage subsided and he realized what he had done. That shock must have spurred him to go on the run. It might even have been the beginning of his extreme need to deny what happened, which could also extend backward to the events leading up to the trauma. His subsequent clumsy disposal of the gun and knife nearby, then later his clothes, also fits. He was eventually found hiding in a run-down motel not far from the crime, fully in denial that he had committed it—a stance he maintained until his survival instinct kicked in, and he figured out that the Shift was his only chance of staying alive.

I'd like to keep Owen alive. If I can nudge the universe, push the invisible skin of the timeline just enough, but not so much that I snap it, I can alter the events surrounding the murder, and save not only James but Owen as well.

There are definite upsides to my job.

The tattooist finishes the last number and quickly cleans the tag. He smears it with anti-bacterial gel and bandages me up good. The last step is injecting the biometric chip, programmed with my tag number, deep into my bone. That one hurts like hell and makes the tattoo seem like a walk in the park.

But it's over quickly, followed by a deep, numbing after-shot to erase the pain.

I ease, gingerly, out of the chair, testing the bandage. It's solid: no chance of coming loose. I pull on my shirt and say, "Thanks."

The tattooist nods and quickly turns away to clean up his equipment.

I don't offer to pay. He'll get reimbursed by the Department of Corrections, once he files the number.

Outside the shop, the LA smog turns the blue sky a hazy white. Even with Owen landing us a couple of hours before the crime, I barely have enough time to get the tattoo before I have to be at the convenience store to fight with James.

I hurry down the street, check the time, and decide to hail a cab. Owen has all of five dollars in his pocket, but I won't need to actually buy anything at the convenience store—the video showed him storming out after the fight with James—so I blow the last of Owen's money getting as close to the store as I can. I still have to hoof it the last half-mile, and the sun is starting to blaze hot, but I keep my long sleeves rolled down. They cover most of the tattoo bandage, and that's one thing I can't afford to lose. Getting a tattoo is no big deal; getting a Death Row tag is a whole different story.

As I come up on the convenience store, I see James there, already waiting for me, clutching a paper bag. My heart rate kicks up a notch, but the timeline stays smooth: apparently I was supposed to meet him here.

"What took you so long?" James says as he pushes off the crumbling concrete wall. Faded paint behind him says *Aces Up!*

In one of the store's previous lives, it must have been a lotto shop.

I show him the bandage peeking from my sleeve. "Got some ink." I have no idea if this is something Owen would say. This is the trickiest part of all: drawing inside the lines, keeping the timeline plausible until I make the big push to stop the murder.

James shakes his head. "Man, what is wrong with you?" But he says it like I'm an idiot, not like he thinks Owen's body is possessed. "We don't got time for that!" He turns his back on me to stalk to the glass door of the shop, which is nearly opaque with stuck-on advertisements.

I hesitate too long.

"Well, c'mon."

I follow him into the shop and to the back, desperately trying to read his body language for some kind of clue about the fight we're about to have. His shoulders are tense, hiked nearly up to his ears. He cranes his neck as he walks, working the stress out. His hands are stringy and nervous, playing with the pocket of his jacket, or possibly hiding something in it.

Owen's pulse pounds in my head.

James pretends to examine the end cap, but it's filled with baby diapers. "Tell me the truth, man." He's speaking to me but he's staring at the diapers. "Did you take the merchandise out?"

"What do you mean?"

"Oh, c'mon!" He turns to me, anger lighting up his face. "Don't give me that shit."

"I don't know what you're talking about." The timeline nudges me. This isn't what Owen said, but I have no clue what's making James grit his teeth and squeeze his eyes tight, like I'm about to make his head pop.

"You can't shit me about this," James says. "She told me what happened."

Okay. Here it is. The girlfriend.

I hold my hands up, going for innocence. "I don't know what she told you—"

James grabs hold of my shoulder and shoves me up against the diapers. "She said you—" He cuts himself off and darts a look around. There's no one else in the store besides the bored clerk up front, but James still lowers his voice. "She said you took out the *merchandise*. Man, I *told* you not to do that."

Back to the merchandise. Were they dealing drugs? There wasn't anything on the autopsy or Owen's intake report that showed—

James gives me a shake. "You gotta snap out of this, understand? She's not yours. She's not ever going to be yours."

The girlfriend again. I'm getting mental whiplash. But James is warning me off her like a friend. Not the threats I expect if he wants her for himself.

"Maybe she could be," I say, cautiously. "You don't know."

"Shit." He pushes off me and steps back. "You are going to get us both killed, you hear me? *Both* of us. Bullets to the head. Is that what you want?"

"No! I don't want that, man, I swear." I don't have to fake the fear—this is spinning out of control, sounding more like a drug deal gone bad than a crime of passion. I have no idea what's going on.

"You got that right." James calms a little, straightens his shirt. "I've got some buyers. They want the whole set, but not all at once. Too hard to move 'em. So we gotta keep the merchandise cool for a while, you know what I'm saying?"

I nod, even though I barely have any clue. The *set*? Sounds like they're in a smuggling operation, but maybe not drugs.

"I got some more supplies to take care of that problem." He shoves the paper bag at me. It's light, with tiny clacking sounds inside, like it's filled with plastic pens. "You go home, and you take care of it. And don't waste none of that shit. It was expensive."

I'm certain I'm holding a bag full of illegal *something*. The timeline squeezes on me. I'm not supposed to have the bag. James is too calm. We're supposed to be *fighting*. I don't mind diffusing the causes of the murder—at some point that's got to happen—but this feels too soon. I struggle to piece it together, but I'm missing almost all the parts.

"So you want me to go back to the house…" I try, hoping James will fill in a few blanks for me.

He runs a frustrated hand through his hair. "Man, do I have to spell it out for you?"

Yes, please. Instead, I pretend to get angry. "Maybe I don't want to, okay! I don't even know what this shit is!" I shake the bag in his face. Maybe he'll take it back.

He shoves it away, gritting his teeth. "Don't screw this up, Owen."

"Screw you! What, are you the boss of me now?" I push at James's obvious concern that I'm going to blow their whole operation, whatever it is.

James paces the back wall. "Owen, don't do this. Not now, man. We're almost there."

"Maybe I don't want to go there anymore." The more I push back on James, the more the timeline relaxes around me. I turn and march toward the front, hoping that'll force James to reveal a little more about what I'm up against. Because I'm driving blind in the dark with no headlights.

"Owen!" James calls from behind, but I don't stop. He rushes up behind me and jerks me to a stop. He shoves his finger in my face. "Look, you can do whatever you want, but you can't have *her*."

"You can't stop me." The words practically force themselves out, and I know that feeling: it's the timeline syncing me up, forcing me to play the game it's already played. I push back on it, and add, "I can do whatever I want." I'm shaking the bag at him instead of the can of beef stew from the video. *Small changes.* Stretching, but not too much. The timeline eases off its squeeze.

James shakes his head. "If you take her out, man, you're gonna die."

Take her out. What the hell does that mean? But I'm getting no more out of James, so I turn my back on him and stalk out of the convenience store in my artificial huff. The timeline skin lets me pass without clamping down. I'm supposed to do this. I'm supposed to march out of the convenience store in a fit of anger. Only now I have a bag filled with God knows what, and the universe is nudging me back to the house.

There's nothing to do but follow it.

Chapter Three

The location of the murder isn't far from the convenience store. Just a half-mile stroll carrying illegal substances in a paper bag through one of the tougher neighborhoods of East LA. If this were my first travel, I might actually worry about some of that. Instead, I'm keeping my head low to avoid attracting attention, while my mind scrambles to figure out what I'm going to find at the house, what I'm supposed to do when I get there, and what actions will or will not trigger the sequence of events that lead to the murder.

Being from the future actually helps with very little of this.

As far as James knows, I'm going to the house to solve whatever problem he and Owen have with their smuggling operation… no indication of which ever appeared in any of the investigations. And sometime in the next two hours, James is going to show up and do something to throw Owen into a homicidal rage. And the weapons have to come from somewhere. I already checked Owen's body when I arrived: I'm not armed. At the moment, at least. So James is bringing the weapons with him. Which would be very bad. Or possibly they're at the house. That would be better.

I glare at a couple of punk teenagers lurking at the ramshackle house next to Owen's, just to keep them from getting any ideas. About harassing me. Or following me. I'd like to tell them to clear out, but that's not my mission here. Owen and James's one-story rental house next door is just as dilapidated as the punks': the rotted wooden porch looks like it'll barely hold my weight, but the front door is solid, with iron security bars across it. I fish around in Owen's pockets and come up with a ring—it has a passcode sensor and several regular flathead keys on it. I need all but two to get inside.

Three-day-old leftover pizza perfumes the air with moldy cheese. A couple of chairs sit askew around the table, but there's no other furniture. I take a quick tour through the kitchen, poke my head in the back bedroom, and check the bathroom, but there's no one here. A door I thought was a closet ends up being the door to the basement. Which I will give a thorough investigation in a moment, but first, now that I'm off the streets, I open up the bag to see what James has given me.

Needles. Syringes, actually. Single dose, pre-prepared. The kind you use for vaccines, although I doubt these are for whooping cough. For a moment, I think Owen and James are smuggling drugs after all, but... then I realize street drugs don't come in neat sterile packages of pre-dosed something or other. These are stolen from a hospital or clinic. They could sell them on the street, but what did James say? *Got to keep the merchandise cool for a while.*

A chill trickles through my stomach. I look back to the basement door.

It starts to add up, but in a very bad way.

I shuffle toward the door and have to practically force my hand to reach for the knob. It's not the universe that's squeezing me away from the door—Owen's been down these steps before. *A lot.* The timeline's practically shoving me down the stairs. It's my own dread at what I'm going to find down there that's dragging on my feet.

I flip on the lights. The steps are decayed wood, just like the porch. The basement is bare concrete with a single bulb dangling near the base of the steps. As I take one creaky step after another, the moldy smell of the main floor is replaced with the sharp tang of urine. I grimace, force myself to keep descending. At the base of the stairs, the space opens up, and I can see the source of the smell.

Cages.

Filled with *people.*

I freeze, my hand on the stairwell railing, steadying myself.

Two large cages, side by side, made of steel bars and wire mesh, hold at least a dozen women between them. They're huddled together like frightened children. The bottom halves of the cages are mesh, and fingers poke through it, curled around the thin wires. The top halves are narrowly spaced vertical bars. A few hands and arms lean out. The women stare at me while I stand frozen at the base of the steps.

"Baby!" one calls out. "You're back!" Her voice is sweet, with a heavy Slavic accent, and it unlocks my legs. I stumble over until I'm standing in front of the cage, one hand automatically reaching out. I stop just outside the zone where I might touch them—or they might touch me.

"What did he say, baby?" She smiles wide, but her voice has an undercurrent of fear that's as pungent as the urine that permeates the dank room.

If you take her out... I pull my hand back. What in the name of all that's holy is going on here?

"Baby, what's wrong?" Panic blossoms in her voice. The others, the ones holding back, lurking behind her, move a little. My eyes adjust to the dimness and shadows, and I can see the unkempt clothes and bruised faces. The chains on their wrists and ankles. The bucket for a toilet in the corner.

I gag, and for a moment, I think I'm going to be sick. I swallow it down. "Nothing's wrong, I just..." I take a step back and look wildly around the basement, sure that James is going to appear out of thin air and the murder is going to happen *right now*.

Because everything is horribly, horribly off.

Think, Ian, think. There was no evidence of human trafficking in the reports. *None.* No indication there had ever been people living in the basement. And yet here they are, and Owen knows them... knows one in particular very well... and then it clicks.

She's the girl.

She attempts a smile, but her dark eyes are ringed in shadows. Cheeks sunken, skin pale, like she's already a ghost. Her eyes dart over me, dance to the bag, back to my face, sizing me up. I glimpse something feral, as if the smile is just a veneer over a slight wildness. How long have they been in these cages? How long does it take for the bars to start clawing away at your humanity?

Her hand reaches through the bars, inviting. "Did you talk to James, baby?"

James. I look at the bag of syringes in my hand. He sent me here to drug them. Maybe sedate them. Maybe something worse. They're the merchandise, and James has buyers, but we have to keep them cool for a while. Is that what Owen and James fought about? Is that what caused Owen to go into a rage and kill his childhood friend? Because he had fallen for one of the women, and now James was going to sell her into slavery? I knew the horror stories of human trafficking. The women were likely here illegally, and some of them were barely more than girls. There would be no good end for them. Owen had to know it, too.

"I talked to James," I say, measuring my words. What did she think Owen talked to James about?

Hope lights her face and wrenches my chest with an almost physical pain. "Did he say yes?"

Owen promised to free her. I breathe through the tightness. "James doesn't understand."

The hope extinguishes.

My head starts to buzz. How can I fix this? How can I get these women out of here without completely warping the timeline? I run a hand along my face and step back farther from the cage.

"Owen, baby…" She's pleading now. "We can… we can be together, just like I said. James doesn't have to know. We can go *now*." She glances back, and I can tell the others are on high alert. She's the ringleader, and they'll follow her. "You and I can go together. The others can make their own way."

"I want to," I can't help saying. Every part of me wants to unlock the cage and go through and take off every shackle. I want to hug them and hold them… not in the sexual way she's promising, just wrap my arms around them until the tremors I can see from across the room start to calm. I can feel the anger inside me, building. It's the rage Owen must have felt, only he must have had it ten times worse because he had a relationship with this woman.

Before I know what I'm doing, I'm digging through my pocket for the ring of keys. The two keys that weren't required to open the front door… one for the cage, one for the shackles.

I hold them in my hand.

"That's right, baby," she says. "Let's go now. Quick. Before he gets back!"

I step forward, but it's like moving through molasses. The universe is pushing back, resisting. It's stretched as tight as a drum. If I force my way through… if I let the women go… it's going to snap. I can feel it. Then Owen will disappear, James may live or he may not, and the women… I'm not sure what will happen to them. The time around the edges of the extinction event get twisted. The two times I failed, when I couldn't stop the murder without breaking the timeline, things were uneven afterward. Different in my memory than in the actual event. Even if I let the women out, there's no guarantee they'll *stay* out.

But the extinction will get Owen for sure. And if he's gone… they have no hope.

I slowly put the key ring back in my pocket.

The woman's fingers curl around the bars of her cage. She thinks Owen's her one hope... and he is. Just not the way she thinks. I look away from the flat expression on her face and run my hand through Owen's hair, tugging on it. There has to be a solution to this... I just have to find it. If I can't outright let them go, if that would break the timeline—at least at *this* moment in time—then maybe there's another point in time when I could try again. I have to stick closer to the script, not stretch it so far, but I'm completely in the dark here.

The original timeline is nothing like I thought.

I look up from my pacing. The woman is still staring at me with that flat, dead look. It sends a chill through me. But I stride up to the cage anyway and search her face for the light that was in her eyes just a minute ago. The rest of the women rustle, shrink back, but she stays at the door of the cage, eyes widening slightly, but coming back to life.

"I want to help you." I hook the fingers of my free hand around the bars and stand close. "But I need you to help me first. Where is James planning on sending you?"

She frowns. "I don't know."

No, she probably doesn't.

"Did I tell you when he was coming for you?"

"No." She looks suspicious now. I'm sounding crazy, for sure. But sitting here, talking to her... I've done it a million times before. *Owen* has done it before. It doesn't push the timeline.

I press my fist to my forehead, trying to think. In the original timeline, I didn't walk out of the convenience store with the bag—I had a can of beef stew instead. Originally,

Owen went there to meet James about letting the woman go. He left angry. *Without* the sedatives. Which means James probably brought the sedatives back here and dosed the women himself. Then, when Owen came back to the house, maybe he found James hauling his girlfriend out as the first batch of merchandise. That's when the murder happened. But then... what happened to the girls? Did Owen liberate them, tear down all the cages, dispose of those, *then* go on the run in his blood-covered clothes?

That seemed... unlikely.

There's a shuffle behind the woman. One of the others checks on her. The leader nods over her shoulder, watching me like a hawk the whole time. The other woman returns to the huddle. Owen's girlfriend keeps sneaking looks at the bag, which I'm still holding, all wadded up in my fist next to the bars.

"James gave you these before, didn't he?" I ask.

"Yeah." She pulls back a little now, with a *you crazy, man* look. I was probably there—or rather, Owen was—so that's something I should know.

"Is it a sedative?"

"Owen, baby, what's going on—"

"Just tell me," I say, trying to pull down the rising anger in my voice. "It'll help me get you out of here."

"Yeah. It's a sedative. Glazes us out for a while, anyway. Not really asleep, but you don't remember nothing anyway."

My eyebrows shoot up. "You don't *remember* anything?" The memory loss that Owen claimed: he said he was unconscious, couldn't remember anything about the crime.

61

Maybe he really was. But how could he commit a murder in that state? Maybe James dosed him, and he woke up later, in time to—

The woman moves lightning fast. Her hand slips out through the bars and smacks the back of my hand, the one holding the bag. I jerk back and, a half-second later, feel the prick. A single-dose syringe sticks out of the bandage for my tag. I yank it out, staring at it in horror, then look back up at the woman. She reaches for me again, and suddenly there's a half dozen hands clawing through the bars, grabbing hold of my shirt, and slamming me face-first against the steel cage. I struggle to get free. They paw at my clothes, but they can't get to my pockets where the keys are. The wire mesh is blocking their reach. I wrench free and stumble back.

My heart races and my vision blurs. I shake my head, and suddenly I'm two places at once: Owen's dingy, fetid basement, and my well-lit office on the thirty-fourth floor of the Department of Corrections.

No! I focus on the cage, the women, the smell of urine, anything to anchor me here in the past. Slowly, my vision clears. I'm still here. Whatever sedative was in the syringe must not have fully dosed me. I give thanks for well-applied bandages by tattoo artists.

The women seem alarmed that I'm not falling over from their attempt at sedating me. Then I realize: they didn't grab the sedative from the bag. They already had it. They were planning on sedating Owen, or possibly James, *all along*. Only I know that in the original timeline, Owen was the one who had the memory loss. And James was the one who got hacked to bits.

I stare back at the caged women. *They* killed James.

At that moment, I hear the front door upstairs open and close. Heavy footsteps creak across the main floor and pound down the steps. I stand in the middle of the basement, clutching the bag of unused sedatives, as James walks into the room.

Chapter Four

Owen was innocent after all.

This thought paralyzes me as James stalks across the floor, glaring at the unopened bag in my hand.

Owen is innocent.

Well, innocent of the murder. Obviously not innocent of human trafficking. But that means I'm not in control of the murder... because if *he* didn't commit it, then I can't stop it.

I physically shake that thought from my head. There's still a way to save this—a best-of-all-possible-scenarios option somewhere in the myriad. I just have to keep it together and stay in the timeline long enough to figure it out.

James stands in front of me, accusing me with his body language. "You haven't given it to them yet."

"We were... having a discussion."

"A *what?*" He looks mystified, then concerned. "Look, man, I know you're into her..."

She's a murderer. She's going to kill you. I know it was justified... or will be justified. I know they were trying to escape. I know the rage they must feel. I *understand* it. At the same time, it horrifies me. I need to find an outcome where that doesn't happen. Where these women don't have to win their freedom by losing their humanity.

James is still talking. "...but she's bought and paid for, man. You need to just forget it."

I drop my gaze to the bag, nodding, buying time while I flip through the possibilities, trying to find one where everyone lives. I slip one hand into my pocket and find the key that will unlock the cages. I turn toward the women trapped behind steel bars, but even that motion has the universe pushing back on me. *Still.*

Option One: I release the women. I fight the universe, the timeline snaps, Owen goes extinct, we go back to where we started—only without Owen—the women use their hidden syringe on James instead, which may or may not work, they may or may not brutally murder him, losing their humanity in the process, and the only sure thing is that Owen is dead.

Shit. I take my hand off the key ring and the timeline relaxes. I look back to James. He's glaring at me, waiting for me to administer the doses.

Option Two: I convince James to release the women. Maybe the universe won't fight him, the women will go free, and James and Owen will go with them, shepherding them to safety somewhere. The only problem: getting James to go for it. And I'm not entirely sure it won't snap the timeline anyway, jumping us back to Option One, which is no good.

"I was thinking…" I say slowly to him. "Maybe we could just let them go."

"Oh, sure. Yeah. Let's do that." He strides forward and grabs hold of my shoulders with both hands. The stink of his nervous sweat momentarily drowns out the urine smell. "At what point did you see any indication that Armando would be okay with us just releasing his merchandise? We're go-betweens, nothing more. Unless we decide to screw with their system, and then do you know what we are?"

I shake my head.

"Dead." He shoves me away. "I love you, man, but I am *not* dying for you. Or for them." He gestures to the cages. "Now stop being an idiot and hand out the doses."

Option Two is out.

I slowly open the bag and look inside, poking around and buying more time.

Option Three: I dose James with one of the sedatives and let the women go free. Maybe the universe will allow that, because James will still die—once the buyers come after their merchandise. With James dead, there's not as much of a warp in the timeline. Whatever the buyers do to him, it can't be worse than what the women did. At least, I hope so. And the women don't have to lose their humanity in the process. Owen already wanted to help them escape—that's not stretching the timeline at all. The buyers commit the murder, so Owen stays off Death Row. But he's got the tag, so he's in jeopardy of going there if he ever commits another crime. But he knows that. Maybe it'll keep him clean.

It's my best option so far.

I reach into the bag, pull out a dose, and slowly turn toward the cages, like I'm going to administer it. I pause when I get there, examining the dose. It's a simple one-pump-action thing. I flip up the safety cap to expose the razor-thin needle. The women shrink back, all except the leader, Owen's girlfriend. She's glaring defiantly at me. I can see why Owen likes her—she's a survivor, a fighter. She has spirit—a spirit I don't want crushed any more than it already has been. I'm facing her, James behind my back. I give her a quick wink, and her face transforms with the shock.

I drop the bag, whirl around, and rush at James. His eyes go wide, and he stumbles back. I aim the syringe for his neck, but he gets an arm up to block me. James is smaller than Owen, but surprisingly strong. He shoves a fist in my gut. It doesn't have too much power, but still, I'm gasping for air as I grab hold of his shirt, yanking him close to try again. But now he's got a hand on my wrist, holding back the syringe from his face. I let go of his shirt to try to transfer the syringe to my other hand.

I don't see the gun until it's in my face.

I grab that instead, thrusting it away. James and I wrestle, hand to hand. I grimace, reluctantly give up on the syringe, drop it, and work on fighting him for the gun. Finally, my greater size works in my favor, and I'm able to force him backward into the basement wall. I slam his hand holding the gun against the wall, and the shock loosens his grip.

The gun falls.

I'm after it, reach it before he does, stand up.

I back away from him, gun pointed at his chest, my heart about to explode out of Owen's body. I can't get any air, in spite of panting like I've just run a mile.

"Owen, dude, no." James's hands are up. "I wasn't going to shoot you, man, I swear. But *shit*! You were trying to... why'd you have to *try* that, man..." He's almost crying with fear.

I'm shaking. The gun tip wavers a little. I can't tell if it's fear or adrenaline or what.

Option Four: I kill James.

Shit. Shit. Shit.

I swallow.

Option Four: I kill James. James dies, but at least it's not via torture; the women are free with their humanity intact; Owen commits the murder, for real this time, without the extreme circumstances, but he still ends up on Death Row, because he has the tag.

My finger is on the trigger. I give it a little touch, thinking about pulling it. The universe doesn't nudge me to stop me. In fact, I almost pull it by accident, like the universe *wants* James to die. He died in the original timeline. This won't break it.

Because James is already dead, I tell myself. *This way he won't be tortured.*

It doesn't help.

I pull the trigger.

The crack of the shot stabs my ears and whips my hand up in the air with the recoil. James falls to the floor with a hole in his head. My gun hand sinks slowly to my side.

I stare at him. For a long time.

I have a random thought about how seventeen cases has made me a pretty good shot.

Eventually, my breathing slows. I'm still in the timeline. The women stare at me from the cages, wide-eyed. My hand is shaking, but I manage to dig the key ring out of my pants and toss it to them. The universe doesn't break when I do it.

A pool of blood is slowly spreading under James's head. The gun is still in Owen's hand. There's one more thing I have to do before I go back.

* * *

You can't remove a Shift tag. Not without taking off a good chunk of your arm, and even then, a tattoo-removal artist risks losing their license and going to jail for accessory to murder. And then there's the microchip embedded in your bone. No one's hacked off a limb to get rid of that, at least not that Corrections has tracked. And the numbers are all associated with you in the future. You, or your limb, would be found eventually.

You can't escape the future.

But you *can* camouflage a tag, so that it doesn't stand out so much. Corrections—or any kind of law enforcement, really—won't be fooled. But it reduces the stigma. To the casual eye, you've got a leopard with unusual spots, or a peacock, or, in Owen's case, a dragon with diamonds running down its back. Camouflage is also illegal, but you'd be surprised what a gun to the head will motivate a tattooist to do.

It's a large tattoo. Large, painful, and time-consuming.

When I'm done with the tattooist, bandaged up for a second time, I return to the basement. The women are gone. If they were illegals, they've already melted into the cityscape. If not, they might be on their way to the police. I kind of doubt it, though. They're unlikely to want to be the kind of targets that witnesses can become. Either way, I hope they'll be able to piece together a decent life now.

In the original timeline, there were no cages, no evidence of human trafficking. In this timeline? I can't be sure what will happen. Perhaps Owen will clean it up. Or maybe the traffickers will come looking for their merchandise, find nothing but empty cages and a dead body, and decide to cut their losses and erase any connection between them and the crime. However it turns out, the universe must be okay with it now, because it's not shoving on me to clean up the mess.

I stand over James's body, slowly cooling in a pool of his own blood. This is where Owen will wake up. This is when he has to figure out what to do next. I've already wiped his prints off the gun and laid it next to James. If Owen's smart, he'll look at his arm and figure it out. If not, he'll be back on Death Row again, but this time ineligible for the Shift.

Either way, he shouldn't be in my office when I return.

I close my eyes, pull in a couple of deep breaths, and picture the thirty-fourth floor of the Department of Corrections. When I open my eyes, I'm sitting in my chair, under the neural net. The sun has moved to a spot where it's now shining in my eyes, time continuing to march forward no matter where my mind is. I lean out of the glare and peer around at Owen's seat.

It's empty.

I reach for the trash can next to my chair and throw up the contents of my stomach.

Chapter Five

"So where's your patient now?" Alyssa sits across from me. She's my post-travel therapist, and it's her usual opener. I don't know if she's looked into the case file—all she'll find there is the tag number and my travel log.

"Don't know," I say, and it's the truth. I searched for Owen in the Corrections database when I got back—as soon as I stopped throwing up and most of the shakes had passed—but there was no record of him being picked up. "He went off the grid after the murder."

"So the murder still happened," she says. "That's your third failure-to-complete. How do you feel about that?" She gives me a small smile, acknowledging the artlessness of that line. I think she's doing it to lighten the situation, ease the burden of my third washout. At least this one didn't result in an extinction.

I give her a slight smile in return. "Since the throwing up stopped, I feel pretty good."

She frowns, and it mars her pretty face. Her hazel-green eyes are usually inviting, but now they're just full of concern for my mental health. From our previous sessions, I know she's intelligent, kind-hearted, funny, reads philosophy, and has a cat named Leonardo, as in Da Vinci. Just the kind of woman I would date if she weren't assigned by Corrections to monitor my reactions to my travels.

And if I weren't the kind of man who had pulled the trigger to kill someone.

Sickness wells up at the back of my throat again. I swallow it back down, hoping it doesn't show too badly on my face.

"I don't remember you having a physical reaction to your travels before." A subtle way to get me to explain, without the prod of her having to ask.

"I don't normally."

She nods. "This time was different."

I take a breath, ready with the explanation that I reasoned out before, in between dry heaves into the trash can. "He was innocent."

"Your patient?" Her thin red eyebrows hike up. I never noticed their color before. They match the red highlights in her deep brown hair. I wonder if she's Irish. My mom would have probably liked her anyway, but that certainly wouldn't have hurt.

"He was innocent all along," I say, "just like he said."

"You mean in the original timeline."

"Yes. In the original timeline." Of course, there's no record now of Owen claiming innocence, because he was never caught. He was smarter even than I gave him credit for, not only eluding being brought in for questioning—the police went looking for him, based on the convenience store video—but disappearing off the grid altogether. Of course, it's possible he actually extinguished out. But I've never had that happen without knowing I broke the timeline. So I think he's still alive. Somewhere, hiding with his dragon tattoo. If the police had known, they could have checked the local tattoo parlors, but the tattooist wouldn't talk about doing the camouflage—it would be tantamount to confessing to murder, and no one's going to do that.

Not even me.

Alyssa is studying my face in our silence. I hope she's not finding guilt there.

"Is that why you haven't activated his tracker?"

I bite my lip, hoping she takes that as moral indecision. This is where it gets a little tricky. "Yeah, I thought about that. It doesn't seem fair to do that to him when someone else committed the crime."

She leans forward, elbows on knees, delicate fingers holding her chin. "So you know who really did it?"

I shake my head. "Since Owen was innocent, I wasn't there when it happened. And I couldn't nudge the timeline far enough to be in a position to stop the murder. I just ended up back here when it happened." There's no way for her, or anyone else, to know about the torture, since that was only in the original timeline. As far as the record shows, James always died from a single gunshot to the head.

Alyssa nods. "So activating his tracker to bring him in, after all this time, just to have him cleared of a crime he didn't commit…"

"Seems like a waste of everyone's time," I finish for her. "And some unnecessary anguish for a man whose friend was murdered a dozen years ago." That part, at least, is the truth.

She's studying me again. "Seems like a rather unsatisfying end to this case for *you*, however. How do you feel about going into another assignment so soon? I saw you're tentatively assigned to prepare for another patient from the Row starting next week."

"I'm good. I'm ready." I nod a little too enthusiastically, so I stop and try to look merely earnest. That's not too hard. "I know this case doesn't count as a resolution, but I'm really okay to go again. I'm still trying to get to twenty as soon as possible."

Her look of concern is unavoidable. And I need her clearance to keep traveling, so I probably shouldn't have brought it up. But I don't want her to think I'm thrown by this last case, what with the throwing up and the shakes and the strange lack of interest in tracking down my patient.

She purses her lips, taking her time to respond. Finally, she says, "Why do you *really* want to go back, Ian? We've discussed this before. You were just a child. I thought you agreed there was nothing you could do."

But she's wrong. I know she's wrong. Even more so now.

"I just need some closure." I hold her gaze. I see more pity there now than anything. Which makes me cringe a little inside, but it's better than suspicion.

"Your parents are dead, Ian." Her tone is professional, but soft. Empathetic. Sweet almost, even as she's about to deliver a lecture on why, even with time travel, I can't bring back my murdered parents from the grave. She really is the kind of person I'd like to know better, outside of the therapy room. Too bad it can't happen, at least not without some ethics violations and being hauled into Internal Affairs for questioning.

"Even if you reach twenty resolutions," she says, kindly. "Even if you're granted an enhancer dose. You were ten years old. I'm concerned the only thing you're going to accomplish is re-experiencing the murders. And I don't think that's going to be healthy, do you?"

"No, probably not." I pause. "But I don't think I'll know that until I try."

She frowns, a little frustrated, I think. "I'm also concerned you might try to do something that *would* change the timeline, but you won't be able to, because you're just a child in a dangerous and unstable situation. And not just physically, Ian. You know very well that re-experiencing a childhood trauma can leave a person... vulnerable. Emotionally. I'm concerned you won't be as rational as you would like to think. Which only means the risk of extinction will go up."

I nod because, of course, I've considered all of that. And in a strange way, I like that she's so concerned for me. But Alyssa doesn't travel—she just does therapy for those of us who do. And what she doesn't know, what she *can't* know, is that I won't just be a grown man in a child's body.

I'll be a man who already knows what it's like to pull the trigger.

"I'm willing to take that risk." I dip my head, then look up and give her a small smile. "But I still have to reach twenty, first. Five more to go."

She sighs, but pulls out her datapad to tap in a few notes. "All right. I'll clear you for your next patient." Her scowl is meant to chastise me, but my heart lifts too much to feel it. "But we're going to have this discussion again, several times, before I'll even think about clearing you for your own dose."

"Yes, ma'am." I smile with real appreciation. I wish I could offer to take her out for coffee or something, as a thank-you, but I know that's seriously off-limits.

Maybe after five more patients.

A Word from Susan Kaye Quinn

I vowed I would never write a time travel story.

(Which should have been my first clue that I would absolutely write one eventually.)

I grew up with *Star Trek* like everyone else, so I *knew* any writer foolish enough to stumble into a time travel vortex would soon find all her plot threads hopelessly snarled. What madness lay that way? Better to stick with future worlds where everyone reads minds or sucks out your life energy. Or retro ones with muscular steampunk technology. Those stories were much more sensible. Not to mention plottable.

Like any good protagonist, I stuck with my no-time-travel-stories vow until the universe nudged me *hard* in the form of an offer I couldn't refuse. First, you should know this about me: I *like* challenges. Actually, that's a little like saying a drug addict *likes* cocaine. I have serious self-control issues when it comes to thrown gauntlets, fourteen-thousand-foot climbs, and deadlines that make brave women shudder. Secondly, you should know that I'm on social media way too much.

So when Michael Bunker messaged me on Facebook and said,

"Hey, would you like to write a time travel story for our collection?" (Gauntlet: thrown.)

"It would be with this amazing group of authors, edited by David Gatewood!" (Vertical climb challenge: unlocked.)

"And by the way, we'd need it fast, like in two weeks." (Cue deadline impossibilities.)

Well... there was really no chance of me saying *no*.

And, to be honest, I'm so glad I didn't. Given that I'm the daughter of an engineer and a psychologist, it's truly a wonder I haven't written a time-traveling psychologist character before now. But I very much enjoyed creating Ian and the world of "Corrections": in fact, don't be surprised if there are more *Corrections* stories to come. (Then again, if someone challenges me to write a cyborg Bigfoot romance, all bets are off.)

If you enjoyed reading "Corrections" as much as I enjoyed writing it, you'll find similar mind-bendery in my other works, especially my *Debt Collector* serial. In that future-noir, my dark hero sucks the life energy out of people when their debts exceed their future potential earnings, and then transfers it on to *high potentials*, people who supposedly have more to contribute to the world. *Debt Collector* also began as a short novella, like "Corrections," then demanded to be turned into a nine-episode, five-season sprawling enterprise (Season One is currently complete, with Season Two scheduled to begin in September 2014). Which is tremendously odd, since I am actually a novelist. Well, after being several other things (rocket scientist, engineer, NASA employee, mother of three, scolder of cats).

My speculative fiction works span a range of ages, from my middle-grade fantasy *Faery Swap*, to my young adult sci-fi *The Mindjack Trilogy*, to my adult steampunk romance *Third Daughter*. But they all dive deep into the heads of my characters, much as Ian dives into Owen's memories, creating adventure out of those interstitial spaces between *what we can imagine* and *what is real*. I hope you'll come along for a few adventures with me!

You can find all about my works on my website or subscribe to my newsletter to find the latest insanity that I've signed up for (hint: new subscribers get a free short story!). I'd love for you to friend me on Facebook, but only if you promise not to message me with challenges of writing post-singularity robot love stories... wait...

Hereafter
by Samuel Peralta

September 15, 2006

THAT AUTUMN SHE'S back in Toronto, staying at her mom's place, before deployment. At Queen's Quay Terminal, her two girlfriends go inside to grab a coffee, to stave off the late afternoon chill. She stays outside to check in, but the phone at her mom's rings four, five, six times, and she flips her phone closed before it goes to voice mail.

There's a soft crush of wind, and she hugs herself in her jacket. Time for that coffee. She turns, and that's when she sees him. All in black, reminding her of Steve Jobs with his turtleneck and slacks, except didn't Steve wear Adidas, and oh my God doesn't he remind her of that lead in the Bryan Singer movie, and—

He collapses, crumples on the ground. She runs up the steps to him, but already he's pulling himself up, bracing himself against the wall of the terminal building.

Just as she reaches him, he looks up, and their eyes meet. Suddenly, a feeling overcomes her: that this face is familiar, that she knows him, that they've met before. In his eyes there's a similar flash of recognition.

At his feet, a glimmer catches her attention, and she picks it up. A silver medallion, in the shape of a spiral nautilus, on a chain. She holds it out to him. "Yours?" she asks.

He takes it, holding her hand for just a fraction of a moment too long. "Oh God, I hope so," he says.

They break off, both now blushing. She's just decided she should be running off, when his knees buckle again and he hits the pavement. This time she has to pull him up and lean him against the wall herself. Nothing on his breath. Clean-shaven.

"I'm sorry," he says, when he's recovered. "It's just been a long journey."

She hesitates a bit before deciding. "Listen," she says. "I think you need to sit down and get something to eat. Why don't you join me and you can catch your breath? I'll buy." She holds out her hand. "I'm Caitlyn."

"Sean Forrest," he says. "Happy to meet you."

Rotini in marinara sauce at the restaurant inside, and she's chattering away, about the closing of *The Lord of The Rings* stage show at the Princess of Wales Theatre, about Jonathan Safran Foer's latest book, about Spenser and the difference between Shakespearean and Petrarchan sonnets—and wouldn't he like to read one she's written, which she happened to carry with her?—and when her phone rings, an hour has passed. It isn't her mom, it's her friends—wondering where in the world is she?

She tells them she'll catch up with them later at the club, turns back to him, and they pick it up as if she'd never left off.

She talks about James Blunt and Kelly Clarkson, about *Gilmore Girls* and *24*, about conspiracies and terrorists, about North Korean politics, about Middle Eastern food, about how her family makes their own tomato sauce.

He talks about rotini, about patterns in nature, about Gödel and Escher and Bach, about Rachmaninoff and Paganini, about nautilus shells and hurricanes and satellite orbits, about integer series and golden means.

Over coffee and dessert, she asks if he'll accompany her to the Rex, the jazz bar where her friends are going that night.

"I've got to go home tonight," he says. "This was supposed to be a one-time trip. But I'm thinking—" And he stops here, for what feels like a long, long time. Then: "I'm thinking that I want to make it back next year."

"Oh no!" she says. "It'd be amazing, but I'm headed to Kandahar."

He looks stunned, like he doesn't know where that is.

"Afghanistan. I'm with the Canadian team at the R3 MMU. Combat operations field hospital."

He's still speechless.

"Oh heck, it's only for two tours," she says. "I'll be back in a couple. How about we make a date for the future?"

That seems to break the trance. But what he does next is unexpected. He takes off his medallion, takes her hand, and presses it into her palm.

"Yours," he says.

September 17, 2007

Southwest of Kandahar. Earlier that day, helicopters streamed like tremulous wasps into Zhari District, ferrying back remains from a shattered infantry battalion. Under her breath, another whispered prayer. Sometimes prayers are answered by a different god.

Behind blast walls ten feet high, at the edge of the runway of the Kandahar Airfield, the NATO Role 3 Multinational Medical Unit, or R3MMU, is an assemblage of field-deployable hospital structures, shipping containers, canvas tents, and leaking plywood buildings.

Despite this, the Canadian Forces Health Services team tasked with command of the R3MMU is on its way to the highest survival rate ever recorded for victims of war.

But Cpl. Caitlyn McAdams, in the middle of her first nine-month tour, isn't at her regular station that night.

That week they're short-staffed at the forward operating base at Ma'sum Ghar, so Cpl. McAdams and Cpl. Paul Francis are on temporary rotation there from R3MMU, twenty miles away.

It's a tiny clinic on the side of a hill near Bazar-e Panjwaii township, a stopgap measure in an area without another hospital for miles, where anywhere you turn might be a roadside bomb or an improvised explosive device, where snipers are as numerous as wasps.

There's a helipad down the dirt road, where a medevac chopper flies serious cases to the R3MMU.

The statistics here, they're not quite as good as back at the airfield.

This is how she remembers that evening: the night air sweet, the sky bright with stars, the wind blowing warm across the desert. And then, an explosion from somewhere not far from the forward base. Minutes away.

She drops her copy of *Cien Sonetos*, and everyone is running to their posts. In a spray of dust, there's an all-terrain vehicle jamming down the road, stretchers barely hanging on to the front. The gates open within seconds, and the soldiers are unloading the two casualties from the Canadian ATV.

In the cramped area, a team of about a half dozen works on the first casualty.

Cpl. McAdams and another team join Warrant Officer Ian Patrick, who's stripped down the second man on the stretcher-table and wrapped a foil blanket around him.

The man is half-conscious, quivering, babbling something over and over. McAdams is passable in the Pashto dialect, but she can't quite understand what he's saying.

While they work, stabilizing his breathing, bandaging his leg, someone's talking in the background. "IED hit. The Afghan was driving supplies for our road construction site. That other one, he's not from here, but he's not one of ours."

Not Afghan. She looks again, and beneath the grit and sweat and blood the face is unmistakable. Her heart twists inside her. Leaning forward to incline her ear nearer his mouth, she understands what he's saying—

Her name.

Work fast, fast, she tells herself. She should be detached, concentrating. Oh God, keep my hands from shaking. A chest wound, serious. Collapsed lung. Need to do an incision. She can hear gurgling as they open him up. Get a tube in, release the excess pressure.

His body is torn, ripped apart by shrapnel. Left hand amputated—the one that held her own, one year ago, for just that fraction of a second too long. One leg gone from the knee down, the other from the hip. They can't stop the bleeding.

"Damn it, damn it, damn it!"

At her voice, his eyes suddenly open. He sees her, and there's recognition, and then he closes them. He doesn't open them again.

"Medevac!" she hears herself shouting.

But it's too late.

September 19, 2009

Honey-crisp apples, from a basket from her brother Joe, who'd served two previous tours of duty himself, and knew instinctively that for her this would mean *home.*

A week ago, Joe had come out to meet her at the Forces base at Trenton, after her final tour. He'd driven up in his shiny new blue Astra, and waxed eloquent about the immensity of the deal he'd gotten on it, because the company was shutting down. Everything was shutting down—car companies, hospitals, banks. She wished *she* could shut down.

Two and a half hours to her mother's home in Port Credit. She'd piled everything in the back of the hatchback—everything that might remind her of the war, of comrades fallen and lost, of the horrors she'd left behind—wanting to focus only on her brother's voice, the highway winding ahead, and home.

A half hour into the drive, she realized she'd been playing with the chain around her neck, winding it and unwinding it around her fingers. On its clasp, the silver medallion roller-coasted down to her thumb. She began to weep.

Honey-crisp apples. The one she bites into is lovely: tart and tangy. She finishes it, laces up her running shoes, and goes out the back, to the woods behind the house.

The neck-chain swings underneath her shirt. She runs.

Sean's Canadian Forces identity disc had survived the blast. She could see it still—two rounded rectangular halves joined in a square, one half meant to be detached and sent to National Defense, etched in her mind like a gravestone:

823-509-653

S P FORREST

NP O/RH/POS

CDN FORCES CDN

And on the reverse upper half:

DO NOT REMOVE

NE PAS ENLEVER

When they found that it wasn't a genuine I-disc, someone at the med unit thought he might have been from one of the intelligence agencies, but it turned out the I-disc wasn't even a good counterfeit. The metal was wrong, too soft, the embossing uneven across the letters. The number had been easily traceable to someone else, an I-disc splashed out for sale on eBay.

All that didn't matter to Caitlyn. What was clear was this: he had come to find her, even if that meant going into the middle of a war zone. And now he was gone.

She runs.

The banks of the Credit River are embroidered with leaves. They crackle as she passes. The air is crisp, slightly chill as she breathes it in.

She runs.

She passes the birch at the halfway point, and pauses for a pulse check. Her heart is already pumping fast as she catches a glimpse of a man, dressed in black, standing on a promontory about fifty yards from her.

She stops, and shields her eyes from the sun. A man from out of her past.

It hits her like a defibrillator jolt, but her mind calms her down. Out of nowhere, he'd appeared before in another unlikely place, half a world away. If he was real back then, real in Kandahar—then why not right here, right now, in the middle of the woods behind her mother's house, alive?

"Is it you?" she asks.

He comes closer. "Caitlyn," he says.

She leans against a tree, breathing heavily. "Sean. You were dead."

"I'm not dead. Not now."

"But how?"

"Can I come closer?"

"How?" she shouts at him, backing off. "You're not a ghost. I was there, two years ago. You were dead."

He takes a breath. "I traveled into that time. And the first time we met."

"Stay where you are."

"I can't," he says, but he stops moving toward her. "I mean… that first time, when we first met—that started out as a one-time trip. But I could only come back a year later, then it had to be now, and tomorrow it will be three years from now, and five years from then…"

"Wait." She puts up her hand. "Time travel. It can't be done."

"Not now. But tomorrow, yes. Well, to a degree. It's a limited time travel."

He stands there, not moving closer, not moving away, a steady point in space. But he continues. "You know how some satellites stay in the same place in orbit, where the gravity of the earth and moon balance each other?"

She's listening; not frowning, not confused, just listening.

"It's not fully understood, but those perfect balance points exist in space and *time*. They're where and when a person can go in the past without hitting a possible paradox."

"Like the opportunity to kill your grandfather, meaning you'd never exist."

"That's right. You can't travel to a point where that might occur. When we first met, that was a non-paradoxical point."

"But you came to Kandahar. You died there."

"Time and space, they're intertwined. The second non-paradox point in time was then, and you were where you were then. And I came back because—because I wanted to see you again."

She pushes herself off from the tree, turns, and runs. Past the birch tree, past the Credit River, home, home.

When she decides to stop and finally turns back, night has fallen, and he is gone.

September 21, 2012

Three years later, she's on a blanket on a beach in Salinas, California, unpacking a basket. Above her, gulls are beating their wings against a coastal spray.

Now that she's waiting for it, when it happens, she realizes that she can sense the return. The wind picking up, subtly, like a whisper. A swirl of waves in the distance, a subtle spiral. A shimmer, like a lens flare, in the sunlight.

"You're beautiful," he says.

She ignores that, and asks, "How long are you here for, this time?"

"Sometimes it's a few hours, sometimes a few days." He shrugs. "There aren't a lot of statistics."

"Explain it to me again, these points of balance, how they work," she says.

"S. C. Penrose, a professor at Oxford, worked out the theory of it. The next advance came twenty years after that, from a researcher at the Weyman Institute, Alex Morgan. He realized that practical transformation of the space-time sub-manifolds—"

She is frowning, and he laughs. Easy, comfortable.

"It's complicated, but not," he says. "The stable solutions are based on the Fibonacci series."

He picks up a piece of driftwood, and starts writing in the sand—

$$1 \quad 1 \quad 2 \quad 3 \quad 5 \quad 8$$

$$13 \quad 21 \quad 34 \quad 55 \quad 89 \quad 144$$

She nods. "Every number is the sum of the two before."

"When you travel into the past, as you come closer to your own time, the interval between balance points becomes larger; otherwise you eventually do hit a paradox."

"But why does it work that way? With time, I mean?"

"Nature is full of symmetries and patterns. They may be invisible, but they're there. The way trees branch, the way leaves are arranged on a stem, the way a fern uncurls, the way a nautilus shell spirals out."

Her hands reach up to where her medallion hangs from her neck-chain.

On the sand, he draws a grouping of squares, then a spiral—

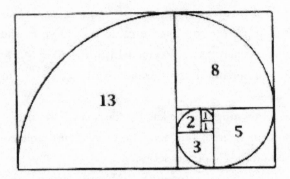

"The golden mean, the Fibonacci spiral—it's the invisible pattern behind a nautilus shell. Why not time?"

"That's beautiful," she says.

He sits down beside her. "Look, I'm sorry for Kandahar. I didn't know it would end that way. I just wanted to be there."

She doesn't answer. It's still something she wants to forget, along with many other things from that era of her life. She thinks of something, takes the driftwood, and crosses out the first four numbers in the sand—

1 1 2 3 5 8

13 21 34 55 89 144

"So after this time, the next time I can see you will be in five years? On this day?"

"Well, there's a precession..."

"Okay, I know. It's not well understood." She looks at him. "You guys haven't figured out everything about this, have you?" It's a statement, not a question.

"We're trying."

She sighs. "Well, now that you're here, make yourself at home."

She holds out a honey-crisp apple.

September 23, 2017

She's on the Bloor-Danforth subway line, on her way home late from work. Except for the conductor in his compartment, the carriage was empty when she got on, so she's a little startled when someone sits down beside her.

"I have a present for you," he says.

She flicks off the touchscreen of her e-reader, and looks up.

He's holding out a book. It's a slim volume of poetry, an edition published—she notes with amusement, as she opens it—just a few years previously.

"Where'd you get this?" she asks.

"Bespoke Books," he says. "Their motto is 'Antiquities and print on demand.' Paper is still pretty popular."

She turns to the page he's marked with a ribbon, and reads:

The Time Traveller's Sonnet

And there you are, at last: your eyes, your face.
Just as swiftly, only a memory,

a star irresolute, the lightning's trace,
a half-remembered verse of poetry.

Still, you are what keeps my atoms in place
against life's centrifuge of anarchy:

your smile, in its sadness a hint of grace,
my hope, my manifold geometry.

To be with you again, I would cross space,
and time, to where began this circled journey:

And there you are, at last: your eyes, your face.
Just as swiftly, only a memory,

a star irresolute, the lightning's trace,
a half-remembered verse of poetry.

The train rounds a curve without slowing down, and for a second the cars jiggle around their connection and the lights go black. The train straightens out and the lights go back on.

"Marry me," he says.

"Are you crazy? The next time we meet, I'm going to be older than you are."

"You're not married, are you?"

"That's beside the point. Why?"

"Because 'you are what keeps my atoms in place against life's centrifuge of anarchy,'" he says.

"Sonnets," she sighs.

September 25, 2025

She's sitting on a park bench at Ron Searle Park, watching the children on the playground. Behind her, the sounds of volleys on the tennis courts. She's scattering the remnants of an egg sandwich to the pigeons on the grass.

When he appears, she flings herself at him, beating him on the chest. "What the hell are you doing here? Get away from me! I hate you!"

As he backs away, a little girl hops off of the slide and runs toward her. "Mommy, Mommy!" She's crying.

Caitlyn hugs her, shielding her from the stranger, speaking to her softly. The little girl is still weepy, but she's nodding. After a while, she's back on the playground, this time at the swings. She swings in a wide arc—high, down, and back—kicking her feet down as they graze the ground, legs up again as she swings up, high, down, back.

Her mother is still fuming as she sits back down on the bench.

Sean waits a few minutes before joining her—taking care to place some space between them. "I'm sorry," he says.

She says nothing for a long time. Then—

"Shauna turned seven in June. And she doesn't even know her father."

He's not sure what to say. "Shauna," he repeats.

"Shauna Catherine. She doesn't deserve this, Sean. She deserves a father who's there for her, who can carry her on his shoulders, read her bedtime stories, teach her how to drive, give her away at her wedding."

He can't say anything, hadn't expected this.

"It's not fair to me." There, she finally said it. "It's not even as if you're in Australia or England, and I can get you on the phone or fly to you. When you're gone, you're *gone*."

"Caitlyn, if I could come back and be with you here and hereafter, I would. I would move heaven and earth to be with you. I would die if that would bring me to you."

She is crying now, remembering Kandahar.

"But I can't," he says, taking her in his arms. "*This* is our hereafter, this is our forever. To the limit of what God and physics allow, I will be with you."

The little girl swings high, then low.

"I may go—but I'm still here. Love remains."

The little girl swings low, then high.

September 27, 2038

She'd been waiting for him at the church at St. Alban's Road, looking back once too often at each of the faces filing in.

Then she'd looked for him at the reception, at the mansion and conservatory at the northwest corner of the university.

Finally, when all the party and most of the guests had gone, she saw him in the garden walk outside Cecil Green, and went out to meet him.

"You're late," she says.

"I'm sorry." He looks around, taking in the afternoon sun and the color of the leaves, the mountains in the distance framing the coastline of Vancouver. "I missed something."

"Only your daughter's wedding," she says, wistfully. Then throws her arms around him. "I've missed you."

They stay there a breath, holding each other, and for a moment there is nothing but the flowers and the trees and the chirp of birds. And the world whirls around them, the world of spirals and hypercatenoids, of tesseracts and planes.

"Oh God, you don't look a day older than when we last met," she says. "And look at me... Men are lucky; you go gray and you don't have to do a thing."

He smiles. "Where I'm from, we don't have to go gray."

They're walking now, through the amazing gardens and terraces, the panoramic sweep of cliffside architecture, and she's telling him everything about the wedding—about the florist who was able to find enough Oceania roses just in time, about how long it took to find the bride's gown and how eventually they settled on a Cecilia Wang design, how one of the bridesmaids dove to the floor to catch the bouquet, how the newlyweds were flying to Paris before heading back to Oxford where they now lived.

"How long do people live, where you are?" she asks.

"Longer, but not forever."

"Have you cured cancer?"

"It depends on what kind of—" He stops, stares at her for a long time.

"Come into the ballroom," she says at last. "Come and dance."

September 29, 2059

She is sitting on a collapsible canvas chair in the middle of a field, a copy of Pablo Neruda's *Veinte Poemas* open on her lap, a bouquet of flowers on the grass in front of her—when he appears.

In the distance, a man watches in a blue spinner, not moving.

Sean walks up to her. She drops the book, and turns.

The hair, the eyes, the face. It's her, but it isn't.

The woman stands, walks toward him. "I was never sure you were real, or someone her mind made up, because of the war," she says. "But it is you."

Sean can't breathe, stares at her in wonder.

"Shauna Penrose," she says. "I'm Caitlyn's daughter."

"I met you when you were seven."

"She told me everything, finally. She told me how you met, how you died, how you lived."

Only then does he realize that the field is marked by small, white slabs—flat, raised-top stone markers—as far as the eye can see.

"I've been coming since last week, on your anniversary. I wasn't sure what would happen, but I came because of her, because she asked me to."

She holds out her hand, palm up, a neck-chain hanging from the medallion.

"She wanted you to have this," she says. "She lasted a long time. Also—she wanted you to know, she waited for you as long as she could."

He takes the medallion and touches her hand—his daughter's hand. And suddenly they're crying, holding each other across the vastness of time and space, comforting each other in the way that only two people can, two people who share something dear that they have lost.

"I've got to go now," she says, finally, gesturing to the man in the spinner.

"Wait," Sean says, but she keeps on walking.

She stops only before she gets in, then turns to him one more time. "There's so much I want to talk to you about. So much I want to know that I don't know," she says. "But I do know one thing: she did love you. Maybe that's all that matters."

And she is gone.

He drops to his knees in front of the space where the bouquet and marker lie, and traces the words in a whisper—

CAITLYN McADAMS FORREST
July 1985 – August 2059
Hereafter, only love remains

A Word from Samuel Peralta

I set out to write a story about a present-day platoon of soldiers pulled forward in time, to fight a future war. "Hereafter" isn't that story.

It's a story that magically appeared while writing that platoon story, a story that a Cpl. Caitlyn McAdams demanded I write. Experience has told me that when a character wants to tell her story, you listen.

Veering away from my original plan cost me precious time—ah, if only I could travel back in time by two weeks!—but I fell in love with the new story as it unfolded, and I hope you find something in it to touch you. One day I may tell the entire story. Alas, it isn't written. Not yet. Right now I'm going crazy revamping my website—and aren't we all?

http://www.samuelperalta.com.

"Hereafter" is partially set in a future I think of as *the Labyrinth*, a world where corporations have expanded beyond governments, where people live in the shadow of surveillance by telepaths, where robots are second-class members of society on the verge of becoming self-aware.

If that world sounds almost familiar, you'd be right. Ever since I fell in love with science and speculative fiction—both the classic writers, including Isaac Asimov and Ray Bradbury, and the more contemporary, including Margaret Atwood and Kazuo Ishiguro—I've realized that what such fiction does so well is to illuminate not the future, but everyday life: life as we know it today.

At the moment my speculative fiction is less well known than my poetry, which includes several collections that range in subject from vampires, in *Sonata Vampirica,* to love poetry, in *How More Beautiful You Are,* to horror and hope, in *War and Ablution.*

Even in poetry, what I found was that, as Hugh Howey says, "I could write about my deepest thoughts, fears, and desires while disguising them as plot." Exploring the bond between a vampire and its victim was really an exploration of abusive relationships. Genetically tweaking avian embryos to recreate dinosaurs became a metaphor for resurrecting a lost love. Fragments from a girl's war diary were a symbol of hope.

We live in a present in fear of the future—of something unknown, dystopian, apocalyptic. I believe that, despite all this, there is promise, there is hope. I plan to write about that, and I hope you'll come along for the journey.

(Oh, and if I do decide I have more to say about "Hereafter," or other stories, a small circle will hear about it first on http://bit.ly/SamPeraltaNews.)

Many thanks to Michael Bunker and David Gatewood for inviting me to be a part of this amazing collection of stories, and to Jason Gurley for the inspiration to raise my hand and say "Choose me!" It's a tremendous honor to share these pages with such talented authors.

REENTRY WINDOW
by Eric Tozzi

"I CAN'T BELIEVE what I'm about to say—can't believe this is really happening. Something's landed here on Mars. Just a half mile from my current position. I watched it decelerate, so I'm certain it's not a meteor. It looked like a parachute deployed, and a piece of it fell away—maybe a heat shield. I don't know what to make of this. There were no other flights scheduled but ours. No way it's from Earth. No way."

Brett Lockwood angled his gloved hand toward the glass of his helmet to read the touch screen on his wrist. His suit had three hours of life support left. Enough time to investigate the strange object. Enough time to make it back to his lander. But after that? He'd have to engage the Mars Ascent Engine, leave the surface, and rendezvous in orbit with his crew in Epoch 1. Once systems checked out, they could start recalculating a trip back to Earth. They'd have to leave now, ahead of schedule. It was too dangerous out here. But based on the orbits of Earth and Mars, getting back home at this point might be impossible.

It was in that moment that Brett felt it sink in, an injection of resignation bleeding into his stomach, possessing his whole body, staking out a stronghold in his mind. *The window's closed, Brett. There's no going home.* The thought came loudly. But he muscled past it. *No. No, there's still a chance!* With a carefully planned gravity assist, they could build enough velocity and make it back to Earth safely.

Brett swept his display to make sure that audio was live, still recording his every word. It was. A tiny waveform at the bottom right of the screen pulsed in time with the sound of his voice.

"Still recording," he said, as if to remind himself to keep talking. He found it to be a comfort—the sound of his voice in that helmet. He'd been waiting for a response from his friend Martin Locke, flight navigator on Epoch 1, or from any of the rest of his crew: Debra Stone, William Chu, Howard Black, Kate Wallace. He could imagine hearing them as clearly as he had on any one of the two hundred days they'd spent together on the flight to Mars, each with their own distinct voice, like instruments in an orchestra. Singing now in his memory. But that's all they were. A memory. They weren't responding to his calls. As if... as if the anomaly had done something to them. Yes, the anomaly—it's why they came here to Mars in the first place.

* * *

Fifteen years earlier, the planetary exploration program had been pronounced dead. Prior to that, there had been plans for a robotic sample return mission, and even a manned mission to set up a permanent habitat on the surface of Mars. But over time, economies tanked, political will failed, people lost interest—and space exploration, whether manned or robotic, was buried and forgotten. One by one, deep-space missions were truncated and spacecraft abandoned, left to die in the uncharitable coldness of the solar system.

It was the Mars atmospheric anomaly that resurrected the planetary and deep-space exploration programs from the ashes of oblivion.

Initially described as merely a strange opening, or window, in the top of the Martian atmosphere, the anomaly soon became the primary target of investigation of the MAVEN Orbiting Spacecraft. MAVEN, or Mars Atmosphere and Volatile Evolution, had been sent to Mars for a routine study of the upper atmosphere; scientists were hoping to learn why the red planet had lost most of its atmosphere over the last several billion years. But MAVEN discovered much more. On a routine orbit, it detected a strong inflow of solar particles moving toward a focal point in the atmosphere—a point that was generating a massive quantum gravity field spike. The phenomenon, as a whole, resembled some sort of vortex.

Readings from the throat of the anomaly were off the charts—a flood of data that no one could interpret. No one knew for sure what it was they were seeing. No one could explain how it got there.

And then, on a subsequent orbital pass, MAVEN vanished.

This wasn't a situation in which a spacecraft encounters a malfunction and drops into safe mode. MAVEN simply ceased to occupy its space in Mars orbit. The phone call from JPL to Washington, DC was brief.

"What's happened to MAVEN?"

"She's gone."

"Sounds like a software issue. It's probably in safe mode, and just needs an update—"

"No, sir, it's not a software issue or a hardware issue or a malfunction of any kind. The spacecraft is *gone*."

Within a few hours, Mars Reconnaissance Orbiter and the Mars Global Surveyor were redirected into new orbits that would keep them at a theoretical safe distance from the anomaly.

Finally, after much debate, the plans for a manned mission to the Red Planet were given the green light, and the ship Epoch 1 was quickly developed and built. The mission was multi-purpose, which made it appealing to those in Congress who finally agreed to pay for it. The flight would satisfy three primary objectives: from a safe orbital distance, it would study the anomaly and catalogue its findings; it would send a lander to the surface of Mars to achieve the first human steps on the Red Planet; and, finally, it would collect soil and rock samples for return to Earth. Three missions wrapped up in one flight. Everyone agreed it was a bargain. Everyone was happy.

A week before launch, Brett and his crew spent an evening at the beach house at Cape Canaveral, just a half mile from the Apollo launch pad. Brett and Martin stood at the edge of the water, looking out over the causeway, watching a full moon rise above the horizon like a looming eye of God. William and the others were taking a short walk along the sandy shore, leaving the two friends alone.

"Crazy, isn't it? Armstrong, Aldrin, stood here eighty years ago and saw that same moon," Martin said.

Brett chuckled. "Is that what we are? Modern day Armstrongs?"

"We're going to be the first people to set foot on Mars," Martin answered. "Well, you at least. Dream come true, huh?"

Brett's gaze floated away from the shore, toward the treeline that rimmed the waterfront. Beyond it stood the Vertical Integration Facility, a fifteen-story steel edifice built to house the new Atlas Heavy launch vehicle that would carry them into space, emancipating them from the bond of Earth's gravity.

"I haven't dreamed in years."

Without looking at his friend, Martin said, "She'd be proud of you, Brett. She would."

"Maybe," Brett replied. "Anyway," he added, quickly brushing the moisture from the rims of his eyes, "I guess it takes something like this."

"Huh?"

"The Mars anomaly... I guess it takes something this bizarre to drive us back out into space. As if our solar system doesn't have enough wonders we could be exploring. Still can't believe we haven't touched the surface of Europa, or Enceladus for that matter. Can you imagine how far we'd be if this anomaly had occurred when we landed Vikings 1 and 2 back in the seventies? If the cameras had turned on and they'd seen fossils or footprints?"

Martin said, "Guess that's why we only made six lunar landings, and Apollo 17 was the end of it. People began to see the moon as something unremarkable."

"And Mars... Curiosity worked for twenty-three years," Brett quipped, "and then—nothing. Like it never happened. Just more rocks and dirt to look at. A dead-end road." He grew somber as the others, bathed now in soft, magnesium moonlight, drifted back toward them.

"Maybe we're the ones that'll reignite this whole thing, Martin. Maybe we'll give the world a chance to believe again."

* * *

A week later, with the strength of nine million pounds of sheer thrust, the five of them were moving at a speed of twenty-five thousand miles an hour, leaving Earth orbit on a sure trajectory that would take them to an intercept with the planet Mars—and the atmospheric anomaly that, as far as remote sensing was able to determine, was still present. Still mystifying.

A voyage to the Red Planet meant two hundred days in space, one way. Two hundred days without seeing blue skies, white clouds, green grass. Two hundred days confined in a space not much larger than a small, one-bedroom apartment. And each day, time dilated. There were no sunrises, sunsets, or any other occurrences that might promise a person that their existence was moving along in an ordinary world. Real-time communications with Earth began to stretch into halting exchanges punctuated by several-second delays. Then fifteen seconds. Then thirty. Then it would take minutes. By the time they reached orbital insertion at Mars, a round-trip message would take almost twenty minutes.

Brett remembered Day 100—the halfway point. It was the day he realized he was adrift on a sea a hundred trillion times wider and more open than the largest ocean back home. Looking out the viewport, he could see nothing behind them, nothing in front of them—only star-dusted infinities on each side. It was the day he felt small, lost between worlds, bound to neither one. Long past a mission abort point, still tens of millions of miles from his destination, he wondered, *My God, what the hell am I doing out here? What have I done?* It was not unlike how he'd felt when she left him.

Carrie had long, platinum-blond hair that framed a kind, youthful face. She was cute. Adorable, in fact. The love of his life. And then, one day, she left. With no explanation. Brett had no idea where she was or what had become of her. Until, many years later, a mutual friend told him about the cancer— and that she was gone. In that instant, Brett slipped through a window that exists between moments—a window into the surreal. He was a man between worlds. Lost.

After Day 100, he busied himself, so as not to dwell on the alarming truth about his celestial position. He went over his previous analysis of the anomaly, and he carefully rehearsed his entry, descent, and landing procedures. These would mostly be executed by software, but still, he ran the drill. Over and over. There could be no errors. No second chances, especially out here. No vehicle, manned or unmanned, had made it to the

Red Planet and back again to Earth. A million things could go wrong. A million things had to go right.

* * *

Day 200 came, and Epoch 1, using an aero-braking technique, achieved a successful orbital insertion around Mars.

"My God," Martin said, a shiver in his voice. "It's Mars. Look at it!"

Brett pressed himself to the viewport, and felt a tide of awe rush in. They were drifting over the Tharsis region of the Red Planet, and centered beneath them was Olympus Mons, an extinct shield volcano that soared eighty-nine thousand feet above the surface of the planet. They'd all studied the pictures of it taken from Mars orbiters over the decades. But as they saw it now, gliding past them, its sheer mass was astonishing—three times the height of Mount Everest back home.

For the next twelve hours the team of scientists settled in: they secured an orbit that would keep them at a distance of twenty kilometers from the anomaly, ran thorough checks of all systems, and unpackaged and assembled equipment that had been stowed since launch.

Finally, they began a comprehensive analysis of the anomaly.

And then, an hour later, it all changed.

"This is crazy," Martin said.

Debra floated past him to her instrument bay, passing a computer tablet to Kate. Kate swiveled away toward another panel, where she performed a data upload that would be sent back to Earth via their high-gain antenna. Howard and William studied their own findings, murmuring between each other.

"It is. But it's accurate," Debra said.

"So what you're saying is… it's gone now." Brett said.

The question hung beneath an unbearable stillness in the ship.

"It looks that way," Martin finally said. "No signature, no traces that it was ever there."

"Maybe that's the problem. It was never there to begin with. The anomaly was a malfunction in our sensors," Howard said.

Martin shook his head firmly. "No. No way that's possible."

"I'd say just about anything's possible, Martin," Howard replied evenly.

Kate added, "It doesn't explain what happened to MAVEN. We're still missing a spacecraft that we know did not deorbit and burn up in the Martian atmosphere."

Brett said, "So the anomaly was here an hour ago, and now it's… gone."

"Shut like a window," Debra said. It was the word *window* that gave them all a moment of pause. Martin locked eyes with Brett, and there was complete understanding between them.

"Maybe it's not gone. Maybe it's just… closed," Brett said.

"So. What now?" Martin asked. The mission prep had been a rigorous exercise in contingency planning, yet the possibility that the anomaly would simply *vanish*… That was one possibility that hadn't been considered.

Brett floated gently to the viewport, stopping himself there, gazing down at the curve of the Red Planet. Mars. They were orbiting Mars—the very first people ever to do so. No one else had ever seen it. Not this close.

"Guys, we're at Mars. The only ones. We've still got surface and sample operations to conduct. I suggest we proceed. We can still make history out here. Our window is still open."

And so they all fell into agreement, and began preparing for surface operations. Brett would pilot the Mars Lander down to the surface and make the first footprints in the soil. He'd do a short-range survey and collect rock and soil samples, each no bigger than an aspirin, and place them in a cache. Then, using the newly developed Mars Ascent Engine, he'd leave the planet and rendezvous with Epoch 1. They were scheduled to spend another several months in orbit. If the anomaly didn't reappear, they'd spend that time doing further atmospheric analysis. And then they'd begin the journey back home.

The surface op began just as expected. Brett safely undocked the lander from Epoch 1 and began a descent toward the upper atmosphere of Mars. All systems were stable, all lights were green. He could hear Martin in the voice-operated switch, or VOX unit, of his helmet.

"Okay Lander, you're in the approach corridor, looking good. No trajectory correction required. You'll be making first contact with the upper atmosphere in just a few seconds."

"Copy that," Brett replied, now feeling an unmistakable tremor in the frame of the lander. Soon, he knew, it would become a far stronger vibration as the enormous force of atmospheric friction began to slow his vehicle. He would feel g forces on the magnitude of seven during peak deceleration, and the heat shield beneath him would reach temperatures as hot as the surface of the sun. For about ninety seconds Brett would become a meteor.

"Okay, picking up strong vibrations here in the lander," he said out loud. Hearing the sound of his voice brought immediate comfort. "Everything's still looking good on the panels."

He felt the pressure on his body as the forces of hypersonic speed crossed swords with friction.

"Ninety seconds of this, twenty seconds of peak deceleration followed by—"

BANG. Brett snapped his gaze toward the sound at the side of the lander. *What the hell was that?* Did something burst? Helium tank? He checked his panels. All green. He closed his eyes and spoke softly to himself.

"Twenty seconds of peak deceleration followed by parachute deploy at mach two point one. Heat shield separation ten seconds after that followed by—"

Brett heard a voice on the radio.

"You've drifted, Lander. Brett, your position is...target landing ellipse...recomp..."

Martin's voice was cutting in and out, his words reduced to mere syllables. Brett fumbled with the VOX icon on the wrist display attached to his suit. It still showed a healthy signal strength.

"Wait. Epoch One, say again?"

There was nothing.

"Martin? Martin? Epoch One, I can't hear you—"

"…an…ly…it's back…an…en…"

Brett shouted, "I can't hear you, Martin! Did you say something about the anomaly? Epoch One, do you copy me?"

All at once, the spacecraft went dark. Every display, every indicator light failed, plunging Brett into iron cold darkness. Then, alarmingly, the forces of deceleration ceased, replaced by a plunging sensation through sheer emptiness. As if… as if the atmosphere itself had opened beneath him and he was falling down a very deep hole. Absolute vertical descent. An express elevator with the cables cut.

Panic sank its fangs into him like a rattlesnake before he even knew it was there. His heart rate broke a gallop, his breath coming in short, staccato gasps. *I'm falling,* he thought loudly. *I'm falling!*

Brett groped with gloved hands until he felt a panel of the spacecraft he could grab hold of. He closed his eyes, feeling motionlessness, yet there remained the terrible sensation of a plunge. *Terminal velocity,* he thought. *I'm a meteor. I'm dead. This is it. Oh, God, if you're real… please… I don't want to die out here. I don't want to die.*

There came another *bang,* a shotgun blast of sound. Immediately, Brett felt himself gain seven times his body weight, and he fell unconscious.

* * *

The light that penetrated his eyelids seemed ashen, the color of a distant, smoldering fire. He felt himself still in his suit, in what he sensed was a supine position, a hard surface beneath him. The ship? Had he crashed? He could breathe; oxygen was plentiful in his helmet.

Still in my suit. Still breathing. Okay, Brett, move. Move.

Carefully he shifted his legs, one at a time. Then his arms, wiggling his fingers inside his gloves.

I can move, he thought.

He rolled slowly over, planting himself on his hands and knees, feeling something there under his hand. A rock?

Open your eyes.

He cracked his lids apart, a boorish, gauzy flare of reddish-pink light striking him. He squinted, allowing his pupils to adjust. Gradually the dust and rocks of the surface of Mars resolved in front of him. Right there under his hands.

Impossible. *The ship... Where's the ship?*

Brett stood and centered himself. He turned slowly around, taking in the rock-rimmed horizon. There, a hundred yards off, was the lander—and miraculously, it appeared to be intact. But how did he get all the way out here? How did he survive? He couldn't remember anything after the sound and the feeling of immense heaviness.

"Epoch One, do you copy?"

Nothing.

"Epoch One, I've reached the surface somehow. Do you copy me? Martin? Deb? Epoch One?"

There was no reply, just the sound of his erratic breathing. And it dawned on him that something must have happened to them. The anomaly, perhaps? Did it really matter? He was alone. Alone on the surface of another planet. It felt wholly ironic: he'd dreamt of this moment nearly his entire life—the first man on Mars—and now, he'd trade it with someone else in a heartbeat if it meant he could be back home on Earth.

Brett looked skyward, into the orange-red haze of the atmosphere. And there he saw something moving very fast above him: a small, dark form. Falling. What was it? Too far away to see. Meteor? But suddenly it sprouted what looked like a parachute, and then a piece of it fell away. It slowed dramatically, small descent engines igniting beneath its rounded hull. A vehicle. Not Brett's. Most certainly not Epoch One. And before he could blink, the form had vanished behind a distant serrated rim, forged of jagged Martian rocks and soil.

"Houston, this is Brett Lockwood of the crew of Epoch One. I'm sending this via my low-gain antenna, hoping you'll pick me up via Mars Reconnaissance Orbiter or Mars Global Surveyor on the DSN. I'm on the surface of Mars. Lander is intact, it seems. I've lost contact with Epoch One. I can't reach anyone. Please respond."

He'd have to wait for a reply, which would be twenty minutes later. If he even got one. Could anyone hear him? The silence that draped him was suffocating. Finally, he spoke.

"I can't believe what I'm about to say—can't believe this is really happening. Something's landed here on Mars. Just a half mile from my current position. I watched it decelerate, so I'm certain it's not a meteor. It looked like a parachute deployed, and a piece of it fell away—maybe a heat shield. I don't know what to make of this. There were no other flights scheduled but ours. No way it's from Earth. No way."

In the lesser gravity of Mars, Brett made his way quickly toward the ridge where the strange thing had disappeared.

"I'm walking in the direction of the object now," he said. "Should be able to make that ridge in fifteen minutes or so. I have no idea if I've landed in my target ellipse. The terrain doesn't look anything like it should. Geology is all wrong. I've got no way to know for sure where I am. This is crazy."

After what seemed like an eternity, he reached the base of the ridge. It sloped upward at a benign angle. He could make it to the top, if he was careful to mind all the rocks. If he were to puncture his suit on a sharp stone, he'd be dead quickly. *Mind the rocks.*

"Made it to the ridge. I'm going to climb it and take a look. See what's on the other side," he said to no one but himself.

Brett ascended the slope cautiously, as loose stones around him gave way, rolling gently away from him. The soil was very soft, powdery, lightly coating the outside of his suit, staining it brick red. When he crested the rim he spotted the mysterious object, and crouched very low.

There it was. Fifty yards out. The talcum-fine Martian dust was hanging over it like a veil, obscuring finer details that might have helped him identify what he was seeing. Behind the lingering Martian haze, the object appeared as a mottled, dark form—squat and mechanical. He thought about the implications of what he was staring at, the magnitude of the moment he was experiencing.

"I have a visual on the object now, although it's... I can't believe I'm seeing this. It's obscured by a ring of dust hanging in the air, not dissipating. I'd have to move closer to get any sense of what this thing might actually be. But the question is… should I? Whatever this is, it's not from Earth, so the only conclusion to draw is that it's alien. Crazy. Probably unmanned, but I can't assume that. I can't assume anything. I don't know what to think anymore. I don't understand what's happening here."

Brett heard a soft alarm. On his wrist panel he saw the words INCOMING SIGNAL, followed by an audio waveform that unspooled across the display. He listened closely as, for the first time since landing on the surface, he heard another person's voice. A voice he didn't recognize.

"This is Dr. Hunter at the Jet Propulsion Laboratory. We don't understand your message. We don't know anything about a Mars Reconnaissance Orbiter or Mars Global Surveyor. We don't know anything about Epoch One. We detected your signal via Viking One's high-gain antenna and the Deep Space Network."

Brett held very still then, trapped in a motionless crouch.

"Wait—did you say *Viking One*?"

It was a beat later when he realized they wouldn't hear him, at least not for another ten minutes. He'd answered on sheer instinct, as anyone would do in a conversation—listen and respond in real time. But out here there was no such thing as real time. No such thing. A chill hit him then, in the very center of his chest. *Time.* What time was it? His display read 12:25:03 UT (Universal Time), converted to local Mars time as 16:45.

Brett drew on his memory. History. Viking 1 had landed... when was it... July 20, 1976 at 11:53 UT. It was now 12:25 UT, and he'd seen this thing fall some thirty minutes ago. *No,* he thought. *No, Brett. You're losing it down here. Probably effects of long-term space travel. Delusions, perhaps?* A psychological break—*my God*—what was happening? And which was more bizarre: that he was experiencing some sort of psychotic episode on the surface of another planet, or that the thing sixty yards away from him was a spacecraft that had landed here over seventy years ago?

He reasoned quickly: if by some crazy coincidence he had landed near the Viking 1 site, the craft itself would still be here—so not all that strange. But he knew that after decades in the sub-zero cold of Mars, Viking 1 had been destroyed. Orbiter images from the past forty years had shown the landing site and the spacecraft both covered in dust, its long robotic sampling arm disengaged from the rest of the craft, canted on its side near the foot of the lander. Viking 1 was a derelict.

The strange dust that had been obscuring the object finally thinned. There was no mistaking it now. The view was clear. There it was: Viking 1—in perfect health—unmolested by the punishing temperatures and suffocating soil of Mars. A phantom reborn into existence, now as real, as new as it had been on July 20, 1976.

"Epoch One, do you copy?"

No answer.

"Martin, do you copy?"

Vacant moments bled together.

"Debra? William? Kate? Do you copy?"

His heart thudded painfully against the inside of his chest.

"Epoch One—does anyone copy me?"

He turned his gaze into the expanse of the Martian sky, a vast, rust-colored void. Epoch One was gone. Or, more precisely, *he* was gone. They'd lost him the moment he'd penetrated the core of the anomaly—a corridor back through time. A reentry window.

And he imagined all of them calling his name on the radio, desperate for the sound of his voice.

"Epoch One. Martin, Deb… all of you… if you can hear me… if by some miracle you can hear me… I'm alive. I can't explain what's happened here. But if this is what I think it is, then I'm about to make history."

Brett decided there was only one thing to do. Because he was dreadfully sure he would never make it back to Epoch 1. Epoch 1 no longer existed. There would be no rendezvous. No rescue. No such thing. This was going to be the only way to prove he existed at all.

Further radio communication was no good. Dr. Hunter at the Jet Propulsion Laboratory would just think he was some whacko that had hacked the channel in order to play a clever prank. The alternative conclusion would be unimaginable. But if they saw it with their own eyes…

The cameras on Viking 1 were meant to capture still images intermittently over long periods of time. There was no video capability. No live feed from the spacecraft. There was no way to tell if or when the cameras were active. It could be hours before they took another image. And that's all he had left now. Hours. Carefully, he stood upright and climbed over the rim, walking directly toward the first human spacecraft to land on the surface of Mars.

* * *

"First color images are coming back! We've got color images coming down now!"

Everyone in the mission support area at the Jet Propulsion Laboratory crowded around their TVs to watch. It had been some twelve hours since Viking had landed on the surface of Mars and sent back its first images. Despite the fact that they were black and white, they had managed to awe the entire world. But the first *color* images would be beyond compare, and the anticipation was electric, as though a million volts were in the air around them.

The image bloomed on the TV screens with a startling suddenness, the reddish, butterscotch tint of the ground, rocks and horizon immediately obvious. Wild applause broke out in the room, along with roars and cheers. There were long embraces, firm handshakes, and tears of joy. Then, strangely, all the noise began to dim, as one by one, everyone noticed something in the image. Something...

"Whoa... what is that? What are we seeing there?"

Dr. David Williams, the Mars mission director, pushed through his colleagues and slipped on his glasses to purchase a better look at the image. A reporter with NBC News tried to shoulder his way toward the TV monitor.

"Dr. Williams? Dr. Williams, can you tell us what we're looking at? Are those... footprints?"

Someone nearby scoffed, hastily edging the reporter out of the way and toward the exit. "That's absurd. These images have to be carefully analyzed. You're in no position to say what we're actually seeing here."

And suddenly all the voices overlapped in the mission support area of the Jet Propulsion Laboratory, July 21, 1976.

"Those are boot prints! Look at the shape—"

"—yes, yes, look... left, right, left, right, leading off—"

"—over that rim! Life! My God, there's life on Mars—"

Someone else shouted, "We don't know that! We can't say that for certain, so don't print that! Are you listening? Don't print that!"

One of the flight technicians approached Dr. Williams quietly and asked, "Sir, what do you think? Is this evidence of life on Mars?"

Dr. Williams never turned his head from the screen. Never blinked. He simply pulled his glasses off the bridge of his nose and replied, "I don't yet know *what* it is. But I'm certain of one thing: we're all going to spend the rest of our lives trying to figure it out. It's a new age we're stepping into. A brand new age. The space program will never be the same."

A Word from Eric Tozzi

Yes, I worked for NASA at the Jet Propulsion Laboratory for five years. And no, I'm not a rocket scientist. Though if I had a dollar for every time someone asked me that question, I could fund my next feature film.

I was a television documentary producer and editor for the Mars Exploration Program. The missions I covered were primarily surface missions: Curiosity Rover, Spirit and Opportunity Rovers, and the Phoenix Polar Lander. Getting an up-close, behind-the-scenes look at planetary exploration greatly inspired my debut novel, *The Scout*, an alien invasion thriller. Exploring that terrain in a book was exciting and felt wholly organic.

Time travel is one of those genres that I've always found absolutely captivating, but decided I would never attempt as a writer. Honestly, I found it intimidating. And then, out of the clear blue, I was invited to contribute a story to this anthology, and I immediately said yes. Ten minutes later I asked myself: "What have I gotten myself into?" I wracked my brain for ideas that first day. Time travel—what do I do with this? Where or *when* do I begin the story? And somehow, my mind drifted to Mars and space exploration.

Between Earth and Mars there is no such thing as real-time. You cannot communicate or send and receive data in real-time. Having a conversation with mission control from the surface of Mars would go something like this: "Hi, we are all fine here. How are you?" Seven to ten minutes later, mission control on Earth gets the message, and replies, "We are doing great. How's the weather out there?" Seven to ten minutes later, Mars gets that reply. For a simple exchange, it's anywhere from fourteen to twenty minutes round-trip, depending on the orbits of the two planets and the distance between them. In space exploration, once you leave Earth, real-time ceases to exist. And that was my jumping-off point for "Reentry Window."

To say I am thrilled to be a part of this anthology is an understatement. More accurately, I'm humbled—humbled to be in the company of such gifted writers. It's my sincere desire that this story gives you a chance to dream, to travel through space and time, and perhaps to experience some of the excitement of an event as extraordinary as landing on another planet.

If you'd like to know more about my work as a writer and filmmaker, please visit my website: www.erictozzi.com

The Swimming Pool of the Universe
by Nick Cole

"THE LAST THING YOU REMEMBER..." Private Dexter Keith asked himself, "is what?"

The question is important. Really important when your mind is scrambled. When time is "messing with you," as Sergeant Collins would say. But the drill sergeant had spoken those words back in the red dirt of a Georgia that now flooded Private Keith's temporarily scrambled neural pathways. A Georgia of basic infantry training; of last year, 2147. A still-living memory of events. Complete with the smells of magnolia and road tar, open-faced turkey sandwiches and grease from the chow hall.

Oven-roasted turkey and magnolia mixing in the heat of a hot day.

Then time had begun to echo.

Time echoes?

"Damn straight, grunt!" yells Sergeant Collins. "Time can echo, reverberate, cavitate. Time can do all kinds of crazy things when one of those phase grenades goes off. *POW*, and things get hazy for a moment or two. Your mind is dancing, for want of a better word. Dancing between the past and the present because of that Spider grenade that just went off next to you. So you got to ask yo'self something, recruit. Something real important I once taught ya." It's a hot Sunday in Georgia when Sergeant Collins tells him this.

Wait—*told* him that.

"But that's the past," Dexter Keith struggles to remind himself.

"You got to understand, a phase grenade messes with your mind, grunt. With your memory. But all you got to do is just remember everything I tell you. You associate concepts in times of crisis and stress, and I'll be right there for you, and you'll live."

Private Keith bangs on the side of his combat helmet and tries to focus on his present situation. Nomad 247. Spiders are overrunning his unit's position.

"Johnson, what the hell are you doing?" yells Sergeant Collins, back in Georgia on that hot morning of turkey and tar. Way back when.

Zip rifle bursts sizzle and crack across nearspace as Nomad 246 tumbles drunkenly through the star field above Private Keith.

"I'm on Nomad 247. That's where I'm at now," confesses Private Keith to himself. "Georgia is a long way away from here." He drops onto the ice as micro-gravity begins to loosen its too-loving, motherly grasp, and the asteroid begins its tumble upward. A wave of phase nausea sweeps over his cold, sweating skin.

Phase-grenade-induced memories overwhelm his explosion-fractured mind.

His mother is holding him in her arms, in the community pool on a hot Saturday in August. They swim into the deep end, where he has been too afraid to go alone. Swimming in the pool with his mother was the only place he would ever let her hold his rigid, strong-willed, little-boy body. He was too independent to let it happen in any other time or place. But in the pool, in the deep end, frightened of the water and the chaos of bigger children splashing, he clings to his mother while she holds him close, in the near weightlessness of the pool.

"I'm on Nomad 247," chants Dexter Keith to himself, in an attempt to clear his thoughts, as he clings to an asteroid tumbling through the vastness of the Near Oort cloud. The asteroid is approaching the pinnacle of its momentary lack of gravity.

"I'm in a combat situation on an asteroid in orbit around another asteroid identified as Nomad 246," continues Keith as he feels his grip on the universe slipping. "I'm experiencing brief periods of micro-gravity brought on by their close orbiting bodies."

"Damn straight again, Keith," calls out Sergeant Collins. "You some kinda brain? I'm gonna recommend you for OCS! Now all you got to do is figure out why you're down there." Another wave of phase nausea, and Sergeant Collins turns away to direct verbal fire onto the nearby, and perpetually slacking, Johnson back in Georgia. Back in basic training. "Johnson! Get down and start knockin' 'em out till *I* get tired!" In the red dirt of Georgia a year ago, Private Johnson drops to the ground and begins to execute the punitive push-ups, counting them out with feigned enthusiasm.

And back on Nomad 247, the Spiders, the mortal enemies of Private Dexter Keith and his squad, alien invaders come to destroy all humanity, are advancing. In the background noise of Keith's combat helmet, the rest of the squad scream like children splashing in the waters of a long-forgotten collection of chlorine and water, cackling with calls of delight. His mother—this asteroid—pulls him closer as gravity resumes its embrace. All about him, technological mayhem, as both human and alien cut each other to shreds without prejudice or mercy. The asteroid, pulling him into itself as the dead and dying are flung off into the void, reminds Dexter Keith of that swimming pool and his mother's arms. In the swimming pool of the universe, gravity is also love.

"Yeah, you're some kind of super genius, Private Keith," begins Sergeant Collins above the battle chatter of the dying squad. "Your parents musta paid good money for them genes. Now the big question is, grunt, what'chu gonna do now that you got knocked senseless by that phase grenade and your mind is wobbling back and forth between Nomad 247 and the past? Seems like a real important question right about now, especially since the enemy is advancing on your position. Might be time to fight back or do something, don't you think?"

"Yeah," thinks Private Dexter, "fight back, let them know who's boss." Gravity begins to let go again, ever so softly, and Private Keith sticks his head up above a black outcrop of deep space-hardened ice and nickel. The edge of the squash-shaped asteroid that is Nomad 247 tracks in his heads-up display, graphing and calculating the lip and contours ahead. Beyond the lip begins the gentle fall toward the waist of the squash, and the enemy gun emplacement firing on the *Lexington*.

"Damn Spiders musta thrown a grenade up here, trying to dislodge our position. We in the deep end now, Private Keith. Looks like we're gonna have to repel an assault," says Sergeant Collins.

"Trooper Keith, this is Doghouse, do you read me? Repeat..." The command net operator sounds distracted, bored, uninterested in the fate of Private Dexter Keith.

"Roger, roger, I read you crystal," replies Keith in transmission voice. The helmet's software recognizes his tone and broadcasts the reply on an authorized net.

"Private Keith, I show you as the only active friendly on Nomad two-four-seven, can you confirm?" Again, the tone is bored.

For a moment, Keith lays his helmeted head down on the rock and ice. He closes his eyes and concentrates on breathing. He knows he's supposed to do this as gravity begins to disappear. But even the sound of his breath fades away as his stomach begins to float. He clings to the rocky surface of the pitching piece of nickel and ice known as Nomad 247 as it flings itself, end over end, through the void.

Johnson, Ferengetti, Reeves, Markowitz—all gone. The entire scout platoon wiped out within moments of jumping onto Nomad 247. And Sergeant Collins? He's gone too.

"I ain't gone, knucklehead. I'm still here, you stupid grunt," roared Sergeant Collins.

"No, Sergeant, you're dead too," whispers Keith to a vast universe with a gift for loneliness.

"Listen up grunt, how about I crawl over to your position and *show* you how dead I am. You got to get back in the game, soldier. You're Airborne—*we're* Airborne, we don't just roll up and die when those Spiders toss a grenade at us. We're death from above! It's time to start killing, grunt! Or are you just some 'leg,' waitin' for orders? If so, why don't you jes' dig in and make yo'self comfortable."

"I ain't no leg," whispers Keith, gritting his teeth as he dismisses the worst insult an Airborne Trooper can be called. A leg. A mere infantryman.

"Then good to go, Private Keith, Airborne! Right now you're the only one of us Command can talk to. You're also about to get yo'self overrun by Spiders. So here's what we're going to do. I'll flank to their right and try to get them to shift fire. I want you to lob some chaff grenades past the lip. Those things will mess with their commo for a moment or two, and then, when gravity resumes, I want you to assault through their position. Roger?"

Private Dexter Keith feels his body trying to leave the asteroid, as once again the massive piece of space rock tumbles skyward. Out in space, he sees the *Lexington* taking heavy fire for a brief, dizzying second.

"Roger that, Private Keith?" barks Sergeant Collins again.

"Roger that," intones Private Keith, blotting out thoughts of imminent death on a tumbling ball of ice and nickel. Alone and far from home.

"Say again, Private Keith. Your transmission is coming in broken and distorted." It's Doghouse, the comm operator aboard the *Lexington*.

"Command, I have a status update for our squad." Private Keith reaches back along his web gear, searching for the magnetic clip dispenser that will release two of his six chaff grenades. "I have contact with Sergeant Collins. His communication and telemetry equipment seem to be malfunctioning, but he assures me he's combat ready."

"Be advised, Private Keith, that we are tracking multiple Spiders converging on your AO. Fire mission upon request."

"Don't let them use those damn cannons," hisses Collins. "They'll kill you, Keith. Just one of them heavy-caliber depleted-uranium rounds from the main rail guns will turn this whole rock to powder."

"Negative, negative, Doghouse, do not, repeat, do *not* fire on our position. We are engaging the enemy."

"Damn straight," says Sergeant Collins. "Now, on my command, pick your butt up and attack, and make sure to use them grenades first, Super-Brain. Just like training back in Georgia."

Private Keith hurls the two chaff grenades forward into the rising lip of Nomad 247, as the gentle hug of gravity returns. "Forty-five seconds before zero-G returns," mumbles Keith to himself. Information from the Op Order that has survived the effects of the phase grenade. The chaff grenades seem to hang for a moment as he retinally cues his HUD to track them. Then with a deft flick of his eye reticule, he directs the grenades downward beyond the rapidly descending ledge of the asteroid. A second later, they disappear over the lip of his temporary horizon, and a moment after that, the faint crumple of aluminum foil can be heard in his ears as the comm channel picks up traces of their explosion. He leaps up and leans forward, running toward the falling lip of the tumbling asteroid. Above him, Nomad 246 falls toward the horizon, its scarred face suffering even more violent revolutions than those of Nomad 247.

Bounding over the lip, he encounters two Spiders picking their way forward. One cautiously holds a heavy zip gun between its two forearms, while the other carries a pistol and another phase grenade. The one with the heavy weapon has probably been watching the lip as they make their approach, but the suddenness of Keith bounding over the ledge has taken it completely by surprise. Keith's HUD highlights the chaff grenades' explosion radius farther downslope.

For a brief moment, the two Spiders and Private Keith do nothing, while Nomad 246 sinks queasily below the horizon of midnight ice. Then the Spider with the pistol begins to fire, rearing up on its back legs. The first shot goes wild, sizzling off into the void, and the next would surely tear a gaping hole in Keith's battle gear and body armor. But even as the Spider aims for its next shot, depleted-uranium rounds spit forth from Keith's autorifle in a brutal sewing machine of bright fury, ripping the two Spiders to shreds, and flinging their various parts, along with torn suit fragments, out into the void at the edge of the solar system.

Seconds later, gravity has disappeared, and Keith is grappling with disintegrating ice and crumbling rock. He clutches frantically at the brittle surface of the pitching asteroid as his mother whispers comfort, and murmurs a forgotten song to him, back in the deep end of that pool on that long-ago hot summer day. In front of him, at the far end of the rising landscape, a full cohort of Spiders, ignoring the loss of planetary embrace, scramble forward, their eight major limbs grappling with rock and ice effortlessly.

"Damn Spiders everywhere!" shouts Sergeant Collins.

"Damn Spiders everywhere," thinks Keith. And now the phase nausea rushes at him again, intense like a swarm of softly buzzing bees. Turkey and grease in the air, Johnson doing push-ups near the pool's edge, on the hottest day of summer at the city pool back in Oakland, California. Memories from the heart of the solar system, far from the edge where the *Lexington* now barely holds her ground, engaging the three Spider Hulks that twist and roll crazily above, in the spinning microcosm that is another struggle for life and death above Nomad 247.

Time bends like a reed and snaps as the single-mindedness of warfare commences. Was there a time before this? Will there be an "after"? The scout platoon, just like the Spider cohort, had deployed onto Nomad 247 only forty-five minutes earlier, sent in to secure the spinning piece of rock and ice for the tactical advantage it might prove itself to be. If gravity is love in the swimming pool of the universe, then what are time and its inherent memories? Tender mercies of things past in the relentless hell of a moment?

Sergeant Collins screamed, exhorted, cursed, and urged Keith on as he fought the Spiders, first using up all his depleted-uranium ammo, then his remaining grenades, and finally deploying the spring-loaded, industrial, diamond-bladed bayonet from his rifle. He slashed and hacked at the physically weaker Spiders, removing limbs and antennae, gouging out endless eyes, and feeling the rifle find purchase in the pulp beneath the mesh of their fibershell environment suits.

Chaos.

Anger.

Red murder.

Nomad 246 said "hello," and "hello" again, like some jolly, ageless uncle that galloped above the battlefield. The Spider Hulks erupted in blue fire as their once-impenetrable point defense networks collapsed beneath the onslaught of the *Lexington*'s main guns and multiple launch system turrets.

Beyond that, the stars swam like children in a pool, laughing and beckoning on a hot, long-ago summer day that promised to never end.

"Damn straight," said Sergeant Collins to the universe, and then he too was gone.

* * *

"What you're experiencing," said the psych officer during Private Dexter Keith's last session at the VA, "is a form of

PTSD. It's called association cavitation." Dexter Keith, now a civilian UberMart manager, focuses on those words as wave after wave of housewives, most trailing screaming children, brandish their PDAs in coupon mode at the harried checkers.

The store telemetry system has fritzed out due to solar activity, and now the Transactors aren't recognizing the PDAs' coupon signals. Beautiful women, bronzed and reinforced with all the latest offerings in cosmetic efficiency, snort and cackle among themselves as Dexter Keith works on the broken Telecomm box. Sweat streams down his jowly face in rivulets. He has gained more than a little weight since leaving the Expeditionary Corps.

Lately he hears Sergeant Collins cajoling and cursing at him in crisis situations, which now seem to be the norm for the newly promoted manager of UberMart, New Las Vegas.

At first it bothered him. He never wanted to be reminded of the horror of Nomad 247. He didn't want to hear the screaming of that day anymore. The cries—and other, pulpier sounds—of both friend and foe had plagued him for his first six months back on Earth. As always, there was Sergeant Collins reminding him to "hang tough," "gut it out," and in time—someday—he, Dexter Keith, would get better. But ten years later, he was beginning to hear the voice of Sergeant Collins more and more often.

"It's a minor side effect," the kind young psych officer had assured him at the veterans' hospital, "of your training." The way the psych officer used the word "training" made it seem as though Private Dexter Keith's long-lost instruction in basic infantry training had consisted of fighting with sticks and heavy rocks. "But the training programs today are much better. The Sergeant Collins program has been removed from service. The tendency for soldiers to hold on to Sergeant Collins caused some unexpected adjustment problems once they were returned from active duty." Sorrowful warmth painted the smile he offered Dexter.

"He saved my life," mumbled Dexter in reply.

"If it helps, there never was a Sergeant Collins. He was just a program written at WonderSoft to teach trainees, like yourself, how to fight and survive in space. From the day you first entered basic training, you were inundated with all kinds of subconscious programming to encourage you to respond to him. His African-American straight talk and his Mississippi mud accent were all contrived to make him seem both familiar and terrifying. When you simmed in Virtual he was always there, punishing you when you did wrong and rewarding you when you accomplished a task.

"It was thought," droned the psych officer, "that if soldiers were ever isolated on the battlefield—overwhelmed, as it were—the Sergeant Collins program would kick in and give the soldier the illusion of help. A form of security, as it were.

"I know events that day were horrible and that you feel bad, but there are things to feel good about. Those days were a fight for our lives. I mean, I was still in elementary school, but I remember the war. It was a fight for the very existence of the human race. We were *that close* to going over the hill and into history. But what you did that day, along with the entire crew of the *Lexington*—and in fact, the whole effort of the human race—turned the tide. That's something to be proud of. *You did that, not Sergeant Collins.*

"So just remember, when Sergeant Collins starts talking, it's just association cavitation produced in a time of crisis or stress. It's just a harmless medical condition brought on by the phase grenade injury you sustained, and the result of bad programming we didn't have the time to test back in the early days of the war. It's only a minor side effect. Ignore it, and in time it will probably go away. And if it doesn't, I can write you a prescription for Blissadol."

* * *

Now, back at the UberMart, petulant housewives are starting to mock him. He sees what they see, and in a way, he agrees with them. A fat man scrambling to meet their insatiable needs on one of the hottest days of the year, with everything he does going wrong, exploding in his face like a series of gags in some silent film. It's almost laughable. It could be something from the early days of cinema if only it weren't happening to him. It's a comedy of errors—and sadly, it's his life.

"Now stop that talk, Private Brain. You're going to break my heart with all your bellyaching. Put it in gear, son, and get it done. Time's a-wastin'," barks Sergeant Collins from across the folds of Dexter Keith's combat-fried brain and antique faulty combat programming.

"Excuse me," says one platinum-blond, BlueChem-eyed housewife over her monstrous breasts. "Is there someone else in charge here? Someone who knows what they're doing? I really have a lot of very important things to do besides sit here and watch you fumble with what seems to be a very simple procedure."

"Tell her to eat depleted uranium and die, Private Keith," hisses Sergeant Collins.

No can do, Sergeant. Customer service is critical at UberMart, whispers Keith.

"Damn me, Private Keith, I never thought I'd see the day when one of my grunts ended up like this. Runnin' an UberMart. I bet you think you're somethin' and all."

No, Sergeant. Not at all.

"Well, we'll see what we'll see, but first you'd better extricate yo'self from this mess you seem to be in. What'chu gonna do, Private Keith?"

"Excuse me," says Monster Breasts. "What's your name and employee ID number? My husband golfs with the regional head of this crappy little store and..."

"Smack her around, Keith."

No can do, Sarge.

"All right then, ignore her. She's harmless. The most important thing right now is that you work the problem. Not the equipment. You know what I mean, young trooper. Just like a rifle malfunction. The equipment works; it's just that there's a problem somewhere in the system—and once you fix that problem, the equipment will work like its s'posed to. Roger?"

Roger that, Sergeant.

Keith finds the problem, and seconds later the Transactors go online. Housewives clap for themselves and say things like,

"Honestly," and, "It's about time!" Keith smiles his fat man's smile and mops the sweat from his forehead. Delora, the head checker, gives him a thumbs-up and a grateful victory smile. An honest smile, a good smile. A smile he thinks about late at night when he sits on his back porch in the cool breeze of the Martian night and thinks about not being alone anymore.

Later in the afternoon, on the loading dock out back, Dexter Keith smokes a cigarette and leans against the red sandstone wall.

"It's days like today..." he thinks, but doesn't finish.

"It's days like today," whispers Sergeant Collins out of the silence, "that make me proud to have trained such a fine soldier as yourself. You done good, son! You just been too hard on yourself lately. Don't let things mess with your head."

I won't, Sergeant Collins.

"Damn straight. I won't let you. Now what about that pretty young thing up front, what's her name?"

Delora, Sergeant Collins.

"Ah, Delora. Sounds real nice when you say it like that. I think you in love, Private Keith."

Maybe, Sergeant Collins.

"Well, tomorrow we gonna start training. Oh-dark-hundred we gonna run, Private Keith. We're going to get back into fighting shape and show that Delora what an Airborne trooper looks like. I'm'a make one hundred and eighty pounds of rompin', stompin', death from above outta you again. And what do you think you're doin' smoking, Private Keith? Crush that thing and start knockin' 'em out! You owe me some push-ups, recruit."

Push-ups, Sergeant Collins?

"Did I stutter, Private Keith? Count off so I can hear you." Dexter Keith lowers himself to the hot grit of the Martian stone, and for the first time in a long time, begins to exercise. It feels good.

If gravity is love in the swimming pool of the universe, and time a tender mercy in the unrelenting hell of a terrible moment, then what is Sergeant Collins?

One, two, three... one. One, two, three... two...

Sergeant Collins?

"Yeah, Private Keith?"

"Thanks."

Perhaps a voice in the dark. Someone to hold onto in the deep end of the swimming pool of the universe.

A Word from Nick Cole

I believe that real readers are often found with a collection of short stories at hand. To me, people who read short stories are special; they do it for the love. You can tell they're looking for that brief, whirling moment through another world, and they don't care about passport stamps or spoons from some tourist trap. Or even a T-shirt with a LAGUNA BEACH LIFE-GUARD logo stamped across it. No, short-story readers are not like that at all. Short-story readers are like scouts scanning the horizon, searching for lost cities and hidden treasures. Like dancers dancing to a song at some sudden wedding they just happened into in some unfound village of happy and good people.

No, short stories don't make the big lists. They seldom get invited to the movies, and no one makes a miniseries out of them. Short stories are usually personal, for both reader and writer. We—both of us—do it for the love. Thank you for taking the time to read our stories.

But that doesn't mean we don't like the big books. The books we can sink our teeth into. The books we can settle down with, and even live and love in for a while. So, if you'd like to read some books I've written, they're collected in a series called *The Wasteland Saga*.

In 2011 I wrote a book called *The Old Man and the Wasteland*, and people liked it. So, I wrote two sequels. The second book in the series, *The Savage Boy*, is available as a stand-alone, and the final novel, *The Road Is a River*, is available as part of the completed trilogy *The Wasteland Saga*. (It's a pretty good deal! Three books for the price of one.) And this August, HarperVoyager will publish a brand new sci-fi novel I've written called *Soda Pop Soldier*. It's basically *Call of Duty* meets *Diablo*.

To find all of my books, and to learn how to obtain them in your favorite format, just go to the Nick Cole page at Harper Collins Publishers.

Thank you for reading our short stories. Let me know how you like them on Twitter @nickcolebooks or on my page on Facebook. Or swing on over to my website for backstory and (coming soon) post-apocalyptic swag at nickcolebooks.com.

And I hope you enjoyed the story of Private Dexter Keith. I think things are going to work out for him.

The River

by Jennifer Ellis

2012

"HOW MANY MILES today, oh exalted exercise goddess?" Paul gave her his usual sly grin as he sidled up to her in the park.

Sarah snorted and bent forward into a deeper stretch. "How could you not know? It's in the schedule. Ten miles, of course. We're tapering." Her body felt taut, excited, wanting to go further—ready to rip off the band-aid and feel the pain of exertion and leave Paul aching behind her. Which of course was exactly the point of a taper. The Ironman was in a week.

"I have my mind on other things. I depend on you to know what we're doing." Paul jogged in place lightly. He wore a fitted white running shirt and tight navy shorts. She almost laughed at his muscled perfection and the tongue-in-cheek horseshoe mustache he occasionally sported. Every single woman they passed today, and probably some of the men, would be completely dazzled by Paul. She'd seen it happen. She, unfortunately, remained unmoved. Dead baby sisters had a way of damping the libido and emotions. Still, something in Paul's eyes caught and held, as it sometimes did when she wasn't on guard.

"Someday, I'm going to say screw the program and just keep running and see if you can keep up," Sarah said.

His sky-blue eyes flashed with the challenge, but he gave her a broad smile. He'd like that, she realized with another catch.

"I'm sure you'd leave me wasted in your dust," he said. "But I know you'd never lie, so I have no fears of that."

"Don't be so sure about that," she said. She lived nothing but lies. But he didn't know that. She turned away, dropped into the warrior pose, and remained silent for several minutes. Behaviors become habits, habits become characteristics. Negative self-talk can be overcome. Go easy on yourself. She could hear multiple therapists talking to her at any one time, but she didn't listen to any of them.

Paul never seemed to take offense.

"So who do you think it's going to be for the gold in the marathon—Gelana or Keitany?" Paul said, as they set off down the wide trail.

Sarah checked her running watch to ensure they were at pace. "Well, don't count Straneo out, but after Rotterdam, I'm putting my money on Gelana."

They automatically turned left at the trailhead to take the forest loop, away from the grasping, swirling waters of the Looking Glass River. They never took the trail that followed first the Looking Glass and then the Grand River. Sarah had said something about optimal elevation change on their first run, and Paul had never asked questions.

They completed their run quickly and efficiently, with little chatter other than to check their lap rate. Their trained, toned bodies were high on movement, flying down the path in unison. She expected him to do well in the Ironman. Not as well as her, of course. The men's field was deeper and broader. He would never feel the victory to which she was accustomed, even though he was just as fast, if not faster, than she was.

"Our last lap was off pace," she said. "Too fast."

"I thought we wanted to move faster in the taper."

"Not *too* fast. The idea was to get you used to a seven-minute pace. That's your goal, remember?"

Paul grunted something inaudible and crossed one foot over the other to stretch his calves. She admired the curve of his thigh.

They were both all about the exercise. She knew he had a job, that he was in fact a physicist of some renown at Portland State University. She never asked him about it. He was her training partner, and former client. And he was younger than she was, after all. Only four years—but at their age, four years to a man was probably an eternity. She supposed he might think them friends in a way. Paul was the only person who knew she'd always wished she had gone to college. He didn't know about Charlotte, of course.

Mostly they just trained.

"So, do you think I'm ready?" It was his first Ironman.

"Just remember," she said. "Run your own race. Don't get intimidated by everyone else around you. We're not solving world hunger here. We're just learning how to push our bodies. There will always be another Ironman, or triathlon, or race. Do your best, and just have a redo if it doesn't turn out how you wanted." It was her standard personal-trainer patter. She wanted her clients to feed off the exhilaration of strength, not victory.

"Absolutely, Coach." He winked at her. "So, I was wondering if you wanted to have dinner with me tonight at the new Thai place?"

"What?" she said. This was so unexpected that she couldn't even grasp a social nicety to attach to it.

He cracked her his customary grin. "I wanted to talk to you about some training stuff, and other things. Five o'clock? I know you don't like to be out late."

She almost said no. It wasn't in the routine, but the edge of nervousness in his smile changed her mind. "Fine, but let's make it the new vegetarian place on Fifth. I need to eat clean this week."

* * *

Sarah ran her clients through their paces. The stay-at-home moms in the morning and early afternoon gave way to the working women in the late afternoon. All chronically worried about their bodies, about how husbands and boyfriends perceived them, about aging. Few of them were really willing to push until it hurt. Few of them did it solely for themselves. They didn't get the rush of being powerful, of muscle fatigue, of effortlessness. But they were her mainstay.

They were always hungry for advice, for just the right formula to have Sarah's body. She watched them watching her, tracing the curves of her quadriceps and deltoids with their eyes—a scrutiny akin to lust, but not quite. Sarah didn't know what to tell them. Eschew personal relationships, make pain your friend, and bury your emotional damage in exercise?

She showered, pulled her hair into a ponytail, and donned a warm-up suit—but then caught her image in the mirror and thought it might look a bit too severe and Soviet-gymnastics-trainer for a restaurant. She relented and put on a pair of jeans. She left her hair pulled back.

Paul was wearing perfectly fitting jeans and a checked dress shirt unbuttoned to the sternum. She almost had to look away. He ordered a beer. She declined.

He raised his beer in salute to her water, took a long draught, and then winked at her. "Screw the Ironman clean-eating regimen. I'm celebrating for one night. I had a big breakthrough in my work today."

This tossed Sarah onto uneven ground. Face to face, they talked stretches, distances, food, races, times, and gear. Personal talk they saved for twenty-five-mile runs when they weren't looking at each other, and even then it was limited and sketchy on detail.

"How so?" she said carefully.

Paul glanced around, as if to make sure there was nobody who could overhear, and then leaned closer to her. "I've invented something. Something important."

"And what would that be?"

"A handheld time travel device." There was satisfaction in his blue eyes, but she detected something else: a faint hint of appraisal. Why was he telling her this?

"You're kidding. For particles, right?" Even she knew enough about quantum physics to know this.

He showed a flash of teeth. "For people," he said firmly.

"You're pulling my leg." Her mind scrambled at possibilities. Did he need a test subject? One who had few personal relationships to worry about if something went wrong? Was that what this was about?

He flashed more teeth and arched an eyebrow. "Would I do that before Ironman?" he said, but then grew more serious, looking at her in an earnest way that she found unsettling. He was probably just being borderline friendly, but in her warped and solitary world, she wouldn't know the difference between friendly and outright lecherous. "You've heard of the grandfather paradox of time travel, right?"

She shrugged. "Let's say I haven't. I've been fairly narrowly focused on, you know, running shoes, body fat ratios, stride length…" she trailed off, hoping this would divert him to one of their usual topics. One of their safe topics.

"The grandfather paradox is where you travel back in time and kill your grandfather, and then you cease to exist and so your time travel wasn't possible." Paul took another slug of beer. "It's always been one of the main problems of time travel."

"Why would you kill your grandfather?"

"Well, ideally you wouldn't. That's an extreme example. The point is, anything you change in the past could set off a string of events that changes the timeline and results in you not even existing, and therefore never traveling in time in the first place. And yet, there you are back in time, unable potentially to return, because you no longer exist. There's also the problem of you running into—and probably scaring the bejesus out of—your past self." Paul cast her a broad smile.

"No kidding," Sarah said weakly. Where was this going? He couldn't possibly be serious. She should be doing her evening crunches and jump-ups and getting ready for bed.

She watched his fingers curve around the amber beer bottle as he spoke. "Let's just say that I've created a device which deals with all of that, because it only allows time travel within your own lifespan and allows for temporal merging. When you travel to your past, you simply merge with yourself until you decide to return to the future. And if you by accident change the timeline in such a way that negates your future time travel—like if you killed me, say—well then you've already merged with your past self, and you just have to relive your life. Potentially irritating, but not a life-threatening outcome. This avoids a lot of the uncomfortable bits associated with time travel. It essentially allows for redos."

"Redos?"

Paul's eyes met hers. "You can fix your mistakes."

"Right. And it works?"

"I tested it myself this afternoon. In fact, I did our run twice today. And I'm just fine."

"That's overtraining," she said automatically. Then she flagged the server and ordered a single-malt scotch.

He winked at her. "The second time I asked you out. The first time I didn't. You don't even remember the first time. So I changed the timeline."

"And where do you keep this device?" she said, with a meaningful look at his shirt pocket. She kept her voice light. "If we go now, we could do a whole week of extra training for Ironman."

He smiled. "It's in my condo. Let's just say it wasn't a university project."

She tried to make her smile friendly, flirty, and unthreatening, the way she had seen other women smile at men. "I want to see." She downed the first scotch in a few burning gulps.

* * *

He took her back to his condo, a sleek brown and cream affair that was unusually cozy and tidy for a man. After showing her how the device worked, he started telling her about the physics of time travel and some of the glitches he was working out. He hadn't figured out how to travel to the future yet, unless you were returning to the future from the past, but he was working on it.

Sarah tried to listen attentively, but all she could think was: *Charlotte.* And: *Mom.* The album of a local band played low on the stereo, and their cover of Madonna's "Crazy for You" came on. Sarah rose with trembling hands, stood in the pale light that streamed in the window from the street, and asked Paul to dance. He hesitated and cocked his head at her, assessing, but then set down the device and came and slipped his arms around her. He was smaller than she had expected, and she felt the soft rasp of his stubble against her cheek as her nose met his earlobe.

He smelled like night air on a river, and she closed her eyes against the faint suggestion of tears, as the solidity of muscle, bone, and sheer intoxicating masculinity pressed against her.

It didn't take long for her lips to find his, for their desire to unfurl. Their bodies fit together and moved in such synchrony that *this* seemed like the moment they had been training for, not the Ironman.

Paul seemed surprised but not unenthusiastic about her sudden ardor. The sex was vigorous, athletic, tender, and shockingly enjoyable considering she had three scotches under her belt and had sworn off men.

* * *

When he was asleep, she rose, huddled shivering in the shadows of the living room for a few seconds, and then collected the device from the coffee table. "Sorry, Paul," she whispered as she eased her way out into the building corridor, and then she ran home in the dead of night, her hard supple legs propelling her easily down the dim streets. She made a mental note to drink scotch before her next race, then realized she was drunk and stupid. She collected her passport, packed a bag, sent an email to all of her clients that she would be away for a while, withdrew as much money from her bank account as the ATM limits would allow, took a cab to the airport, and got on the first available flight to Vegas. The device, a modified smartphone that raised no security questions, weighed heavy in her pocket.

Sarah checked into the MGM Grand as "Serena Parker" and slept for four hours.

Then she rose, made herself a strong coffee, and ate the Doritos and salted almonds from the minibar. No need to keep eating clean.

On any other weekday, she and Paul would be completing their morning run. Today would be a slow, seven-mile jaunt, continuing their taper. She wondered if Paul would know the schedule in her absence. She wondered if he had run on his own, knowing that she betrayed him.

She wouldn't have predicted that she would miss Paul. She had known that she enjoyed their morning runs, but before today she would have said it was the running she enjoyed, and the comfort of knowing that she had someone who could keep up with her beside her. But now, Paul's absence yawned before her.

He wouldn't want to run with her anymore anyway. She had just stolen his life's work.

He had been so excited when he'd shown her how to set the date and time on the device and simply push a button to move back and forth through time. He did it, apparently, in front of her, claiming to have moved several books from the coffee table to the kitchen counter his second time through. She hadn't noticed. And he hadn't vanished, but rather simply continued on, claiming to have gone back and returned. That was the beauty of it, he said. Nobody other than the time traveler will even notice anything has happened.

His eyes had been such a limpid blue when he showed her the device, and then later when he held her. The sex had been unbelievable.

She didn't miss him; she was just feeling bad. And it was necessary. If there was any chance she could deal with the guilt that had crippled her for what seemed like her entire life, she had to betray Paul.

She contemplated starting to work with the device right away. But she decided to go for a run first so she could start with a clear mind. She ran seven miles, their scheduled training distance. Just enough to take the edge off. Though running without the steady rhythm of Paul's feet next to her, driving her to carry on and go faster, was almost disorienting at first. She wanted to keep going, to run until it hurt, but it was too hot and she had to get started.

Back in the room, she showered and towel-dried her hair while sitting on the bed. Her fingers fell to lips that had been, just a few hours ago, on Paul's. She tried to vanquish the fantasies of him kneeling in front of her, pulling the towel away, and the heat and press of skin.

She twitched to check her email, to update her Facebook status, to scroll through the incessant thunder of meaningless news with which she had become accustomed to distracting herself. She had always peppered her Facebook page with motivational training quotes, because, sadly, the majority of her friends were clients. She often posted quotes that said that running and training were, like life, a journey with ebbs and flows. Like a river.

But she tried to stay away from river metaphors.

What would she update her status to now? "Just stole a time device from the hottest guy ever." That seemed consistent with the chirpy climate of Facebook. She could even update her relationship status from "single" to "really really complicated."

But she'd left her phone and computer behind. Too traceable. Paul would probably know how to find her right away, if he was looking.

What she really wanted to post was her favorite Lance Armstrong quote: "If you ever get a second chance in life for something, you've got to go all the way."

For herself.

At eleven, she sat on the bed and pulled out the device. Studied it for a few minutes. She would start small. Paul had said that when he went back in time to their run, he could remember doing it the first time. She would go back a few minutes in time, move the channel changer from one end of the entertainment center to the other, and then return.

At quarter after eleven, she entered the date and time with sweaty fingers, hit enter, clicked "yes" in response to the "are you sure" prompt, and then pushed the final red button at the bottom of the device, staring at the red numbers on the bedside clock.

It felt like nothing happened. She remained sitting on the bed. Except that she could clearly see that the time now read eleven o'clock. She moved the channel changer to the far end of the entertainment center. Then she entered the numbers to return to the time she had just left. She pressed the button, and the red numbers on the clock changed to 11:15.

She spent the morning experimenting with going a few minutes back in time. She moved everything she could think of around the room. Sometimes she used the device to return to the time from which she had started, and sometimes she just waited it out. It all seemed fine.

* * *

Over the next two days, she started taking larger leaps: a half hour, an hour. She sat at a table in the hotel sports bar and experimented with changing the timeline in a public space. She knocked her drink off the table, ordered and consumed several glasses of scotch, and made a fool out of herself asking a man to sit with her. And then she undid it all.

She supposed that curing hangovers was probably not the intended use for the device.

It all seemed so shockingly simple that Sarah decided to make a larger jump. She went back to her room, entered the date from three days prior, and—before she could chicken out—pressed the keys required to initiate. She closed her eyes.

This time the air temperature around her changed dramatically, and the hum of the air conditioner vanished. The feel of the bed beneath her shifted. She took a deep breath, risked opening one eye, and nearly screamed. She was sitting in her home office in Portland, looking at her client schedule. Her eyes went frantically to the date on her computer.

June fifteenth. The date she had set. Three days prior, at quarter after two in the afternoon, this was exactly where she had been. After a panicked moment, she registered that she still held the device in her hand. She tried to control her breathing.

So. The device took the user back in time to wherever they had been at the time set on the device. This was unexpected, but not surprising. She supposed Paul had essentially told her this with his talk of temporal merging. Was her present self still sitting on the bed in Vegas? She supposed so, unless she did something now to change the timeline.

Paul was only six blocks away at the university. He didn't yet know that she had taken the device. She *hadn't* yet taken the device.

She punched in the numbers to return to Vegas, to return to the present, although she had to say that the past felt remarkably like the present, and the present like the future, at the moment.

Either way, she felt very uncomfortable being that close to Paul with the device she stole, and she had to fight the urge to run to him and tell him everything.

When she arrived back in her hotel room in Vegas, the power was out. But once she'd checked to make sure everything remained where she had left it, she lay back on the bed and closed her eyes. The power flicked back on about ten minutes later.

She had an actual functioning time machine that allowed for redos. She could correct mistakes. She could go back to the day she had made the biggest mistake of her life—and fix it.

And then, perhaps, she could have a normal life, and not have to wake up every day feeling sick to her stomach that she had killed her little sister.

There were the glitches that Paul had told her about. If a person went back beyond the creation date of the device, they could alter the timeline such that the device could cease to exist, which would mean that they were stuck there in that time, living out their life in the past—within that new timeline. A life they had already lived. Except for what they chose to do differently.

It seemed like a minor risk.

She would try a few more jumps. Working up to longer ones before going back to that day. But first, she needed money. And in Vegas, with a time device, that seemed like a remarkably easy thing.

She decided roulette would be the best bet. It didn't require the skill of poker, and one win at the highest-stakes table would be sufficient. She dressed in the red silk dress she had purchased in the hotel boutique earlier that day, pulled her hair into some semblance of a chignon, and headed downstairs.

She watched the roulette ball bounce from section to section on the wheel. She would lose the first four times, and then on the fifth time, she would watch where the ball went, go back in time, and place all of her chips on that number.

It all went as planned, and the crowd let out a huge raucous cheer at her victory. The man running the roulette table scrutinized her, and finding nothing amiss, gave her the chit to go collect her winnings. She rose carefully—no need to rush—

and turned directly into a white-faced Paul. He wore that same checked shirt, open at the neck, and his eyes seemed dark with anger, but the way they quickly flicked down her body in that dress sent a shiver down her thighs. He held another device, a carbon copy of hers, in his left hand. So, he had another one. No need to feel as guilty for stealing the first one then.

"You can't do this, Sarah," he said. "You need to give me back the device."

She forced her voice to be haughty. "I don't know what you're talking about." She started striding away from him, as fast as she could go on the ridiculous and unstable four-inch heels the boutique woman had convinced her were the perfect match for the dress.

"Please, Sarah. Stop." He easily kept pace with her. His fingers closed around her arm. She shook him off and broke into a run. Two security guys emerged from the shadows of the casino and approached Paul.

"This man is bothering me," she said, and continued her trajectory toward the women's washroom. The lights in this section of the casino were out, and emergency lights kept the hallway illuminated. She quickly glanced over her shoulder and saw Paul speaking angrily with the two security guards.

In the bathroom, she typed the numbers into the time device. She would go back to this morning. This evening would never happen. Paul would never find her, because she would never be in the casino.

* * *

At noon the same day, or rather the same day repeated, after she had lain on the bed and gotten control of her breathing, she donned a hat and sunglasses and concocted the most unusual outfit she could out of the clothes she had hastily packed. She went to a drugstore and purchased sable hair dye, reading glasses that made her eyes water, makeup, and a paisley scarf. She dyed her hair, applied her makeup with a heavy hand, put on the glasses, and then, shortly after midnight, headed out to a casino in another hotel.

It all went the same as before: the four losses, the small jump back in time, the return to the present, the win... and the arrival of Paul, with a strained and hurt look around his eyes.

She suppressed a cry of alarm. But she was more prepared this time, with the numbers already entered into the device.

"You don't know what you're doing," he hissed. "This was not how this device was meant to be used. Please stop. Come back to Portland with me."

The accusation stung, and tears sprang to her eyes that he would think her so shallow. "Sorry. Can't," she said. She darted into a row of slot machines. She was wearing flats this time. Paul followed at a measured pace, trying not to look like he was pursuing her, while he called her name quietly. She wove in and out of the tables—laid out so as to be confusing and repetitive, to draw the gambler in, to make sure they never left. She managed to put a few feet between herself and Paul, ducked behind a half wall in the almost empty casino, and pressed the button on the device to take her back to that afternoon, just after she had dyed her hair. To erase her win, and to erase Paul finding her.

In the cat-and-mouse game of time travel, the mouse always had the advantage. But perhaps only slight.

She collapsed on the bed of the hotel room in frustration. This continual jumping back in time was exhausting. She was living each day twice—three times—and sleeping only once, and she still didn't have the money she needed to get her mother out of debt and away from Jake, so her mother wouldn't die.

She had to rethink her strategy. How was Paul finding her?

It must be the size of her wins, she concluded. He was tracking big wins by women, which probably made some sort of news or list, and then jumping back in time to the time of the win. Had he figured her for a gold digger and known to go to Vegas? The possibility cut her to the core. But then again, she *had* established herself as a thief and a liar, so gold digger probably wasn't too far a leap.

And now that he knew she was here, he could potentially use his device to be in every casino, every night for the next two weeks. It would be exhausting, but doable.

She could go for small wins, then, or go someplace else entirely. There were other gambling places in the US, or even Europe. She had always wanted to go to Monte Carlo. But she was already running low on money, and using her passport to fly would be too risky. She couldn't get to Europe. She couldn't see any way the time device would allow her to rob a bank or jewelry store. She was sure there was probably some way, but her mind couldn't unravel it. Winning big in the lottery would be theoretically easy, but the check would have to be made out to her real name, and that would result in activity on her bank account—which Paul, or somebody, could potentially be watching.

She couldn't go back in time to before Paul gave her the device, not yet, as that would take her back to Portland, or all the way back to Maryview, and could result in her changing the timeline such that Paul would never give her the device in the first place. She might only have one shot at jumping a long distance back in time, and she had to make sure it went perfectly. She thought that Paul had seemed to hedge slightly when he'd said he hadn't worked out traveling to the future yet. Like maybe he actually *had*, but wasn't going to tell her about it. But trying to go to the future seemed too uncertain, too dangerous, and she wasn't sure she wanted to know where she would end up. Permanently alone with her hand weights and running tights, probably.

This time travel thing was giving her a blinding headache.

Horses. She could try horses.

Tomorrow she would go to Phoenix, where she was sure there must be a horse track, determine the winning horse, and then go back in time to bet on that horse. She would sleep first, though.

The next morning she forced herself to apply her makeup even more garishly. Then she withdrew the remainder of her savings—no need for secrecy, Paul already knew she was in Vegas—and bought a Greyhound bus ticket. In the bus station, she checked newspapers and listened to the TV news to see if she had been reported missing. But there was no indication of anyone being concerned. It was indicative of her largely solitary life that nobody—other than Paul—would be alarmed by her sudden disappearance. And Paul probably wasn't alarmed. He was probably furious.

But she had to do this. For Charlotte.

Charlotte had been so headstrong, even as a three-year-old, but perhaps the brain had a way of changing memories to rationalize, to justify. To excuse negligence. Perhaps *all* three-year-olds were headstrong. Sarah couldn't be sure. All she knew was that her stepfather, Jake, had been right: *You've fucked up so royally that you've destroyed everyone's lives.*

And she had. In the wake of Charlotte's death, her mother had drifted into a grief so deep that she couldn't be revived, and her stepfather had sunk into a sullen rage that bled through when he was drinking and resulted in more bloodshed. Sarah's. Her mother's. Until finally he killed her mother with his fists and went to spend the rest of his life in prison.

She could go back to before her mother even met Jake. Give her mother enough money that she would never consider marrying Jake. But that would negate Charlotte, and Sarah had loved Charlotte with all her heart. No. She would go back and undo that one moment of inattention—no, of *negligence*—when she ran into the house to answer the phone, thinking it might be a boy she liked—she couldn't even remember his name now—and left Charlotte alone in her sandbox.

She checked into the Land's End Motel in Phoenix, her dwindling bank funds now becoming an issue, bought a hideous sunhat and floral dress, and made her way to Turf Paradise.

She had never watched horse racing before, and the pounding hooves made her own calves ache for a hard, driving run. She watched the first race—noting the first-, second-, and third-place finishers—and then went back in time. She tried to decipher the illogical odds, and placed some small bets. She won, pocketed the cash, and returned to the motel, all the time looking over her shoulder. Paul didn't show up.

She placed larger bets the next day, and collected her ten thousand dollars. On the third day, she waited until the last race of the day, then put the ten thousand dollars for a win on the winning horse—one that had been given long odds. She decided against an exacta or trifecta bet on the second- and third-place horses. Too risky. She struggled to do the math—she had sleepwalked through algebra—but knew that the payout would be big.

Even knowing the outcome, having watched the race twice, her heart was still clamoring in her chest as the first-place horse, *her* horse, a horse named Vertigo Charlie, thundered across the finish line.

When she turned away from the payout window, shoving her winnings into her purse, Paul stood right behind her, his breath on the back of her neck somehow a cross between a caress and a threat.

"I'm just going to walk with you. I won't touch you," he said, falling into step beside her. "Please don't jump."

"No way," she said, picking up her speed. "How are you finding me?"

Paul sighed. "The device pulls a huge amount of energy from the local grid. I can watch for spikes and nearby outages and then figure out where you are. And you've obviously established a pattern... of looking for money..." he trailed off.

She had thought that the power failures she had noticed at the MGM were because the hotel was under renovations. "It's not what you think," she said. She walked faster.

Paul hastened his pace in order to move slightly in front of her. "It doesn't matter. I really need it back. I haven't perfected it. It wasn't meant for doing multiple jumps in a day. What you're doing is dangerous for you *and* for other people." The disappointment in his voice made Sarah nauseated. All her life, people had been disappointed in her.

She turned, grabbed hold of Paul's elbow, swung her leg around, and dropped him to the ground. She saw the shock on his face. Then she started to run.

"Fuck you, Paul. I need it. You don't understand."

Paul scrambled to his feet and called after her. "Please stop, or I'm going to go back and not invent the device."

Adrenaline and fear coursed through Sarah's veins. She ran harder. She had a head start, and she put every bit of training that she'd poured into that Ironman, which was happening that day in Coeur d'Alene, into her pace, as she fumbled with the device.

Paul leapt to his feet and started after her with his tight, efficient gait. She ran faster, and the distance between them narrowed and widened as each of them pulled out bursts of speed, Paul calling her name as he ran. Finally, she was able to fully enter the right date into the device: the day before the date that had been echoing in her brain ever since the moment Paul had first told her about the device.

August 14, 1990. The day her sister died.

She raised her finger to push the button that would take her twenty-two years into the past.

Paul's hand closed around her arm; his blue eyes seemed to burn her. She shook him loose and her legs automatically launched into an adrenaline-fueled race-finish sprint. "Sarah, wait. You don't understand. I invented this device because of you. I lo—" Sarah's finger punched the button, and Paul's last words were cut off.

1990

It felt like she fell into her thirteen-year-old body from a height, but in reality, she probably arrived as she had every other time she'd made a jump: smoothly, with no sense of change at all.

Except every part of her body felt different. She had become so used to tautness, to muscles that were poised and inexhaustible at all times. To be in the slack growing body of a thirteen-year-old girl was wrenching.

She had timed her arrival for the middle of the night, when she knew she would be in bed. The room was darkened and she lay under a layer of sheets. Her eyes traced the outlines of the blinds on the window and tried to find a recollection of them. She calmed her breathing. This was her old bedroom, she was sure of it. She felt around frantically for the time device in the bed. But it was gone. Her purse with the hundred thousand dollars was gone, too.

So—her actions *had* changed the timeline. She wasn't a time traveler anymore; she'd simply merged with her younger self, and would now re-live her life. Paul must have followed through on his threat, and gone back in time and never invented the device—or just never told her about it, or never became friends with her in the first place. Not surprising. Her efforts to get money to rescue her mother had been for naught, and worse, had contributed to Paul's decision to go back in time and prevent her from ever obtaining the device.

Or was that even possible? She'd gone back in time to way before their meeting at the track; if that meeting now never happened, maybe Paul didn't go back and change anything. In fact, if everything went as she hoped, her life would be completely different. Maybe she would never even meet Paul.

Which would explain why she didn't have his device.

Is that what happened? Would happen? She had no idea.

What had he meant he invented the device because of her?

Sarah felt carefully down the length of her body. She wore the tank top and flannel pajama bottoms that she would have been wearing when she was thirteen, not the dress she had worn to the track. Perhaps the device didn't allow for the transfer of any "things"—only the device, and the traveler? Why had she never noticed this before? She cursed her own stupidity. All of her test trips had been short ones—to an earlier moment when she'd been wearing the same clothes, holding the same things—and because the device always moved along with her, she'd just assumed...

But when she went back in time three days to Portland, she had arrived wearing her warm-up suit, not the jeans she had been wearing in Vegas. She had been so frantic to get out of there, she hadn't processed this critical fact. So it was true: you can't take things with you. Oh God, she had been so stupid. All her efforts to get money had been a complete waste from the start—and made Paul believe the worst about her.

Paul. She might never see him again.

But she was here, and she knew what was going to happen tomorrow, and that was all that mattered.

Sarah rose and staggered in the direction of the bathroom, navigating by patches of light and dark, trying to remember which way to go in the dim array of doorframes and rooms containing sleeping bodies. Down the hall to the right? She pressed her hand against the hallway wall, tried to feel her way by grooves and bumps, her night mind grappling with a flood of conflicting body memories.

She flicked on the light in the bathroom and nearly fainted at the sight of the blue walls, wood finishing, blackened grout, and peeling paint, so familiar yet so out of place and time, like an impossible caricature of itself. She looked in the mirror and reeled as if she had been punched in the gut. This creature with dark eyebrows, plump, pimpled skin, and wild, thick hair could not be her; the cheekbones she had become accustomed to seeing had been buried beneath youth.

There was an insolence and an innocence to this image in the mirror. The sardonic undertones and lacerating self-judgment that decorated her adult affect had vanished, but so too had the confidence and the determined set of her jaw.

She felt her mind and body start to spin out in strange grief at the loss of her thirty-three-year-old self, but she clutched the edges of the vanity, looked directly into the mirror, and smacked herself hard across the face.

"Get ahold of yourself. You're still old," Sarah ordered under her breath. She probed her memories. They remained intact. She was still her thirty-three-year-old self. But then she felt the surge of something else: a willful, hopeful, impetuous, thirteen-year-old self. She was undeniably that girl too. A girl whose life would in so many ways end tomorrow. *Had* ended, she corrected. But perhaps not *would*.

She wanted to sink to the floor and sob for her thirteen-year-old self.

But she didn't. Instead, she held on to the sink and stared fiercely at herself, like she would do again in a few years to sort herself out when she crawled into the house drunk, wallowing in sorrow and self-hate. *Had* done, she corrected again.

She was here to change tomorrow. And everything.

On the way back to her room, she slipped into Charlotte's room. Her sister lay in her toddler bed, a tangle of blankets and stuffies around her, her blond curls matted across her forehead with the sweet sweat of babies.

Sarah exhaled a sob and sank to her knees, pressing her lips against Charlotte's soft, fat cheek. She wanted to crawl into bed with her and snuggle up to her sister's warm, breathing body.

"I won't fail you this time," she promised.

* * *

Sarah woke early the next day. Her mother and Jake got ready for work as expected: her mother wan and resigned in her pale green diner uniform, Jake agitated and hopped up in his jeans and tool belt. Sarah analyzed Jake's moves coldly through a twenty-year lens of hindsight. She saw rage and contempt in the way he expected her mother to serve him, in his posturing around the kitchen, in his arrogance with his boss on the phone. How had she not seen this before?

She recalled the fear and confusion of her nine-year-old self when her mother had introduced Jake as Sarah's new father, and he'd moved into their house with his collection of guns and swaggered around as if he owned it and them. She had thought then that that was just what dads were like. She had commenced a campaign of appeasement, shifting ghost-like around the house at her chores, never talking back, trying in vain to avoid sparking his fury or mockery.

But perhaps a killer is always easier to spot when there's a body.

The day proceeded as it had twenty-two years before. She fed Charlotte, cleaned the kitchen, and played with her tiny sister with damp palms. The run-down squalor of their home jarred her. Had she known then that they had been so poor? Or had everyone lived like this?

The appointed hour came. The hour when Charlotte had declared that she wanted to go out and play in the sandbox. The hour before their driveway would be filled with emergency vehicles scattering red, blue, and white light over walls and windows. When emergency personnel, neighbors, her mother, and Jake would all be pointing their finger in blame at her.

When they would find Charlotte's small body in a small bend in the river half a mile downstream. When Sarah would want to die herself.

Sarah proposed playing Strawberry Shortcake or Care Bears; she offered Lucky Charms and *Barney*. But Charlotte kept running at the patio door, exclaiming "Sanbo, sanbo," before collapsing by the door in a minute heap of rage.

So they went outside. Charlotte alternately tossed sand out of the sandbox, charged at the creek, and punched Sarah in the leg, in the obnoxious willful way of an adored toddler. Sarah shrank further inside herself as she watched Charlotte's behavior. Had she been angry with her sister? Tired? Envious? Had any of these factors contributed to her decision to leave Charlotte alone in the sandbox?

The river slid relentlessly past, a murky torrent of accusation.

Or had it simply been about a boy, and teenage invincibility?

The phone rang. Sarah still didn't remember who it was she thought would be calling. She didn't answer the phone.

Charlotte played on in the sandbox, her candy-floss blond hair rippling in the breeze. Sarah watched with a pounding heart, expecting that at any second fate would intervene and lightning would strike, the river would flood, or terrorists would come and carry her sister away.

But none of that happened. Evening fell and her mother and Jake came home, and Jake strutted around the kitchen drinking a Budweiser, grabbing Sarah's mother's ass, and spouting about Saddam Hussein and the fact that the US should invade. And Charlotte lived on. And nobody knew that anything had just *not happened.* Sarah bit back sneering comments regarding the Persian Gulf War. Because, of course, it hadn't happened yet.

Instead of feeling relief that she had saved her sister—or rather, not been the cause of her sister's death—Sarah felt profound terror. She had changed the timeline. Charlotte hadn't died that day in August. But what if timelines were more robust than that? What if Charlotte was destined to die at Sarah's own hand? What if it was only a matter of time?

* * *

As the days and weeks passed, and the Montana summer gave way to the reds and yellows of autumn, Sarah became more and more obsessed with Charlotte's safety. She stood behind Charlotte while she walked, cut her food into tiny portions, and used Clorox on every surface in the house.

And then there was the matter of her mother.

Nancy Williams worked her tables in the Maryview Diner each day beneath a palpable mantle of exhaustion, tolerated Jake's slights and cuffs because that was what she had come to expect from men, and went about her household tasks and mothering with a quiet edge of desperation. Sarah had wanted money to enable her mother to get away, to go to school, to have options. But that hadn't worked out.

Sarah had thought that saving Charlotte would change Jake, that he wouldn't be so angry, so liberal with his punches. But she saw now that she may have been wrong. Perhaps

Charlotte's death had only exacerbated Jake's deep-lurking fury and disdain for the world. Perhaps her mother's death was still coming.

* * *

Sarah worked up the courage to approach her mother one night as she bent over the sink, finishing the dinner dishes. Jake was out bowling, and Charlotte was in bed. Sarah had already checked on her and then checked the patio door to ensure it was locked.

"Mom, are you happy with Jake?"

Her mother hunched her shoulders and twitched as if she had been shot.

Her voice was sharp. "Sarah, that's none of your business."

"It *is* my business. I don't like the way he pushes you around."

"It ain't your business. Since when did you become little miss worldly and hoity-toity? You see what it's like with two mouths to feed. Jake's all right. He's the best we got. Don't you go ruining it for me now."

Sarah's adult sensibilities wanted to take her mother by the shoulders and shake her. The child inside her slunk away wounded. Perhaps she couldn't change everything.

* * *

Sarah started to work out, train to be a long-distance runner, and study harder. She joined a bunch of brooding, socially awkward boys in the hunter-training course offered in their school. She would become a doctor and a bodybuilder, and she would learn how to use guns.

Despite her chronic siege of apprehension, it was odd and yet exciting to engage in the activities of the teenage years without the saturation of grief and guilt that she had carried heavy on her shoulders the first time through. She occasionally let up on her Charlotte vigil to attend dances, hang with friends, and go out with boys. Always, she would rush back to the house before too long, tangled in a deep skein of guilt for something that hadn't happened.

It was strange, this living twice. She had thought she would have been better at it—that released from the undertow of tragedy and operating with adult knowledge and attitudes, she would be happy. But she discovered that redoing something doesn't totally release you from the experience and memories—the *reality*—of the first time. She recalled the quote that she had posted on the wall of her office when she'd started running long distances: "You have to forget your last marathon before you try another. Your mind can't know what's coming."

She had changed the timeline. Her mind didn't know what was coming. Yet still she braced for it.

Nevertheless—and she was never sure why; perhaps it was the ongoing effort of playing the role of a teenager and being treated as one, or perhaps it was the chemical soup and biorhythms of youth—her younger self started to assert its dominance. The memories, habits, and confidence of adulthood faded, and she became more willful and reckless. She even allowed herself to feel, tentatively. Boyfriends, and friends that she'd never had, eked out a comfortable existence on the periphery of her life. She drank too much, partied, and made mistakes. She almost became a teenager—just one with a darker and more lengthy past than all of her peers. But she continued to train, study, and practice her marksmanship doggedly.

* * *

One night Jake grasped her arm as she emerged, wrapped in a towel, from the bathroom, her blond hair dripping down her back.

"You better watch it. You're starting to look like a she-man." His eyes glittered with the sharp edges of six Budweisers. He had a handgun tucked into his pants, like he did sometimes when he "heard noises" in the backyard and had to protect his property, or spent the evening shooting beer cans off a stump.

Sarah snatched her arm away and was pleased to see she had knocked him backward slightly.

He leered at her and teetered a little. "Men don't like a woman stronger than they are."

"I guess that's their problem, then," she said. She wanted to wipe that shit-eating grin off his face, wrench him to the floor, and break him. She wanted to eliminate any chance he would still kill her mother. There was no reason for him to now. He wasn't deep in a tailspin of grief and alcohol. Charlotte was alive. Sarah repeated this to herself over and over.

"Watch your mouth, girl," he said.

"Watch your ass, man," she mouthed silently as he turned away.

* * *

The day that Jake had killed her mother passed without incident, and aside from occasional bouts of temper and a black eye delivered to her mother on Mother's Day in 1993, Jake mostly saved his fists for bar fights. Sarah's mother kicked him out a few times. But he would simply go and sit on the picnic table in the driveway and smoke—sometimes for hours—watching the house, until his cigarette was just a faint amber glow in the night and her mother felt bad, or scared, and let him back in. And Charlotte grew into a precocious and gorgeous drama queen, alternately adoring and raging at Sarah in the chronic, grating ebb and flow of sibling life.

Sarah sucked in a small hollow swell of comfort. Maybe she had changed enough. Still, allowing herself to feel too much relief brought strange panic attacks and nightmares. So she was careful.

But as the ghosts of her mother and Charlotte faded, and their real live selves became more firmly entrenched in Sarah's mind, another ghost arrived to flit around the edges of her consciousness whenever she drifted in and out of sleep, daydreamed, or started to hope.

Paul.

Paul, with his witty, serious, and attentive ways; his deep-blue eyes and slender muscled body that had made her gasp when she finally saw it unclothed. He trailed her like a phantom through all her dates, all her encounters with boys. He had been so tender and passionate that one night. She nearly wept from wanting him, her mind a volatile cocktail of womanly wants and teenage hormones.

Paul wasn't dead; he existed somewhere. But at this point in time, he was only fourteen to her eighteen.

He invented the device because of her. What had he meant by that? And then she had stolen it from him and betrayed him. There was no hope for a relationship. Except that he didn't know what she had done. Might never know.

She tried to convince herself that her mind had manufactured him—that her hazy adult memories had embellished him, bestowed him with astonishing looks and a sparkling personality, and tricked her into thinking she had cared for him. But despite her best efforts, she couldn't erase the curve of his jaw or the taste of his lips from her dreams.

1995

When the time came to select a college, Sarah found herself accepted with entrance scholarships to each place she had applied.

She made noises about not going. About staying in Maryview with her mom and Charlotte... and Jake. Her mother snapped.

"You have one chance to get out of this godforsaken life, and you are damn well going to take it. Don't you dare live my life."

Her mother had probably meant "don't you dare live a life like mine." But there was the double meaning. For two lifetimes now, Sarah had been living three lives: her own, her mother's, and Charlotte's. It was probably unsustainable.

Sarah chose the University of Oregon, with plans to go to med school at Oregon Health Sciences University, clinging to a scrap of hope that perhaps she could find Paul in a few years. But what would she say? "Hi, we knew each other in a different timeline. I stole your time travel device, and I'm really sorry. By the way, I think I love you." She barely knew anything about his past, where he grew up, how to find him. Why had she never asked him? She knew he had done his master's and Ph.D. at Portland State. But right now, he would still be in high school.

She left Maryview with trepidation. But Charlotte was eight, and her mother was alive. Perhaps she could live her own life now. For the first time.

2003

In her second-to-last year of med school, Sarah took to studying in the physics department at Portland State. It required a commute. It was ridiculous; she felt like a stalker.

She had tried to look Paul up during her undergrad. But there were too many Wendlands in the phone book, and the Internet hadn't yet sufficiently evolved to the point almost anyone could be found anywhere. She needed

Facebook, Google, Twitter, or LinkedIn. She should invent one of them—and then, when she was a billionaire, find Paul.

The first time she saw him she nearly leapt from her chair. He sauntered past, ten years younger than when she had last seen him. But he showed no sign of recognition—why would he?—while she knew the outline of every bone in his face.

She continued to study at Portland State instead of the posh library at OHS, she joined the running group he belonged to, and she made her friends go to physics department pub nights.

And yet he persistently ignored her. Or simply didn't notice her. Occasionally he would offer a vague smile, as if he had seen her around somewhere but didn't know where. And she couldn't work up the courage to speak to him.

They had originally met when he'd signed up for a triathlon training group that she was running. But she was a med student now, not a personal trainer, and as fit as she was, she no longer had the time or the credentials to organize a training group. She trained for herself, but it didn't come close to the gut-wrenching determination she had put into it before, when she had to feel physical pain to erase the emotional pain. She occasionally considered quitting med school to go back and be a personal trainer, but that seemed like too much of a sacrifice for a relationship that could go nowhere.

She followed Paul sometimes, lurking in bushes and behind bookshelves as he ambled around the campus. She snapped a picture of him while he walked past the library one sunny afternoon, his vulnerable but sensual face wrapped in thought.

She almost laughed at herself. She had become the cat and he the mouse. Who was this cipher that she was pursuing? He was from a different timeline.

She fell into step with him one morning during running club. In her previous life she could easily keep pace with him. She was still easily the fastest woman in the club, but medical school had cut into her training time, and she had to push to match his speed. She tried to remember how easily she and Paul had fallen into jibes and sprint challenges.

"Hey," she said, hoping her face wasn't a brilliant red.

"Hey," he responded.

"I'm Sarah," she said.

"Paul," he returned.

"What department are you in?" she said.

"Physics," he said. "You?"

"Med school."

"OHS? You're a little far afield."

"I live around here," she lied. Then she waited, because Paul had always carried the conversation before. Or had he? Had she structured their conversation by outlining drills and distances, and he'd eased his way in with quips and questions? She drew a blank. She smiled at him. He smiled back, and for a second she hoped that she saw some flicker of interest in his eyes.

"I was wondering if you wanted to have coffee sometime, and talk about, you know, training," she said. She wasn't sure if her voice was thin and high from the exertion or the nerves.

Paul lowered his eyebrows, looking bemused. "I guess..." Then, "Just so you know, I have a girlfriend."

She gasped back a small sob of humiliation, and forced her lips into a bright smile. "Oh yeah, no. I just wanted to find out how often you run, get some tips, you know..." She trailed off. "But don't worry about it."

They had reached a hill and he started to pull out in front of her. He glanced back with an eyebrow uplifted, the polite running partner code for "Can I go ahead?" She doubled her effort to keep up. But it was no use.

At the end of the run, everyone stretched. A bunch of skinny, sort-of neurotic people contorting their bodies into various shapes. Running culture almost made Sarah laugh now. They were all too serious. She still loved running, but she wasn't quite as compulsive about it this second time around.

Paul approached as she eased into a deeper quad stretch.

"You going in any races this season?"

"I'm not sure. Maybe the Portland Tri."

"That's good. You're super fast. Just remember to run your own race," he said with what appeared to be almost an apologetic smile, and then jogged off.

Run your own race. Live your own life. Maybe that would have to be a life without Paul.

She didn't quit running group, but she no longer tried to keep up with Paul and she stopped stalking him at the university. She trained harder, and one day she passed him with a small wave on the hill where she had tried to ask him out.

He didn't say anything to her after their run that day. He just passed her with a tight little smile.

* * *

Sarah's mother called one night as Sarah prepared for final exams.

"Charlotte's in trouble," she said. "She's been using drugs. Jake and I don't know what to do. Can you come and talk to her?"

Sarah drove out in her little Hyundai. Charlotte was seventeen. Sarah hadn't been home much in the last two years. Too much studying and running. She cursed her negligence as the miles passed between Portland and Maryview.

When Sarah arrived home, Jake was slurring his words and staggering around the kitchen. The cigarettes had hardened and yellowed his skin, and his eyes smoldered like two pieces of coal inside a stiff exoskeleton. Her mother seemed to have lost thirty pounds. Sarah tried not to cringe at the dinginess of the green shag rug, rough wood cabinets, and dusty macramé planters in the dim light of evening. Charlotte was out.

"We tried to keep her in," her mother wailed. "But she won't listen."

Sarah found Charlotte giving a blow job to a dark, heavy man with tattoos in an alley behind "the Pump and Grind," the local nickname for the Break in Time, the grimiest bar in town. When Sarah called out for them to stop, the man shot back into the bar, not keen to partake in a family drama. Charlotte rose to her feet—almost skeletal in her impossibly tight jeans and stilettos—offered Sarah a menacing toothy grin, and made as if to follow the man. Sarah grabbed her and started to haul her back to the car. Charlotte fought like a wild woman, punching and kicking her sister with a strength at odds with her mass. But Sarah persisted, and had endurance on her side. In the car, Charlotte glared at Sarah from beneath a heavy layer of eyeliner, her pupils too large for the light level. She was agitated and refused to do up her seat belt as Sarah pulled away from the curb.

"Fuck you," Charlotte said.

"Fuck you back," Sarah responded and started driving home. "What are you doing, Char?"

"None of your business." Charlotte contorted her words in the careful enunciation of the impaired. Her left hand bounced and jittered.

"You need to clean up." Sarah hated the words coming out of her mouth. She could find none of the comforting suggestions that she had learned doctors are to say in clinical practice. She pulled back and tried to refocus. "I'm sorry. Forget I said that. Tell me what's going on."

Charlotte lapsed into silence in the seat next to her. The streetlights lit her mascara-streaked face and baleful expression.

"What did you take tonight?"

"None of your business."

"I love you, Char. Please, talk to me."

"Fuck you, Miss Perfect. Miss Doctor. Oh no, I can't drink, I'm training," Charlotte extended the word *training* into a mocking slur. "You can't keep me here. You aren't the police. I could jump out at the next red light." Charlotte fumbled with the door handle.

A bile of panic rose in Sarah's throat. She slowed, but there was no place to pull over and too many cars behind her.

Charlotte had her hand on the handle and opened the door a crack. The rush of air and the dark, ruthless, moving pavement beneath the car sent a shot of adrenaline through Sarah's system. The red taillights in front of her blurred and she tried to ease the car into the right-hand lane. "Stop it, Charlotte, just stop it. I gave up everything so you could live. Don't you dare throw your life away like this."

The door closed a bit. "What are you talking about?"

Sarah found an opening and, trembling, pulled the car into the outer lane, looking for a place to pull over. She had to keep talking, but she almost didn't know what she was saying. "There was an accident, when you were three. I came back in time to save you. I gave up the man I loved to do it, the man who invented the time travel device. Please just live. That's all I want from you."

Charlotte began to laugh hysterically. "And you think *I'm* high."

Sarah spotted a place up ahead to pull into and put on her signal light. "Look, forget it. I know it sounds ridiculous. It *is* ridiculous. I probably imagined the whole thing. Let's just get you home and sobered up, and then we'll talk."

"Oh, well, thanks a lot for coming back in time to save me and leaving me with the biggest bastard of a man who ever lived. Do me a favor. Maybe next time put fucking Jake in the time machine and send him back to the Jurassic period."

Charlotte gave one last crazed burst of laughter, pushed the door open wide and flung herself out onto the black pavement.

* * *

After the ambulance took Charlotte away, Sarah drove home with trembling fingers. She had to collect her mom and Jake because Jake was too drunk to drive and her mom had night blindness. Jake downed two more beers while Sarah and her mom tried to corral him into Sarah's car.

"She's in a coma." Sarah repeated what she'd told her mother on the phone. "Abrasions, broken arm, concussion. We need to get back to the hospital. Now."

"Well, you fucked *that* up royally," Jake said. "The fancy doctor. I guess you're not that good at it after all."

"Leave her alone, Jake," Sarah's mother said.

"Leave her alone, Jake," he mimicked.

"Stop it," Sarah ordered. "We need to get to the hospital."

"Always so righteous," Jake murmured. "Sarah's always the adult. Aren't you glad we always have an adult with us, Nance?"

"That's enough. Just get in the car," Sarah said, pressing her hand against the small of his back to guide him in the direction of the back seat. At the touch, Jake's hand snapped out and grabbed her arm. Sarah wrenched her arm out of his grip reflexively.

"Oh, aren't you the tough one?" Jake said, puffing his shoulders up into his fighting stance.

"Jake, just get in the car, please. Leave her alone," Nancy said.

"That's right, Nancy. Just take your daughter's side as usual. Sarah and I were just having a little conversation, weren't we Sarah?" Jake lunged forward and grabbed Sarah by the elbow. Nancy reached out and tried to pull him back.

Jake whirled and swung out wildly with a loosely fisted hand, catching Sarah's mother hard on the chin. Nancy Williams fell backward, hit her head on the edge of the car door, and toppled to the ground.

"Mom!" Sarah yelled. Her mother lay motionless. Blood streamed from her head.

Jake lurched and bent, his arm pulled back at the ready, as if he meant to finish off her mother, and Sarah snapped. She wrenched his arm backward, swung her leg out to take his feet out from under him, and plowed her fist into his face.

Jake, caught by surprise, fell hard to the ground. He rolled over onto his stomach before Sarah could come at him again, and when he returned to his back, he held a handgun in one hand.

"Stupid little bitch. This is your fault," he said. He fired, but he was too drunk to focus and the shot sailed over her head. Sarah kicked the gun hard out of his hand before he could fire it again.

Jake rolled over and grabbed her ankle, snapping her feet out from underneath her. She fell on top of him, and they rolled over and over on top of each other down the gentle slope of their driveway. Each was grasping for the gun, and then there was a tooth-rattling bang, and the blood from Jake's body was drenching her as his grip on her arms loosened.

Sarah pushed Jake's body off of her and crawled, sobbing, over to her mother. She felt for a pulse, but got nothing.

* * *

She knelt in the grass snorting hysterical tears and emitting guttural, almost feral wails as she pounded her mother's chest in some sort of pathetic facsimile of chest compressions, her hands slippery with blood. The ambulance was taking forever. Jake lay motionless a few feet away. Charlotte was probably dead in the hospital. This wasn't a redo. This was worse than the first go around.

"Sarah! Sarah!"

She almost didn't hear the voice until a hand closed gently on her shoulder.

She whirled.

Paul stood there in the dim light, his blue eyes luminous and tortured.

"I'm so sorry I'm late. I got lost. I meant to be here half an hour ago."

"What are you talking about?" She continued to pump furiously at her mother's heart.

Paul held up a time device. "I came back to prevent this. But I didn't know the exact time, and I had to travel from Portland, and I misjudged. I'll just go back a little bit, and I won't get lost this time."

Sarah didn't let up on her chest compressions. "No way. How do I know you're not going to make it even worse?"

"How can it be worse?"

Sarah shook her head furiously through her tears. "How did you even know this was happening? You don't even know me."

Paul glanced at the blood covering Sarah's arms. He spoke in a hurried voice. "I think we should talk about this later. A few months ago a woman came to see my 2013 self. She told me what happened. Gave me a picture taken of me in front of the library when I was in undergrad. Her name was Charlotte."

"Charlotte?" The thrall of sirens cut through hum of the night air.

"We need to do this now, Sarah. Charlotte said both your mother and Jake died tonight, and that you were jailed for Jake's murder. I need to undo this now. I don't want you to experience any more of this timeline."

"You mean redo?" she said faintly. The sirens were closer now. She could see a police car behind the ambulance.

Paul tore a hand through his hair. "Yes. I'm going back." His finger reached for the button on the device.

"Wait! I'm going with you. I need to know this happened, so I can make sure it doesn't happen." She leapt from the ground, snatched at his other hand, and held fast even as she felt it jerk in hers.

* * *

She was back in her car driving from the hospital, about a mile before the turnoff to her mother's house, trembling so hard that the car wobbled and careened on the deserted road.

She edged the car into her mother's driveway and cut the engine. She could just turn around and go right back to the hospital, but if she did, maybe Jake would still deliver the punch that would kill her mother. She pulled the key out of the ignition and slowly eased open the door. A cool breeze from the river traced through her hair.

Paul slipped out of the darkness and joined her, the moonlight casting shadows beneath his cheekbones. He had made it on time this time. Her body almost shuddered in relief, but then she tensed up again. What if they didn't get it right this time either? Their lives could become an endless series of redos. What if Paul got shot this time? Or if she did? They could erase it and try again. But what if with each successive redo, the outcome became worse? A perpetual, progressively grimmer Groundhog Day.

"Did you just jump with me?" he said.

She nodded.

"So you know what we're going to redo?"

She nodded again and choked back a sob.

Paul's hand found hers, and squeezed. "We'll fix this," he said.

* * *

"Charlotte's visit was the push I needed to finally invent the device," Paul said, as they sat facing each other on separate beds in a darkened hotel room in the shadow of the humming hospital, their knees almost but not quite touching.

With Paul's help, Sarah had managed to convince Jake to go to bed and dry up, and then, once he was passed out, they took her mother to the hospital. Charlotte had regained consciousness and was stable. They were taking shifts by her bedside. Sarah just hoped she could convince her mother and

Charlotte to move back to Portland with her. To never return to that house with Jake. She wanted to call the police and tell them that Jake had killed her mother and pulled a gun on her. But of course she couldn't, because he hadn't. That was the crappy part of redoing the past.

The time device sat on the bedside table. So addictive, this possibility of redo. So dangerous. How could she undo Jake completely—make sure he never entered their lives—without undoing Charlotte? Was there some other way to erase him?

"But how did Charlotte know to come to you?" Sarah asked.

Paul's silhouette shifted. "There was an article about me in the Portland Press saying I was theoretically working on the idea of time travel. Charlotte said she found my picture in your stuff, and that you had told her some crazy story about going back in time. She was desperate to help you… She admitted she was grasping at straws." He stopped and cast a shadowy glance at her, waiting.

Charlotte. Charlotte had saved *her.*

"So now you want the story of how I went back in time," Sarah said. Her chest tightened and her breath came in shallow puffs, not the deep restoring breaths she had trained herself to take when under stress. "I stole the device from you. Not in this timeline. In a previous one. Then by jumping back twenty years in time, I changed the timeline somehow, and you no longer invented the device, or you did it a few years later, or you didn't tell me about it, so I no longer had the device. I'm sorry. I did it to save Charlotte. She drowned when she was three, in the river. It was my fault. You and I were friends."

Sarah paused. They had been more than friends. "Good friends. When you told me about the device, I saw my chance to save her, and I betrayed you and I am so sorry." Sarah pressed her face into her hands.

A sliver of light from between the heavy hotel curtains fell on Paul's hands as he reached out and placed them on her thighs. His weight felt heavy and solid, and she wanted to slip off her bed, fall to her knees, and wrap her arms around his waist.

"I know most of that, Sarah. I went back in time too, that day when you went back at the racetrack. I had something in my life that I had to try to redo, too. My dad died of lung cancer when I was twenty. I went back and took another shot at getting him to quit smoking. I had figured before I even went to the track in Phoenix that you were planning to do something like you did, and that you might negate the timeline and my invention of the device, so I already had my device set to the time and date I wanted to go to before I approached you. When I saw you push your button, I pushed mine."

Sarah lifted her face and looked at him. "So you have all your memories of our friendship, of me being your running partner, of the night I stole the device?"

Paul's full lips tilted up in a slight smile. "Yes, I do."

A crushing wave of hurt fury washed over her. "But you never gave me any acknowledgement in Portland! I was practically stalking you, and you acted like I was invisible. Why?"

Paul rose and walked to the window. "That was pretty hard. But I felt I had to. First of all, you stole the device from me. If you had just asked me for it, and told me why you wanted it, I would probably have let you use it. So I was pretty hurt. And let's face it Sarah, you were in Vegas trying to game the system. You didn't tell me why. I didn't know about Charlotte. When you came up to me last year, I thought you might be trying to get close to me again to steal the device a second time. And you always told me that you had wanted to get a university education and be beholden to no man. And there you were doing it. I didn't want to stand in your way. It was just easier to pretend I didn't know you."

Sarah sniffed out a sob. "I see." She did, sort of. "And when Charlotte came to you—why didn't you try to save her? You could have come back earlier and prevented her from jumping out of the car."

"Charlotte said that jumping out of the car and having to go to rehab made her get her head on straight. She cleaned up. But I don't know how much you going to jail helped with that. There's always a risk of redoing too much and changing the timeline completely. I didn't want to do that."

"I see. Well, thank you for coming back today and helping me. I assume you're going to go back to 2013 now."

Paul turned. "I'm not sure about that. Charlotte told me something else."

Sarah lifted her chin. "What was that?"

Paul hesitated, staring at her with his brilliant blue eyes. Sarah stood up and risked approaching, skirting him like a skittish cat, her legs wobbly, a small ember of hope springing to life in her heart.

"She said... she said you had feelings for me."

"Oh."

This was hopelessly inadequate, but Paul continued talking. "I had loved you for so long, all those years of training together. But you seemed so damaged, so impenetrable. I had given up hope."

"I was."

"And now?"

Sarah sifted through her collection of memories. Redoing things couldn't completely erase them. Charlotte's death, her mother's death—twice—and Jake's murder all still threatened to drag her under. "I'm still damaged," she said slowly. "But I'm not impenetrable."

They stood and looked at each other for a few seconds, not saying anything, the tips of their fingers touching.

"Did you find that when you went back, your memories of the previous timeline faded?" he asked, finally.

She nodded. "Just a bit though. It was like new memories were being written on top and my body was resetting to be my younger age. The memories just got a bit fuzzier and maybe less important, just like really old recollections of my childhood. I forgot details, but I don't think I forgot any of the important things."

Paul pressed his lips together. "It was like that for me too. And for some strange reason, Madonna's 'Crazy for You' became my favorite song this time around. My buddies had a good time with that one." She saw the flash of his white teeth in the dim light, but then his face grew more serious. "Listen. I could go back to 2013. But I'm not sure if I want to." He paused and took a slightly firmer hold on her hands. "I don't know if you could come with me. For you, that would be traveling into the future—using the device I brought back from my 'present.' And even if you can travel to the future, we have no idea where you'll be—or with whom—in 2013." He paused. "I was thinking maybe we could stay here—together—and try to get this relationship right this time."

The fragment of possibility in her heart blossomed into a cathedral of hope. She risked taking a step closer to him until the edges of their clothing and bodies grazed each other. He pulled her the rest of the way to him, and the lips it seemed she had been waiting a lifetime for found hers.

When he released her, she was breathless and shaking, and had no doubts about how she felt about him.

"When you showed up in Phoenix, you said something," she said. "You said you invented the device because of me. What did you mean by that?"

Paul offered a faint smile. "It seems I invent the device in every timeline, so there must be a lot of factors that drive me to it. But in that timeline, it was all your talk of redoing races, that you always have a second chance. It got me thinking about second chances..." Paul trailed off, and he lowered his eyes to stare at the floor. "There's something else I need to tell you." She stiffened, but he didn't let her go. "I don't know what the physiological impact of living over again has on the body. If I stay, I'll be living this period of my life again, and

I'm…" His voice broke slightly. "I'm not sure how many times I've done this."

"What?" This admission threatened to sink her. Only the closeness of his body kept her from going under. Just. A small life preserver in a turbulent current.

Paul lifted his eyes to hers again. "I'm not sure how many times I've gone back and relived my life. It's possible I've done it maybe four, maybe five times, maybe more. The memories keep writing on top of each other, and my body keeps rejigging. It seems like I remember the most recent timeline—the one just before the one I'm living—fairly well, but even parts of it start to fade, and I only have a vague sense of the previous ones, or that the previous ones even exist. It becomes addictive, the opportunity to redo. Thank God I haven't tried to change history, or who knows how much I would have bollixed things up."

"Oh." This wasn't what she had expected. Had he had countless other lovers, wives, children?

He tightened his grip on her hands, and it sent shivers down her spine, but her head spun from his proximity and his words. "When I went back in time when we were both in Phoenix, I'm not even completely sure it was about my dad, although I told myself it was. It's possible that I was more afraid that if you went back and changed the timeline—such that we never met and I never invented the device—I would lose all my memories. I think maybe I was hanging on to those jumbled memories like a junkie. So I jumped too. And then my device disappeared for the first time ever, so it seemed like the timeline had finally been changed such that I wouldn't invent the device. And I swore I wasn't going to. I was going to stop the cycle. So I didn't pay attention to you, and eventually you stopped running with the group—I didn't know it was because you were in jail—and then 2012 came and went, and I didn't invent the device like I had before, and I thought I had stopped the cycle." He took a deep breath. "But then Charlotte found me, and told me what happened to you, and... I had to. So it wasn't that I hadn't invented it, I just did it a year later—in 2013, which I think is why it disappeared when I made the jump from Phoenix in 2012 in the previous timeline."

"I see." She let go of his hands, stepped a few feet away from him, folded her arms over her chest and shuddered.

"Wait," he said. "You don't understand: the one constant, through all my timelines, has been wanting you. Each timeline has brought me closer to you. I thought we were finally going to be together the last time, and then you took off, and I was stupid. But now we're together... and maybe we can finally get it right. Please, let's give this a chance. I'm going to throw the time device into the river and we can just be together."

He moved closer to her again, and she could feel the warmth of his body and see the glitter of his eyes. She wanted to wrap her arms back around him, but she didn't let herself.

She let out a whimper before she regained control of her voice. "But the fact that it's still here, now, means that you *will* invent it in the future, right?"

"I think so. Maybe. It's confusing. I don't want to, but..." He sighed. "Yes, I think that's what it means."

She met his eyes. "If it's so addictive, how do I know you won't use it when we have an argument, or something goes wrong for you at work, or you just want a redo? What about when the magic of our relationship fades and you just want to experience the early days of it again, or when you meet someone else and want to go back and have a relationship with her while you're young?"

Paul tore his hands through his hair. "I love you. I have *always* loved you. I don't want to redo anything. I just want you. I promise."

Sarah almost laughed, would have laughed, if she hadn't been shaking so hard. Hadn't countless hapless cowboys crooned those very words to mistreated wives and girlfriends? And they only had access to beer and other women, not time travel devices.

"Go to the future and get me one then. Program them so they're linked together. So if one of us goes back, or forward, we both go."

Paul frowned. "I don't think that's a good idea."

"Consider it like mutually assured destruction."

"Oh, that's a good way to start off a relationship."

"I don't think we have any other choice."

Paul sat heavy on the bed. "I won't be able to invent them until 2012 at the earliest. There are some breakthroughs in quantum physics and some developments in plastics that need to happen first. Why don't we destroy this one and buy ourselves eight years to be together without worrying about it? Then we can revisit this conversation in 2012."

He looked up at her, his eyes earnest. Sarah stared at him, this man that she loved, and memories flicked through her mind, memories of her practicing medicine alone, of other men, of Charlotte and her mother, of being in this room before. She had had these moments previously. She had always thought they were just some strange imaginings or déjà vu... but perhaps it was multiple lives of redoing.

"Wait. Have I...? Have *I* been doing this, too?"

Sarah saw the flash of alarm in Paul's eyes before he buried his face in his hands. "I don't know. I don't know. All I know is that we're together right here, right now, and whatever happens in the future, I want to have this time, these eight years, and maybe forever. Please, please can we throw the goddamn device away?"

"But what difference does it make, if you can invent the device in 2012, what's to stop you from coming back and living this life again? I would never know. This could be the third or fourth time we've had this conversation. Our lives could be an endless loop of redos. We don't have eight years." Sarah's voice had taken on a panicked edge.

Paul crossed the space between them and took her hands in his. "No, no. Stop." He took a deep gulp of air and seemed to steady himself. "You're right. We don't. But what relationship ever does? We have right now—that's all anyone ever has. This very moment. I love you, and I want nothing more than to be with you, even if I do it a hundred times." His voice cracked. "Please, please say yes."

She stood and stared into those beautiful blue eyes that she had looked into so many times, maybe more times than she even knew. Could she keep doing this? Should she?

Slowly she let her forehead fall into the curve between his shoulder and his neck and breathed him in.

"Did Gelana win the marathon in London?" she murmured into his sternum.

She felt his body shudder in a slight sob and his arms snake around her. "You better believe it, and she broke the record."

* * *

They tossed the device into the St. Mary a mile downstream from where Charlotte had drowned a timeline ago, or perhaps many timelines ago. Charlotte was safe in the hospital, recovering from her jump from the car, cleaning up. Her mother had agreed to leave Jake and come back and live with Sarah in Portland for a bit.

Paul's hand in hers felt absolutely right. Solid, like there was no chance of time travel. Like he would never leave her.

Had it felt absolutely right before? She might never know.

Perhaps they had both become cats chasing the mice of perfect lives.

As the gunmetal waters rushed past, Sarah tried to quell the fear that moving water always wrought deep within her psyche. Memories, like water, had a way of seeping into fissures and breaking things down, dissolving the present with the floods of the past.

Perhaps it was time to try to jettison all the memories and start fresh.

The river of time had once seemed to her to be inexorable, but now it seemed filled with loops, eddies, and backwaters. Or perhaps it was more like the ocean: endless, with no clear navigable path.

The time travel devices would resurface in their lives. Somehow. She knew it, and he knew it. But for now, having the ability to change pasts and futures somehow had made the present moment, and Paul's body next to hers, seem all that more precious.

A Word From Jennifer Ellis

Although I tend to think in novel-length arcs, I do write short stories. Since I tend to frame everything in a skiing context, I liken writing novels to skiing big open bowls, where you have the luxury of taking long, beautiful, swooping turns. Writing a short story is more like skiing the trees, requiring tighter turns and more careful maneuvering. More thrilling perhaps, but riskier. And writing a short story about time travel throws a bunch of potential sinkholes and cliffs into the mix. Fortunately there is no shortage of those on which to train at my local ski hill.

Being from Canada, and having done most of my informal training in the CanLit tradition, I have often worried that my short stories are not sufficiently gritty. My first experience writing a short story that had a happy ending was for a reading at a Christmas event, and the audience actually cheered when I finished. Of course I then turned around and immediately rewrote the same piece with a grimmer ending to submit to literary magazines. In the spirit of taking risks, I decided to go with a more positive conclusion for my piece in this collection.

I have written about time travel before. My middle-grade series focuses on the question: What would you do if you could see your future? How would you live? The first novel in the series, *A Pair of Docks*, was released in 2013, and the second novel, *A Quill Ladder*, will be out in December 2014. I wanted "The River" to focus on the opposite question. What would you do if you could change your past? Just because you *can* travel in time, does that automatically mean you will? It seems that I spend a lot of time imagining both potential futures and pasts. My adult novel, *In the Shadows of the Mosquito Constellation*, set in a dystopic climate-changed future in the Canadian West, will be available in May 2014.

Links to my novels, tips on indie publishing, and general musings on the writing life can be found on my website: www.jenniferellis.ca

I am very grateful to David Gatewood for inviting me to be a part of this anthology. I am honored to be part of a collection with such amazing independent authors.

A Word in Pompey's Ear
by Christopher G. Nuttall

BEING A WOMAN IN ACADEMIA can be quite a chore.

It's not so bad if you want to take Women's Studies or Cultural Relativity 101, but it's really quite dispiriting if you wish to study Ancient History. Yet I've always been fascinated by the Roman Republic, thanks to a father who read Cicero and Caesar to me when I was a little girl, so studying it seemed a dream come true. Or it would have been, if it hadn't been for some of the academics I had to impress.

"Julia, I read your paper with the greatest of interest," Professor Rowe said. "But the idea that Pompey could have saved the Republic is mere wishful thinking."

Stung, I retaliated at once. "Pompey was the defender of the Republic during the Civil War, and he managed to impose a workable settlement over Asia," I said. "Given the chance, he could have applied those skills to Rome."

"But he never had the chance," the professor countered. "And the passage from republic to empire was pretty much inevitable."

He paused. "It was a very well-argued paper," he added. "But not convincing."

I stood, collecting my papers as I rose. It had taken me nearly a month to write my proposal for a study of Pompey's life and just how significant he was throughout the varied problems facing the Roman Republic. And the professor had taken less than an hour to read through it and then dismiss it with a handful of well-chosen words. I understood his point—Pompey had never had the chance to reshape the Roman Republic, not after Caesar chased him out of Italy—but how could he simply ignore the possibility? History's lessons are about what *might* have happened as much as they are about what *actually* happened.

And Pompey fascinated me, more than I cared to admit. He seemed like a character out of myth, almost the reincarnation of Alexander the Great. He'd built an army, fought for the dictator Sulla and then for the Roman Republic... and had then been forced into battle by the Senate he'd helped to flee from Rome. What would history have been like if Pompey had managed to get his way?

I walked into the cafe, ordered a hot coffee, and sat down to think about my next move. My paper hadn't been *precisely* rejected, but it was unlikely I would get any funding for a long-term research project. It wasn't a sexy project, nor was it something the faculty would fear to deny funding to, out of concerns about accusations of racism or the like. I had a feeling that I'd have to go back into serving as a research assistant—or, more likely, find something else to do with my life. But there are few calls for an ancient historian outside the universities of the world.

My thoughts were such a blur that I barely noticed when someone else sat down at my table, facing me and resting her long fingers on the tabletop. It wasn't until she cleared her throat that I looked up—and stared. She was timeless, her face both stern and beautiful. Her hair fell around her face like a halo, distracting me from her smile. She was so beautiful that I found it hard to look at her directly.

"I read your paper," she said. There was something faintly Italian about her accent, something that sent shivers down my spine. "Do you really believe Pompey could have made a difference?"

I don't normally defend my research papers to anyone, apart from my supervisors, much less a complete stranger, but her faintly mocking tone goaded me to respond. I never even questioned who gave her my paper, I just launched into full-on defense mode, going point by point through my entire thesis, claiming that Pompey was the man with the right vision at the right time to save the Roman Republic from Caesar and Augustus. It felt like I went on for hours. And then I told her that if *I* had been there, I could have steered Pompey toward saving the Republic.

"Really?" she said, musingly. "Could you have even *talked* to him?"

I nodded. "I speak Latin."

"Not the right sort of Latin," she said. "But you will. Never let it be said that I didn't give you a fair chance. Or that you didn't ask for it."

I opened my mouth to ask what she meant, but it was too late. She jabbed a finger at me—and the world went away in a flash of blinding light. And then there was commotion all around me. Men were staring, rooted to the floor in shock…

"Well," a thick voice demanded. "Who are *you*?"

I looked up… and found myself staring into the face of Gnaeus Pompeius Magnus, otherwise known as Pompey the Great.

He wasn't quite what I'd expected, certainly nothing like anyone from my time. He was clearly old, yet there was a youthful determination in his posture that reminded me that he'd definitely struggled hard to keep in shape and share the privations of his legionnaires. His famous blond hair was going gray, but the quiff he wore in an attempt to imitate Alexander was firmly in place. Did Rome have hair dye? I honestly couldn't recall.

"I'm… I'm Julia," I said. Too late, I remembered that Julia had been the name of his late wife. His face darkened for a long moment, then faded back into inscrutability. "I was sent to aid you."

Pompey's gaze swept the room. "Out," he said. Two of his guards made to protest, but he silenced them with a look. "Leave us."

He waited until everyone was gone, then turned his gaze on me.

"Explain," he ordered.

And so I did.

* * *

Pompey was very far from stupid. He might not have understood all I tried to tell him about the modern world, but he understood the opportunity I was offering him. And, as I'd arrived in a flash of light, he seemed quite willing to believe that I was a gift from the goddess Venus herself. But it wasn't going to be easy. Caesar had crossed the Rubicon a day or two earlier.

I'd honestly never quite grasped just how long it took for news to flow from one part of the Roman Empire to another. The Roman Empire seemed so small by the standards of the British Empire, but because the Romans didn't have any form of fast travel or communication a Roman commander might be out of touch with the Senate for years, and an army might arrive hard on the heels of the messengers warning of its arrival. By the time I'd convinced Pompey to listen to me, Caesar's army of veterans was already heading toward Rome.

But Pompey had known that, of course. His plan to leave Italy and retreat to the east was still good—after all, it had come very close to success. My sanction—and that of the Goddess—was all he needed to overcome a handful of lingering doubts. It helped that he wasn't fool enough to believe untrained men a match for Caesar's legionaries.

It would have gone perfectly, I thought, if it hadn't been for the interference from the Senate. I wasn't allowed to meet with them, but I heard enough muttering from Pompey to understand that the Senate was torn in two. The whole idea of abandoning Italy was horrifying to them, and some of the idiots wanted to make a stand. Cato, in particular, was stubbornly refusing to budge. It took all of Pompey's powers of persuasion—and a threat to resign—to get the Senate moving southward to a point where they could take ship. By then, Caesar was hot on our heels.

The Romans weren't quite sure what to make of me, particularly the ones who hadn't seen my arrival. I'd forgotten—or, rather, I'd overlooked—just how misogynist the Romans were, particularly the stubborn old traditionalists. Famous Roman men are famous for the right reasons; famous Roman women are famous for being... well, sluts and whores, and for daring to put themselves on the same level as men. It was maddening to discover that I wasn't allowed to attend war councils, even though my knowledge of what had happened in my past was effectively foreknowledge of the future. I spent far too much of my time in a cart or a restricted handful of houses as we made our way southward. If it hadn't been for Pompey's wife, who was a good-natured woman, I suspect I would have gone insane. And Pompey, for all his faults, genuinely loved her. For some reason, the Romans snickered about this behind his back.

But we made it to the ships and escaped before Caesar could lower the boom. I didn't blame Pompey for running, even though some historians alleged that Pompey could have won if he'd turned and fought. I watched from my cabin as we left Italy behind and headed east, leaving Caesar with an empty treasury—I'd convinced Pompey to take the treasure with us— and a countryside stripped of everything it needed to feed itself. Pompey's ruthlessness, alas, had not echoed down through history as much as it should have.

The sea voyage was absolutely terrifying. There was nothing like it in the modern world, certainly not in my experience. No GPS, no outboard motors, nothing but sails or rowers powering us through the water. I looked in at the slaves and shuddered in horror when I saw them chained to the benches, providing the power to keep us moving. They were utterly broken, following orders and little else. And the stench was appalling. I tried to explain to Pompey that slavery was wrong, but he just looked at me blankly. He didn't even comprehend what I was trying to tell him.

It was easy to say, I realized grimly, that the Romans had a more progressive view of slavery than the Confederated States of America. They did; it wasn't uncommon for a slave to be freed, then start rising in the ranks of Rome. But for every slave who made it, there were a hundred who lived and died as slaves—either taken as captives by the Romans, or simply born into slavery. Nor were there any laws governing the treatment or mistreatment of slaves. A slave had no rights, no freedoms. Being worked to death—or raped—was also far from uncommon.

By the time we reached our destination, I was almost a nervous wreck. Pompey, of course, was disgustingly enthusiastic as he strode ashore and started issuing orders, rallying the troops and his loyal clients from Asia to his banner. His wife took me with the other wives; half of them were boring, while the other half spent most of their time calculating ways to advance their husbands' careers. But it wasn't easy for a woman to wield any overt influence in Rome.

A man who paid too much attention to his wife would become a laughingstock.

But Pompey listened to me, enough that we could start planning a trap for Caesar. When the rogue general crossed the waters in pursuit, we were waiting. A sea battle in the ancient world was a chaotic affair, and Caesar himself managed to slip out of our grasp, but we sank a number of his ships and killed a vast number of his men. Naturally, he landed anyway, as we'd blocked his line of retreat. And then we started to advance toward his base camp.

At first, the battle didn't go our way. Caesar's men were far more experienced than ours, even though we had far more men to use in combat. The battle might have been lost, if Caesar and his men weren't so badly drained. But we hung on, and two weeks later, we launched a second offensive, forcing Caesar to retreat. This time, there was no food for him to take from the land, and the local cities all closed their doors to him. He was in the middle of trying to storm one city when Pompey's armies finally caught up with him. It was a savage battle, but—pinned against a sealed city—the outcome was never in doubt.

I'd long lost any hope of the Senate being graceful in victory, yet they managed to shock even Pompey by their attitude toward Caesar and his men. Caesar's body was dragged out from where it had fallen, and was then dismembered, while his men were summarily executed or sold into slavery. There was no honorable treatment of the defeated. Even the Romans who had fought beside Caesar received the same brutal treatment. Afterward, when the killing was finally done, Pompey cried in his tent. Caesar and he had been bound together by ties of friendship and love— he'd married Caesar's daughter—and part of him would always regret the outcome.

"They forced him into fighting or dying," he told me afterward. "They wanted him dead—and they got their wish."

I knew he was right. Caesar had been confronted with a choice between fighting or going to his execution like a lamb to the slaughter. How could anyone blame him for fighting?

* * *

Our return to Rome was more like a victory parade than anything else. Mark Antony, who had remained behind in Rome as Caesar's deputy, didn't have the forces to put up a fight, particularly with the whole country turning against him. Instead of trying to hold Rome, he took his loyalists and headed northward, back to Gaul. Pompey and the Senate marched back into the city, took control of the fortifications, and returned to their homes without a fight. And then the killing began.

I'd only heard whispers from the other women—and grumbles from Pompey—about how the senators had carefully planned their return, divvying up positions of power and the estates of those they considered rebels. Now blood washed the streets of Rome as the victors wreaked their revenge on the vanquished. Cato, stern and unyielding, pressed for the sternest of measures against the defeated, removing hundreds of men from the senatorial rolls for not having been enthusiastic enough about the war. Others were killed simply because they had land and property the victors wanted. Rome hadn't seen anything like it since the days of Sulla. And Sulla had reshaped the world.

I bore some of the guilt, I knew. I had named many who would serve Caesar in future—and many who would serve Augustus after he became the first true emperor of Rome. Augustus himself—Octavius, as he was at the time—was brutally murdered, even though he was just a sickly youth. I tried to convince Pompey to spare some of the men I knew would have talent, but he was remorseless. And so was the Senate. The warnings from the goddess would be heeded.

It was harder for me to follow the politics, once the war was won and we were back in Rome. I no longer had any foresight, now that history had changed. Pompey seemed... well, not entirely unwilling to listen to me, but not quite willing to take everything I said on faith either. I was, after all, a woman. No matter how much I tried to talk him into making changes Rome desperately needed, he refused to listen, or was unable to make the changes. I couldn't help thinking that the defeat of Caesar had changed nothing.

And we had enemies. Pompey, as was his wont, had disbanded most of his armies once we had returned to Rome, keeping only a handful of legions in being to hunt down Mark Antony and secure control over Gaul. His enemies had seen this as a display of weakness, a sign the great and old man could be brought down. Cato and Cicero, unlikely allies, had combined their forces to cripple Pompey. They feared powerful citizens, I knew, but they feared powerful women much more.

"I hate the Queen," Cicero said, bluntly. No one doubted that he meant me.

But what else was I supposed to do? Be a good little Roman woman: seen but not heard? I hated the restrictions on my life imposed on me by my gender; they might have thought I was a gift from a goddess, but I was still a woman. Pompey wanted to keep me close—and the Roman Senate sniggered about that too—and yet he didn't quite seem to know what to make of me. I tried to teach him ideas that might help Rome— everything from the English alphabet to primitive steam engines—but he never listened. And he found the whole idea of democracy laughable.

I didn't understand until after his wife died. Pompey wasn't interested in raw power, unlike either Caesar or Sulla. He wanted *acceptance.* He wanted the confirmation that he was part of the Senate and the people of Rome. And the Senate, torn between jealousy of his achievements and fear of his power, was unwilling to clasp him to its bosom. By the time Pompey gave up the thought of marrying a senator's daughter and offered to marry me instead, I understood just how thoroughly they hated him.

The Romans had no real concept of political parties, certainly not in the modern sense. Political life in Rome was an endless struggle between individuals: everyone wanted to rise to the top, while everyone else wanted to drag them down. Rome had a long history of fearing men with power; every time a Roman General was no longer needed, his enemies would turn on him and unseat him from power. No wonder Scorpio wanted to be buried in Greece. His ungrateful country had turned on him after Carthage was safely destroyed.

Marriage to Pompey was odd. He doted on me, just as much as he had doted on his other wives, but he still didn't *listen*. And it was frustrating as hell to watch while Rome slowly turned against the man who'd saved it more than once.

The next political catfight started after Mark Antony smashed two legions in quick succession and started threatening to advance—once again—on Rome. I didn't understand why they didn't simply give the command to Pompey. He might have been old, even by modern standards, but he was still as sharp as ever. Besides, nothing I'd seen or read had given me much regard for Antony's abilities as a general. Unless the Romans of old had been right, I conceded, and Cleopatra had indeed sapped his strength. But, whatever the truth, it hardly mattered. All that mattered was parrying Antony before he could threaten Rome. In the end, they gave the command to an up-and-coming senator, someone who wanted a military command to burnish his chances of future glory. For the Romans, that was quite understandable. They had no concept of separating the military from the civilian sphere.

I didn't know him. It struck me, from time to time, just how many Romans I didn't know, but this one should have been recognizable. My best guess was that he had been a very junior aristocrat who'd died during the war against Caesar, back in the original timeline. But it didn't really matter. Pompey and I watched as he led his troops out of the city and headed north—and then we went back to our home. For the first time, it struck me just how old Pompey truly was. He was reaching the end of a long and very eventful life.

But the Senate gave him no peace. They hounded him relentlessly. For the first time, there were suggestions of inquires into the source of Pompey's staggering wealth, the exact terms of the settlement in Asia, even the truth behind my appearance. I watched as Pompey grew older and grayer with every new attack, as if he'd lost the spark that had kept him going.

And then word came from the north. Antony had won yet another battle, and Rome herself was threatened once again.

And what did the Senate do? They called for Pompey.

Pompey was tired, but not unwilling to serve. He amassed a new army, placed his oldest son in a high position (his youngest had gone into the navy, on my recommendation), and gathered a hundred other young aristocrats to help him lead. One of them was Brutus, which should have worried me more than it did. But Brutus was loyal to the Republic, and so, in his way, was Pompey. He worked hard, harder than anyone else, to build up a colossal army, one capable of beating Antony by weight of numbers. Pompey might not have been a great general, lacking the flair Caesar had brought to the battlefield, but he was an organizational genius, all the more impressive for lacking computers, radios, or anything else a modern general would take for granted. By the time he led his army out of Rome, it was the most powerful and capable army Rome had sent into the field since the end of the Civil War.

I stayed behind. The battlefield, Pompey said, was no place for a woman. And, besides, I was in no danger if I remained in Rome. Women might be considered second-class citizens at best, but they were rarely harmed, no matter who their husbands were or what they had done. But still, I wanted to be there.

News filtered back slowly—very slowly. There had been a battle and Pompey had won. Mark Antony had been killed. The last traces of Caesar's faction had been stamped out. And then the shit *really* hit the fan.

It was nearly a week before all of the pieces fell into place. The Senate had seen a chance to get rid of two birds with one stone. As soon as Pompey had won the battle, Brutus and his allies had surrounded him and stabbed my husband to death. They hadn't known, of course, that that was how they would kill Caesar in the original timeline. Instead, in the world I had created, they killed Pompey instead. But they'd reckoned without his son. Pompey the Younger had killed the assassins, rallied the army, and was now marching on Rome. And the Senate had nothing to put in his path.

They came for me, of course. I didn't try to fight as they bound my hands and led me through the streets to Rome's very first prison, built right next to the Senate House. Instead, I just waited as they put me into a cell and left me there, perhaps intending to try to use me as a hostage. Somehow, I found it hard to care.

And then, when the doors opened, I saw *her* standing there.

But I was beyond shock at that point. An odd detachment had fallen over my mind. If they'd dragged me out for execution, I wouldn't have resisted. Instead, I just waited to see what would happen.

"Come with me," she said.

No one barred our path as she led me up a long flight of stairs and onto the roof. Outside, I could hear the sounds of shouting as the Senate tried hard to rally a defense of the city. A few hundred armed men were running toward the walls, while weapons were being distributed and veterans were hastily being pressed back into service. But morale looked low, from what little I could see, and many of the veterans wouldn't be enthusiastic about fighting Pompey's son. Rumors of how he'd died had already spread through the city. The Senate might have hated him, but he was a hero to the ordinary citizens—and to his men.

"The city will fall," she said. "And they brought their fate on themselves."

I nodded in agreement. The Senate had played with fire once too many times. In the original history, Caesar had been pushed into rebellion and eventually won the war. Now, my stepson would be leading the fight to show the Senate just how idiotic it was to provoke a man with an army—and with an awareness that defeat or surrender meant certain death. Would Pompey the Younger be better or worse than Octavius? In the end, it didn't matter.

It was over. No matter what I'd done, the Roman Republic was dead. It had committed suicide.

I turned to face her. "Who *are* you?"

The woman smiled. "Don't you know?"

I shook my head. Pompey had speculated that she might be the goddess Venus, but I'd never been raised to believe in the Roman gods.

"I am Nemesis," the goddess said. "And I cannot be denied."

Historian's Note

Historically, the Roman Republic—particularly the Senate—was suspicious and fearful of military commanders who managed to win fame and fortune, creating an odd atmosphere where individual achievement was both praised and punished by society. (And serious problems were allowed to ferment because no one could be trusted with the military might to handle them.) As the Roman Republic reached the height of its power, its politics became increasingly dangerous for military officers.

Pompey did not have the mindset of a new emperor, despite serving Sulla during his dictatorship. He wanted to be loved rather than feared—thus his attempts to please the Senate rather than impose his own order. Unfortunately, this made him look weak, and daggers (metaphorically) were drawn. The Senate, at first fearful of Pompey's colossal army, relaxed and started trying to marginalize him as soon as he disbanded the army. Caesar, when faced with demands that he disband his army and return to Rome as a private citizen (which meant disgrace and exile at the very least), decided it was safer to go into revolt than surrender to the Senate.

Sadly, it is unlikely the Roman Republic could have endured for much longer, even without Caesar. Those with the talent to succeed were unlikely to tamely accept attempts to cut them down indefinitely.

A Word from Christopher Nuttall

I've always enjoyed historical debates about what could have happened if something had been a little different, but—at the same time—I've studied history long enough to know that there are some places in history where the outcome is almost completely immutable, no matter what happens. The Roman Republic was doomed to fall simply because of its internal contradictions; Caesar might have been the chosen executioner, but someone would have taken his place if he'd simply never impinged on history at all.

For those interested, Nemesis was one of the Greco-Roman goddesses, specifically charged with punishing hubris—in this case, that of both Julia and the Roman Republic. Short stories are really not my thing, so I think I may redo the story as a full novel at some point. Comments and thoughts are always welcome.

And me? I've been writing since 2004 and I've recently had some success on Kindle, as well as with a couple of small presses. You can download free samples of some of my books from my site (www.chrishanger.net) and then download them from Amazon at a very reasonable price.

Rock or Shell
by Ann Christy

"HEY! YOU, OVER THERE! Can you see me?"

The girl, perhaps sixteen or seventeen, looks startled for a moment—then hunches down as if she can hide behind the thick mist that surrounds us. Her near flinch tells me just about all I need to know about her. At least all I need to know to make contact.

"Don't worry. I'm not like some of the others. I won't hurt you," I say, and motion her forward in my most non-threatening manner.

She shuffles forward warily a few steps, and then stops—eyeing me, my piles of stuff, and the forest of wires attaching me to those piles. I can't blame her for that. I'm probably not the only one who's figured out this trick—this method of hanging on to possessions in this no man's land where time is in constant flux—but I don't think there can be many others.

Now that I get a good look at her, I can see that she's a bit lost at sea, so to speak. She's certainly a teen—or close enough that it doesn't matter—but she has the eyes of a girl who's seen too much. Her lips are cracked and dry, her cheeks sunken; her hair is greasy at the crown and her face is in need of a good wash. And her jeans and fashionably thin t-shirt aren't the best clothes to be trapped wearing, in this in-between of time and nothingness.

But she isn't covered in filth like some of the others that have happened across my nest. And she's upright and moving. She couldn't have been roaming about in the mist for too long or she'd look even worse. More likely she'd be dead.

Yet the most remarkable thing about her is her weary eyes. The hollows beneath them are so profound and dark that I know she hasn't slept since landing here.

And here I am, lounging on a giant mattress surrounded by stuff.

She looks longingly at my mattress, at the cup in my hand. She gives a sniff, as if the aroma of the coffee has finally reached her. That seems to settle the matter, and she walks those last few steps toward me without any hint of hesitation.

I carefully maneuver myself backward on the mattress to make room, always keeping my great harness of wires in mind, and I give the mattress a little pat to let her know she's welcome to sit.

With the grace of youth, she folds herself onto the surface, and a sigh escapes her that almost breaks my heart. I hold out the cup of coffee I've been sipping and say, "It's got cream and sugar. The cream is just the powdered stuff, though."

Tears spring into her eyes so quickly that I know she must be exhausted almost beyond reason. She accepts the cup with one hand, the other remaining tightly fisted in her lap, and drinks it down without even testing the temperature. Under the cup her throat bobs, and I see how thin it is. Her jeans look as if they're gapped a bit at the waist, and there are hollows in her cheeks and temples. Perhaps she's naturally thin—or perhaps she's been here much longer than I had first thought.

The cup is upended once more, so she can drain every last drop, and then she regretfully holds the cup out for me to take. Her nails are dirty and ragged, and the lines in her fingers are starkly outlined by ground-in dirt.

"I'm Gertie," I say, and take the cup from her.

Her eyes grow nervous once more, and she takes quick glances around: at the many five-gallon pails around my mattress, at my hands—most likely checking for a weapon—and then into the pale mist that encloses our island of color and substance.

"I'm Sarah," she says at last. "Thank you for the coffee. I've not had anything to drink in a long while."

Her voice is rough, as if she hasn't spoken in a while, but what surprises me is her accent. It isn't just British, it's posh TV British. It's the kind of accent you only get from just the right sort of expensive schooling in just the right place. Of the ones I've come across who speak English, most do so with a decidedly North American accent.

"Then you're probably hungry," I say, and her eyes tell me her answer. "Well then, let me get you some food. First, let's get the ground rules out of the way, shall we?"

Sarah tenses a little, but doesn't pull away. "Ground rules?"

I wave toward my wires and then all the other things around us and say, "You know that whatever we're connected to—even if only through some conductive medium—comes with us?"

She looks a little confused and shakes her head.

"Well, it does. It's too late now, but you could have brought things. These wires are what keeps it all here, so you mustn't touch them or anything." I pause, and pull up the hem of my shirt to show her the wide belt of coiled wires that circles my belly. Given that she's already trusted a total stranger enough to join them on a mattress, I probably don't need to add a warning, but I feel I should. "This is where all the wires connect to me. If I should die—well, you've seen what happens then, right?"

She gulps and blushes, then nods. That also tells me she understands at least a little of what's going on here in the mist.

"I, uh, saw someone disappear," she says quietly. The fist she's had clenched from the moment I saw her tightens, the knuckles whitening.

"Okay, we can talk about that later. Just no touching the wires, okay? And the only other rule is no yelling or being loud. If anyone comes near enough to hear but not see, you could lead them right to us. Got it?"

She nods and looks into the mist once more. A deep sigh escapes her, and she says, "I'm very happy to follow those rules. I've not sat down on anything but that mist in days. I never thought I'd see a mattress again, let alone sit on one."

I give her a smile and then scoot around toward my little gas stove, which rests on a couple of pails. I brought a whole load of those small green bottles of gas, but I try to use them as sparingly as possible. I get water from one of my many containers, a cup of macaroni from another, and I let the little stove do its work.

Pointing to a bin just behind the girl's back, I ask, "Can you grab me a packet out of that, please?"

Whatever object the girl's been gripping in her fist, she now transfers it to her mouth, so as to free up both her hands. The object rounds out her cheek—*like a squirrel's,* I think. The girl carefully lifts the lid, taking care not to jostle the wires, and when she looks inside the bin, she gives a little gasp at the contents. She lifts out a freeze-dried meal bag and gazes at it for a long moment, her eyes scanning the colorful photo of a tasty-looking meal, before handing it to me. She doesn't let go until my own hand is firmly on the packet.

"The tricky part is getting things into other things," I say, to break the silence.

She doesn't understand me, so I point to the macaroni. "When I dump anything in, if I'm not careful, it's suspended for a moment and… poof. Everything has to touch something."

Sarah transfers the object from her mouth back to her hand, and squeezes her fist closed before she speaks. "Sort of like this, only the opposite." She lifts her fist so I'll know she's speaking of the object in her hand.

I nod and stir the macaroni. Food preparation here is very hard to accomplish, but I've learned a few tricks to make it easier. Several small metal clips are attached to my shirt, and each one has a wire wrapped carefully around it, connecting it back to my harness. I take one off, raise it for her inspection with a smile, and then clip it to the bag she just retrieved.

She laughs and says, "You've thought of everything!"

"Shh," I say, but gently and with a smile so she knows I'm not angry. Her face has lost years in the minutes that she's been here, and her posture is relaxed, almost slumped. I can see she's itching to lie down, relax, and sleep. Whether it's because she's just worn out, or because I'm probably about the same age as her mother would be, she seems to have decided to trust me entirely. And no matter the many comforts I may have, I confess that I'm delighted to have company. In this unchanging place, the most oppressive thing is the solitude. I don't even have a dawn to cheer me, or a sunset to mark the passing of a day.

When the food is ready, we settle in and share it right from the pot. Sarah is a good guest, careful to fill her spoon only as much as I fill my own, and take only one bite for each of mine. It's an impressive show of restraint, since I know she must be starving.

After a dozen small bites, I sigh and lean back, and say, "You have the rest. I can't eat as much as you young people."

More than half the food is left in the pot, and she tries to hide the eagerness she feels, but her tongue darts out to touch her lips in anticipation. While she eats I fill a bottle with water, and I wait until she comes up for air before offering it.

With only one hand free—her object is still clenched tightly in her fist—she takes a moment to be sure the pot still has its clip before setting it down. Then she drinks until I think she might drown. The water bottle is back in my hands less than a second before Sarah's head is back at the pot, shoveling in bite after bite.

While she eats, I look out at the mist, making sure no one is coming upon us. It isn't really mist, of course. There's no water to condense on the skin, like with a true mist. And it's not a haze either. Yet those are the two most common terms used to describe it. One time a professor from a university in Hamburg happened upon me. He spoke excellent English, and his fascination with this place made him almost immune to the situation he found himself in. We shared a meal, just like I was now doing with this girl, and he told me that he felt the mist was something explainable, even if he couldn't explain it.

He told me that the distance one can see through the mist is directly related to the size of the area one occupies, which might be the reason why I can see as far as ten paces from my nest, while others say they can see only five or so. He was a kind man.

"Be careful, you're losing some," I say when I see her losing her focus. Just as I say that and she raises her head, we both see a piece of pasta fall off the side of her spoon and disappear as if it had never existed. In fact, it *hasn't* existed now. It is gone from space as well as time.

Like everything else in the world. Unless I'm right, and everything works out like I hope it will, that is. And for that, I will need this young girl.

"Oh," Sarah groans, mourning the loss of that bit of food. She looks back at me, perhaps expecting me to be upset, and says, "I'm sorry. I'll be more careful."

I see her hand grip the spoon more tightly, either because she's trying hard to lose nothing or because she doesn't want me to take it away from her. I just give her a nod and sip some of the water from the bottle, waiting for her to finish.

We're left with a dirty pot, which Sarah licks almost clean—even going so far as to wipe her fingers around the bottom where she can't reach using her tongue. When she's finally done, I do the "easy clean-up" trick, to put her at ease and lighten the mood. After a thorough wipe-down with a wet paper towel, I toss the dirty wipe into the air above us, where it disappears. I toss the empty food packet after it.

Sarah smiles and says, "Well, there's always something good to be found in every situation."

I nod. She gives a yawn, and I know she must be exhausted beyond belief, but I don't want to wait to find out her story. People who are tired—and I discovered this long before winding up here in this world of no time—are more likely to simply get things over with and tell the truth when questioned. Once rested, they may be more coherent, but they're also more likely to put up their defenses.

"Sarah, I know you're tired, but before I sleep this close to someone I don't know, I'd like to know a little bit about you. How you wound up here and all," I say. It's a reasonable request.

She stretches and then grips her stomach in sudden discomfort. I might think it a ploy, except that I can hear the gurgling even across the giant mattress. Her stomach has been without food a long time.

"How long have you been here?" I ask.

"I don't know. I tried to keep track, checking out there to see when it was dark or light, but I lost track. I think at least five days," she answers, her voice soft.

Time is relative here, so I know that doesn't mean much. I've been here for nineteen days in my time, based on my watch, but for her it may be only five. Even that long without water would leave her dead or barely alive. Yet she's walking and talking.

"What have you been eating and drinking?"

She flushes again, but this time with embarrassment. "I've had nothing to eat. I popped out to drink a few times, and..."

The way she trails off, I guess that she's been forced to recycle a little fluid. I'll leave that line of inquiry alone. I'm much more interested in her popping out.

"You could breathe out there? What was it like?"

Looking out into the mist again, she grows thoughtful and distant. Her voice becomes so soft and quiet that I have to lean forward to hear her next words.

"No, you can't breathe out there now. There's nothing." She pauses then and looks at me, her eyes intense. "It's just rock, covered with this dark sand. In some places it's very deep, and other places it's just bare rock. There are pools of water all over, and steam comes up from them when it first gets light."

That confuses me, because the last time I went out there it was much like she described, and I couldn't tolerate it for more than a few seconds. Certainly not long enough to find a clean patch of water. I'm not sure I would drink it anyway. Who knows what's in it? And popping out is impossible for me now that I'm tethered like I am—at least, if I want all that I have to remain intact. I lost several of my pails once when they fell away from the uneven patch where I landed.

"How did you stay out there that long?" I ask, genuinely curious.

Now it's her turn to have information that I don't, and she's eager to share it, to pay for her meal and place on the mattress. She smiles and says, "You can travel. All you have to do is think it when you pop in and out."

At my expression she waves a hand out at the mist and says, "It's something about this place that does it. I pop out—you know, just focus on dropping back out—and then take a quick look to see if there's water, and then come back in. If there's no water, then I just keep doing it until I *do* see water somewhere, and then I just focus on that location and pop out right there." She shrugs then, both of us understanding that all of it is entirely inexplicable. Our common language of life in the mist is all that we have.

She looks up at me from under her stringy hair and asks, "When's the last time you were out?"

"A while," I say, trying to give the impression that I'm not clear on the time rather than tell her how long I've been here.

Now we've gotten some of the prelude aside, and I think she knows I'm going to go to the heart of the matter. Given our situation, she must know I'm going to ask. Her shoulders are bowed over her lap and her fist is tight around her object, her other hand clasped over it to be sure she doesn't let go.

Her tension is palpable, so I decide to take a detour before getting right to the question. I hold out both of my empty hands and ask, "Notice I don't have to carry one?"

That draws her out of her anticipatory funk, and she looks me over, searching for a bulge in my cheek or some other indicator of where I've got my object stashed. "How? You don't have one at all?"

It's a risk to show anyone this, but really, what does it matter? If my heart stops I'll disappear anyway, and she doesn't look like the sort to dig it out of my body while keeping me alive just long enough to get my object into her hands.

At least one of the bad ones out there does this. I learned this from another man I encountered in the mist, a man who had run into the bad one and barely escaped. Bleeding and frightened—and quite understandably terrified of any new person, including me—he had been hard to help. It was only when I held up the medical kit that I was able to persuade him to come forward and let me tend to him.

After that, he'd been eager to share his story, to show me the long gash the man had made to dig out his object. It was his story that gave me the idea in the first place. The bad man, who I'd taken to thinking of as Cutter, wanted to control all the objects. He apparently believed that would give him the ability to change things back.

I unbutton the top few buttons of my shirt, and laugh when she gives me a look exactly like a teenager should. Folding back the top wedge, I show her the top of my chest and the little bulge there. An angry red line crosses it, and I still have pieces of tape over the top and bottom of the cut. It's healed, but I can't be sure how strong it is yet, so I won't risk it working its way out.

Sarah gasps and leans forward, stopping abruptly when she nears my web of wires. Her gaze is on the lump, and I can see her working out the geometry of my object and the mechanics of what I've done. When she leans back, her fist tightens again and she asks, "What is it? Yours, I mean."

"A little green pebble. I found it on the beach. Yours?"

She opens her fist so cautiously that I can almost hear her joints creak. Her fingers don't straighten all the way. They've been curled into a fist for too long, and there are dark lines of grime along each joint. In her palm rests a small shell of a type I've never seen before. It's tiny, no more than an inch long, and beautifully whorled with colors that would have attracted any eye.

I ask, "Did you find yours at the beach, too?"

It's a good a way as any to broach the subject.

"No. A man gave it to me while I was waiting at the tube station," she says, and I know she must dwell on that moment a great deal.

"Ah," I say. I've heard of that before. Some that find the objects get themselves into such a muddle that they can't take it anymore, and would rather disappear than keep going. Or they think they can make everything go back to the way it was if they give it away. I've never figured out how or why they get these ideas.

We sit in silence for a moment, the ever-present soft sound of nothingness around us—and it does have a sound, although one that can't be described—absorbing what's been said and shown. I see her eyes dart back up to the area where I've stuffed a rock under the skin of my chest, and I ask, "How did you figure out what it was? Aside from what must have happened to the man that gave it to you."

Sarah sighs and says, "Because I was mad at my mum, I found out right away. When the man held my hand like that, he scared me. He was dressed nicely but he looked frantic and sort of sweaty. He grabbed my hand and said that I was young and couldn't have too many regrets. He pressed the shell into my hand and let go. Then he just disappeared." She makes the *poof* motion with her hands—or rather, with one hand and one fist.

"There had to be more to it than that. You could have just dropped it."

"Yeah, but he said not to," she says and shrugs. "And then everything just changed, like it shifted or something. The walls had been tiled but full of these huge murals. I know it was like that. I remember it. But then they weren't anymore. It was just white tiles, all streaked with black like they are, covered with loads of flyers and billboards and such. And I remember that, too."

"And no one else noticed, right?" I say, knowing the feeling. Holding an object takes you out of the loop of repercussions when something changes. Letting go of it means it all catches up with you. No one is absolutely sure what dying with an object does, but I think I have a good idea. Some things change back, but it's all dependent on what else got changed by someone else in the meantime. That's my theory.

She nods and smiles at me. "Exactly. I was completely freaked out. I mean, who wouldn't be? But then I did the exact wrong thing. I wasn't supposed to have taken the tube that day. My mother, like always, called at the last minute and canceled on me, so I didn't have a ride. I was really irritated at her—and when this happened, the first thing I thought was how stupid she was for not showing up, making me end up having to see a weird guy disappear and the walls change. I thought about how I wished she wasn't my mother."

"Oh, no," I answer, because that's all I can say. I know exactly where this leads.

She nods again, but her smile is so completely gone it's as if it had never existed. "Yeah, exactly. All shifty weird, and then when I got home it wasn't my home. Some other family lived there. My mum's law office wasn't there, and I couldn't find my dad at all.

"But you kept the shell?"

"Of course! That man said to keep it, and once the shifty weird thing happened I knew something was going on. At first I thought it was like a magic lamp or something. I didn't understand that it was rearranging time." She waves a hand again, like she's going to tell an old story. And in a way it *is* an old story. "I tried to fix it. Kept putting things back. But you can't control your head, you know."

"The old brain does it to us all," I answer.

"Do you know what this is? How it works? Why they're here?" she asks. It's clear that if she's met any of the others in here, she hasn't had a chance to really talk to them.

No one knows what's really going on, of that I'm quite sure. Some say it's supernatural or divine; some say natural. But most think it's from beyond Earth.

I've had more time in comfort than anyone I've met, time when I can just think about it and try to reason it out. In my life I did that for a living: divining the future aims of others based on the outcomes of their past actions. It paid great money. It allowed companies to predict what people would do, want, or buy next. I've been using that skill while sitting here and stewing on my mattress in the midst of the end of everything.

"I can tell you what I *think* it is, but I can't prove a bit of it," I offer.

"Please."

There are no blankets on my mattress, because that would create too much risk of them getting tangled with my wires, but I do have two pillows, and I carefully move one of them through the tangle toward Sarah. I plump up my own and lie down on my side, facing her. She does the same. It's incredibly comfortable, and she's relishing it—if the groan that escapes her is any indicator.

"Let's just say you're looking for great places to live, and you find this planet. It's perfect: lots of water, the right amount of heat. The only problem is that it's covered with life. Life that doesn't match whatever passes for DNA in your species, and is utterly useless to you. And it's everywhere. Every nook and cranny. What would you do?" I ask her.

Her eyebrows lift, and her crooked grin tells me that she's hearing something new—and not particularly believable. "Really? You're going with aliens?"

"Okay, I know it sounds weird, and maybe the motive isn't malevolent. Just go with me here," I say, and she nods. It's only one of my many theories, but there's something about this one that rings more true to me than the others. Not completely, because I'm surely missing a whole lot, but in general principle.

"Right, so if you're smart—and let's face it, if they got here they *are* smart—you're going to study the dominant species of the planet. That would be us. What's the one thing that you can always count on with humans?"

She thinks for a moment and says, "That we're assholes."

I laugh because she's utterly serious in her answer, and counter with, "That we're curious and grabby."

Again she looks dubious, so I add, "If you find a bag of money on the sidewalk and you're a nice person, you might hesitate to pick it up, or you might call for someone else. But if you find a pretty rock or shell, you wouldn't hesitate."

She opens her fist a little to look at her shell and then says, "Yes. I can see that."

"And there's something else about us that is utterly consistent. Our brains are a running monologue of regret and wishes for change." I finish by gesturing toward her, referring to her first experience with her own object.

Instead of agreeing with me, she shakes her head and says, "No. I don't think that's true. That was just a fluke what happened to me."

I shake my head back at her and say, "Not a fluke. We regret things all the time. All day, every day. We just don't know it."

"How do you figure?" she asks.

"I found out what my little rock did almost from the moment I picked it up, just like everyone else I've talked to did. I picked it up, and when I stood up, the stinging from getting my legs waxed bothered me. Though I have no conscious memory of anything specific, I do remember thinking I was stupid for getting it done right before I went to the beach—with all the salt and so on."

She nods and waits, her hand tucked under her head as she sinks further into the pillow.

"Well, you know what happened then. Everything went all shifty and blurry, and I felt like I wasn't balanced or something. It felt like vertigo. So, naturally, I dropped the pebble."

"You did? What happened?" Her voice still sounds wide awake, but her eyes are getting heavy.

I laugh, breaking my own rule about noise, and clap my hand over my mouth. "Oops. Well, it wasn't a huge thing, so all that happened was that I was suddenly standing there with all the hair that had been removed right back on my legs where it had been before. What a waste of pain that was!"

She grins. It lightens her features and smooths the lines of strain for a moment. They return almost immediately and she says, "So you picked it back up."

"I picked it back up," I confirm, but even *I* can hear that flat tone of regret in my voice. "I figured it out right away. You can move the time to make whatever it is you're thinking about not happen, but it won't affect you so long as you're holding the object. Like you, I thought I'd stumbled onto some sort of weird magic lamp or something. At first I tried to control it. Little stuff, like going back and not dating the guy that wound up wrecking my car while drunk and getting my insurance jacked up. Stuff like that."

I had done so much more than that, but how to explain it to a girl who has never driven the crowded freeways around my city or pressed through crowded sidewalks or waited in long lines for coffee? How can I explain the moment someone cut me off in traffic and I thought—for only the briefest of moments—that it was payback for cutting someone off the day before? *Poof.* I could remember both the bad-mannered cutoff and also being late for work because I'd stayed in my lane. A thousand such thoughts pass through our minds every day— and for three days, a thousand shifts came unbidden. Sarah's voice breaks through the thoughts that roll pointlessly around in my head.

"I never thought of that," she says. "I just freaked out, but then all the other changes started happening so fast and I had nowhere to go. And then I was here."

"Oh, for me it took a lot longer than that. I must have been one of the early ones," I say.

She's looking at me intently, and I can hear the question she wants to ask just from her expression. She wants to know what happened that was bad. Because, of course, there has to be something bad somewhere in there.

I press my hands underneath my pillow and snuggle my cheek into the cloth. It's getting dirty and smells a little of sweat, a little of dirty hair in need of a wash. I may have brought a lot of stuff, but I'm slowly losing the battle to maintain myself all the same. Dry shampoo is a stopgap; it wasn't meant for weeks in this chronological limbo of ours.

"It's the consequences of erasing the bad that wind up getting us in the end," I say.

Sarah seems to withdraw for a moment, looking into herself and her own past. The only thing she has conscious memory of changing was a whopper, and one that certainly fits the bill. Her eyes refocus on me, back in the present, and I try to give her a supportive smile, though I know it's weak.

I press on and say, "That bad boyfriend, the one I went back and un-dated?" She nods. "After the shifty bit, I realized all that I had lost even though I'd regained my old car. I could see the key fob for it on the rack on the wall, back where it should be. I could remember both the boyfriend and the wreck—but also me telling him I wouldn't go out with him on that first date. Both at once."

Again she nods, the side of her face pressed into the pillow so that it pushes one cheek up, giving it a look of roundness that the thinning of her body has taken away.

"Then I looked again and realized my dog was gone, too. No bed covered in little hairs, no toys scattered into the corners where he liked to stash them. The bowls were gone. Everything."

"Oh," she says. I can tell by the way she says it that she's mentally comparing it to the loss of her parents, and my loss is coming up wanting.

"I know, a dog. But that's not the point. The point is that I got Bumpy while I was dating that guy; I got him when I saw a flyer at work about him needing to be adopted because he was about to be put down. Do you see what that means?"

She doesn't answer directly, but I can see the wheels turning, so I wait. It's important she understands that it's more than the loss of a dog.

Finally, she answers, "It means your dog probably died and you either never saw that flyer or you ignored it."

"Right. That's exactly right. And yet I know I must still have seen it, since it was up at my work—so that means I must have ignored it. It means… It means that even though that guy was a dick who didn't treat me well and eventually wrecked my car, he made me a better person. A kinder person. The kind of person that doesn't ignore a plea for help to save a dog's life."

Sarah is starting to understand now, and it's so very important that she understand. She says, "The bad stuff is what makes us better?"

"Sort of. Maybe not all the time, but it's like everything else that happens in our lives. It has ripples. And all that we are is contingent upon what happens to us without our knowing it will happen. The unplanned beauty of it all," I say.

We fall silent again and I watch her. I can see a look—not quite peace, but more a sort of acceptance—settle over her features. She's no less grimy or tired-looking, but she does appear less worn, and perhaps less burdened.

"Where does it end?" she asks.

This is where I need her to go. This is the question I need her to ask.

"I think the last one alive is the one who will decide that," I answer.

Her brow crinkles, and I think she must realize the math doesn't quite work out. "But everything doesn't come back right when people die. At least, not perfectly."

"No, not exactly. There's a trick to it," I say, and see the interest in her eyes. "The person has to die with their object… and be focused on wishing they had never picked it up."

Her laugh is bitter. "I wish that every moment of my life." She stops talking, and the thoughts in her head are churning almost visibly. Then her body stiffens, she looks at me as if taking my measure, and asks, "How do you know this?"

"Oh, I don't *know* it," I say, making my voice light to ease the tension I can feel coming off of her. "It's a supposition on my part. I've been alone a while, and have had a lot of time to think."

The tension does ease then, and her frame relaxes into the mattress again. It's a slight change, but one so visible to another human that it might as well be a spoken word.

"There must be a lot already dying, if they have nothing, like me," she says, the words rising at the end a bit like a question. "But it's still the same out there. Dead, lifeless. And that *is* the present out there, not the past, right?"

This is one of the problems that bothers me most. We don't feel the shifts in here, in the mist, and I can't pop out like someone less encumbered can, but enough have told me the same story of our unchanging and lifeless world for me to form a theory. I know that whoever the nihilists are—the ones still filled with the idea that life should never have developed on Earth, the ones who have gone back far enough so that life simply never took hold—are still alive and well in here somewhere. I'm betting one of them is Cutter. I nod but say nothing.

This girl is a bit more perceptive than others I've met, able to think beyond the first level of consequence. She says, "And some of them are probably dying without thinking that they should go back and never pick it up."

She looks to me for approval or confirmation, so I nod again.

"So those changes won't revert, will they?"

"No, Sarah, I don't think they will," I answer. "I think we would have seen more shifting if that had happened. But you said it's still just rock and water out there."

"So then, how will the last person alive be able to change it? Get it back?" she asks.

I hate to break her heart, but I owe her whatever truth I can offer, even if I'm only using a theory as my truth. "I don't say that they can get it all back. I only say that the last person will be able to decide what happens. What *happened* in the past."

Her face crumples in disappointment and sadness, but there are no tears. I think she's well beyond that. "What will they be able to make, then? Something close to what we had?"

"No. I don't think so. There are too many variables for that. Whoever is the last one with an object would have to be able to undo every action by every object in the exact order it was done. No one can do that. But a cautious and careful person, one with good intentions and an understanding of consequences, might be able to make something quite beautiful in its own right."

She nods again. She sighs a long, relieved sigh. It's so deep that she seems to grow smaller as it leaves her body. The way her eyes meet mine after that sigh tells me that she understands what I've been moving toward from the moment I saw her frightened and hunched form coming out of the mist.

"Will it be quick?" she asks.

"Instantaneous," I answer confidently. "We don't have to right this minute."

She eases up from the pillow to sit cross-legged on the mattress and I do the same, ready in case some fight-or-flight impulse makes her come for me. She isn't armed, but I'm constrained by my web of wires. I'm more like a bug trapped in a web than the spider that spins it, and she's young and unfettered. But there's nothing to worry about. She eases a clump of my wires out of the way of my foot as I try to get comfortable. It's a solicitous act by someone with a good heart.

Once I'm settled, Sarah looks at the mattress and its plain blue sheet, and smooths a hand across the surface. She seems to feel the plastic underneath the fabric of the sheet for the first time. There's a question in her eyes.

"We'll need to step off the bed," I say, and pull the gun out of my waistband. It has been there, at my back, since the exact moment I saw her. Before then, it had rested on the mattress no more than a few inches from my hand. It's never far from me. You never know what a new person passing by will do.

Sarah gets off the bed without hesitation. She holds my wires for me so I can scoot off and stand at the edge of it where there's a gap in my fort of supplies. We stand close to each other, face to face, and for some reason I can't define, I reach out and fold her into my arms. The hug I give her is the kind reserved for mothers, daughters, and those we love more than we can adequately express.

When we disengage, I say, "Move back about two steps. No more."

She does, then asks, "What should I do, just wish for it all to go back?"

I shake my head and say, "No. Just focus on never letting that man give you the shell. Focus hard on it. Close your eyes and cover them with your hands so you can focus."

She pops the shell into her mouth and moves it to her cheek, which is a smart move, because even a head shot doesn't mean that death will be complete before the hand opens and the object falls. She turns to the side a little, which I didn't instruct her to do, but she's a young girl and the thought of getting shot in the face is probably just too much for her.

Around the shell, she says, "Make sure you're the last one."

"I will. I won't give up. The Earth needs life and life needs the Earth."

She gives one more approving nod and puts her hands over her eyes. I can see how hard she's focusing; the lines of her mouth are as tight as her shoulders. I fire.

She disappears almost before the sound of the shot is over, so I know it was a good shot. She's so completely gone that there's no hint she ever existed. I can't feel any shifting here, but that doesn't matter. It's one less object giving conflicting directions to the world outside the mist. And that is good.

Sound carries strangely here in the mist, so I swivel around in my web of wires to see if there's any darkening anywhere that would signify the presence of another person coming into view. But there's nothing save uniform white, and I sigh in relief.

After a different shot—a shot that had erased another who had come across me and my mattress—I had turned to find an old man staring at me from only a few paces away, a look of horror stamped on his features. He'd shuffled backwards so quickly I'd had no chance to explain, and I've not seen him since. He's probably dead by now, given how frail he had appeared even then. And he'd had nothing with him save the clothes on his back that I could see.

Most aren't like Sarah, willing to end what has become a nightmare instead of a life. I can usually tell which way they'll go. Most of them, I have to trick. With some, I claim that I can help: that I've stayed behind with my giant nest in order to help those still inside to get out. Depending on their story, I might tell them it's a prayer, or a meditation, or a way of using their object. Eyes closed and a wish in their minds is all I need to do what needs doing. It doesn't make me feel good about what I do, though.

For now, all I can do is wait for the next one to happen by. I'm so tired that I can barely function, and Sarah's visit has drained every bit of my energy reserves. I need sleep, but sleep is dangerous. Anyone could come upon me. Maybe even Cutter.

I work my way back up onto my mattress and pull the motion sensors out of their storage box. They aren't connected to me, precisely. Instead, I've worked wires from the sensors to the heaviest of my containers, and joined those wires to the one that connects it to me. It's filled with rice, so my small movements when I sleep won't jar it and set the motion sensors off. At least, not usually.

Once I'm set and all the sensors are in place, I put my gun on top of a container near my arm and lean back on my pillows. The pillow on top smells different now. It was the one Sarah used. Even through the smells of sweat and dirt, I can detect the faint scent of someone different. Some things do remain behind.

All I can do now is sleep and wait for the next person to find me. I have my support system, anchored by my wires and my mattress, and I doubt there are too many others who managed to get so organized before the mist took us permanently away. I'm confident I can outlast most—and maybe all—of the others out there with their objects. I'm committed, and that gives me another edge.

Unless he dies on his own, loses a fight with someone else, or finds me, one day I'm going to have to seek out Cutter. There are still more out there, but I have a feeling that in the end, it will be me and him deciding the issue—with force. Me on the side of life, and him on the side without it. It's almost poetic.

But no matter what happens, no matter how long it takes, I want to be the last. Biology may not be my strong suit, but I'm patient and I understand consequences. I'll guide the planet back through time and let life lead the way. Erase what comes to destroy it if I can. It probably won't end in humans, or even anything I can recognize as remotely *like* humans; but I know I can leave the Earth with something that can see the world and understand the glory of life. That's all I can do.

And after that—well, I've got a knife. I won't need my little pebble anymore.

A Word From Ann Christy

I have a confession to make. I'm an accidental author.

As a career naval officer, I'm adept at telling myself stories. When it comes to thinking up new worlds or fantastic tales during the dark midnight watches on the bridge of a ship, I'm a champ. But never did I think to write them down.

That all changed when I read *WOOL* by Hugh Howey. After reading it, I made up my own "silo story," set in the world of *WOOL*, and felt so excited about it that I asked him if I could write and publish it. Writing the *Silo 49* series has been such a gratifying experience that now I simply can't stop. That so many people liked my writing amazes me anew each and every day.

My writing slate is full, with many new releases in the works for the next year and a half. Yet when I was asked to provide a story for this anthology, I happily dropped everything to jump in with both feet. It is outside my comfort zone and short stories are a challenge I relish. Leveraging the reader's imagination with only a few words is work of the most enjoyable kind. What I most enjoy is hearing what the reader saw—and comparing it with what I saw while writing it.

I call writing a form of mental zombie-ism in reverse. I get to put a little piece of my brain into yours and stay there with you for as long as you remember the story. It is my hope that you enjoyed the meal.

You can contact me and find out about new work at my website: www.annchristy.com

The Mirror
by Irving Belateche

AFTER MY MOTHER DIED, I decided that it was time to go for broke. I would raise my station in life by moving to Manhattan and making something of myself through hard work. If the American Dream was alive, I'd be its poster child. *Poor boy from Maury, Indiana moves to the big city, and through pluck, desire, and hard work, makes it big.* Even to me this sounded corny, but all big dreams sound corny.

I'd stayed in Maury to take care of my mother, just as she'd taken care of me. Not only did I *want* to take care of her, but I felt I owed it her. She kept insisting I go out into the world and make my mark, but I knew it wasn't right to abandon her in her time of need. She'd sacrificed for me, worked long hours so I could go to St. John's rather than the neglected public school down the block.

She'd also saved enough money for me to go to college, where—though I didn't excel there—I discovered I had a knack for sales. People trusted me, listened to me, because I always educated myself about whatever I was selling. And maybe, in part, it was also because I was basically a loner. I liked to spend hours reading, watching movies, and listening to podcasts. So sales was my outlet for all that time spent alone, and I poured all my energy into it.

My first two months in Manhattan were a slog. I couldn't sell the one thing I needed to sell most to get a job: me. I didn't get a single job offer—not even one word of encouragement. No one gave a shit about my college degree, or my pluck, or that I enjoyed a good book or movie.

I'd walked from small business to small business—Internet start-ups, independent financial services firms, boutiques, art galleries—resume in hand, the old fashioned way, asking for a ground-floor opportunity. And it turned out the ground floor was packed. The down economy provided an endless number of overqualified applicants, and when I wasn't competing with them, I was competing with Ivy League grads with connections.

I was determined not to look for employment with a large company, because I knew that was no way to make it big. I was willing to work hard, but only in a business small enough to make a difference. Yet as it stood, the whole endeavor was beginning to look foolish. It was time for a reality check.

Why not try a smaller town?

There were plenty of small towns and small businesses across the state of Indiana, as well as in upstate New York. But just as I was seriously considering the move—googling small cities with vibrant start-up sectors, making lists, comparing living expenses, et cetera—the tide turned.

I was on my way to an interview with a company that two NYU film-school grads had started. Their business catered to the wealthy by making films on demand, written and directed by their clients. Apparently this was becoming a hot thing among the one percent.

On the way to the interview, I passed a small antique shop. The words *Remembrance of Things Past* were embossed in faded gold lettering across its bay window. And judging from what I saw through that window, the business wasn't doing too well. The antique furniture inside may have been valuable, but it was scattered about as if it were part of a Saturday morning yard sale thrown together at the last minute. There was no organizing principle behind the presentation, and anyone taking a cursory look would assume the pieces were nothing but junk.

Before I moved on, a man stepped out of the shop and stuck a handwritten note on the door. *Sale! Going out of business!* The man made eye contact with me. He had a kind face; laugh lines edged his blue eyes. Those lines were now taut with worry.

"I'm sorry," I said, motioning to the sign.

"Don't be. I should've wrapped this up years ago. You want to look over the inventory? I've got some wonderful closeout deals."

"I'm more of a seller than a buyer."

"What are you selling?"

"Right now, I'm selling my ability to sell."

"You're a little late. At least when it comes to *Remembrance.*"

"Better late than never, right?"

He chuckled, and his laugh lines relaxed.

* * *

Ten years later, *Remembrance* was thriving. Inventory had expanded, we had a long list of regular clients, and the small shop now boasted a quality showroom whose layout often enticed clients to buy more than they'd intended to when they'd first set foot in the shop.

Melvin Tishner, the owner of the shop—the man who'd hired me on the spot that day—was planning to retire in two weeks. Though he'd enjoyed every minute of the shop's revival, he said he was feeling too old and tired to participate actively in the business anymore. By this time he trusted me with every aspect of running the shop, and he never stopped marveling at how I'd been able to turn the place around.

From day one he'd taken me under his wing, gradually teaching me everything he knew about antiques. Each day, Melvin had given me a specific lesson. From recognizing types of wood finishes to understanding the difference between a highboy and a chest-on-chest, his lessons were designed to help me acquire the knowledge I'd need to become a bona fide antique dealer. And each evening, as soon as the shop closed for the day, I'd go online and do more research into the lesson of the day.

When I wasn't learning about antiques, I was employing every method of sales I knew to move the store's inventory and keep the business afloat. And when my knowledge of antiques finally caught up to my sales abilities, that's when the business took off.

In addition to a good paycheck—and what I hoped would eventually be an ownership stake in the business—there was another benefit to working at *Remembrance*. It made me a frequent guest at dinner parties, cocktail parties, gallery openings, show openings, and other gatherings sponsored and attended by Manhattan's wealthiest residents. Old money, new money, famous and infamous. It wasn't as if I were part of this Manhattan royalty, but still, I got to move in some pretty rarefied circles.

It was quite a different story when I retreated to my Upper West Side apartment. There, I was still the boy from Indiana—the boy who loved nothing more than to spend his time reading a good book or watching a good movie. I also discovered movie revivals, which were a real treat, as I'd never imagined I'd get to see some of my favorite movies on a big screen.

It was in my tenth year of working with Melvin that my life took a major turn. I was working late as usual, when our new employee—Dolores, whom I'd hired myself—came into the back office, now my office, to let me know that a Rebecca Ward was on the phone and wanted to have *Remembrance* broker a sale for an antique mirror she owned. Ms. Ward wasn't a regular client, so I asked Dolores to email her a questionnaire. It was a routine set of questions to help determine whether a piece was worth appraising.

Ten minutes later, Dolores returned with the questionnaire already filled out. Apparently Ms. Ward was in a hurry to sell this mirror. She'd had Dolores read her the questions over the phone and had supplied the answers on the spot. I perused the form and determined that it was worth a trip uptown, not just because the answers indicated the piece might be authentic— including a proper chain of title—but also because Ms. Ward's address indicated wealth, and that increased the odds that this piece was genuine.

On Friday afternoon, I left the shop in Dolores's hands— Friday afternoons were the slowest hours of the week—and took a cab to the Upper East Side. Ms. Ward lived in one of those grand old Manhattan buildings where the apartments have more rooms than sprawling country estates.

Rebecca greeted me at the door to her apartment. I was immediately taken by her pale gray eyes, her lush raven hair, and her extraordinary beauty. She reminded me of a rare, exotic bird.

She led me through the apartment, explaining that she lived there with her parents, and that the west part of the apartment was hers, complete with its own kitchen. On our way to the mirror, I noticed a variety of antique pieces— Hepplewhite, Queen Anne—throughout the tastefully adorned home. Not only did this trip yield the benefit of meeting Rebecca, but it looked like it might also be good for business.

We stepped into her living room, and my eyes immediately fell on the mirror in question—a stately cheval, framed in mahogany.

"I bought it at an estate sale," Rebecca explained. "And I'd like to sell it. It just doesn't quite fit in the way I thought it would."

I scanned the rest of the furnishings. She was right; the mirror didn't fit in. But it wasn't just that it didn't fit with *these* furnishings; I wondered if it would fit with *any* furnishings. Something about the mirror seemed peculiar. Yet, as an antique dealer, it wasn't my job to vet a piece using my personal taste; I'd brokered the sale of plenty of pieces that I didn't care for. Also, to be honest, my mind wasn't really on the job: I was already planning to appraise the mirror just so I'd have a reason to talk to *her* again.

"In the questionnaire you said you had the last two bills of sale."

"Sure—you want me to get them?"

"Please."

She left the room, and I took a closer look at the mirror, swallowing my distaste. From the craftsmanship and the appearance of the wood, there was no doubt that this was either the genuine article or an excellent forgery. When Rebecca came back with the bills of sale, I told her as much, then went on to explain the procedure for appraising the mirror's value. The bills of sale would help establish a pedigree, especially if it had been part of an antique collection already. I'd also try to trace the chain of title further back.

"So, you'll take it on?" she said, her gray eyes sparkling with hope.

"Sure," I responded, "but only if you'll do me a favor."

"What's that?"

"Go out to dinner with me tonight."

She smiled, shyly and also a bit sensually, though that might have been my wishful thinking. She brushed her lush hair away from her face. "It's a deal," she said.

"Great. I'll have Sammy and Mario pick up the mirror in the morning. Will someone be here?"

She nodded. "Do I need to wrap it up so it doesn't get damaged?"

I grinned. "Don't worry—we're competent. They'll pack it properly, so you don't need to do anything else. It'll take a couple of weeks to value the piece, and if goes well, we'll get the word out that it's on the market. Do you have any other questions?"

"Is tonight going to be casual or formal?"

"Casual."

* * *

And that was how I met the love of my life. It was the classic whirlwind courtship. We saw each other two or three times a week right from the start, and within two months, it was almost every day. We'd take long walks in Riverside, her favorite park. We'd have languid dinners and take in old movies. We'd make love—she was a sublime lover: playful, sincere, dirty or sweet, depending on the occasion—then lie in bed, reading late into the night.

And not only was she beautiful, she was also clever and down-to-earth, very much a small-town girl—if such a stereotype really existed. Even though she'd been raised in

Manhattan, and her parents, Robert and Amanda Ward, were wealthy—both scions of old Manhattan money—and she'd attended Columbia, she was nevertheless the most earnest person I'd ever met. Maybe that was the quality I'd seen on that first day.

Sometimes I wondered if she was too good to be true. Was she putting on a show just for me, seducing me with ease with her gray eyes and raven hair, with a personality designed just for my psychological profile? Did she know me better than I knew myself?

Even now, I don't know if I could have stopped what happened next by taking those questions more seriously. And I guess it doesn't matter. Since I didn't.

* * *

The first strange incident occurred during a romantic getaway in Avon, upstate. We were staying at a small boutique hotel, and everything was going well. We'd gone hiking, visited the Five Arch Bridge, and eaten quail and lamb, each with a different rare wine, in a charming restaurant nestled in the woods overlooking the Genesee River.

I'd been working long hours over the previous month. A number of the shop's long-term clients had pulled some of their money out of the stock market, fearing a bubble, and wanted to invest that money in antiques. As a result, I'd been scouring other shops, auction houses, and private collections looking to fill that demand. We'd only made love twice over the previous few weeks, and both times had been hurried.

But after that fantastic day, Rebecca had planned a fantastic night. The room was lit by candlelight, and the fresh scent of wildflowers drifted into the room through an open window. She wore nothing but a sheer camisole and silver earrings, and when the candle flames flickered and the shadows of light and dark played off her smooth pale skin, I was spellbound by her sensuality.

We made love, and it was all-consuming. A strong breeze blew into the room, stirring the candle flames into a wild dance. My eyes went from the wild flames to the dresser mirror, and I saw our bodies entwined. I was about to turn away, self-conscious, when I saw something that sent me into a panic.

My breath caught in my throat and my heart started pounding.

In the mirror, the woman I was making love to looked nothing like Rebecca.

She had auburn hair and green eyes, and when I focused more closely on her features, trying to convince myself that this was just Rebecca reinterpreted by an odd trick of the light, another breeze blew into the room, sending the curtains billowing in front of the mirror.

The curtains cleared, and I saw I was once again entwined with the raven-haired love of my life—Rebecca.

"What's wrong?" she said.

"Nothing," I quickly answered, still a bit shaken. "Mixing those two wines at dinner must've made me a little drunk." But I didn't feel drunk, not that I was especially familiar with the feeling—I rarely drank. Still, I convinced myself that the wine must've caused the strange hallucination.

I was able to get back in the mood, somewhat, but an uneasy feeling stayed with me for the rest of the weekend. So did the image of the woman with the auburn hair and green eyes.

A few weeks later, I decided to ask Rebecca if she'd marry me. I assumed she'd say "yes." She appeared to be as in love with me as I was with her. We were happy and comfortable with each other. Also, her parents had welcomed me into the family and didn't seem to mind that she was dating "below her class." I'd seen how some of the other old-money families disdained the beaus their daughters dated and/or married because the beaus didn't have the proper pedigrees.

I was so confident that Rebecca would say "yes" that, rather than discuss the proposal with her in advance, as most couples did nowadays, I planned to propose to her the old-fashioned way: surprise her with an engagement ring over dinner.

On the chosen night, as I was closing up the shop, I glanced at the cheval mirror that had brought Rebecca and me together. Rebecca had joked that my only fault was that I hadn't been able to find a customer for the mirror, even though it had turned out to be a rare piece from the Middle Ages. Roman Myers, a specialist in glass antiques, had dated it to the fourteenth century.

I had tried hard to sell it and was eager to be rid of it, not only for Rebecca, but for myself. Over time, the mirror had gone from being a piece that felt merely peculiar to one that made me feel downright uneasy whenever I glanced at it.

Maybe Rebecca had felt the same way about it and that was why she'd wanted to sell it. And that possibility wasn't so farfetched, because even though it was prominently displayed in the shop and several customers had been tempted to buy it, no one had pulled the trigger yet. Maybe *everyone* felt uneasy around it.

I closed up and headed uptown to our current favorite restaurant, a small, undiscovered Italian restaurant on Amsterdam. In my pocket was a diamond ring—a French Victorian given to me by Melvin, who was ecstatic that I'd found the woman of my dreams.

I had the cab drop me off a few blocks from the restaurant so I could walk off the day's stress before meeting Rebecca. It had been a hectic day. I'd had to deal with Christie's on a Chippendale armoire, which I'd promised I could deliver to a client for a certain price. Turned out I couldn't.

But with every block, my chest lightened and my thoughts drifted away from business and toward the restaurant and the proposal. Night was falling, and the city was bathed in purple twilight. The sidewalks were busy with young couples out for the evening and Columbia students laughing and joking with each other.

Nothing seemed out of the ordinary until I looked down an alleyway and saw a figure skirting the shadows. Silhouetted by the purplish light, he looked like he was wearing a long black robe, a brimmed hat, and a mask shaped like a bird's beak. The sight sent a creepy chill down my spine, but I kept right on walking and told myself that I'd just seen some odd configuration of shadows. My backup explanation was that I'd seen a man headed to a costume party.

For the rest of the walk, a feeling of disorientation stayed with me. I tried to shake it off, but didn't succeed until I arrived at the restaurant and a more pressing concern took over. I was about ten minutes late, yet Rebecca hadn't arrived yet. This was odd, because Rebecca was *never* late, and I wondered if this was a bad omen. *The night I plan to propose to her is the first time she's late.* That was silly and I knew it. It was just the lingering unease from the figure in the alleyway.

I waited for fifteen minutes before texting her, then waited another five minutes for a return text. When there was no return text, I called her. She didn't answer, so I left a message, trying to hide the anxiety in my voice—and doing a bad job of it. After ten more minutes passed, spent trying to convince myself that all was well, but knowing that this was unlike Rebecca, I finally called her parents.

I heard myself explaining to Robert, her dad, that Rebecca was late for dinner—well aware that I was coming across as unduly worried, perhaps even a bit obsessive, like an overly controlling lover. Still, he was friendly and said that he'd seen her earlier in the evening, and not to worry.

But as it turned out, my concern was justified. She never did show up for that dinner.

* * *

The next few days were a haze of increasingly panicky inquiries and horrible scenarios playing themselves out in my head.

I looked everywhere for Rebecca, but she was nowhere to be found. The police got involved almost immediately because everyone who knew Rebecca—her parents, her friends, and I—insisted that her disappearance was highly unusual. She was far from the type to take off on a lark.

Detective Bill Moore was assigned to her case, and at first I thought it was his gruff manner, in combination with my own lack of sleep and raw nerves, that gave me the impression he was targeting me as the prime suspect.

But after three weeks or so, when some of Rebecca's friends started to treat me more coldly and with less sympathy, and the police themselves were slow to return my calls and less forthcoming with information, I realized that my initial impression had been correct. And all doubt was erased when Detective Moore called me in for questioning.

He interrogated me about every facet of my relationship with Rebecca. From the gist of his questions, it was clear that he was building his case around the theory that I was obsessed with Rebecca, and that I'd asked her to marry me and taken it badly when she'd turned me down.

Melvin was still in my corner, and up to this point, so were Robert and Amanda, but her parents were about to have a change of heart. Their sorrow over their missing daughter permeated every one of our conversations—which of course, under the circumstances, was appropriate. They had been so close to Rebecca that at times I'd been jealous. Unfortunately, Detective Moore had somehow picked up on that emotion and used it to further bolster his theory. He saw this as yet another trigger for my anger at Rebecca. If I couldn't have *all* of her, than no one could have *any* of her. I finally decided I needed to visit Robert and Amanda to counter Detective Moore's propaganda against me. From the last couple of phone calls I'd had with them, I sensed that they needed to be reassured that I loved their daughter more than life itself.

Robert greeted me at the door. "I'm afraid we're not very good company," he said, reaching out to shake my hand.

As I took his hand, I felt a couple of bulbous, gelatinous lumps on his palms, and I instinctually jerked my hand away, leaving him visibly startled.

"I'm not the greatest company either," I said quickly, hoping to mask my awkward reaction to his handshake. But it was too late. He was already taken aback.

I followed him into the living room, and on the way, I tried to catch a glimpse of his palms. I wasn't able to get a good look until we were both seated, and when I did, I saw—there were no lumps. And that sight turned out to be even more disturbing than if there *had* been, because I was left wondering what it was I'd felt just seconds earlier.

Amanda came into the room, her cheeks sunken and her eyes weepy. "Would you like something to drink or eat?" she asked.

"No, thanks."

"Are you sure?"

"Yeah."

She sat down next to Robert and her eyes met mine. "How are you doing?" she asked.

"Hanging in there. Barely."

"Join the club," Robert said, rubbing his hands together anxiously, a habit he'd picked up since Rebecca's disappearance.

I didn't want to look at either of them for too long because the hopelessness etched on both their faces drew my own feelings of despair right to the surface. I realized right then that it had been a mistake to come over, and that realization became even more obvious when I found that I also couldn't bear to look at the family photos that lined the mantelpiece. The last time I'd visited, I'd taken solace in those photos of happier times—Rebecca's family intact—and had still held out hope that the police would find her.

Now, that hope seemed distant. And I was the prime suspect in her disappearance.

Not wanting to focus on Robert or Amanda, or the photos, my eyes fell on Robert's hands just as he pulled them apart—and my heart suddenly starting racing. Scattered across his palms were bulbous lumps, black and red. Oozing.

"Are you okay?" I said.

"No, I'm not," he said, defensively.

"I meant your hands."

"What about my hands?" he asked, and glanced at them, then at Amanda.

"Is something troubling you, my dear?" Amanda asked me.

"Yeah—" I said, checking out Robert's hands again. They were fine; the lumps were gone. "I mean, 'no'… I guess I can't stop replaying everything, looking for clues."

"There aren't any, are there?" she said.

I shook my head and my eyes fell back on the photos. And what I saw made my throat tighten and my stomach ball up into a knot. I couldn't fathom what I was seeing. I blinked a couple of times, then rubbed my eyes, and felt the heat of anxiety on my skin.

In the photos, everywhere that Rebecca had been, just seconds ago, was another woman—a *completely different woman.* Smiling in front of the Wards' summer house in the Hamptons, waving from under a cherry tree in Riverside Park, holding her diploma in front of the Alma Mater statue at Columbia. Even the portraits of Rebecca—as a child, as a teen, as an adult—were now portraits of this new woman as a child, as a teen, and as an adult.

A woman with auburn hair and green eyes.

The woman I'd seen in the mirror in Avon.

What the hell was going on?

I couldn't help but get up and approach the mantelpiece. A closer look at the photos didn't change a damn thing. My heart was racing and nausea was starting to well up from my knotted stomach.

"Who *is* that?" I blurted out.

"Who's what?" Robert said.

"The woman in all these pictures."

"What are you talking about?" he said.

I looked back at him. "What happened to the original pictures?"

"Son—You'd better tell us what's going on." Robert's voice wasn't sympathetic.

"The girl in all these pictures—" I wasn't sure how to put it without sounding like a lunatic. I wanted to shout out, *This isn't your daughter*, but maybe I was mistaken. Another scan of the pictures confirmed that I wasn't—there just wasn't any resemblance at all between Rebecca and this woman.

Robert stood up. "Is there something you need to tell us?" he asked firmly.

I knew exactly what he was getting at. A confession. My erratic behavior was proving to him that Detective Moore was on the right trail.

"Mrs. Ward—Amanda—" I said, looking for support. "Don't you see that this woman isn't—?" I stopped myself. There just wasn't any way to ask the question without sounding delusional.

"I'm sorry," I said. "I've got to go." I headed toward the foyer, trying to come up with an excuse for my quick departure, and ending up with the always lame, "I'm not feeling well."

I thought they might say something before I stepped out into the foyer, and when they didn't, I glanced back—and could tell that the tide had turned. Robert was standing tall and unyielding, ready for the battle ahead. He had his arm around Amanda, who was now slumped, as if the revelation that I might be guilty was too much for her to bear.

I hurried through the foyer and let myself out.

* * *

I had many of my own photos of Rebecca, so I took them to the restaurants we'd frequented. The maître d's and waiters stared at the raven-haired woman in the photos, then shook their heads. They'd never seen her before. On the other hand, when I showed them a photo of the auburn-haired Rebecca Ward, which I'd downloaded from her LinkedIn profile, they all immediately recognized her as the woman I'd been dating.

This was true of everyone who'd seen us as a couple.

I was baffled and couldn't confide in anyone, even Melvin, for fear of being labeled psychotic. So I scheduled a couple of sessions with a psychologist. He said I was basically of sound mind, though he did prescribe medication for what he said was normal depression brought on by Rebecca's disappearance. When I pressed him for a diagnosis based on my strange symptom, he told me he'd never heard of a case like mine and that this symptom wasn't associated with any of the classic psychological disorders.

My visits to the psychologist, plus my new obsession with finding someone—anyone—who'd seen me with the raven-haired Rebecca, prompted Detective Moore to call me in for another talk/interrogation. Melvin suggested I hire a lawyer, which might have been the smart way to go, but I went with the stupid way: relying on the fact that I was innocent.

Detective Moore and another detective led me into an interrogation room, where Moore started asking me questions about a seedy neighborhood in Queens. I had no idea what he was getting at, but I should've figured it out. Looking back, it was clear he'd been trying to connect me to a lead that had come in.

He pressed me hard and added another layer to his theory of the spurned obsessive lover. He said I was a social climber who'd slowly clawed his way up from poor Indiana country boy to high-class antique dealer, and that this tough journey had taken a mental and emotional toll. My seething jealously toward my wealthy clients and my repressed insecurity about my background were violently discharged on the night Rebecca refused to marry me. Her rejection had been proof that I was worthless.

This was so far from the truth, and I was feeling so penned in and distraught, that I did the unthinkable: I told Detective Moore that the woman I'd been dating wasn't Rebecca Ward. I didn't know Rebecca Ward. I had never *met* Rebecca Ward.

"What kind of shit are you trying to pull?" he said. "If you wanna plead insanity, you gotta confess first."

"I can't explain it. I know Rebecca's parents. I know her friends. They all saw me with the Rebecca Ward you're looking for. Same with every place we went to. But I was with a different woman—every time. The entire time. A woman who looked nothing like Rebecca."

Moore shook his head, disgusted. "So your story is, you're sitting there with Mr. and Mrs. Ward and this other woman, sitting there all cozy, just the four of you, one big happy family, and her parents don't notice she's not their daughter?"

"I don't get it either," I said, and pulled out my wallet, then showed him a photo of the other woman. "She's the one I was dating."

He looked at the photo, then got into my face. "So where—pray tell—is this other Rebecca? She missing, too?"

"I don't know..." And I *didn't* know. I knew nothing about this other woman.

Until that night.

I locked up the shop, but lingered because I didn't want to head back to my apartment just yet. All afternoon I'd been worried sick about what Moore had said when he'd dismissed me earlier: my arrest was imminent, and the DA would be easier on me if I confessed.

The shop was deathly still, and the purple dusk seeping into the shop's bay window threw an otherworldly glow over the showroom. Running away was on my mind, and though living the rest of my life as a fugitive wasn't appealing—in fact, it was shameful and tragic—I was beginning to think there was no other way out.

I walked over to the antique mirror. Lately, I'd kept away from it. What had once brought me joy now brought me sorrow. I stared at my reflection, pale and gaunt from weeks of worry, and wondered how it had come to this.

And then she was right there, staring back at me from the mirror: the raven-haired beauty whom I'd known as Rebecca, the love of my life. But instead of her earnest smile, she now boasted a malevolent smirk, openly mocking me. A beat later, she was gone—and I was left staring at my shocked reflection, my eyes wide with confusion and fear.

I knew immediately that this hadn't been a hallucination. After all the creepy things that I'd witnessed, I had no doubt that I'd just seen Rebecca in the mirror. She'd *wanted* me to see her. But why had she chosen to appear in the cheval mirror?

Within a minute, I was on the phone with Roman Myers, trying to set an appointment with him. He wanted to meet in a couple of days, but I told him it was an emergency. I needed to see him right away and would pay triple his rate. *And* he didn't need to come down to the shop. This was about a piece he'd already evaluated.

He agreed to meet right away, but I sensed he was worried that he'd authenticated a forgery. So I put him at ease and told him that I was calling about the cheval mirror from the Middle Ages and needed to know more about its pedigree for a possible sale.

Then I hopped into a cab and took it up to Riverside Drive, where he lived. When I stepped out of the cab, I heard a dog barking, incessant and disturbing, from Riverside Park below. I might've ignored it, but there was a violent wind sending trash and leaves swirling madly up and down the road, so I thought the dog might be lost or injured.

I jogged across Riverside Drive and peered over the retaining wall, down into the park below. The tree branches were swaying aggressively in the wind as I tried to locate the barking dog. Suddenly it darted out from under a large oak. Even from a distance, I could tell the mongrel was in bad shape, mangy with an uneven gait. Then three men, wearing body-length black overcoats, brimmed hats, and bird-beak masks, emerged from under another tree.

The men quickly caught up to the mongrel. One man took it down, another helped him hold it down, and the third pulled out a knife—and slit the poor mutt's throat.

"What the hell are you doing?" I yelled out.

The men didn't look up. They just calmly moved away from the dead dog and back underneath the trees.

The dog lay there in a pool of blood, while I did nothing but stare down at it, incredulous, burying my instinct to clamber down the long staircase into the park. Instead, I replayed what I'd just seen. These men had been dressed like the man I'd seen in the alleyway on the night of Rebecca's disappearance. It didn't take a genius to realize that both incidents were related not only to each other, but also to Rebecca *and* to the mirror *and* to the bulbous lumps on Robert's hands.

I hurried back across Riverside Drive, and buzzed Roman's apartment. Roman, a small compact man in his forties, had been an art history major who hadn't been able to land a job out of college. He'd fallen in with a private investigator and done well, and eventually combined those skills with his art history background to establish a business in authenticating glass antiques. His skills were in demand all over the world.

When I stepped into his apartment, he told me he'd already started putting together a more detailed pedigree for the mirror. "I went back as far as I could this time."

He invited me into his "war room," which was a mix of old school and new school. He had hundreds of reference books that hadn't been digitized, and a T1 line feeding three high-speed computers capable of sifting through billions of pieces of data in a flash.

"Okay," he said, breathless and excited. "Luckily there aren't many pieces like it, so even when the trail went cold, I was able to pick it up again by skipping even further back. I got four new owners before I lost the trail in the seventeen hundreds."

I was impressed, though I shouldn't have been. This is what Roman was known for. The first time he'd authenticated the mirror, he'd traced it back to an English nobleman who'd purchased it in the late nineteenth century.

"I got some paper on all four of them, tying them to the mirror, so that's nearly two hundred more years. You're definitely good to go at whatever price you're charging. No question about it."

I could have beat around the bush, trying to draw more information out of him, the kind of information I was really looking for, but after what I'd just seen in the park, I got right to the point. "Did you find anything strange about the mirror itself?"

"Strange? Well… no… except for a weird coincidence. A pattern with the owners. They all ended up in prison. Every one of them was convicted of a serious crime. Including the English nobleman."

I suddenly felt sweaty from panic and my heart started to race. I had to sit down and take a deep breath. Was I destined to be convicted of kidnapping, or worse?

"Do you want some water or something?" Roman said, concerned.

"No thanks."

"Listen… I'm sorry I haven't called to check in on you. How have you been holding up?"

"Some days are better than others," I said, then got back on topic. "Did you find anything else unusual?

"Nah. But isn't that unusual enough?" He moved over to his desk and grabbed some papers. "I printed out the bills of sale. I'll email you the PDFs."

I took the papers.

"Who's the buyer?" he asked.

"Can't say yet."

And since there wasn't much I *could* say, I thanked him and beat a hasty retreat, still reeling from the knowledge that I was destined to be the next in a long line of the mirror's victims.

* * *

I lived just a few stops away, so instead of taking a cab home, I walked over to Broadway and headed down into the subway. The train arrived within minutes. I boarded, sat down, and tried to give some thought as to how Rebecca was tied into all of this. Around me, all was normal, the subway car filled with the usual eclectic mix of people.

The train pulled out of the station, but as soon as it entered the tunnel, it stopped. The lights went out, and many of the passengers groaned. I didn't think much about it—this was a fairly common inconvenience—but when the lights came back on, all the other passengers—Hispanic, Caucasian, Asian, African-American, young and old—were shivering with feverish tremors. Some were breathing hard, their tongues, coated in white, hanging from their mouths.

My heart was pounding and I told myself that this wasn't really happening. But it was just as real as anything I'd ever seen.

Blood vessels beneath the passengers' skin began to burst, and the blood that pooled under their skin quickly turned black.

I got up, ran to the door at the end of the car, and tried to pry it open. It wouldn't budge. Then just as I was about to give up and run to the other end of the car, the door slid open—and a huge man, with soot on his face, dressed in rags, stepped into the car.

He was carrying a lit torch.

I stood there in shock.

The man went over to the nearest passengers—now dead, and covered in sub-dermal black sores—and lit them on fire.

Horrified, my knees wobbly, I turned, ready to race through the open door, when the lights flicked off—sending the car into total darkness—and just as quickly flicked back on again.

Everything and everyone was back to normal.

Except every passenger was staring at me.

The train suddenly lurched forward, and I grabbed a handle and tried to gather myself.

By the time I stepped into my apartment, I still *hadn't* gathered myself. My mind was racing, trying to connect everything I was seeing—or imagining, or hallucinating—to Rebecca. I fired up my computer and started googling what I'd seen. My perfunctory research revealed that the men I'd seen earlier—the ones wearing bird-like beaks, wide-brimmed hats, and ankle-length garb—were dressed like "plague doctors" from the Middle Ages—which connected directly to the mirror's origin. In the fourteenth century, doctors had no idea what caused the plague, but they were sure it was contagious, so they came up with this early kind of bio-protective suit, including the headpieces with beaks. Those beaks were filled with vinegar and sweet oils to counteract the strong stench of the dying plague victims. And the people I'd seen in the subway car bore the horrific marks of those infected victims.

But I still had no idea how Rebecca fit into this. So I decided to go back to the source of this nightmare: the cheval mirror. I took a cab back to the shop and didn't even look out the window along the way, for fear of hallucinating again.

Inside the shop, I picked up the mirror and hauled it to the back—so that my presence after closing hours wouldn't raise the suspicions of passing pedestrians—and inadvertently set it down opposite a mirror that hung on the back wall. The two mirrors reflected into one another, creating that hall-of-mirrors effect.

And what I saw in those infinite reflections was startling: other men—dozens of them—all staring into the mirror. From their clothes, it was clear that they spanned the centuries; and from their faces—fearful, sweating, and panicked—it was clear that they were the other victims of the mirror, struck down by its curse.

I half-expected the raven-haired woman to make her own appearance—to smirk at me, lord her beauty over me, mock me for falling for her—but she didn't.

One by one the other men disappeared from the reflections. I immediately called Roman, desperate to understand how and why I'd been sucked into some cursed supernatural world along with these other victims, and looking for any slim hope of avoiding my fate—spending the rest of my life in prison.

I asked Roman if there were any kinds of superstitions or legends associated with mirrors in the Middle Ages. He was quick to answer.

"As a matter of fact, yes—one that was quite popular in its time, now long forgotten. A lot of people in the Middle Ages believed in reincarnation. They thought souls traveled from one body to another after death—"

"But how did that play in to mirrors?" I interrupted, impatient, knowing the clock was running out on me.

"Well, some people believed that you should never leave a mirror in a room with a dying person. And if you did, you should turn it away so it wasn't facing that person."

"Why?"

"I'm getting there. If you didn't turn the mirror away, it would capture that person's soul when it left his body. Then that soul wouldn't be able to enter a new body, and it wouldn't be cleansed of its previous life. Anyway, that's the theory, based on what historians found in diaries from the Middle Ages."

Was Rebecca a soul caught in the cheval mirror? And if she was, why did she ruin the lives of those men? And why had she targeted me?

Then, as if she was at last ready to move to the final stage of her plan—now that her secret had been revealed—there was a sudden pounding on the shop's front door. I looked down an aisle to the bay window at the front of the shop. An NYPD cruiser and a plain-wrapped detective car were parked at the curb.

The end had come.

I didn't want to turn myself in, but going on the run didn't seem like the smartest strategy either. Still, what choice did I have against a supernatural foe?

The pounding on the door continued. Had Detective Moore connected me directly to the kidnapping of Rebecca Ward, a woman I'd never met? It didn't seem possible—but then again, *none* of what was happening seemed possible.

And facing that truth was enough to convince me to flee. I considered trying the back alley, but decided Detective Moore would have that covered, and opted to go for the roof exit instead. I took a step toward the back stairwell—

And felt something grab my arm.

I looked down. Stretching from my arm back to the mirror was a long stream of flowing glass—a smooth, reflective, *living* tentacle. It had coiled itself tightly around my forearm.

And it was pulling me in.

I fought to rip myself free of its grip, but I never stood a chance. As I passed through the mahogany frame and into the mirror, a chill cut through me.

And then, I was *inside* the mirror. Facing out, unable to turn, and barely able to move. I could only stand—and stare.

And what I saw, through the glass, most definitely wasn't the shop. I looked out instead on a small room, furnished with antique pieces—chest, bed, chairs—all solid, large, harsh, and rectilinear. All from the Middle Ages. The mirror would fit right in here.

The door to the room suddenly swung open and two brutish-looking men hurried in, carrying a struggling woman, bound and gagged. The men were wearing short, coarse wool tunics fastened with leather belts, while the woman wore a rough-looking gray dress with a gray apron.

The men dumped the woman on the bed—it was Rebecca.

What the hell was going on?

The men untied Rebecca then bound her hands and legs to the bed's posts. When she was secure, one of the two men—large, muscular, with a grubby face and a piggish nose—said, "I'm taking out the rag, miss. If you scream out, we've been told to kill you."

Rebecca nodded, terrified. The man then pulled the rag from her mouth, and she spoke quietly, wary of the warning. "I do not have the Black Death. I am not sick. Please. Please let me go."

"That's not up to us, miss," the pig-nosed man said.

Why was I being forced to watch this?

Rebecca struggled to free herself, but it was futile. Again, I tried to break out of the mirror—this time to help her—but my attempt to free myself was as futile as hers.

Then two men left the room just as another man entered. He was older and effete, with a refined face, and dressed in a royal blue surcoat, the attire of a wealthy man.

The fear on Rebecca's face turned to anger. "Nicolo? You? *You've* done this?"

"You've done it to yourself," Nicolo said. He was holding a metal cup in his hand.

"Let me go. Now!" She fought against her bindings.

Nicolo smirked and grabbed her jaw.

She swung her head from side to side, throwing his hand off.

He slapped her hard. "Stop, or I'll break your neck right now." He grabbed her jaw again, this time more firmly. "Drink this. You need it."

"Why are you doing this?"

"Because you are still with child. I understand that you intend to keep it. I told you not to."

Nicolo raised the cup he'd been clutching and put it to Rebecca's lips. She kept her mouth shut, so he wrenched her jaw open and forced the cup's contents into her mouth.

After a few seconds or so, during which Nicolo quickly retreated from the bed to the other side of the room, I saw the expression on Rebecca's face turn to horror—she began to spit, cough and gag.

On the sheets of the bed were the results of her spitting— spots and splashes of crimson blood.

"You're the devil!" she shouted. "You have fed me the Black Death!"

"As a physician, I have taken an oath to do no harm," Nicolo said from the safe confines near the door.

Rebecca glared at him with hatred, which quickly turned to fear. "Why should you punish me so? Your own flesh and blood is within me."

Nicolo didn't answer. He stepped over to the mirror and looked at himself—I saw the cruelty in his eyes.

Then he turned the mirror around, and I was plunged into total darkness. I tried to move, but I was still trapped.

In the blackness, I heard Rebecca's voice, steady, somber, and captivating...

My transgression came back to haunt me. But you see, I'd had no choice. I hadn't been able to find work for such a very long time. Employers, like everyone else, were frightened of strangers—you never knew who might bring the Black Death to your doorstep. Few would even talk to a stranger for fear of contracting the disease.

Nicolo hadn't offered me a job. Instead, he'd wanted a mistress. His wife was old, dried up, and mean. I'd visited him five times—and when I discovered I was pregnant, I told him the truth, believing in my heart, as my mother had taught me, as she had named me—Carita—love—that there was more love in the world than hate. I believed that he'd take the child, even if he discarded me. The child would have a life without struggle, a life of privilege.

But he did no such thing. Instead, he told me to get rid of the child before it took its first breath of life. So I hadn't visited Nicolo again. As you saw, this wasn't enough for him.

He kept me a prisoner for days, or maybe weeks—I couldn't be sure. I became rail-thin. My skin became an ocean of black lumps and red pustules. Nicolo didn't return to the room since infecting me, and the only mercy he showed was allowing one of his servants to bring me water, and, when I was too weak to move, to untie me.

I was resigned to my fate, and eagerly awaited my final breath. In was then that my gaze was forever fixed on the back of the cheval mirror—the dark world where you now find yourself. I would study the rich grain of its mahogany, the only beauty in this room of sickness and death. The only good.

When the day of my last breath finally arrived, and my soul could no longer hold on, I had but one goal. The Black Death had rampaged through my flesh, sapped it of life, except for one waning spark. And before the Black Death completely extinguished that small spark, I knew what had to be done.

I strained to slide toward the edge of the bed. My withered muscles barely responded. I didn't even have the strength to swing my legs onto the floor, so I didn't try. Instead, I slid off the bed— oh—how my bones ached when I landed on the floor.

I dragged myself ever so slowly, painfully, toward the back of the mirror, toward the beautiful mahogany. The dull throbbing I felt didn't start in any one place or end in another, but consumed every inch of me. I wanted that spark of life to die right there, and see where my soul would go.

But I dragged myself to the mirror, where I rested for a minute and considered my destiny before I changed it forever.

What would my life have been like if I hadn't met Nicolo? Would I have found true love and proved that love was stronger than hate? That love conquered all? Or was that just a terrible lie that my mother had believed in and taught me to make life bearable? I would've preferred to have believed in that lie, to have lived a long life, to have found my love and raised my family even in poverty. But Nicolo robbed me of that life.

So with the little strength I had, I reached up and turned the mirror back around...

The world spun and the darkness vanished. I was once again looking into the small room, but Rebecca—Carita—was no longer on the bed. She was now prone, motionless, on the floor, directly in front of the mirror. At first I didn't recognize her. The Black Death had destroyed her beauty. She was emaciated, her skin ravaged with sores, and her raven hair matted and knotted.

I wanted to turn away, to avert my eyes from the cruelty of her fate, so painfully visible, when I saw a faint ethereal wisp rise from her lifeless body and take shape: Rebecca—Carita— the woman I had loved. Her soul, her spirit, her essence intact, and her beauty restored.

She—her spirit—approached the mirror and entered it—I watched her float right through the glass. But she wasn't in the mirror with me. Somehow she'd disappeared.

I pushed at the glass. It wouldn't budge. I tried to move forward, but I was still trapped.

As I pushed once more against the glass, the door to the small room swung open and a man walked in, dressed in the strange uniform of a plague doctor. He looked down at Rebecca's body, then looked at the mirror. He reached for the mirror as if he was going to turn it, but stopped and instead slowly lifted the beak headpiece off of his head—revealing the creepiest part of this nightmare yet.

The man was *me*.

I held my breath, stunned, trying to grasp this.

Then the man wiped his brow, and I saw that he no longer looked like me. It was Nicolo. He quickly exited the room.

Again I pushed on the glass, and this time my hand went through. Without hesitation, I lunged forward, out of the mirror, and found myself back in the shop just as Detective Moore and two other officers, guns drawn, were rushing to the back of the store.

* * *

The arrest was a blur. During the car ride down to the precinct and the booking, I was focused on understanding the real story of what was happening, not the story Detective Moore had put together.

Carita had forced me to see Nicolo as a reflection of myself—so I'd know that my soul had come from him. My soul was traveling the normal path: with each new life, each new person it inhabited, it was cleansed of the memory of all of its prior lives—including the life of this murderer. But Carita's soul received no such cleansing. She was cursed to forever remember the tragic end to her life and to seek revenge century after century, lifetime after lifetime.

In the holding cell, I wondered if there was a way out.

Melvin came to visit and told me he'd found a good lawyer. The DA was going to charge me with kidnapping and attempted murder, and it was time to start building a defense. The NYPD had found Rebecca Ward, the real Rebecca Ward, in an abandoned building in that decrepit Queens neighborhood Moore had questioned me about. She'd been imprisoned there and was now lying in a hospital bed, in a life-threatening coma.

Melvin insisted that the evidence against me was all circumstantial and emphasized that Rebecca could still come out of the coma and clear me, but I knew that neither of those outcomes were in the cards. Carita would make sure she got the conviction, just as she'd done with all the men who'd come before me bearing the plague doctor's soul. She would create hard evidence against me. In fact—though I didn't know it at the time—she already had. And if Rebecca did recover from her coma, I knew Carita would somehow get her to identify me as the perpetrator.

My only hope was to make amends with Carita. I had to make her understand that even though I had the plague doctor's soul, I wasn't him. *But how?*

My first hearing was two weeks away, so I had plenty of time to come up with a plan. What I finally decided on would surely sound insane to anyone who hadn't experienced what I had: I planned to meet Carita in her own world, on her own terms. And to do that I needed the cheval mirror.

There was no way the NYPD was going to let Melvin bring the mirror to my holding cell, so I asked Melvin to bring it to the hearing. When he and my attorney asked why, I lied to them, telling them I wanted to present it as evidence. There were markings on the mirror that pointed to another suspect. Of course, Melvin had Roman check out the mirror, and Roman came up empty. Still, I insisted he bring it. He finally agreed, and cleared it with the courthouse security detail in advance.

On the day of the hearing, I arrived in court, handcuffed, and sat quietly as an assistant DA read the charges against me.

A few minutes later, I learned that Carita *had* created incriminating evidence: my fingerprints had been found in the room where Rebecca had been held captive. On a mirror.

As the ADA and my attorney sparred over bail, I scanned the room, plotting out the logistics for my plan. The mirror was at the back of the courtroom, near the door, where a police officer stood guard. Up front, another officer was stationed at the door that led into the judge's chambers. Both officers had weapons. I checked to see if there were any other armed officers. There weren't. I had hoped there'd be more, but I had to work with the cards I'd been dealt.

My attorney was still fighting for reasonable bail when I suddenly blurted out, "I'm innocent! I didn't do it. Why would I—?"

The judge banged his gavel. "Don't interrupt the proceedings."

I jumped up from my seat. "But I would never do some—"

The judge banged his gavel again. "You can't—"

"You don't understand what's really going—"

"That's enough!" The judge banged his gavel one, two, three times, and I turned and jumped over the railing onto the first row of the spectator benches, then ran toward the aisle.

The officer at the back of the courtroom snatched his revolver from his holster and shouted, "Stop! Now!"

I didn't stop. I had no intention of stopping.

I made it to the aisle and ran straight toward the officer.

"Stop!" he shouted, training his gun on me.

I kept running toward him, believing with every ounce of faith I could muster that this was the only way to save myself—and that, like Carita, I had a soul as well as a body.

"Stop!" the officer shouted again, and this time I saw panic spread across his face as he realized he was being forced to make the biggest decision of his career.

He fired two shots.

I felt a burning in my chest and heard a ringing in my ears. A tingling numbness spread through my body as I stumbled and fell forward. I hit the floor hard. But before losing consciousness, I forced myself to focus on the mirror, just a couple of yards away from me—and I thought about my soul.

The colors of everything around me started to lighten, to desaturate, and the people closing in on me—Melvin, the officer, and others—were moving in staccato slow motion, halting and fragmented. Their words, their shouts, were long baritone yawns of incomprehensible syllables.

Then everything around me turned pure white, and the sounds all disappeared.

I was with her.

In the mirror.

Carita was as she'd been: the raven-haired beauty with the pale gray eyes. But the small-town-girl quality that I'd fallen in love with was gone. Her eyes were hard, her face severe, and her body rigid. She was vengeance embodied.

"I'm not the doctor who murdered you," I said.

"Oh—but you are."

"You *know* me. You came into my life. You saw who I was."

"I saw your soul."

"But *this* is my soul. Right here. Standing in front of you. Isn't it?"

Confusion flickered in her gray eyes. She looked out from the mirror, into the courtroom. Everyone was harried and distraught, moving to and fro. My body was sprawled out on the floor and Melvin was holding my hand, tears running down his cheeks.

"Doesn't a soul learn and change through its lifetimes?" I asked, pleading.

"You haven't learned."

"I'm here to show you I have."

Paramedics rushed into the courtroom, and one of them knelt down over me and opened his kit. The other unfolded a stretcher.

"I'm sorry for what that doctor did to you," I said. "But me, here, this soul—I love you."

The paramedic who was kneeling over me checked my eyes, then grabbed a hypodermic needle from his kit. He prepped it, stuck it in my chest, and pushed the plunger.

"You must've felt it—out there—when we were together?" I said. "I thought—I hoped—I *still* hope—that you feel it. I love you, and I will always love you, Carita."

The paramedic checked my eyes again, then glanced at his partner. "We're losing him."

Carita turned to me. Her face had softened, and a gentleness had returned to her eyes.

"Carita. I want to be with you. That's why I'm here. Love is more powerful than hate."

She reached out and touched my face and—I was staring up at the paramedic. I blinked a couple of times, disoriented, and he smiled.

"Hang on, pal," he said, then went to work on my wounds.

I looked past him, into the mirror, and saw Carita walking away.

* * *

A month later I was still in the hospital. The officer's bullets had done some serious damage, but I'd recover. My breathing would forever be hampered from the damage to my right lung, so there'd be no marathons or hikes up Mount Everest for me. Still, for the most part, my life would be normal. Especially because the visions from the Middle Ages had stopped haunting me.

Rebecca Ward had come out of her coma and had cleared me as a suspect. She told Detective Moore she didn't remember much of what had happened to her. On the night of her disappearance, on her way to our undiscovered Italian restaurant, she'd felt faint and had blacked out just as she was passing the alleyway where I'd had that first vision. The next thing she knew she was a prisoner in a room in the decrepit neighborhood in Queens where the NYPD had found her. She had never seen her captors and no one had ever explained to her why she'd been kidnapped. The only details she could recall from her captivity were a pervasive scent of vinegar and a mirror hanging on a wall.

The first few times Rebecca and I saw each other again, it was awkward—not so much from her side, but from mine. She remembered our relationship as it had been and wanted to put this entire nightmare behind her. But when I was with her, eating in our favorite restaurants, walking through Riverside Park, lying in bed, I kept looking for signs of Carita hidden beneath Rebecca's auburn hair and green eyes. It took me a while to accept that Rebecca *was* Carita—or at least, she was the part of Carita I'd fallen in love with: the clever and down-to-earth woman, the one who somehow embodied the earnestness of a small-town girl even though she'd been raised in Manhattan.

I asked her to marry me, and she accepted with joy.

As for the mirror, Melvin decided to buy it from Rebecca. He swore that when I was lying on the floor in the courtroom, on death's door, right after the paramedic had said, "We're losing him," a flash of pure white light had leapt out from the mirror, and a second later, my eyes had blinked open. Melvin wasn't superstitious, but, as he put it, "You wanted the mirror there that day, and it did its job. Seems like a good idea to keep it around."

A Word From Irving Belateche

"The Mirror" is one of those story ideas that's been in my story file for a long time. Most of my story ideas make it to my story file because they have one of two elements: either a science fiction element or a supernatural element. "The Mirror" is no different. It's based on a little-known superstition.

But for a story idea to actually make it out of my story file, it has to deliver great characters. Characters that a reader wants to follow. "The Mirror" did that. It delivered two characters who would never have met were it not for this superstition. And that led to the story you have here.

I've always loved science fiction and supernatural thrillers. For me, those stories heighten the emotional journeys that we're all on in our own lives. Good science fiction and supernatural thrillers always reveal something about human nature. Something that we recognize in ourselves and in others.

If you enjoyed "The Mirror," please check out my novels and other short stories listed on my website (www.irvingbelateche.com) and/or join my newsletter.

I want to thank David Gatewood and Michael Bunker for inviting me to participate in this anthology. I'm honored they gave me the opportunity to have my story included with the stories of such accomplished authors.

Reset
by MeiLin Miranda

I'M SO SORRY I haven't seen you since you got back, Janelle. I've been so busy with the probate and the move and the new grandkid. Anyway, thanks for coming. Tonight's the end of a tough year.

I know you've heard a little about my friend Catherine since I got the house. I don't know why you never met—well, yes, I do. I'm embarrassed to say it. There's always your one friend who's too weird to introduce to people. You know what I mean? That was Catherine.

This is what I wanted to show you. These boxes here were hers. They're filled with drawings of children. Seven boxes, one kid per box. I have them memorized by now: Margaret, Jess, Amanda, Tim, Aaron, Maya, and Emily. I have no idea who they are.

Catherine didn't have kids, never married. Never had a boyfriend as far as I know. We went to grade school and high school together. I've known—I *knew* her most of my life. I'd know if she had one kid, let alone seven, even if she gave them all away. I did know about the drawings but I didn't know she'd done this many.

She was a really good artist, huh? Catherine couldn't draw a straight line before we turned sixteen. Then suddenly, right after her birthday, she started drawing these kids over and over, all different ages. Nothing else, and they're really, really good—like, photographic. Who were they? She'd only say, "Kids I have to draw before I forget them." She'd start crying, and that's all I could ever get out of her.

Catherine was normal before then. Boys, college plans, the usual. Getting her first car. Music—she was totally into Bowie. And then the drawing started, and she withdrew.

Her parents called it sulking. I think they were worried, but they didn't know what to do and they didn't like the idea of sending her to some doctor who might send her to the nuthouse. It was embarrassing. These days it's hard to think of getting help as embarrassing, but it was back then. You're lucky you're a little younger.

I tried to help. I'd say, let's go down to the record store, Bowie's got a new album out, and she'd say, no, heard it a million times already. "Wanna watch *Fantasy Island*? You love that." No, waste of time, seen it.

Seen it already, she said that to everything. *Star Wars*? Seen it. "How can you have seen it? It just came out, there are lines around the block. You have totally not seen that movie!" Nope, seen it.

Catherine lost a lot of friends that year. She hardly talked to anyone but me. She'd been my best friend since kindergarten, and *someone* had to be her friend. She wasn't a bad person. Something just switched off in her brain.

Or maybe something switched on, I mean, she was always smart, but suddenly she knew everything. She challenged all her classes. Finished them before they even started. I had no idea she knew so much Spanish, or American history—or chemistry. What the hell? Catherine hated chemistry. She just said she always brushed up on everything in the months before she reset.

That word. She'd use it every once in a while. *Reset.* I didn't know what she meant. Anyway, she graduated a year early. They couldn't really keep her.

Once she got out of high school, she came back to life a little. She talked more. I was the only high school friend she stayed in touch with. She said I was her constant. How would she say it? "Sandy, you're the one thing that never really changes, no matter how many times I go through this." Go through what? I'd ask. "Never mind," she'd say. "You never believe me." How could I not believe her if she never told me?

She went to community college for a while. You have no idea how embarrassing that was for kids from my high school. Catherine could have gone anywhere. Yale or whatever. I went to Northridge. She took a couple classes at night and worked. Secretarial stuff—she was a doctor's receptionist right before I graduated from college. She still lived at home.

And then all of a sudden she had money, lots of money. She moved out of her folks' house and stopped going to school. Her parents asked me about it. "Is Catherine into drugs? If it's drugs you have to tell us so we can help." Drugs.

It was okay to get help for that. Betty Ford and all those guys had just gone into rehab.

So I go to her and say, "Catherine, what's up? Where's it all coming from? Your parents are asking questions and you're gonna get your ass thrown in the Betty Ford clinic or something." She smiled and said, "Yeah, I've got it all right here, let's go." Big accordion-type folder right there next to her purse, like she'd known I was coming.

So we drove down to Catherine's parents' house, and she spread it all out on the dining room table because it was the only space big enough, and she had bank books and account statements and all this financial stuff. She'd been playing the stock market. She was already worth more than a million bucks. I just said, wow.

Her dad understood all the paperwork, which was good because I didn't. He said, "How'd you do this?" She said she had a good memory. Meaning what? She just shrugged and said she'd kept an eye on some companies over the years.

Some of the stock buys went back to when she was in high school, the year she changed so much. She'd put her babysitting and birthday money into the stock market, forged her dad's signature to get around the under-eighteen thing. Boy, was he mad. She said, "How mad can you get when I've made so much money?" I think it still took a few years for him to start asking her for stock tips. She was never wrong. Never.

Catherine bought this house, right on the water, just when the market was at its lowest. I loved coming here to visit. I can't believe she left it to me. I just can't believe it. We lived further inland. Now that I think about it, I was still living there when you and I started working together, right after Gene left. Catherine told us when to buy our first house, and then when to sell it, but Gene wouldn't listen and he handled the money. We got hosed like you wouldn't believe.

After the divorce, you bet I listened to her. He screwed me out of everything and I had to fight all the time to get my support payments on time. Catherine's advice was the only way I got Josh through college.

I know, I talk about it too much. You'd think by now I'd be over it. She told me not to marry Gene, and I did it anyway. She said I married him every single time and it never worked out. I thought she was talking about karma or something, Catherine said woo-woo stuff all the time.

I always wondered why she didn't go out or anything. At first I thought maybe she was gay, and I told her she could tell me if she liked girls, I'd never tell anyone. This was when being gay was like the worst thing. She said, "No, I just can't go through it again."

I said, "Dave didn't break your heart that bad, did he? Let it go. We were fourteen."

That wasn't it, she said. "Last time I decided not to get involved and it didn't hurt so much when I reset, so this time I thought I'd do the same." Reset. I didn't ask by that point, it was just Catherine. We'd stopped talking about it.

Anyway, a couple nights before she turned fifty, Catherine called me up and said can I come over the night before her birthday, have dinner. Sure, why not. Empty nest, not doing anything. I'm not dating, that's for sure. Done with dating. Catherine was alone and she seemed pretty happy. Painted a lot. See the one over there? That's me. She painted it when we were thirty. Yes, the nude. She got me drunk and talked me into it. Anyway, that's my story.

Catherine never painted those kids, though. I never even saw her draw them after high school. Then that last night before her birthday, the night she and I had dinner together here, she pulled out these boxes. And then she started pulling out portfolios, one after the other after the other, all the way from when we were sixteen to that afternoon. "You always asked me why I draw these kids," she said. "I keep drawing them because I'm afraid I'll forget what they looked like. Right around the beginning of 2011 I start drawing them a lot, more than usual, because if I reset again I have to start over. I want them fresh in my mind."

I said, "You used to talk about resetting, and I don't know what that means. I mean, I know what it means, but I don't know what you're talking about." She smiled kinda lopsided and said I wouldn't believe her but it didn't matter, either way she'd be gone tomorrow. I started to get a bad feeling and said, "Okay, then tell me."

She said they were *her* kids.

"You don't have any kids."

"Not this time," she said.

I got so frustrated! She'd said stuff like that for years, since we were teenagers, since just before she left high school. "What the hell happened to you, anyway?"

Then she told me the weirdest thing: she said she went to bed the night before her fiftieth birthday and woke up on her sixteenth. She said it'd happened over and over again. That's what she meant by "resetting."

Well, what the hell am I supposed to say to that? "Like… like one minute you're fifty, and it's 2011, like now, and the next minute it's 1977 and you're sixteen? How do you pull that trick?"

"I don't know," she said. "I wish I did because this is the seventh time I've had to go through this and I want it to stop."

And I'm like, "Why would you want it to stop? You get to be young again just when your body starts falling apart and life's getting really shitty! Why would that be a bad thing?"

I was saying it, but I didn't really believe it. Life doesn't work like that. But she was my best friend, my oldest friend, and I was scared stiff worried for her at this point. I thought, I better just keep her talking.

Catherine banged the table so hard all the drawings jumped. "Because of them," she said. "I was stupid the first few times and kept trying to get my kids back."

It went like this: The first time it happened, she left Margaret and Jessie behind. She found their father, I don't remember his name, and tried to marry him again. But she was twenty outside, and fifty-four inside. She wasn't the same person he'd fallen in love with. She didn't get past the first date.

So she started drawing the two kids she wouldn't have that time around and married this other guy instead, and they had the twins, Amanda and Tim. I guess twins ran in his family or something.

I don't know where she got this stuff. She was obviously really creative, but if I'd known this was what was going through her head this whole time I would've worked a lot harder to get her some help, I mean, almost thirty-five years of this.

Then she had Maya with this guy from Santa Cruz one time through, and Aaron with a half-Puerto-Rican guy from New York the next. Emily was her last, with someone named Louis, who she said was the one she'd loved most of all. I guess that's why I remember his name.

Every time she "reset," she'd draw the kids she left behind so she wouldn't forget them. She said it'd been so long, she was starting to forget what Margaret and Jessie looked like. God, that just gives me the shivers.

I kinda laughed and asked her, if she got married five times was I ever a bridesmaid? She said I was her maid of honor each time. Sometimes the matron. Once, she said, I was pregnant out to here.

I was freaking out by then but I stayed calm on the outside. I was thinking maybe she started drinking before I got there or something. I guess it must have shown on my face, because she said I never did believe her, and she'd told me five lifetimes already.

"Maybe I'll believe you next time," I said.

Catherine looked so sad. She said, "I don't know what happens when I reset—if I die in the life I'm leaving or if it all just disappears like it never happened or what. And I don't know what happens to you, like if you just kept going all those other times in a different time line. I hope so. I don't want to think you or my kids just disappeared because I reset."

She asked me to hold still. She started drawing me holding my glass of wine, and I finally noticed the pile of textbooks on the end table. Calculus, biology, Spanish, history, chemistry.

I got really creeped out. I decided to stay the night because, Jesus, something's broken in her head. Maybe in the morning I could get her into treatment or something but right then the only thing open was the ER and we were sure as hell not going there. She didn't seem violent or even all that agitated.

So I said, "Time for bed, honey, let's put you down and I'll stay in the guest room. Tomorrow's your birthday. I know it's early but you've had a little too much. It'll be better in the morning. I'll clean up out here, okay? And then we'll go out for birthday dinner tomorrow, the sushi place on the pier."

She said she wouldn't be here in the morning.

I said, "Sure you will, honey, I'll be right here with you, nothing's going to happen. No one's going to make you reset, or whatever."

She said, "If I'm right, I won't reset this time."

Wow, what a relief, I'm thinking, maybe it's something that comes and goes. So I put her to bed. I just wish I'd stayed in the room with her. I wish…

Hand me the tissues, please?

So.

So I put her to bed, and I sat on the back deck. It was a gorgeous night. I finished the last of the bottle of wine. Catherine had really, really good taste in wine. Taught me a lot.

And then I went to bed.

When I woke up the next morning, she was dead. The coroner said it was sleeping pills, way stronger than you can usually get, but Catherine had a lot of money. Stupid amounts of money. She could get her hands on anything. She drank a bottle of vodka on top of it. She hated vodka.

There was a note. She said she was sorry to leave me with this mess if things actually kept going after she was gone. She didn't believe in suicide, but thought maybe if she died just before she turned fifty it'd stop the reset. That word. She said she wanted to make sure I was okay, just in case I was still here, and to look in her old accordion file.

That's where we found a copy of her will. Her parents were already gone and she was an only child. She left me everything. The house, her stock portfolio, her savings... everything. I'm set for life.

It was awful, the way they picked me apart at the inquest. I wish you'd've been here. No, no, that was a once-in-a-lifetime trip, Janelle, don't you dare feel bad. Catherine left behind plenty of evidence to clear me—she put stuff in places I could never have gotten to. She'd planned this for a long time. The executors finally gave me the keys two months ago.

I just gave my old place and everything in it to Josh, and got myself all new furniture. I think his wife's pissed off because I didn't buy a fancier place for them, but she can go to hell. My grandbaby Tomas has a trust fund now. He'll get it when he turns twenty-five. I don't think it's good for kids to grow up with piles of money and everything handed to them. I don't even want him knowing the trust fund's there. And if Josh needs help I'm here and he knows it.

All Catherine's stuff is in storage, except the boxes. Well, I got out the paintings and put them back up, too. I don't know what I'm going to do with the boxes. I don't even know why I brought them home from the storage unit. I just keep thinking about the children Catherine thought she had. I looked through all the drawings last week for the first time. I have my favorites pulled out in a separate portfolio. I might frame them.

Look at this little round-faced girl in a straw hat. She turns into a beautiful young woman with an impish smile. That's the one she called Jessie. Looks just like Catherine. And then this little guy, Aaron. What a stubborn face. Grew up to be a handsome boy in his later pictures. He always looks kind of gangly. I think he was still a teenager when Catherine reset. Reset, or…

I don't know. I don't know.

But this is the weird part, Janelle, the part that just gives me goose bumps. I found this box when I went to the storage unit. It's labeled "Sandy." A note inside in Catherine's handwriting said, "These are so I don't forget all the versions of my best friend."

There aren't as many drawings in it as there are in the kid boxes, but there's plenty. In the pictures I'm fat, I'm thin, I'm pregnant, long hair, short hair, dyed hair, with kids, with Gene, after Gene. None of them look like I do now, or like I've ever been, but they're all definitely me. Each one has a little description, like me in a cast with "Sandy's broken leg" written on the back, or me in a bathing suit with "Sandy in Acapulco" on the back. I've never been to Acapulco. Never broke my leg, either. Okay, so maybe she made up a bunch of stuff about me, too, right?

But then this one. "Sandy with her daughter Chelsea"...

Oh, Janelle.

I've never told anyone this, ever, and don't you ever repeat it to Josh. I always wanted to have a daughter, but I had a son instead. I love him, I love him terribly, but I always wanted a daughter, and I wanted to name her Chelsea. I never told anyone that, not even Catherine. Oh, look at how pretty she is. All that curly black hair. My eyes. Dimple in her chin, like Gene's mom. I wanted a daughter so bad...

Excuse me. No, it's all right, I'll be okay, the whole thing just makes me sad. She was just... she was a really good artist, huh?

Tomorrow's Catherine's birthday. I know she couldn't have reset like she said she did, but sometimes I wonder if she's sixteen again, drawing me with the glass of wine in my hand so she doesn't forget.

I miss her. I bet I always miss her.

Well. We should eat. Let's have dinner out on the deck. You've been to Acapulco. You can tell me about it, I'm thinking of going in the spring.

And I'll open a bottle of Catherine's wine. Amazing wine. Really, really good wine. She always knew which years were the good ones.

A Word from MeiLin Miranda

"Reset" is based on a recurring daydream (daymare?) in which, like Catherine, I am flung from my current life back into high school. At first, it was fun to think about. At my age, starting over again with a grown woman's maturity and a teenaged girl's vitality is an irresistible idea.

In time, it dawned on me what a horrible fate it would actually be. I'd have to sit through high school again, for starters. But worse, I would lose the life I have now with my husband and daughters, who are the joy of my existence.

It horrified me. I couldn't shake it, so I wrote this story to stop the daydream. It worked, but I still can't read this without crying.

My main series is a sprawling epic fantasy family saga filled with magic, sexual politics and intrigue set in a Victorian-like world. Its books weigh heavy in the hand.

By contrast, my short stories are under five thousand words and almost always set in the present or future. They tend toward magical realism rather than straight-up fantasy or science fiction. Though I am considered a pretty funny person, they're also invariably melancholy. I don't know why that is. Perhaps it's some inner melancholy that expresses itself only when the words available are limited.

I've been a writer all my life. I wanted to write fiction but worried about letting anyone see my true self. The writer cannot help but expose that self to the reader, and I was afraid readers would mock what they saw.

So I went into journalism instead and was miserable. I did it for a long time anyway; at least it was writing.

In 2006, I died and was revived—a long story for another time. As I floated between this world and the next, along with my anguish over leaving my family came the awful realization that all the stories I had inside me would remain untold. When they brought me back, I knew what I had to do, scared or no. Recovering my health is a fight I'm still waging, but in late 2007 I was well enough to start writing fiction. I dove in with a ferocity that startled even me.

I'm not afraid any more. The worst that can happen has already happened. If someone doesn't like what they sense of my heart, I won't die; they can always close the book (though I hope *you* like it, reader). I'll keep writing anyway, until I die for the final time.

The Laurasians
by Isaac Hooke

HORATIO HORACE, ADJUNCT CURATOR of Paleontology at the Museum of National History, was hard at work deep in the bowels of the museum. His team had been extracting this particular specimen for weeks now, ever since the delivery truck had dropped off the huge chunk of sedimentary rock, and in every spare moment Horatio had returned here to his love.

Ah, paleontology. He wouldn't trade it for anything in the world. Paleontology was like a surgery of sorts: removing a dressing of stone to reveal the fossilized bones of a majestic titan underneath. It was delicate work, and required men and women of a particular bent. The biggest requirement was patience.

It always felt to Horatio like he was revealing something of epic importance. It was exciting, because he never really knew what he was going to uncover within the rock. Maybe a bone that would help fill a gap in one of the existing skeletons in the archives or on display. Maybe an entirely new species never discovered before.

So far this one looked to be a carnosaur of some kind—possibly an *Allosaurus*, judging from the size of the leg bone. Secretly, Horatio hoped it might be a *Tyrannotitan*, because only a very limited, partial skeleton of that genus had ever been found. Imagine the prestige it would bring his museum if his team were to become the first to uncover a nearly complete *Tyrannotitan*. This sedimentary rock came from a region known for its tyrannosaurids, so with luck…

He was exposing an interesting part of the fossil at this very moment. It seemed to be a rib bone of some kind, though it was strangely out of proportion to the rest of the skeleton. Long and thin like the pole of a tent. Intriguing. It was possible this was a bone from an entirely unrelated species—perhaps some hapless mammal the carnosaur had eaten before it died.

Horatio heard footsteps behind him. By now he could recognize the footfalls of all his colleagues without looking, but this impatient tread proved unrecognizable to him. A museum visitor perhaps, wandering around in the off-limits area.

"If you're looking for the tour guide, I'm afraid you're well off the mark," Horatio said.

"Horatio Horace?"

Horatio paused. Who could be bothering him?

He hesitantly put down his rock hammer and chisel, and turned around.

The visitor looked like he could have been cut from rock himself, with that face of rough peaks and weathered valleys.

He dressed in the suit and tie of a blue service uniform; shoulder boards on his pea coat indicated a military rank of some kind.

"I'm Captain Abraham Ford," the man said. "And I'm putting together a team."

* * *

Horatio was panting. Heavily.

He wasn't built for this crap.

Everything had been great up until now. The buffet dinners, the planning, the build-up to the Event. But after they arrived here, things immediately soured.

The insertion site was a barren, hilly landscape of treeless shale, stunted shrubs, and scraggy rocks. Megan Brocks, paleobotanist (and former student of Horatio's), insisted she needed fauna to study, not rocks. She wanted to leave the insertion site immediately and explore this great undiscovered country.

Horatio stressed that it was far safer to remain close to the insertion site. That going out there was the equivalent of suicide. But Megan wouldn't hear it.

Horatio didn't like Megan. His former student was one of those people who always believed she was in the right, even when she was wrong. Megan was charismatic, and crafty to boot. She played on the warrior mentality of the military escort (Horatio thought of them as an escort, but in reality it was he and the other civilians who were the tag-alongs, much as he hated to admit it). Megan questioned their manhood. She said something like, "Are you men, or are you mice? Are we here to explore? Or cower?"

The Travelers had promptly loaded into the Hummers and barreled onward, caution be damned.

"Come on, Horatio," she'd said at the time. "Live a little."

The barren landscape soon fell away, replaced by oversized conifers. Proto-pine trees. Megan had her fauna.

The Hummers halted some distance inside the forest. An appropriate site for the "Forward Operations Base" was picked out, and the Travelers piled out of the Hummers.

Horatio had been forced—indignity of indignities—to lug all his heavy equipment from the Hummer by himself, including his bulky tent. No one would help him. No one! All these strong military boys around him, and none would lift a finger to help a middle-aged man. They were too busy "securing the perimeter," as it were. Whatever.

This was still the opportunity of a lifetime, Horatio had to admit. A chance to get up-close and personal with *living versions* of the creatures he'd studied his entire life. He would confirm once and for all the validity of the theories regarding these prehistoric animals. He hoped to put to rest the debate on protofeathers—or "dinofuzz" as some of his lesser-esteemed colleagues dubbed them—and to prove exactly which species, at least in this time period, had them. He also hoped to verify some of the leading theories regarding dinosaur behavior, such as pack mindset and pecking order.

The foliage was thick, and it could almost be called a jungle—of cone-bearing conifers, anyway. Pine needles were everywhere. The trees had them. The shrubs had them. Proto-leaves.

Megan must be pleased.

The air was tepid and heavy with humidity, so that by the time he settled on a spot for his tent, he was drenched in sweat. He chose a location close to the center of the camp, near the captain's tent. Horatio figured he'd be safest there.

He flung his equipment to the ground and wearily unzipped the tent bag. He tossed the tent rods to one side, sending a herd of some small creatures galloping away through the thick undergrowth. Startled, Horatio watched the branches and proto-leaves sway as the things fled, but he couldn't actually discern any of the creatures beneath the thick foliage.

One of the navy boys had set up his tent nearby, and he bent over and caught one of the creatures as it hurried past. He brought the struggling animal over, cradling it in his arms.

"Lose something, Doc?" The navy boys all called Horatio either Doc or Professor, even though he didn't have a degree.

"What is it?" Horatio said, somewhat afraid. He himself certainly wouldn't have picked up any random animal he found in this time period. He lacked the temerity for such things.

"You tell me."

It was a small animal, roughly the size of an adult cat, with hooves, a short mane, and a relatively hairless tail. All in all, it was similar to a modern horse or deer, except in miniature. Even its muted neighs were a subdued version of the real thing.

"Amazing!" Horatio said, feeling his excitement build. "And to think, the commonly held belief is that the *Hyracotherium*, the ancient forerunner of the modern horse, existed solely at the end of the Cretaceous period, after the dinosaurs died out! Ha! Hold still!" Horatio delved through his bag, searching for the approved digital camera. All of their equipment was specially made—the cameras, even the guns— of biodegradable materials. That way if someone misplaced something, the timeline wouldn't be affected.

That was the theory, anyway.

The rules clearly stated no personal, non-biodegradable electronic items could be brought on this trip, but that hadn't stopped Horatio from sneaking his smartwatch along. He was secretly wearing it even now, under his sleeve. He didn't go anywhere without that smartwatch, and he wasn't about to do so now just because some pompous, self-important navy captain told him to.

The Travelers had been given other, more reasonable rules. They were here strictly for observational purposes. No killing of any life whatsoever, except when facing extreme duress. Horatio could agree to that. The Travelers even had to be careful about uprooting or trampling too many shrubs. Sure, whatever.

Despite all these rules, accidents could still happen. What if one of the Travelers inadvertently stepped on and killed a small rodent or monkey that turned out to be the precursor of the modern human? Maybe the tiny *Hyracotherium* the navy man was holding was the actual genetic forebear of modern horses.

And maybe it was about to have a heart attack.

What a terrible thought.

Horatio found the prescribed digital camera and took a snapshot, followed by a quick video. "Good, good. Now let it go. Let it go!"

The navy man shrugged and set the tiny horse down. The thing immediately galloped away into the undergrowth.

Horatio took some pictures of the foliage for good measure.

"Finish setting up your tent, Doc," the navy man said. "Supper's at seventeen hundred."

"Ah, the regimented life of the military. It's why I never signed up, you know." Horatio's own life was regimented to the extreme, but he wasn't about to admit that. "What's your name, son?"

"LPO Franks, sir," the man said.

"Ah yes, that's right," Horatio said. He'd been introduced to everyone earlier, though for the most part he'd forgotten everyone's name the instant after it had been spoken. "No acronyms, if you please. I'm not a Navy SEAL."

"Call me Franks then, if you want," Franks said.

"Very good, Franks."

While he was setting up his tent, Horatio heard sporadic gunfire near the perimeter of the camp. He rushed over to find out what it was (despite Captain Ford's very specific orders restricting civilians to the center of the "base").

When he got there, Horatio was told that some dinosaur was making exploratory tests of the perimeter, and that if he didn't want to be devoured alive, he should return to the camp center pronto.

He did so. Grudgingly. He was a palaeontologist, after all—and dammit, he wanted to see a dinosaur.

Horatio didn't hear any further gunfire, and assumed the dinosaur had been chased off. Too bad.

He took his time setting up the tent and unpacking his equipment, so that he was the very last person to join the other Travelers for supper. He was never a big fan of food anyway. It was just a rather crude vehicle for enabling nutrient absorption and caloric energy replacement. Necessary, yes, but highly inconvenient. He usually delayed eating for as long as he could, and often forgot about food entirely, much to the detriment of his health. Especially when he got caught up in his work.

Someone had jury-rigged an air conditioner to the battery of one of the Hummers. The team was gathered around it, eating their MREs in the cooler air.

"So how are you tonight, my fellow Laurasians?" Horatio said, sitting down.

Someone threw him an MRE. Meal, Ready-to-Eat. He caught the parcel, ripped it open, and examined the contents with a shrug.

The "meal" proved to be a disgusting hodgepodge of pasta and meat that was supposed to be *spaghetti alla bolognese*. It had the texture of string beans dipped in lumpy tomato sauce, and it smelled like diarrhea. Though, since Horatio had never tasted diarrhea, he couldn't say whether the taste matched the smell. But it must be said: it did taste fairly horrid. Even so, he forced himself to down the stuff. Nutrient absorption and caloric energy replacement, after all.

About the time he reached the halfway mark on the MRE, a giant insect—roughly the size of his face—buzzed past.

Horatio ducked in terror.

The insect hovered above the air conditioner.

"Relax, Doc." Franks plucked the insect out of the air. The navy man was a quick one. "Just a dragonfly."

Franks tossed the insect toward Horatio, who barely shielded his head with his hands. Those giant, papery wings rippled across his forearms before the insect flittered away. Laughter ensued.

"Funny," Horatio said. "Torture your elders, would you?" He shivered involuntarily. "I hate bees."

"It wasn't a bee, dude," Franks said.

"Ah, yes, yes. You are right. I'm merely *overreacting*," he said dryly.

"You are. When you find yourself face to face with an aggressive dino in camp, that's when you can start shitting your pants."

"Harrumph." Horatio wrinkled his nose. "Do you have to convey yourself so rudely? Please, keep the swearing to a minimum."

"You ain't heard swearing yet, bro," Franks said. "Believe me."

"Oh, I believe you." Horatio took another forced gobble of his fecal-smelling meal. He seriously began to wonder if one of the navy boys hadn't purposely defecated inside it.

A distant roar arose, and everybody froze, listening nervously.

The sound didn't come again.

"We shouldn't be doing this," Megan said into the nervous silence that followed.

"Doing what?" Franks said. "Teasing the 'ol' doc?"

Megan frowned. "No, you can tease the bastard all you want. I mean traveling back in time. It's wrong. We could return to a future where humanity doesn't exist. A future where some dinosaur-like species has assumed dominance. Or we could all die out here. Let's go back."

Horatio gasped, and looked at her in disbelief. The damn girl was so mercurial. First she wanted to come out here and leave behind the safety of the insertion site, and *now* she wanted to go back? She'd been the same way when she was his student. Always so fickle. It's why he swore never to date any of his trainees ever again.

"A bit late for second thoughts, isn't it?" Franks said, putting words to Horatio's thoughts. "A few hours ago you were all gung ho about marching ahead. What was that you said? Are we here to explore, or cower?"

"That was before dinosaurs started testing our perimeter."

Franks hefted his heavy gun. "We're big boys here. From the future. I think we can handle ourselves against some prehistoric reptiles."

One of the Hummer drivers spoke up. His name was Wilson, Horatio thought. "If we returned to a changed world, it wouldn't be so bad. Sure, we'd have to listen to crocodile rock, watch crocodile TV, and get used to everyone speaking crocodile slang, but hey, we'd be celebrities."

"Assuming the crocs didn't decide we'd make better TV dinners than celebrities," Megan said.

Franks grinned ironically. "And you do realize, Wilson, if we returned to a future where humanity didn't exist, that would mean the only girl in town was Megan."

"Like I said, wouldn't be so bad." Wilson gave her a wink.

Megan rolled her eyes and got up. "I'm going to take a nap."

Captain Ford held up a raised palm, and Megan stopped. He glanced at the lieutenant commander, one Douglas James. "Is the perimeter watch set?"

Lieutenant Commander James nodded. "It is, sir. The motion detectors are in place, and we've got men on patrol."

Captain Ford scratched his chin. "Seems too quiet out there. I don't like it. Any news on the *T. rex*?"

The lieutenant commander shook his head. "I think we scared it off."

"*That* was the dinosaur your men encountered out there?" Megan said, eyes widening. She glanced at Horatio. "A *T. rex*?"

Captain Ford nodded. "I wasn't going to tell you civilians, but you have a right to know the situation."

Horatio felt his own dread rising. "Wait a second, a tyrannosaurid was testing the perimeter? I was under the impression it was a herbivore. Maybe a *Triceratops*, or *Ankylosaurus*?"

"Nope." Captain Ford studied him. "Something on your mind, Professor? Something we should know?"

Horatio examined the Travelers. Hard, military types. Some were still smiling, though they could surely read the fear in his body language and tone.

"Don't be so sure you scared them off," Horatio said. "Let me explain something to you. tyrannosaurids weren't stupid. We've done skull casts. Their brains were three times larger than those of most dinosaurs living at the time. They were far more dangerous than most people imagine. They weren't simply dumb brutes; they used strategy to take down their prey. You military men take pride in your small-unit tactics, but these tyrannosaurids were the ones who *invented* them. I believe they hunted in bloodthirsty packs, with each tyrannosaurid assuming a different role. The young were swift and agile, and chased down the prey. The slower adults would bring up the rear, and deliver the crushing mortal blows."

"What are you saying?" Captain Ford said, a bit too coolly.

Horatio stared him down. "If a tyrannosaurid was probing our outer perimeter, then we're in big trouble. Because he was doing so for the rest of the pack. Prodding our defenses, looking for a weakness. To the tyrannosaurids, we're fresh tuna inside a can. Just because they don't have a can opener doesn't mean they won't find a way to peel open the lid and get access to the meat. No matter how many machine gun turrets and rockets you think you have guarding the perimeter, the tyrannosaurids will find a way inside. Eventually."

The mood among the Travelers darkened. No one was smiling condescendingly at the middle-aged paleontologist anymore. Good.

"See, this is exactly why we brought him along," Captain Ford said. "Douglas, I want you to fortify the perimeter. Now."

"Yes sir. Bravo Platoon, with me!" The lieutenant commander stood up, saluted, and hurried off with half the navy boys.

Megan sat back down. "Suddenly I don't feel like napping so much."

Horatio finished his MRE in silence.

"Tell me, Professor, what do you think so far?" Kichio Mato said into the conversational void that followed. He was smiling slightly. Maybe the Japanese physicist felt culturally obliged to brighten the mood, or maybe he hadn't actually understood what Horatio had just said.

Kichio Mato. He had invented the time machine, while Captain Ford's navy had paid for it.

"What do I think of all of *this*, you mean?" Horatio said.

Kichio nodded indulgently.

"Despite the risks, I think it's amazing. It's stupendous. Time travel is a boon to humankind. It will change everything. Research. Paleontology. *Everything*. Thank you, Kichio, for inventing this."

The physicist inclined his head.

Now if we can just get back home in one piece... Horatio thought.

"I still don't understand exactly how it works," Megan said. She was trembling somewhat. Still afraid, because of what Horatio had said about the tyrannosaurids. Wanting a distraction. Some reassurance that everything would be all right.

A pack of tyrannosaurids prowling the outer perimeter, probing our defenses. Horatio didn't blame her for being afraid.

"It operates on the principle of the Matryoshka wormhole," Kichio told her.

"And what is that exactly? In English."

"How about Japanese?" Kichio grinned.

No one got his joke. Well, Horatio got it, but he didn't find it funny, especially not now. Horatio kept eyeing the tree line, expecting a tyrannosaurid to come racing out of the foliage at any second.

Kichio let his smile fall away. "The Matryoshka wormhole. Twenty-two hundred chambers, nested one within the other like Russian Matryoshka dolls. Each separated by a minute distance. We implode each sphere at the same time—initiating the Casimir effect within them and creating negative energy. We use that energy to open wormholes between the chambers via space-time foam. And the very first sphere—the arena-sized chamber where we and our vehicles and equipment are stowed—Travels. And here we are."

The Travelers could return only via that sphere. Unfortunately, they'd left it behind at the insertion site—it was simply too big to bring along, which was why Horatio had been so adamantly against leaving the site in the first place. If things got nasty out here, they'd have to withdraw all the way back to the sphere, potentially fighting every step of the way.

"There's one thing I've been wondering," Horatio said. "How come we can Travel only to this specific date and time?"

"The date is determined by the number of spheres, and the size of each one," Kichio explained.

"But can't we go to different eras by changing one of those two variables?"

Kichio shook his head. "Too few spheres, or too many, and the Casimir effect collapses. Same thing if we vary the size. This is the only point in time we can ever travel back to. At least until our understanding of the physics involved improves. I actually discovered time travel by accident, you know. I was trying to create a portal to an alternate universe, and instead I created a portal to the past. Imagine, *dinosaurs!*" He giggled, like it was the biggest joke in the world.

Again, no one else laughed with him.

"That's all well and good," Horatio said. "But if our mission ended successfully, how come we haven't encountered any other time travelers?"

Kichio opened his mouth, and promptly shut it. He glanced at Captain Ford, who pressed his lips firmly together.

"Get packed up, people," Captain Ford said. "I want to return to the insertion site within the hour. I think we've had enough 'exploration' for the time being."

Normally Horatio would have complained that he'd just unpacked everything, but like everyone else present, he was more than happy to get out of there.

* * *

Drenched in sweat, Horatio awoke from his quick nap to the sound of sporadic gunfire in the distance.

The tyrannosaurids were testing the perimeter again.

He had dreamed of the tiny horse. It had returned with friends. They had run him down in a pack, sprouted sharp teeth like little dogs, and viciously torn his body to pieces.

It was silly. Horses were herbivorous. He wasn't going to let the dream trouble him.

Time travel.

Who would have thought it was possible?

And yet here he was, waking from a bad dream in the Cretaceous period, on the continent of Laurasia. Simply amazing.

Like he'd told Kichio, time travel was going to change everything. Probably literally.

As he rubbed the sleep from his eyes, he noticed something: the gunfire was increasing in frequency.

He also heard the occasional scream.

A distant rumbling sound came now, like a geyser begging to break the surface.

Not good.

He barreled out of the tent and started to pack his supplies. He cursed himself for not doing this earlier when he had the chance. When he'd reached his tent after supper, he'd been all groggy from the food (that was another reason he didn't like to eat—it made him sleepy), and the prospect of packing everything up hadn't seemed very appealing. The captain had promised them an hour after all, so Horatio had decided to lie down for a quick nap before packing. Just a teensy, tiny nap.

Whoops.

Navy boys rushed past him as he hauled his supplies one by one from the tent.

The all-pervasive rumbling was growing louder.

"Forget the tent!" Franks said as he sprinted by. "Get your ass to the Humvee!"

Horatio heard a terribly inhuman whoop, so loud it edged into roar territory. Birds were direct descendants of theropods, which included the tyrannosaurids; Horatio's analytical mind vaguely noted that if he took a chicken's cluck, slowed it down a hundred times, and amplified it a thousandfold, he could reproduce the sound he had just heard.

The roar-whoop came again. It seemed about thirty paces away.

He promptly abandoned the tent and raced after Franks.

The rumbling grew behind him until it sounded like he was being pursued by a roomful of massive machine presses firing out of sequence.

He glanced over his shoulder.

A pack of tyrannosaurids bore down on him, their immense feet shaking the earth, their roar-whoops reverberating in the air.

A part of his mind noted triumphantly that protofeathers were sheathing the backsides of the tyrannosaurids, while reptilian scales dominated their undersides. Just oversized birds, in the end, as he had always suspected.

The other part of his mind reminded him that these oversized "birds" meant to devour him with extreme prejudice. If ever there was a time to ignore the "don't kill the dinosaurs" rule, it was now. Except everyone was too busy running to kill anything.

Waving him on, Franks waited for him beside the back door of the closest Humvee.

Horatio dove inside.

"Go go go!" Franks leaped in after him, shutting the door as the Humvee squealed away.

Other Humvees took off around them.

"To the insertion site!" Franks said to the driver. "Floor it!"

Horatio was sandwiched between Megan on one side and Franks on the other. Franks shook his head, hugging his chest like he was suddenly very cold. "We should've never abandoned the insertion site. Forward Operating Base, my ass. Let's spread ourselves thin. Ingenious. It was you scientists who demanded we explore this place. Goddammit."

"That's the fault of Megan Brocks!" Horatio said. "Paleobotanists always insist on doing irrational things, even when those things put everyone else in danger! She did it just to defy me! I know she did!"

"That's just like you, Horatio Horace," Megan said. "Always accusing me. Always calling me the troublemaker."

"That's because you are!"

She shook her head sadly. "I did it for you, Horatio. I wanted you to see the dinosaurs for real. I wanted you to live your life outside the museum for once. That's why I insisted on leaving the insertion site."

He could almost believe her.

The roar-whoops continued above the Humvee's revving engine. Horatio also heard machine-gun fire from the navy man who manned the turret on the roof. If Horatio looked back, he could see the legs of the turret operator in the back seat.

"Switch seats with me," he told Megan firmly. He wanted the window seat.

She shrugged, opening her seatbelt. She was pretending to be calm, though the terror was obvious in her eyes. "You want to be more exposed, suit yourself."

"Hey, I'm being chivalrous."

"I didn't think you knew the meaning of the word."

He and Megan switched places, and Horatio sidled up to the window.

He couldn't really see much from this angle. The dinosaur pack was too far back. Still, he caught occasional glimpses of the sleek, massive forms that pursued through the conifers.

He had to get some pictures.

Horatio slyly glanced at Franks, and then pulled back his sleeve to expose his smartwatch, which had a built-in camera.

Franks noticed immediately. "Where did you get that? Doesn't look mission-sanctioned."

"Uh, Captain Ford said I could bring it," Horatio lied.

Franks regarded him dubiously.

"Why are you worried about something like a smartwatch at a time like this?" Horatio said. *Military bastard.*

Franks shook his head, then looked back out his own sealed window.

Horatio got close to the glass and took a photo. Because of the angle, all he captured was his own reflection. If he wanted to get a good picture, he'd have to open the window. But there were no obvious buttons or turn-handles underneath it…

He glanced at Franks. "Uh, how does this open?"

Franks shook his head. "You're not opening the bulletproof window." To the driver: "Can you speed it up?"

The sound of gunfire from the turret above continued relentlessly. The pack didn't slow, however, judging from the roar-whoops, which were actually increasing in intensity. The forest was growing sparser outside, Horatio noted.

He studied the window. It had locking pins and latches. He had an idea of how he could open it. But he didn't want Franks to catch him...

He glanced surreptitiously at the navy man, and pretended to take another photo with his smartwatch, though he was actually eyeing those latches the whole time.

The Humvee swerved suddenly, and hit a terrible bump, jolting everyone out of their seats. Horatio's head almost hit the ceiling.

Franks leaned forward. "What the hell was that, Wilson?"

The driver, Wilson, glanced over his shoulder. "Dunno. Looked like a small dinosaur, sir."

Horatio took advantage of the distraction to pull the locking pins on the window. He followed that by quickly turning the latches.

"Wait!" Franks shouted at him.

Horatio pushed on the window.

The bulletproof glass plate promptly fell away, vanishing into the trailing undergrowth.

The window was certainly open now.

And would never close again.

"Uh, hadn't quite expected that," Horatio said sheepishly. "I thought the glass would stay connected. Like the windows people have in ordinary cars, you know?"

"Damn civilians," Franks said, shaking his head.

Horatio leaned out the window, smartwatch camera at the ready.

"I'd get back in here, if I were you," Franks said from inside.

Horatio ignored him.

The tree line fell away entirely.

Horatio surveyed the situation behind him. Only three other vehicles followed this one, in scattered positions.

Horatio glanced forward, confused, wondering where the remaining Hummers were. But he saw no one else.

That wasn't good.

The tyrannosaurids abruptly burst from the tree line and closed on the trailing Hummer. These dinosaurs were roughly the same size as the vehicle. Younger ones, then.

The man operating the turret atop Horatio's vehicle fired back at the pack, trying to protect the trailing Hummer.

Horatio plugged the ear that faced the turret with one finger. The distance was too far, he thought. None of the bullets from this turret were hitting.

As he watched, two tyrannosaurids closed in on both sides of the trailing Hummer. The first dinosaur took a good dose of machine-gun fire from that Hummer's turret, and swung its head sharply away as bullets drilled into its skull. The second tyrannosaurid closed—

The trailing Hummer's turret operator attempted to swivel his machine gun toward the new threat—

Too slow. The second tyrannosaurid chomped down and scooped him right out of the turret.

A third tyrannosaurid swooped in and bit into the machine gun itself, trying to break it off—no success there.

Tyrannosaurids approached the defenseless Hummer from both flanks, repeatedly bashing their heads and upper bodies into the sides.

The vehicle swerved as the driver attempted to run the leftmost tyrannosaurid off the road. The dinosaur leaped on top of the vehicle, then slipped off, crashing to the ground.

But then the rightmost tyrannosaurid lowered its head and got in a good bash, completely flipping the Hummer, which skidded to a halt.

Three of the dinosaurs instantly converged on the upturned vehicle, while the rest pursued the remnants of the convoy.

Beyond them, in the distance, Horatio saw several large, adult-sized tyrannosaurids lumber from the tree line. They were approaching the upturned Hummer, and seemed eager to finish the job.

As he watched all this, Horatio felt a strange sense of detachment. He was horrified by the loss of life, yet both relieved and validated at the same time. His theories were exactly right. The tyrannosaurids hunted in packs, with the young leading the charge and the old cleaning up from the rear.

Little good it would do if no one found out he was right. He wouldn't let the deaths of those men be in vain.

He removed his smartwatch and directed the camera toward the pack, taking several pictures of the tyrannosaurids. He then switched to video mode, leaned slightly farther outside, and began narrating.

"This is Horatio Horace, Adjunct Curator of Paleontology, Museum of National History. I am currently in the Cretaceous period, continent of Laurasia. I am part of a convoy of Navy Marines—err—Navy SEALs. Here you can see several tyrannosaurids in pursuit. Our precarious situation notwithstanding, you'll notice these tyrannosaurids are rather small, about the same size as the Hummers. They are the younger members of the pack, and—"

One of the tyrannosaurids unexpectedly closed from the side—

Horatio barely had time to pull himself back inside the vehicle before those jaws munched down, and the dinosaur crunched empty air instead.

The driver abruptly swerved to the right, hitting the tyrannosaurid—

The creature jammed its giant head through the open window.

The tyrannosaurid, now wedged within the window frame, pulled the Hummer sharply to the right with its sheer weight. It half-ran, and was half-dragged, alongside.

The dinosaur couldn't open its mouth, because the metal borders of the window frame were just the right proportions to constrain its jaws.

Franks fired his pistol at the thing, point-blank.

Meanwhile Horatio and Megan were just panicking.

"Ahhhhh!" Horatio said.

"Uhhhhhh!" Megan said.

The tyrannosaurid pivoted its head left and right, trying to break free. Its lower jaw moved over Horatio's lap.

"Ahhhhh!" Horatio shouted. "The eye! Get the eye! Ahhhh!"

Franks just kept shooting. To his credit, the tyrannosaurid's nearest eye exploded, splattering Horatio in proto-blood.

The tyrannosaurid broke free and dropped to the ground.

Horatio tentatively peered outside.

The dinosaur's corpse receded behind them.

Horatio couldn't stop shaking. "Th-th-that was rather c-c-close."

Megan's face was pale. But when she heard Horatio's words, anger crept over her features, overriding any fear.

"No thanks to you, you selfish bastard!" Megan said. She switched to the low-pitched voice she used when mimicking him. "I know! I'll open the window so I can get some good photos! Who cares if I put everyone's lives at risk? All I care about is getting my perfect picture, so I can show it off to all my friends back home, and brag about how great I am and how right all my theories are!"

Horatio inclined his head. "Y-y-you're right. I'm sorry." His hands were still trembling.

She tried to grab the smartwatch from his fingers, and nearly succeeded. But Horatio was the quicker, despite the shaky aftereffects of his overtaxed adrenals, and he managed to stuff the watch into his pocket.

Anger was beginning to replace his own fear, now.

"How dare you!" he said. "I almost paid for those photos with my life, and here you are scrambling for my smartwatch, trying to destroy it and all my precious pictures. By my rights, I should—"

He noticed something.

"What?" Megan said mockingly. "What should you do?"

"It's gone."

"What?" Megan said, nonplussed.

"The gunfire," Horatio said. "From the turret."

Megan cocked her head. "You're right." Her voice trembled.

The two of them glanced back nervously, toward the back seat. The legs of the operator were no longer there.

Horatio looked up into the turret. There was a splatter of blood around the rim.

"This isn't good," Megan said.

"Maybe one of us should man the turret?" Horatio gazed at Franks.

Franks was on the radio. "Captain Ford, do you read, over? Captain Ford?" He noticed Horatio looking at him. "What?"

Horatio nodded toward the back seat.

Franks looked. "Dammit." He piled into the empty back seat.

Horatio glanced out the window.

Behind them, the other vehicles were nowhere in sight.

The tyrannosaurid must have dragged them farther off course than Horatio had thought when it got stuck in the window. Either that, or the other Hummers had already been overturned, and their occupants killed.

Five young members of the pack remained in pursuit.

They were gaining.

Free of the restraining binds of the foliage, these young ones really cranked out the speed now.

Horatio pulled himself inside and gazed at the speedometer. Incredible. The theoretical top speed of the entire species would have to be revised.

"How far to the insertion site?" he asked the driver.

"One klick," Wilson, the driver, said. "Give or take."

Horatio didn't think they were going to make it.

Franks had shoved himself up into the turret position now, so that only his legs were visible in the back seat. He was firing at the pursuers—

Those roar-whoops abruptly increased in pitch and intensity—

Franks was unceremoniously yanked from the roof with a loud *crunch*.

Megan screamed.

A tyrannosaurid approached the Hummer on Horatio's side.

Horatio protectively shoved Megan away.

The dinosaur slammed its body into the Hummer, tossing the vehicle violently.

Another tyrannosaurid hit the vehicle on its opposite flank.

The two dinosaurs kept bashing the vehicle, ramming it back and forth between them. They would bow their heads, then lift their necks on impact, striving to flip the Hummer like two dogs trying to topple a garbage bin full of offal behind the butcher shop.

Two dogs…

Dogs liked to play.

Horatio buckled his seatbelt.

"Does anyone have a grenade?" he said matter-of-factly.

The driver tossed him a grenade. "Pull the pin, let it cook, then toss it."

Horatio pulled the pin.

"Fetch!" he yelled, tossing the grenade out the window.

The nearest dinosaur hurried off in pursuit, panting like a dog. The tyrannosaurid bent over, clutched the grenade in its teeth—

The explosive detonated, tearing the dinosaur's jaws apart.

Maybe Horatio had just killed the genetic forebear of the modern chicken. No more cockfights. No more fried chicken.

Somehow he doubted it, though the world would just have to do without chicken if he had.

"Another, please," Horatio said.

The driver tossed him a second grenade.

Horatio waited until the next tyrannosaurid came in close, then he yanked the pin and threw the grenade at the dinosaur's face.

The tyrannosaurid eagerly caught the grenade in its mouth, like a dog catching treats from midair. It promptly swallowed the explosive.

A few seconds later the tyrannosaurid's belly ripped open in a gush of blood and intestinal loops, and the beast dropped.

"This is rather fun," Horatio said. "I think I've found my second profession."

"What, you've moved on from digging up dinosaurs to killing them?" Megan said.

"In so many words, yes."

The barren terrain became hilly, and Horatio knew they were close to the insertion site now.

He was about to ask for another grenade—when one of the tyrannosaurids hit the Hummer ferociously, and he felt the vehicle lift and begin to flip.

The Hummer, now inverted, smashed down hard to the ground, landing on its roof. Horatio felt his brain slam against his skull as he and Megan dangled upside down from their seatbelts.

Momentum continued to carry the upside-down Hummer forward for a bit, and then the vehicle hit a steep incline, skidding downward.

Finally, the upturned Hummer slid to a halt.

The navy boys in front recovered immediately, and opened their quick-escape bulletproof windows to pile out.

The ground shook—

Horatio heard a sickening thud, and he knew one of the navy boys had been taken down.

Horatio unbuckled his seatbelt, and crashed down onto the ceiling (which was now the floor). He reoriented himself, opened Megan's seatbelt, and caught her. She had a bloody wound on her head, and was unconscious.

He dragged her from the Hummer.

Amazingly, no jaws clamped around his body.

He hoisted Megan into his arms and ran. He glanced back. The other tyrannosaurids seemed preoccupied with their fresh prey.

For the moment.

Megan moaned quietly in his grasp.

"You're going to be okay, Megan," he said.

It was funny. He disliked her intensely, yet now when it came to it, she was the last person he wanted to see harmed.

The world needed people like her. *Good* people.

The ground shook—

Something rammed him forcibly from behind. It felt like a wrecking ball had slammed into his back. He stumbled forward a few paces, lost his balance, and fell, dropping Megan.

A terrible vise clamped around his left leg. Pain shot through his calf.

He heard heavy breathing behind him, and felt air press against his clothing as massive nostrils exhaled.

He glanced over his shoulder, knowing what he would see. Fearing it.

A tyrannosaurid had pinned him below the knee. Only a baby, though still as big as a small car. It was saving him for the bone-crushing teeth of an adult.

A Hummer zoomed past, and the remaining tyrannosaurids dispersed, chasing after it. They had failed to notice Megan. Or maybe they *had* seen her, but had dismissed her as inconsequential: no need to restrain someone who's already unconscious.

The roar-whoops faded around him.

He heard the occasional, distant sound of frantic gunshots. Then a crash—

The sound of the final Hummer being taken out.

Captain Ford had promised that Horatio would get to see living and breathing versions of the fossils he so dearly loved. And now he was living that dream.

Just not in the way he had expected.

Filled with a curious mixture of respect and awe, Horatio stared over his shoulder at the baby tyrannosaurid. Such a beautiful creature. And strangely, he wasn't all that afraid. He somehow managed to emotionally detach himself from the situation: as far as he was concerned, it wasn't his leg, but the leg of someone else that was firmly fixed in the mouth of the one-ton predator.

That detachment helped him to think with crystal-clear clarity.

And he thought of a way out.

It was a long shot, but it just might work.

He didn't have much time now. Not before Daddy came.

He fetched his smartwatch from his pocket. He set the volume to maximum, and then played one of his daughter's favorite songs, a little ditty by some trendy boy band. He tossed the whining watch at the baby tyrannosaurid.

The dinosaur released his leg and ran away in terror.

Horatio stood up shakily, hoisted Megan into his arms, and then ran, limping heavily, toward the insertion site.

"We're going to survive this, Megan," he said. "We're going to make it."

Her head flopped lifelessly.

He could see the arena-sized sphere just ahead, its doors left invitingly open.

The way home.

The sporadic sound of gunfire and explosions erupted in the distance behind him. Some of the Travelers were still alive out there. Regrouping, hopefully.

338

Horatio promised himself he would wait for them as long as he possibly could, once he reached the machine.

Almost there…

An adult tyrannosaurid leaped down from the sphere, landing in front of them with an earth-shaking thud.

A *Tyrannotitan*.

It stood between Horatio and the only way home.

Well, he'd tried his best.

"I'm sorry, Megan," he said to the unconscious woman, as the giant lumbered forth for the kill. "I guess we're not going to make it after all."

* * *

McMillan Motabu, assistant to the Adjunct Curator of Paleontology at the Museum of National History, was hard at work on the latest find. His lead, Horatio, had been curiously absent for some weeks now, and McMillan was continuing the excavation of the specimen.

At this moment, he was working on the same section of the fossil Horatio himself had been focusing on before his disappearance. McMillan had removed enough of the outer rock by now to realize that this was not bone he was uncovering in this area, but rather some unknown material. Maybe a resin of some kind? But if so, it was no resin he had ever encountered before. The pieces were thin, rod-like. Similar to tent poles. Yes, that was the best description.

It was all very curious.

He would have to have a fragment sent for testing later.

He received a call on his smartwatch, and set aside his tools to plug in his earbuds. He could work while on speakerphone, but then everyone would hear, and he would also make mistakes. Besides, the call was from his wife, and she demanded his full attention.

He had the habit of pacing when he talked on the phone, and by the time he hung up he'd walked halfway across the work hall.

One of his students was just entering. Sasha. A pleasant girl.

McMillan removed his earbuds to greet her, but she spoke first.

"McMillan," Sasha said, her mouth dropping. She pointed at the sedimentary rock behind him.

He glanced at it.

Odd.

He hadn't noticed before, but from this angle the rods he had uncovered this morning seemed to form actual letters.

What were the chances?

No, of course it was random.

McMillan heard footsteps behind him.

Some kind of military man entered the hall. Dressed in a blue service uniform with a suit and tie, the hard-faced visitor seemed like a man McMillan wouldn't want to cross.

"I'm putting together a team," the man said.

McMillan glanced once more at the fossilized letters behind him:

S.O.S.

A Word from Isaac Hooke

"The Laurasians" was inspired by a *Choose Your Own Adventure* book I read as a child, in which the main character was a time traveler. In *Choose Your Own Adventure* books, you can make different choices, and depending on those choices, you influence the outcome of the book. For example: *If you want to hide from the animal, turn to page 8. If you want to confront the animal, turn to page 22.*

Anyway, one of the "bad" paths led to the hero dying in the belly of a dinosaur, and one hundred million years later, a paleontologist digs up the dinosaur, and finds the hero's bones.

In the first draft of the Laurasians, Horatio returned to the present and, while pondering whether he would ever return to the past again, discovered a bone in the belly of the fossil he was excavating. He recognized that bone, because of the steel graft attached to the tibia—he had a similar graft on his own tibia, because of the surgery he'd undergone to repair his leg from the tyrannosaurid attack. I changed the ending because I wanted Horatio's fate to be left up to the imagination of the reader.

There is no such thing as a Matryoshka wormhole (yet), though the time travel machine was based on the concept of the "traversable wormhole," which utilizes a similar "nesting of spheres" idea. The Casimir effect is also real.

About the Author

Isaac Hooke is the author of the military science fiction novel *ATLAS*. His experimental genre-bending action novel *The Forever Gate* was an Amazon #1 bestseller in both the science fiction and fantasy categories for a (very) short time when it was released in May 2013.

When Isaac isn't writing, publishing, and blogging, he's busy cycling and taking pictures in Edmonton, Alberta, Canada.

He's been writing since 1997, and he has a degree in Engineering Physics.

You can follow Isaac on Twitter @IsaacHooke and his website IsaacHooke.com. Sign up to be notified of his new releases here: http://bit.ly/atlaslist

The First Cut
by Edward W. Robertson

I GRADUATED to the Cutting Room fourth in my class—of four. Maybe it's not as bad as it sounds; there were twenty-two dropouts. It was the best day of my life and I was allowed to tell no one. After the ceremony—a crisp, no-frills affair on the top floor of Central, with a speech from Davies himself—they stuck us in a tube and popped us off to our new home.

In an ideal world, we would never have had a single case. But not even Primetime is perfect.

I was assigned to Mara Riesling. Senior agent, though not much older than me, and pretty, which mattered to me at the time.

"What now?" I said.

"Now, you practice."

"Then what was the Academy?"

"A test for the real test. A school for the school. Do you understand what's at stake?"

"The futures of billions," I said. "And?"

She smiled. "Why were you fourth?"

She took me to the Pods. The room was as clean as you'd expect but much simpler. White hemispheres big enough to camp under. She nodded me inside one.

I poked my head from under its canted lip. "Going to bother to tell me where I'm going?"

"It will tell you everything you need."

"Then let's go save some worlds."

"The only world you're going to is a virtual one. Deep immersion. Indistinguishable from the real thing."

"But without the ability to ruin any fragile causalities."

"Bingo. See you in a week."

She spoke a command, and the Pod closed me in.

Vertigo tilted every neuron in my brain. I emerged in another world. Another time. My tablet had all the details, downloaded from my Pod: Early Information Age; the island known in most worlds as Manhattan. What was known was that, in the original timestream, Leslie Larsen had died of heart failure at the age of eighty-three. Yet in seven days, she would die of heavy metal poisoning, at the age of twenty-eight.

Simple case. Yet seven days later, when the Pod opened and I was back in the white room of the CR, I hadn't found the trespasser.

"You failed," Mara said.

I rubbed my eyes. Felt swimmy from the transfer. "Did seven days pass here, too? Or just simulated?"

"Full. We want everything to be real except your screw-ups. What happened?"

"I couldn't get close enough. The net profiles were no good. They were so thin it made *everyone* look like a trespasser."

"That didn't seem to trouble Jackson." She pointed to the front of the room. A broad whiteboard listed our four names, handwritten: Jackson Propher, Wella Nunez, Ben Wilhelmsen, Blake Din. Jackson had a "1" under his name. Wella and Ben had no results yet. Mara strode to the board and traced a circle through the air. An enormous "0" appeared on the board below my name.

"Guess that's why he was tops in class," I said.

"It was the doorman. Okay? The doorman."

"Shit," I said. "How was I supposed to know that?"

"His teeth? The buttons on his jacket? His *haircut*?" She stared at me, head tilted. "You hung back, Blake. You can't be afraid to dive in."

"I thought that was the prime directive. Any intrusion, no matter how slight, causes damage."

"The question is whether it's worse than the death you're there to stop. Passive surveillance and collation isn't working? Time to hit the streets."

After that I had two weeks off from the Pods. Not as punishment, but because your head can get Untethered if you spend too much time away from Primetime. Not to say it was a vacation, either. Quite the opposite. Drudgework, theory. I couldn't wait to get back to the Pods. When I did, the board had been updated: Wella had a 1, and Ben had joined me with a 0.

"You can't always get it," Mara said. "No one whose career has lasted more than twenty cases has come out batting above .500. But at *least* try to fail well."

The Pod closed. The case was another murder. Another young woman. They tend to be: those trespassing from Primetime with the intention of doing violence are usually in it for thrills, revenge, power plays. They target the weak (children, the elderly) or those who made them feel powerless (women, overwhelmingly so). I knew the theory inside and out, yet when my seven days were up, I wound up on the heels of the wrong man when the bullet entered the woman's skull.

"Why not send us back with nine thousand flycams?" I groused, climbing from the Pod. "Or just have the Pods watch the whole goddamn thing themselves?"

Mara just stared. "If that's a serious question, you're further behind than I thought."

"And if you thought it was serious, your opinion of me is lower than *I* thought."

"Indulge me."

"Dropping future tech into a world can disrupt it far worse than any murder. The very act of *observing* changes the observed. We get one chance. Pure, clean. A footprint like a cat on the ice."

She nodded, mollified. At least she didn't insult me by asking why we only got one shot. "What went wrong?"

"Not much in the way of digital resources. Which seems to be a running theme of these tests. I pinned down the guy who was supposed to meet her at the time of death—but she was killed hours before the police report stated."

"You trusted a police report?" Mara cackled. "From the twentieth century?"

"Pardon me for having professional respect."

"These places don't have Pods. The reports are educated guesses—at best. Build your case from the ground up. No assumptions."

On the board, Jackson's score had climbed to 2. Wella whiffed, but Ben had tied her at 1. Mine remained a round empty nothing.

I had two weeks to dwell on it. Studying old Cutting Room cases. Things we never had access to at the Academy. Fascinating, but I wasn't in the mood. My weekly assessments began to suffer, too.

Don't even ask about the third case. When the Pod opened on me, Mara's eyes could have popped me and served me at the movies. "You stayed with the victim."

"I saved her."

"You're not supposed to *speak* to the victim. You kept her in a hotel room all week!"

"And *saved her.*"

"Who gives a shit?" Mara stalked a circle around me, jabbing at me with her index finger. "All that means is the trespasser gets spooked and comes back after you've left the timestream. And you've blown your chance!"

"The victim's already dead," I said. "If we don't execute, we can be damn sure they'll stay dead. If I save them and spook off the killer? There's no guarantee he'll be back."

"So you traded that possibility in exchange for massive damage to the stream?"

"I told her we had a credible threat from an ex-boyfriend. I thought I was being creative."

She closed her eyes, holding up her hand for silence, letting the anger dissipate from her face. "These are sims. *Training.* That's the point. This is the last time you break the rules like that."

The scores updated. A neat countdown: 3, 2, 1, 0. Mara's steps departed from the room. A second set replaced hers. Jackson, smiling, the tips of his canines peeping from beneath his upper lip.

"Planning to join us at some point?" he said, towering over me.

"Do you think this is a competition?"

"The way you're playing? Not in the slightest."

I whirled, grabbed his collar, slung him against the whiteboard. He went for a low kick, but I arrested it by jamming my knee into his. I buried my elbow in his throat. "Pray they wash me out."

He stared back, daring me to hurt him. I stepped back and let go. He straightened his collar. "Doesn't look like God needs me to convince him."

Another two weeks off. Mara was up in rotation when a real case came in, leaving me to study under the care of a taciturn man whose attitude suggested he was on the verge of retirement. I rededicated myself to the work, but found myself staring through the screen, absorbing nothing.

For the fourth case, we got something new. Kingmaker scenario. A nobody from Primetime flits off to a backwater to play out their fantasies of grandeur. Rarely happens in modern days—things are more settled than they used to be, it's much harder to fly under the radar when you're disrupting things on that scale—but it still crops up here and there. For some, utopia isn't enough. They want *worship*.

In this case, the virtual trespasser was entangling herself in a world where everything was jittering like a three a.m. Sunday comedown. Roughly mid-twenty-first, by standard reckoning. Too many living in desperation and too little funding to keep the violence corralled. Within this framework, the trespasser had spurred a joint rebellion in both Baja and Southern California. Due to her intrusion, tens of thousands would die in the fighting, and the area would crash twice as hard as in the pure version of the timestream.

And I had to find her within a paranoid, violent underground who had consciously isolated themselves from the surveillance and public online presences that tended to make that era so easy to navigate.

I was three days in and (I felt sure) one move away from her when everything went white. As I was pulled from the simulation, there was no swimmy, vertigo-inducing disorientation. Just Mara, dropping her face below the rising edge of the Pod.

"I'm going in," she said. "Real case. Answer now: Will you go with me?"

"Of course."

She nodded, handed me a plain black backpack, and ran from the room at a dead run. We crossed into a hall into a second chamber of Pods, dressed ourselves in period-appropriate clothes the Pod had waiting for us, and climbed inside. The vertigo of the transfer was three times worse than it had been in the sims. I felt like I was turning inside out, like my teeth were flipping up from my gums to swallow my head. Next came the numb non-being of betweenness.

Then I was there.

"There" was a forest, dark—the Pods can't directly observe conditions on the ground without damaging their pristine state (and risking exposing themselves), so they have to pop us out in the middle of nowhere, where there's virtually no chance our arrival is witnessed. Makes the first few hours of a visit a real pain in the ass. There in the woods, Mara knelt and dug into her pack, withdrawing a sheaf of paper, the margins perforated. My heart sank.

"Tell me there's a tablet hidden in there."

Scanning her printouts, she smiled wryly. "Full-on analog, baby. I'm afraid this asshole knows what he's doing."

"This is ridiculous. Why didn't we poke our eyes out before hopping in the Pod, too?"

She got what she needed—directions, I assumed—and started jogging through the trees. "We're not operating completely blind. This knife cuts both ways."

I followed her through the undergrowth. The smell of fallen leaves was tremendous. "Why me? Why not Jackson?"

"What happened between you two? At the Academy?"

"What would it matter?" I cocked my head. "Unless you heard about our little disagreement."

"I hear everything, Blake."

"I'm sure the Pods help. For the record, he was being a poor winner."

"And at the Academy?"

"He hurt a friend of mine," I said. "I straightened him out. Okay, your turn."

"Don't you understand?" Mara slowed, eyes skipping between mine. "The trespasser. It's Jackson."

I stumbled on a root. One that might not have been there. "You're joking."

"It's not unprecedented. Get in the Cutting Room, and you've got access to everything."

"Including an education in how not to get caught," I muttered. "So what'd he come back to do?"

"Murder," she shrugged. "Penny Clarke. Twenty-five. Ten days from now, she'll be reported missing. She's never found."

"That's it? Would have expected more from Jackson."

Mara gave me a look. "It's easy to look down on these people. They still use phones, for God's sake. Attached to *walls*. And you, you're Primetime. In a week, you'll walk out of here, same as you'd walk out of a theater and back into your real life. But Penny Clarke—she's a real person, too. Just as much as you. Always remember that."

I was quiet a minute. "If I drop this one, am I out?"

"If you keep worrying about yourself instead of the victim, you will be."

We crested a ridge, but the trees blocked our sight ahead. Far away, a train whistle pealed through the night.

"Better hurry," Mara said.

The ground sloped down for a few hundred yards, then leveled. The trees quit, revealing iron tracks under the stars. We jogged down to the platform just in time to greet the screeching metal monster pulling to a stop. Inside, scattered passengers gazed out the windows. Some read paper books and glossy magazines, also paper. A kid with long, greasy hair and a flannel jacket wore bulky, round things over his ears. Headphones.

We were in public and there wasn't much to say, so we didn't. Within half an hour, a million lights sprang into view. It was unique, as always, each iteration sporting its own geography of towers, yet the Manhattan skyline was recognizable on any world.

"Neither of us have been here before," Mara said, as if reading my thoughts. "You think you know it, but you don't."

We detrained at Norfolk Station. It was getting on in the evening, but people streamed around us as Mara examined a subway map and proceeded to navigate us to a Brooklyn hotel a few blocks from the Clarke woman's apartment. While Mara left to fetch a car from an all-night rental place, she posted me in the diner at the corner down the street from the woman's apartment. Mara was gone more than two hours, and I was glad for the chance to drink some coffee, bad as it was, and let my mind adjust to having been yanked from a simulated world and dumped into a real one, neither of which were mine. I saw two people enter the apartment, and jotted down their descriptions.

In our musty-smelling hotel room, Mara waved her printouts at me. "Our file is as thin as the stuff it's printed on."

"The net?"

"In its baby phase. Not nearly big enough to have enmeshed the culture yet. Maybe our job's as simple as waiting for Jackson to expose himself, but he knows we'll be watching. He'll have brought a mask."

"Then how do we recognize him?"

"We watch from the street. Follow Penny Clarke, see who she meets, then take a sniff at them and see if they're wearing Eau de Primetime."

She gave us a quick haircut to make us less obvious, then handed me a pair of sunglasses. She drove, parking up and across the street from the apartment. The Pod had culled several pictures of Penny Clarke from obituaries and such and

I memorized these as the hours ticked away. The neighborhood was quiet but unfriendly, single men wandering past without destination. By the early hours, both of us were nodding off. Mara told me to head back to the hotel for a nap. I was grateful, but it wasn't long enough; when I spelled her, I had to bite the insides of my cheeks to keep from falling asleep.

Morning light hit the street, dirty and yellow. Mara popped the passenger door, startling me.

"Well?" she said.

"Nothing."

She glared across the street. "Grab us some breakfast. Anything with bacon."

I returned to the diner, paying with one of the bills the Pod had printed into my wallet along with my ID, and brought back our food. The bacon tasted even better than it had in the simulations.

"Here's where she works," Mara said, passing me an address. "See if she's in. Don't get made."

I wasn't overjoyed about running solo through a strange city where every other one of the barbarians was carrying a gun, but that was the job. The job I'd been working toward for six years of secondary school and another three years in the Academy. I climbed out of the car. The street smelled like old, damp laundry. I jogged past brick walkups and struggling trees guarded by short black iron fences. Her work was only a ten-minute jog away, a bodega with attached cafe.

Clarke wasn't in. That, according to the guy behind the counter, was because she hadn't worked there in weeks.

I jogged back to the car and clambered inside. "I don't get it. *Weeks*, Mara. Is she already gone? How could the Pod have screwed that up?"

She narrowed her eyes in disdain. "Got any change? Watch and learn."

I handed over all the coins in my pocket and followed her to the street. She found a hilariously antiquated booth sporting a large plastic receiver attached to a flexible metal tube as thick as my little finger. She consulted one of her printouts, dropped coins in the box, and dialed.

Moments later, her eyes lit up. "Mrs. Clarke? Hi, this is Kenya. Kenya Andrews. I'm a friend of Penny's, we went to school together. That's right, Washington. So, reason I'm calling—oh no! Nothing like that." She laughed brightly, waving a hand in the chilly air. "*Much* less frightening. Except for her when I ask why she changed her number without bothering to tell me. Do you have it? Oh, wonderful."

She turned and scowled at me, palm held up, scribbling above it with an imaginary pen. I rustled through my pack and produced writing instruments.

"Okay, I'm ready." Mara wrote down numbers, then smiled as if Penny's mother were right in front of her. "I'll tell her just that. Thank you so much, Mrs. Clarke." She hung up and rolled her eyes. "I fucking hate the Analog Age."

"I don't see why we can't lock Penny Clarke in a room, but you can call her mother. What if that delay in her day means she steps in a crosswalk two seconds late and gets mowed down by a truck?"

"Shit happens. Meanwhile, she can be happy her little girl's moving up in the world. She's got a new apartment—Manhattan."

Turned out she hadn't climbed *that* much higher. Her new digs were across the river, but they were in the dubious stew of streets downtown and east: grimy brownstones mixed with buildings whose residents didn't like to admit they lived in project housing. In a small stroke of luck, a motel sat across the street from her place. The carpet in our room was so worn you could see the glue in places, but the view was right. A few hours in, Mara hadn't taken any notes on the people going in and out. I asked as much.

She pointed to her right eye. "Camera. We'll see about getting you one later. If you stick."

"I thought anacs weren't allowed."

"It's not *really* tech. Purely biological. Cut me open and you won't know what you're seeing unless you already know what you're looking for."

It was nearly five p.m. and a full day into our visit before we first saw Penny. She was young, blond, as pretty as her pictures. We followed her into the subway. She got off a few stops south and walked to an Italian restaurant, waiting on the sidewalk, looking north and south. A few minutes later, a tall man with dark hair and a crisp suit walked up to her, grinning, and kissed her hard.

"That look like Jackson's build to you?" Mara murmured.

"Thereabouts."

"They kiss like they just met last week."

I eyed her sidelong. "This counts as intelligence?"

"In this era? I'll take whatever I can get."

With the possibility that the man was Jackson, and no way to surveil them from out on the street, all we could do was take up space at a table on the patio of another Italian restaurant while we waited for them to finish dinner. By then, it was early evening. The man held the front door for Penny, waving inside to the staff. He headed north, and we followed on the opposite side of the street. At the avenue, he raised his hand for a cab. One swerved to the curb. They were off and lost in traffic before we'd even made it to the street.

I stared down the bustling avenue. "What the hell do we do now? We don't even know his name."

"No," Mara said. "But the people who just fed him do."

She turned around and headed back to the restaurant. I was made to wait out in the gusty street while she spoke to one of the staff, who eventually led her deeper into the building. I put my hands in my pockets, inhaling basil and garlic bread.

Mara emerged with a smirk. "Name *and* address. Never underestimate what those who work for pennies will provide in exchange for real dollars."

She pulled a similar trick with the doorman of his midtown apartment. The man's name was Anders Rik. He had lived at his current residence for less than a month. The doorman had first seen Penny a little over a week ago. Rik got no mail and rarely received visitors besides her. When Mara checked the phone book, he wasn't listed.

We took the subway back to the motel. As soon as we got there, Mara set herself beside the window. "What do you think?"

"Definite candidate. Maybe *too* definite."

"How so?"

"If it's Jackson, wouldn't he put more into his cover? Go back further, plant more of a footprint? From what we've gleaned, this Anders Rik didn't exist a month ago."

"Maybe he thought a month would be enough," she said. "Or maybe he's not as smart as you."

"Does that mean I passed?"

Mara snorted. "I'm dead on my feet. Take the window while I take a nap."

It was a long night. Trapped behind the window while everything else thrived. I didn't know why I cared. Most of the city smelled like urine or worse, the lights were gaudy, the traffic never really quit. Beyond that, the very *era* was horrifying, barbarous. People with no choice but to live on the streets like mongrel dogs. Many were a mere step or two above that, packed into bug-infested rooms, eating processed meals from plastic packages. Sirens yowled constantly, reminding us all how much crime and death roamed the streets at all hours.

Even so. There was a pulse to it. It was alive. More than that: it was my first world besides my own. I wanted to be out in it, immersed in it, part of it. Not caged behind a window watching over a woman I'd never met.

That thought was what brought me back. The reason I was here—the reason I was *allowed* to be here—was because I had spent years preparing to protect these worlds from my own. Primetime: alone in the ability to reach back to other wheres and whens. And no matter how good we made things—we had repeatedly altered our own past to achieve the best possible now—there remained those of us like Jackson.

Which meant there had to be people like me.

That was our first day. On the second day, Penny Clarke saw no one besides the employees at the bodega two buildings down. It was a Wednesday, but she didn't go to work. On the third day, Penny walked to a park multiple blocks west, a far more upscale place where people ate lunch on benches without fear of sticking themselves with a discarded needle. Halfway through her falafel, she was joined by another young blond woman.

During a lull when Penny had been in her apartment alone (a common circumstance), Mara had made a supply run, bringing back a bevy of recording and surveillance gear. It was dishearteningly oversized, and the fidelity was horrendous, but after some experiments, I was feeling less pessimistic. I found a seat on a bench behind the two women, separated by a well-maintained hedge. I set my pack beside me and maneuvered it until the shotgun mic blared their voices into my earbuds.

Most of it felt like empty chatter, but it did provide us with a first name for Penny's friend (Cecilia) and notice of their upcoming plans. What caught my ear, however, was our next introduction.

"So what do you think of Dean?" Cecilia said. "I mean *really*."

"He's nice," Penny said. "Cute. Respectful. But he should cut his hair. Don't tell me you're having second thoughts."

Cecilia laughed. "Not exactly. More like... I'm thinking of asking him to move in."

"*Move in?* How long have you been dating, a month? Why not ask that dude with the skateboard while you're at it?"

"Because I really like him? And he's in that place in Greenpoint. He's going to get stabbed. If the rent doesn't kill him first."

Penny lowered her voice, but she wasn't able to hide her judgment. "Has he found a job yet?"

"Well, that's the other thing. As much as he sleeps over, why should we pay rent on two places? Another few months of this and he'll have to move back to Pittsburgh."

Penny was quiet a moment. "Just be careful? You think you know a person, but they're only showing you what they want you to see."

"You're one to talk," Cecilia laughed. "How long have you known the Golden Goose?"

"Quit calling him that," Penny said, but she was laughing, too.

I followed Cecilia home and nabbed her full name from the listings at her apartment building. Mara did some calling around, learned she'd been in the city since college, same job and apartment for the last three years. Her boyfriend was Dean Sarnak, a newcomer to the city. Mara was able to confirm he had a birth certificate in Pittsburgh, but other details—like family, for instance—proved wanting.

"That doesn't mean they're not there," Mara said in our hotel room, staring down at the assorted notes we'd gathered to date. "Question is whether one of us wants to burn the time to check them out."

"Dean and Anders are our only probables, right?"

"Along with the general wild card of 'literally everyone here but you and me.'"

"But right now, the favorite is one of those two. Why not try to rule one out?"

She pinched her temples. "I'm not taking my eyes off the girl. You want to see Pittsburgh, go buy a plane ticket."

It was a gamble: between travel and legwork, I was looking at two days away, maybe three. We had seven days until Cecilia would report Penny missing, but Penny didn't have a job to be missed at. No family in the city. As far as we knew, she might be killed this evening.

I rolled the dice. The plane to Pittsburgh had *propellers*. I closed my eyes and focused on my breathing. Somehow, we managed not to crash. I ran down both sets of Sarnaks in town, confirmed they were real and that Dean belonged to one of them, then returned to the city.

"So it's Anders or the field," Mara said once I rejoined her. "Good news: I bugged her phone. Sketched out a timeline."

My eyebrows shot up. "Do you know when she's taken?"

"Listen to this. Today is Friday. Four days from now, on Tuesday, Cecilia reports Penny missing. Meanwhile, Penny's schedule is all booked. They're on for a group date tonight, then Cecilia's going apartment hunting this weekend and Penny's going with. Saturday *and* Sunday, with a date with Anders on Saturday night."

"I bet she misses the Sunday apartment hunt," I said. "Someone flakes on you one day, it's no big deal. Cecilia probably figures she's off with Anders. But when she can't get ahold of Penny on Monday or Tuesday either, that's when she goes to the cops. If we stick to Penny after she leaves Cecilia on Saturday, we can nail Anders as soon as he makes his move."

"I can buy that."

I nodded vaguely, working this over. A timeline was a huge find. It was a strong pointer toward the identity of the killer, and we would know to step in the instant anything looked awry. Endgame.

Mara got up for another cup of coffee. "You look dead on your feet. You want to catch a nap or come with? Our little crew's going to the movies together."

"I'll sleep when they do."

Mara smiled and got her coat. "Now imagine doing this on your own."

There was a subway stop right beneath the theater, but we took the car. After we'd circled the block three times in search of a spot out front, I realized we'd be watching from the street. An unexpected disappointment settled on my shoulders. Even in my place and age, we remember the Golden Age of the Movies, and I'd looked forward to joining the crowds seated between the projector and screen and sharing two hours in another world.

Eventually we found a spot. Penny and Cecilia arrived together. They stood on the sidewalk, Cecilia smoking a tobacco cigarette, cheeks puffing. Dean showed up, scruffy-faced, jeans torn, and then Anders, who towered over the three of them. They went inside.

I pressed my face for a better look at the theater. Four-story multiplex. Lights for days. "This is crazy, you know? What if Anders takes her out back and shoots her while we're out here?"

"Normally, we could stick a little closer." Mara glanced at the car ceiling; it had begun to rain, tapping the roof. "But you see why the agency save rate hovers below fifty percent."

"And we only get one shot."

"After that, the trespasser's back in Primetime, interacting with the world. Returning here to try again would thus fuck with *our* stream."

I nodded. "Wonder what Penny Clarke would think of that."

"I imagine very little, as she'll be dead. You know, there are people who argue we shouldn't be here at all. A waste of time that only leaves Primetime open to exposure." Mara pressed her lips together. "You want a hot dog? I want a hot dog."

"Maybe later."

She popped the door, pulling up her collar against the rain, and jogged to a cart on the corner across from the theater. Penny's life depended on so much going right for us. Yet if the Cutting Room had never existed, Jackson might never have had the opportunity to come for her.

Mara got into the car bearing two foil-encased hot dogs and began to chow down. The car filled with the smell of mustard and boiled meat.

"Ilya," I said. "Ilya Bostov."

Mara wiped sauerkraut from her mouth, talking around a half-chewed bite of hot dog. "That supposed to mean something to me?"

"That's what happened at the Academy. Our first year, she and Jackson were friends. Good friends. He wanted more. But there was always something in the way."

"Another man?"

I nodded, tapped my chest. "I never thought much of him. But you can't tell your girlfriend to quit hanging out with a guy. Not without looking jealous. Insecure. Maybe she starts to think you *should* be insecure. Especially when the other guy is the type to invite us all to Mardoune for the summer. Ilya, me, a friend of hers named Laury. And Jackson, of course. He has this incredible downtown apartment, view of the river, young, hip neighborhood. Two weeks in, we're having the time of our lives.

"That night, the four of us go out to a restaurant. Like normal. Come home, drink more, also normal. Laury falls asleep on the couch and I nod off too, but I wake up just long enough to remember I'd gotten us tickets to the Dolande exhibit in the morning, and even though Ilya's going to be too hung over to make it, *I* don't want to be the one to catch the blame. So I take the dose of Clear I've been hoarding. Even then, as soon as I sit down, I'm heading back to dreamland. Too heavy to stand back up.

"Then I hear a clink. Metallic. Jiggling. Furtive. That's enough to get me up. Jackson's not in the room. He's got a bedroom, but I *know*. Ilya's door is locked. I kick it in. The clinking was his belt; his shirt's off, pants on. She's wearing nothing. Jackson and I fight across the apartment, but the girls hardly stir. Takes a neighbor to break us up."

Mara stared down at her hot dog as if she'd just heard what it was made of. "Why wasn't he expelled?"

"Same reason he had a downtown apartment in Mardoune."

"Money and the name?"

I nodded. "He hadn't actually committed a crime yet. Except for whatever he'd drugged us with. But it washed out of our system before we could get tested. In the morning, I tell Ilya exactly what happened. Ilya flies home that day. I leave the day after that, but she won't talk to me. When the Academy resumes, she's not there. I got a call from her six months later. Haven't heard from her since."

Rain pattered the roof of the car. "I'm sorry."

"Gave me more time to study," I shrugged. "Tell me there's something in there you can use."

"Well, it's going to make me feel a lot less guilty if I have to shoot him."

I laughed and leaned back in the seat. My stomach began to rumble, but I ignored it. I'd eat when we were back at the hotel. Anyway, if I ate much right then, I was pretty sure I'd fall asleep sitting up.

The rain intensified. The second-story windows flashed— lightning?—then vanished in an eruption of black smoke. Glittering shards spun through the air, a background note against the explosion thundering across the night. I yelled out, throwing my hands up over my face.

Mara reached for the door handle. "Let's move."

Car alarms went off along the street. "I thought she wasn't supposed to disappear until this weekend!"

"You think this is coincidence? *Move!*"

I rolled from the car into the rain. People were screaming inside and outside. Smoke roiled from the broken windows, carrying the smell of burnt plastic. Pedestrians ran down the sidewalks, gawking over their shoulders. Mara loped across the street and into the theater lobby. My nerves burned along with the building. People were already rushing out through the smoke-choked lobby. Others staggered down the escalators, shrieking senselessly, holding their shirts over their mouths.

I glanced from face to face, eyes stinging. Passengers thundered up from the subway entrance, thickening the hundreds of people pushing across the lobby. Many were already outside.

"There!" Mara pointed through the haze.

Across the wide space, Anders lurched along with the crowd, standing a full head above most. Mara fought her way nearer. Something tickled in my gut. I held near the doors. On the escalator, blond hair flashed through a momentary hole in the smoke, accompanied by Cecilia. Cecilia was smiling, teeth peeping from beneath her upper lip.

I drifted forward, turning my shoulders to fight through the oncoming masses. At the base of the escalator, Cecilia hooked around, heading to the back of the building, dragging Penny behind her. Shoulders jostled mine. A wave of smoke blew over us, accompanied by fresh screams. When it cleared, I glimpsed Penny and Cecilia exiting the south corner of the building at a run.

I barged forward, drawing shouts and shoves. I hit the street and slowed at the curb, peering into the rain. People fled down the streets, faces warped with fear. A block away, a blond ponytail swung as its owner rounded a corner and disappeared behind an apartment.

I ran ahead, suddenly aware that I was unarmed. We hadn't expected an event tonight and had left our pistols in the hotel. I swerved around the corner, slowing as soon as I saw the two women walking briskly down the sidewalk. Penny was glancing over her shoulder, waving back in the direction of the theater. Cecilia put an arm around her shoulder and guided her on.

We passed a small park. Pedestrian traffic thinned. Too late, I realized I should have dropped back; at a scuff of my shoe, Cecilia turned around. She picked up her pace. Knowing she could bolt at any moment, I kept up.

As they passed a tall red building, Cecilia beelined for the front doors and disappeared inside with Penny. I broke into a run. Inside, a woman behind a high desk swung her face to inspect me. I smiled tightly, gesturing out at the rain, and moved through the rudimentary security system.

I stopped, taken aback. The middle of the building was nothing but open space. The ceiling hung two hundred feet above the patterned marble floor. Railed balconies looked down from three sides. On the ground floor, the lobby's edges were fronted by reading desks, nine-foot shelves of books, and booths with bulky, cubical monitors and equally bulky headphones. Scattered people sat quietly, absorbing media. I walked quickly to the elevators. None were moving. I opened the stairwell, heard footsteps far above.

I moved inside, easing the door closed behind me, and headed up as fast and as silently as I could. The library was an odd choice, yet as canny as it came. The slightest scene would draw far more attention than I wanted. If I pursued, Cecilia could lose me in the stacks; if I lurked near the door, she could take a back exit, or wait for me to be ejected by security. Even if my wrench in her plans saved Penny this night, Cecilia could return later for a second pass after I was back in Primetime.

Their steps echoed above me.

"What are we *doing*?" Penny said.

Cecilia's voice was so soft I could hardly make out her words. "Waiting here, where it's safe. We don't know what's going on out there."

"It's *fine*. We're five blocks from the theater."

"Give me ten minutes, okay? My heart's about to explode. Then we'll go home."

"What are we doing in a library?" Penny's voice bounced from the walls. "I'm going to Anders's."

"Penny! You're shaken up, that's all."

Footsteps clapped down the stairs. I saw my chance. I had paused a few landings below them, but I began to climb, doing nothing to disguise my steps. The sound of another set of shoes rang down the stairs. Ascending. I reached a landing. Above, Penny's eyes widened. I smiled politely, passing her. Upstairs, a metal door closed with a bang.

I ran up the steps. The door opened onto a maze of towering bookshelves. I hustled to the balcony running along the edge of the stacks. The lobby sprawled fifty feet beneath me. A nipple-high railing protected me from stumbling into the vastness, but the very sensation of so much vacant space was dizzying, as was the repeating geometry of the stone floor far below.

The level appeared to be empty; Friday night. I moved forward, feet whispering on the carpet. Clothing rasped from somewhere up ahead. At the corner of the stack, I hesitated. Smelled perfume. Heard perfect silence. I slipped a book from the shelf and lobbed it over the stack.

It thumped against the next row of shelves. I spun around the corner. Cecilia whirled toward me, gun in hand. I grabbed it and twisted, slamming her hand into a row of books. She slammed her fist into my chin. I lurched back, but I had fifty pounds on her. I twisted harder. She cried out, her grip relaxing. I wrenched the pistol away.

Cecilia backed toward the entrance to the row. "Look at you."

"Look at *you*," I said, happy to have a little more space between us. "Where'd you get the body?"

"How did you make me?"

"Your tobacco. You weren't inhaling. Puffed it in your cheeks, like you didn't know what to do with it or didn't like it."

She laughed in disgust. "No way was that enough."

"Enough to get me watching. Then, after the explosion, you forgot yourself and grinned. Showed your teeth. You may have changed bodies, Jackson, but you didn't change *you*. Why Penny?"

"Haven't figured it out? No wonder you couldn't pass a single sim."

"I don't have to get the answers myself. Central will slice every last one from you. Right before they vacate your brain. Then I'll get to see those teeth while you're smiling, swabbing floors and toilets, too scooped-out to know you were ever anything more."

She rolled her eyes. "You idiot. Then I'm already dead, aren't I? The only question left is whether you're willing to pull the trigger—and lose your life in prison here?"

She grinned and moved toward me, rolling her hips. Pulling the trigger would bring every eye to me. Get the place locked down. Maybe I'd make it out and maybe I wouldn't.

I charged into her. Lifted her up. Slung her over the railing.

Before she began to scream, I ducked back into the stacks. Her wail pierced through the vastness of the library. I headed toward the stairs, wiping off her gun, and stuffed it behind a dusty pile of books. By the time I got downstairs, they'd closed off the doors. But to them, it was a probable suicide. I told them I'd seen nothing. I gave them my information and left.

At the hotel, the room was dark, empty. Mara didn't call the room until three a.m.—she'd been on Anders the whole time. I told her it was over. I could tell she wanted to ask more, but she restrained herself until she got back to the hotel. I told her Jackson had been Cecilia. That once I confronted him, he'd forced my hand.

"How did you know?" she said. I explained about the smoking, the grin. Mara frowned. "Awfully thin to abandon me in the middle of a chase."

"It was a calculated gamble. You were already on Anders."

"And what if you'd been here by yourself? Which one would you have followed then?"

"The same. Anders didn't feel right."

"Oh, bullshit."

"Jackson planned the trip to Mardoune for weeks. Months, maybe. He wasn't going to put less effort into *this*. Anders was too easy. A false lead. Jackson meant us to follow him while he—Cecilia—made off with Penny."

She nodded at this, then frowned again. "But the Pods saw Jackson climbing inside. That's how we knew it was him. I can believe he was carrying a mask, a nose kit, that sort of thing. But how did he change his *height*? His whole body?"

I didn't have an answer for that. We didn't figure it out until we got back to Primetime. His Pod didn't show one jump—it showed two. He'd gone to another world for the body job, jumped back to Primetime as a young, vibrant woman, and without exiting the Pod, had then made the jump to Penny's world.

"God damn," Mara said. "He would have made a hell of an agent." She glanced at me sidelong. "But so will you."

We were able to turn up a few more answers. According to newspaper records culled from the time, the theater explosion had taken place in the original timeline and hadn't been Jackson's doing. We surmised he'd taken advantage of the event to throw off the observers he'd known would be following him. As for duping us with the Cecilia identity, we discovered the real Cecilia Evans had died three months prior in a wholly legitimate car crash. His absorption of her identity might have unraveled if we'd dug further, but his new gender had been the perfect ploy to get us to dismiss Cecilia as a suspect.

I searched everything—Jackson's search logs, his communications, his home. I've built theories, but I've never learned why he did it. Why it was Penny Clarke. Maybe some day, I'll learn enough for the pieces to fall into place.

Until then, I keep going. Keep using every trick I've got to undo what should never have been done. Until I reach the point where I never come back without adding a "1" to the board I keep in my head—and I, like all of us, am so far from this—I see his teeth, I see her falling, I see the face of every one I've failed to save.

A Word from Edward W. Robertson

Technology's what sci-fi is all about, but it isn't always a boon for other genres. Back in the early 2000s, cell phones threatened to put an end to horror movies as we knew them.

Being trapped with a killer doesn't mean much when they can be foiled with a text message. Fortunately, screenwriters had access to an eldritch trick known as "hand-waving." Oops, your battery's dead. Oh dear, turns out Camp Crystal Lake doesn't have 4G coverage. Nullifying cell phones is easy (for now!), but the technology is so ubiquitous and disruptive it has to be addressed or the audience will be distracted by questions all movie long.

Screenwriters haven't done as well with the Google Problem. Back in the day, if your character wanted to learn more about the strange bump under his skin, or the obscure Babylonian demon possessing her son, they *at least* had to visit the library of an eccentric expert. Now? A normal person will travel no further than the far-flung land of their desk. To consult the venerable Wizard of Google. And there is no such thing as an exciting Google scene. Not even with safe search off.

I've got a similar issue in the Cutting Room universe. If Blake has access to a time period with a robust internet, to avoid messing with the timeline he's going to spend 98% of his investigation in front of a laptop, tablet, or his ocular implants. His case, in other words, would closely resemble his author's life. That's not an entertaining prospect. Not unless you're into the high-stakes drama of zooming closer and closer on Google Maps until it won't zoom any more.

Drama is about making your characters' lives hell, though, so the behind-the-scenes story of the Cutting Room series is about me minimizing Blake's internet access—or taking it away altogether.

I'm starting to wonder if it's a time travel series at all. Sounds more like a horror story.

The Dark Age
by Jason Gurley

THEN

I CAUGHT HER.

The doctor gave me a textured blue wrap. Frannie looked alarmed and said, "No, no, skin—skin-to-skin, I want skin-to-skin," and the doctor assured her that this was only for me, so that I wouldn't drop her. I lost track of what I was supposed to feel, and I bent over the bed, only dimly aware of Frannie's feet near my head, her toes splayed wide as she fought. I heard her scream like I'd never heard her do anything before. It was primal, and I felt like a hunter on the savannah, standing over my kill, like a warrior, head thrown back and the taste of blood in my mouth.

And then she came to me, like a child on a water slide into my arms, slippery and dark and blue, and I caught her, and her tiny face looked like the wrinkles of my knee, almost featureless in her surprise, and she bawled rapidly. She pierced my heart and my ears with her cries, and a nurse clamped and clipped the cord, and I carried her to Frannie and laid our daughter on her breast.

She wailed and clung to her mother, her tiny fingers opening and closing against Frannie's skin, and Frannie breathed heavily and said, "Elle."

I didn't want to look away from either of them—Frannie dripping with sweat, her hair in damp rings on her face, and Elle, pushing against her mother's skin like a fresh piglet—but the movement at the door caught my eye, and I did, I looked up, and for the rest of my life I wished that I hadn't.

Frannie saw, and looked, too.

The man in the doorway smiled regretfully, and waggled his fingers at me, and nodded.

I met Frannie's dark eyes, and watched the tears well up, and I felt my heart pull out of my chest and stay behind in that beautiful room, the most wonderful place that had ever been made. I kissed Frannie, but she kissed me back, harder, and then I nuzzled Elle's tiny soft ear with my nose, and kissed her head everywhere, and her small hands. I would have stayed in that room forever if I could have.

But I followed the man out of the room, my ears ringing with sadness, an enormous hole in my head and my heart, and that was that. We both knew that it had to happen, but we'd pretended it wasn't going to. And then it did.

I followed his dark suit through the hospital corridor. I couldn't feel my hands. My feet moved on their own.

He said something, but I don't know what it was.

We stepped out of the building and into the light, and the cold wind turned my tears to ice.

* * *

NOW

Elle taps the camera, and I watch her fingertip, large enough to crush worlds, grow dark and obscure my view. I laugh, and she giggles, and this makes her laugh harder, and then she begins to hiccup wildly. She rocks back on her bottom and puts her hands on the floor behind her, and reclines and stares at me, hiccuping and laughing, and I laugh with her.

"You're silly," I say to her. "Silly, silly Elle."

She babbles at me, and in the stream of muddled sounds I hear something that sounds like *a-da*, and I say, "Frannie!"

Frannie turns the camera on herself, and her smile is big and bright and threatens to push her eyes off of her face. "We've been working on it all week," she says. "She can't quite make the *d* sound work, so all we've got is *ada-ada*, except, you know, it's more like *atha, atha*."

I turn away from the camera and wipe at my eyes.

"Daddy's crying," Frannie says. I look back to see her turn the camera to Elle, who thinks this is hilarious. She pats her round tummy and laughs harder, and then the hiccups take over in a big way, and a moment later Elle burps up breakfast.

"Oh, uh-oh! Uh-oh!" Frannie singsongs, and she says to me, "We'll be right back, Daddy!" and puts the camera down.

I watch Frannie's feet, then she scoops up Elle and whisks her out of frame.

I sigh and push off of the wall and turn in a slow flip, waiting.

Sarah comes in through the research wing hatch and sees the camera and says, "Oh, shit—I mean—oh, *goddammit*, I—fuck! Shit."

I laugh at her and tell her it's fine. "Elle spit up," I say. "Commercial break."

Her face relaxes. "Whew. Okay. I don't want to corrupt your little girl or anything."

"Did I forget to flip the sign?"

Sarah turns around and leans out of sight. "Well—nope, no, you did," she says, leaning back in and holding up the little handwritten *recording* sign. "I wasn't even looking, I guess."

"What did you need?"

She looks around, scatterbrained, gathering her thoughts. Then Frannie comes back into the room with Elle, singing a bit, and she sees Sarah on the display and says, "Sarah! Hi!"

Sarah looks up at the screen and smiles sheepishly. "Hi, Francine," she says.

"Everything okay?" Frannie asks me.

"Everything's fine," I say.

"I was—I shouldn't be in here," Sarah says, making a slow turn toward the hatch. "I'm sorry. Nice to see you, Francine."

"Bye, Sarah," Frannie says. She lifts Elle's small hand and flaps it at the camera. "Say 'Bye, Sarah!'"

Elle yawns.

"Bye, sweetie," Sarah says, then shakes her head at herself and looks at me. "Really, I'm sorry. I'm sorry. I should've checked first."

"Not a big deal," I say, and then Sarah floats back into the research module and presses the hatch shut behind her.

"It's not like we were having phone sex," Frannie says, chuckling. "Make sure she knows it's fine."

I look at the readout beside the screen. "Time's up anyway," I say.

Frannie's frown is adorable. "Oh, I'm sorry, dear," she says. "We wasted so much time cleaning Elle up—I'm so sorry."

I smile, but I know it's a sad smile, and I know Frannie can tell. "Kiss her for me," I say.

Frannie kisses Elle, a big playful smooch that sets Elle's giggles off again.

"Love," I say.

"Love," Frannie answers, and then she squeezes Elle and coos, "Love! Love!"

The screen goes dark, and I sigh, and look around the module. It's cramped and small, but it's private, at least until Sarah bumbles in again. I point my hands at the floor and push off with my feet, just enough to reach the lights, and I snap them off. The module goes pitch-black, and then my eyes adjust to the faint light from the porthole. And then I cry, the way I always do. The tears stick to my face like film, and when I've cried enough to feel better, I sop them up with my sleeve, and turn on the lights, and get back to work.

* * *

This is the way it has to be.

I was already in the program when Frannie and I met. She sometimes asked me that awful, difficult question: Would I have signed up for this if we'd already been married? And I tell her no, of course I wouldn't, but I would have. I still would have. Some things are important, and then some things resonate through history like a bell, and this is one of those resonant things, being here, aboard the *Arecibo*, crawling through the night.

Then Frannie got pregnant, despite our best efforts and multiple contraceptives, and my answer to that question softened.

When I caught Elle that morning in the hospital room, I knew that it had changed. Frannie saw it on my face, I think, though we've never talked about it since then. But she knew that my heart had changed, and by noticing that, she learned that my earlier answers had been kind lies.

We are a crew of seven, with the simplest of orders.

See what's out there.

So that's what we're doing.

We've all left something behind.

It isn't easy for any of us.

We are martyrs.

I think of Elle's bright eyes and her shock of blond hair, and I wonder what it would feel like to hold her, that hair tickling my face as she falls asleep on my shoulder.

I would hold her for hours and hours and never grow tired.

It wouldn't matter to me if my arms fell off.

Every day I grow heavier with regret.

Every day I hate my younger, star-crossed self a little more.

* * *

Sarah is the scientist. Introverted, awkward, a little odd.

Then there's Mikael, our technician. We wanted to call him an engineer, but he prefers *spaceship guy.* As in, "Hey, spaceship guy, the wing just fell off."

Stefan and Heidi are the pilots. Heidi has a secondary specialty—she's the shrink.

I'm the communications guy.

Walter is the physician and nutritionist. Edith is the researcher.

They are all quite nice.

We have a pact among us—an unwritten one, one that the WSA probably figured would happen but didn't write into our training manuals, or account for during our isolation boot camp in Antarctica—that anybody can sleep with anybody else, and nobody will be jealous, and that our families on Earth will never know. It was Walter's suggestion. Heidi thought it was a marvelous idea, and would reduce tension. So far I think Mikael and Edith have been together, and Walter and Stefan, and the plan has held water. But I think soon someone will feel bad, and then things will be strange.

I told Frannie about the pact. It was our first video chat. She thought it made sense, and told me that she couldn't begrudge me for taking part.

"Sarah seems nice," Frannie had said.

"I don't want to sleep with anyone else," I told Frannie. "I miss you."

"Be practical," Frannie said. "We're talking about the rest of your life here. You aren't a monk. You shouldn't be."

Heidi approached me a few days later. I said no, and she wasn't upset or embarrassed. I didn't tell Frannie. I don't know why I didn't.

* * *

We have all left something behind, somehow. We talk about these things, about our families and lovers, as if it will somehow ease the pain of it all. Mikael had just met his birth parents for the first time. He thinks it would have been easier to have never met them, but Walter thought that it was better to know. "Now you won't spend the rest of your life wondering about it," he said to Mikael once.

Heidi has a husband and two children. They're in college. Her husband writes novels. She thinks that he'll be happier alone. She doesn't talk about her children. Each of us keeps something for ourselves, and doesn't talk about it.

I am just like a new father on Earth. Each time Frannie sends me a video of Elle doing something new, I show everyone. Stefan seems the most enthusiastic about her progress. Edith always watches and nods, and then goes back to what she was doing before. I don't care. I sometimes wonder if I must share Elle with everybody so that everybody will recognize the enormity of my personal loss. I told Heidi that during one of our sessions, once.

Heidi said, "Is that what *you* think?"

Of all of them, Sarah is the closest to a friend for me. She seems to like Frannie, and that makes me like Sarah more. I like that she doesn't talk much, that she prefers to be alone. I like that she considers me the next best thing to being alone.

Sarah seems nice.

Sometimes I think about it.

* * *

Elle gets bigger and bigger. Frannie and I celebrate Elle's birthdays every month, to make up for the many I will miss. The WSA permits only two communications per week, and I look forward to them as much as I did to my own birthdays as a child.

I miss every first.

Frannie will wait for my call, then excitedly tell me that Elle has started walking, that she had her first solid food, that she said her first word. Elle demonstrates all of these things for me, but I feel like one of my shipmates—not a parent, but an audience. I cry every time. The emptiness between us feels incalculably large—larger every time we talk. I see Elle's eyes change from blue to green, her chubby cheeks become slim, her hair fall to her shoulders. She wears the clothes of an adult—pretty sweaters and thick tights and patent shoes, and I feel a terrible fear seize me when I realize what is coming.

Frannie sees it in my face. She doesn't know what to say. She only says, "We love you more than anything." She means it, but I can feel the helplessness behind her words.

The inevitability of the *Arecibo* launch hung over our pregnancy like a pall, like a storm that grew darker and more ominous every day.

But it is nothing like the storm that approaches now.

* * *

"*The WSA* has mandated special counseling sessions for each of you," Heidi says over breakfast a few days later. "Now, I'm inclined to agree—but I'd like you all to tell me if you prefer them to be one-on-ones, or if you would consider a group session."

She studies everyone's faces, and when nobody speaks, she adds, "I think a group session would be more productive."

Everybody dreads the Long Sleep, as they've been calling it. Walter says it's not exactly a Sleep. "It's a dark age," he says. "Literally, it's *the* Dark Age."

Heidi looks around the room and says, "Right. Okay. A group session."

* * *

Sarah sits beside me. We're all gathered at the dining table in the galley. There aren't many chairs aboard the *Arecibo* that aren't attached to consoles, so the galley was the default choice. One by one the crew floats in and buckles themselves into seats at the table. Heidi comes in and sits down and says, "Who are we missing?"

"Edith," Mikael offers.

"Is she coming?" Heidi asks.

Mikael shakes his head. "She doesn't want to talk about it."

Heidi sighs, and thinks about this, then says, "All right. We're on our own out here, folks. WSA can't really do anything to you. Does anybody else want to skip this?"

Silence, and then Stefan unbuckles and leaves. Mikael shrugs apologetically, then follows.

We watch them go.

"So," Walter says cheerily.

Heidi smiles at him and I wonder if they've slept together.

"The Long Sleep," Heidi says.

"The Dark Age," Walter contradicts.

"Whatever. How do you all feel? Who wants to talk about it first?"

I begin to cry immediately.

Sarah pats my knee beneath the table, then leaves her hand there, and I feel my skin flush hot.

Sarah seems nice.

"Maybe this should really be mandatory," Walter suggests.

* * *

Frannie is exhausted. She's alone on the screen, her eyes rimmed red. Her hair is disheveled, and she's wearing her pajamas.

"Frannie?" I ask.

She tells me about her day—Elle has been throwing tantrums, but it's because she has a fever, Frannie thinks, so she's trying to remain as patient as she can, but it's wearing her down. Elle hasn't slept more than a half hour for two days. "Can you hear her?" Frannie asks.

"Yes," I say. The sound of my daughter crying hundreds of thousands of miles away is wrenching. I want to go to her. I want to pick her up and hold her close and say, "It's okay, Daddy's here." I want her to snuggle close and sniffle herself to sleep in my arms.

Frannie says, "It's so hard," and she cries.

"Fran," I say, leaning close to the camera. "Darling."

"I'm so alone," she says.

I strap myself into my bunk that night and think about my sins.

I have abandoned them.

I hate myself.

I unstrap and go to Heidi.

"What if I killed myself?" I ask her.

* * *

The Long Sleep, the Dark Age. One hundred forty-four years of hibernation sleep. Autopilot. Essential systems and life support only. Seven people, quietly stored in airtight sleeves, in a module with countless systems redundancies. Heart rates slowed and monitored. Data transmitted daily back to Earth, for a long slow journey to the WSA's computers for analysis and modulation.

"Well, you shouldn't do that," Heidi says.

"Tell me why," I demand. I'm crying. I'm the most unstable person on the *Arecibo*, I think.

"Because your wife and daughter would know," Heidi says.

She doesn't have to say another word.

But she does.

"If you want to kill yourself when we wake up," Heidi says, "then at least you won't hurt them."

* * *

The possibilities are impossible to predict. The WSA and our native governments have put in place a series of treaties and contingencies, and written a strange new constitutional document that will take effect should any one of those bodies no longer exist when we wake up. A lot can happen in a century and a half. We might wake to find that the WSA has lost its funding. There might have been wars. Earth could have been destroyed by a meteor. Or it might have evolved into a technological utopia. The cure for death might have been discovered, in which case our families might survive to see us again.

But nobody knows for sure.

Frannie says, "What am I supposed to do?"

"What do you mean?"

Elle sits on Frannie's lap, playing with a toy I don't recognize, a plush character from a children's show, and it strikes me again that I am left out of even Elle's tiniest experiences. Does she hold that doll close when she sleeps? Is it her favorite?

"Am I supposed to be alone for the rest of my life, too?" she asks.

I don't know what to say to her.

"I'm sorry," she says, wiping her eyes. "I didn't know it was going to be this hard."

"I'm an asshole," I say.

Her eyes widen and she looks in Elle's direction, then back at me.

"I'm sorry," I say. "Elle, ignore Daddy."

Frannie turns the camera to Elle's face. "Say night-night to Daddy," she says.

My beautiful daughter looks up and smiles and says, "Nigh-nigh, Daddy."

Frannie turns the camera back to her own lovely face and says, "I'm sorry. Don't worry about us. We're going to be just fine. We love you."

"I love you, too," I say, and kiss my fingers and hold them up to Frannie's.

* * *

Sarah is in the research module when I come out.

"I thought everyone was asleep," I say.

She shrugs. "Sorry. Sometimes I can't sleep. Are you okay?"

I touch my face. My skin is tight. "I was crying," I say. "I'm fine."

"You're a sweet man," Sarah says to me.

"I wanted to kill myself."

She smiles sadly. "We all do."

I float past her and go through the hatch to our sleeping quarters, and then I turn and look back at her.

"I'm putting her through so much," I say. "It's inhuman. I can't think of anything worse."

"I can think of lots worse," Sarah says. "But Frannie's wonderful. She'll be okay. She'll find someone."

I look down.

"You have to let her do that," Sarah says. "You're not really hers anymore. She's not really yours."

"I… yeah."

"I don't know what it feels like to be in your skin," she says. "But maybe it helps if you think of them as a story that you're watching. Like on television."

"I'm going to miss every episode," I say.

She nods. "But you'll know the ending tomorrow."

I can't help it. I cry. The thought of my family growing up, growing *old*, dying—and that all of it will happen while I'm asleep—feels like someone has grabbed my ribs and is spreading them apart, pulling as hard as a body can be pulled. It feels like I'm going to come apart, and I double over involuntarily.

Sarah is there, then, and she holds me and we wobble in zero gravity together. She puts her hand on my face, and my tears crawl from my skin to hers.

"You won't lose everything," she whispers. "I'll be here when you wake up."

* * *

The last conversation with Frannie is surreal.

She is wearing the bulky sweater that I liked, the one with the neck that's wide enough for her shoulder to peek through. I stare at her skin and try to remember what it felt like to touch it. I try to remember her smell. I can't.

Elle is wearing a beautiful sundress and yellow rain boots. "Boots!" she cries, pointing at them.

"Boots," I agree, trying not to cry again.

Frannie smiles with shining eyes as Elle runs to her toy chest and picks up a building block, then brings it to the camera.

"Block!" she says. Her eyes are big and she bites her lip, waiting for me to understand.

"Block," I say, nodding.

I wish that I could stack the blocks with her into a great big prison cell, and stay inside of it forever with her. I watch her run to the toy chest. She puts the block down and picks up a squeaky giraffe.

"Raffe!" she says, displaying it to the camera.

"Giraffe," I say.

"Elle, honey," Frannie says as Elle runs back to her toys. "Daddy has to go in a minute. Can you say goodbye? Can you tell him how much you love him?"

I cannot hold back my tears. I suck in deep breaths and stare longingly at the Earthbound room and my girls inside of it.

"I miss you, Ellie," I choke out.

"Daddy misses you," Frannie says.

Elle comes back to the camera and holds up a stuffed pig. "Piggie!" she cries.

I nod like a fool, and she runs away again. Frannie snatches her up and brings her back to the camera, and Elle kicks in protest, and Frannie looks at the camera with a terrible fear in her eyes and says, "I'm sorry, I'm sorry, she's—"

The digital counter runs out, and the screen goes dark.

* * *

Heidi and Walter see to us all, one by one. Walter will be the last into the units, as the ship's doctor.

He stands in front of me, adjusting the monitoring belt. He is close enough that I can feel his breath. He smells like coffee. He smiles at me and says, "It's going to be a pleasant dream. Okay?"

I nod and look away, uncomfortable with his closeness.

Heidi comes by next, after attending to Sarah, who will be in the sleeve beside mine.

"Are you okay?" she asks.

I am tired of crying. I feel as if I have cried a thousand years.

"The first thing Walter's going to do is adjust the gas compounds in your sleeve," she says. "There's a light neuro-sedative in the mix. You'll feel relaxed and carefree."

"I don't want to sleep," I say.

"We all have to," she says.

"I'll stay awake. I'll watch over the ship, make sure everything runs fine. I'll make sure you'll all be okay."

"The ship can do that for itself," Heidi says. She leans closer and kisses my forehead. "You are going to be all right. When you wake, we'll talk. Okay?"

I think about Heidi's family. "What about your kids?" I ask. "Don't you care about them?"

She's unruffled by my tone. "My boys will be fine," she says.

"They got to know their mom," I say bitterly.

Heidi's smile is kinder than I deserve. "Let me help you inside," she says.

* * *

Inside the sleeve is a slim, curved screen. It's fixed to the thick polyglass before my eyes, and it displays a simple message.

You are humanity's finest, it says. *We wish you godspeed and long lives. Make us all proud.—WSA, Earth*

The message disappears, replaced by something new.

Hey. Look left.

I frown, then turn my head.

Sarah waves at me from the clear sleeve next to mine. She says something, but I can't hear her, and I shake my head. I mouth, "I can't hear you."

She points at the screen in front of her face. I understand, and look back at mine.

The message reads, *We can talk until we fall asleep.*

Then another line: *It's voice-activated. Just talk.*

I say, "Hi."

Hi.

I look over at Sarah—weird, strange Sarah—and she smiles.

"You're too happy," I say.

You're the saddest person I've ever met.

"I should be," I say back. "I'm a monster."

Will you be okay?

I hear a dim hissing sound, and outside the sleeve Walter waves at me, then gives me a thumbs-up. He folds his hands beside his face and mimes falling asleep. I nod blankly at him, and then he moves on.

It smells sweet.

I sniff the air. "I don't want it."

I know you're scared. You're a good man.

"I'm not. I'm not a good man."

You're not really the best judge of character. Your own, I mean.

"Sarah," I say, feeling the drift of the gases. "I'm terrified."

It will be over before you know it.

"That's what I mean. When I wake up, my little Elle—"

She will be proud of her daddy. What do all the other dads do that's so special?

"She'll hate me," I say. "She'll die thinking I left her, that I didn't love her."

She knows.

I stare at the screen. To my left, Sarah is drifting.

I say, "Record a message."

* * *

Elle, Frannie—

I hope with all of my heart that this message comes through. Maybe the WSA will see it and make sure. I hope so.

We're going to sleep now. It's about to happen—I already feel woozy. I'm sorry. This is my last message and I'm going to sound like a drunk. I'm sorry, I'm so sorry—

Frannie, my dear, my sweet wife. I have loved you since I met you. I wish that I could hold you forever, but I can't—I have to let you go. Be happy. Fill your days with love. Fill Elle's.

Elle, sweetheart—I'm going to cry, I'm sorry—Elle, there is nothing—I—oh, god, I'm drifting, it's happening—

Elle—Elle—

I hold you always.

I am—I am always—

Elle—

* * *

The message ends, and I blink away tears.

"Stupid," I whisper to myself. "I didn't say anything at all."

Sarah is wrapped in a white blanket beside me. Her eyes are wet, too.

"You said everything," she says. "Everything."

We sit in shock around the table with the others. Each of us leans on another.

Heidi looks the worst, as if she can't believe it's real. "My pretty boys," she whispers.

The table is lit from within, a soft bone-blue glow like a ghost, which is exactly what it is. Before each of us are the messages we sent to our families and loved ones—except for Stefan's. He presses his palms hard to his eyes. Walter rubs his back.

"I didn't know," Stefan rasps, his voice tired from the years of sleep.

"He didn't send any messages," Sarah whispers.

I nod. What a terrible feeling for his family on Earth—to wait for his message, to see reports of the others and their final letters, and to never receive their own.

Poor Stefan.

A gentle tone sounds, and I look down at the table.

2,783 messages retrieved.

"What's this?" I ask.

"You're the communications specialist," Mikael says.

* * *

2,783 messages.

The sum total of missives sent to the *Arecibo* from Earth following our entry into the Long Sleep. Most are reports from the WSA—status updates on major events. It is an otherworldly feeling, thumbing through them and seeing tiny bites of history. They read like fictions: *North Korea. Nuclear detonation. Dissolved democracy.* It's like reading an alternate history, a science fiction novel.

The WSA is gone, we learn. The World Space Association was disbanded in 2142—"They couldn't have waited until we woke up?" Walter asks—which explains the dead air on the networks.

The United States is gone as well.

"All empires fall," says Heidi, but she says it in a haunted voice.

The rest of the messages are personal ones.

Sarah has dozens from her parents. Heidi's boys have recorded hours of video—she's a grandmother. Each of the crew has countless messages. Stefan has many, and this seems to cheer him.

I have one.

* * *

It's a video.

I don't recognize her at first. Her blond hair is brown now, her green eyes steady. She is outdoors, at a picnic table. The sky is pink behind her—dawn over the trees. She's backlit, partially in rose-colored shadow. She stares into the camera, and opens her mouth once, then twice, as if she isn't sure where to begin. A nervous smile, and I see her then: I see her mother in her upside-down smile, the smile that should by all rights be a frown but isn't. I see myself in her eyes. She is older than I am now.

Elle.

Nine hours of video.

"Daddy," she says, looking straight into the camera. Her voice is strong and a little scratchy, like her mother's.

I remember her wrinkled pink skin, her insignificant weight in my hands. Her strange smell, her little fish mouth gasping at the air.

"Boots!"

Her tiny fingers—opening, closing.

A-da.

A tear slides down her cheek. I am struck by her beauty and how much of an adult she has become. I have so many questions for her, and I will never be able to ask any of them.

"I hold you always," she says, repeating my own confused words back to me.

Her tears spill over, and so do mine, my long sleep over, my dark age turned to light.

A Word from Jason Gurley

The Dark Age is one of those stories that is born out of frustration, and worry, and fear—all the emotions that seem to either produce great art or completely drown it before it can take a breath. I wrote this story during a perfect storm of circumstances. I'd lost my job a couple of months before, and I'd just gone on my twentieth or fiftieth interview, and nobody was slapping money down on the table. I was working long, long hours on freelance and book cover design projects, trying to keep some income in the pipe. And I'd just listened to a literary agent tell me that the most important thing I've ever written had "too much character" and not enough plot. Through all of this I was just missing my daughter, who at the time was two years old. My wife and I both work very hard— she works exceptionally hard and long days as a full-time mother to our little girl, and I work as hard as I can to keep food on the table for all three of us. There are days when I leave the house before six a.m. and don't get home until midnight, and every waking hour between is spent working and missing my family.

The Dark Age came from that. Children grow up so fast, and there's nothing worse than discovering that in the moment when you weren't looking, they've learned seven new things—and in the moment that it takes you to light up with joy about these new things, they've grown bored with those new things and have moved on to a dozen more. Keeping up is not easy, particularly when you aren't always there.

I started writing this story one afternoon in a public library. I was supposed to be designing a book cover for an author, and this small idea in my head wouldn't stop nagging me. I set the book cover aside and began writing, and within a few pages I knew that I couldn't keep writing the story in the library. The story was taking a sledgehammer to my insides. So I packed up my laptop, walked outside, and sat in the passenger seat of my Jeep for another hour, and wrote the rest of the story. It completely wrecked me. Two months after writing it, I still can't read it without feeling the same way.

Short stories like this one, at least for me, don't come along all that often. I don't know if *The Dark Age* is good, or if it's sentimental crap. What I do know is that it got under my skin, and that I hear from new readers every week who tell me that it tore their heart out to read it—not literally, of course, though readers have used those words. And maybe a story that has that effect on readers doesn't have to be good or bad. Maybe a story that does that is *true*. I can't think of a better thing for a story to be.

The Dark Age is dedicated to my little girl, Squish. When readers order a signed paperback edition of the story from my website, they don't just get my signature on the title page— they get my daughter's Crayola autograph as well. This story is as much hers as it is mine, and I hope one day she's proud of me for having written it for her.

Afterword

Writing a time travel story… it's almost a rite of passage for a science fiction author. Isaac Asimov, Robert A. Heinlein, H. G. Wells, Kurt Vonnegut, Michael Crichton, Gene Wolfe, Stephen King, Jack Finney, Joe Haldeman, Robert Charles Wilson—all have written stories of time travel. Even Charles Dickens (*A Christmas Carol*, 1843) and Mark Twain (*A Connecticut Yankee in King Arthur's Court*, 1889) got in on the action—trendsetters both, as it turned out.

And in TV and film, stories of time travel have, if anything, been even more popular. *Star Trek* alone, in its many incarnations, has incorporated time travel into a whopping forty-nine different TV episodes and four of its feature films, according to fan site Memory Alpha. Box-office smashes like *Back to the Future* and *The Terminator* have grossed millions and launched franchises. Mind-benders like *Primer*, *Donnie Darko*, and *TimeCrimes* (*Los Cronocrímenes*) have gained huge cult followings. And Bill and Ted's adventure was so excellent that they followed it up with a *Bogus Journey*.

One might think—given all this—that time travel has been done to death. That the well has run dry. That there is nothing left to enjoy, nothing new to learn—no more insights into human nature, no more bewildering paradoxes, no more ripping adventures. No chance of an "original take" on a tired trope—just one more protagonist breaking free of time and traipsing naïvely through history.

And yet.

As the authors in this collection have masterfully demonstrated, "time travel" is definitely not a pre-fab, cookie-cutter story outline that limits the author. There is no finite well of "time travel stories" that will eventually be tapped. These thirteen authors were each given the same instructions—*Write a short story involving time travel*—and yet they came up with thirteen stories that couldn't be more different from one another, more varied, or more original: moving, intellectual, gut-wrenching, gritty, insightful, haunting, and just plain fun. In skilled hands, the time travel device doesn't constrain the storyteller—it liberates her. It allows her, and the reader along with her, to grapple directly with powerful emotions and concepts like regret, love, purpose, and mortality.

It also lets us explore what would happen if a pack of ravenous tyrannosaurs ran into a team of Navy SEALs with machine-gun-mounted Humvees. And that's pretty damn cool.

I want to thank the thirteen wonderful, amazing, talented authors who created *Synchronic*. I'm honored to be associated with them all. And if writing a time travel story is a rite of passage, I'm thrilled to have played a small role in initiating such talented authors as these into the club.

And a special thanks to Michael Bunker, my partner in bringing *Synchronic* to life. This anthology was his idea in the first place, he recruited the bulk of the talent, and I'll always be grateful to him for bringing me on board. Michael's readers already know that he's a brilliant author, but I can assure you that he's more than that: he's also a talented collaborator, a good man, and my friend.

David Gatewood
May 2014

A Note to Readers

Thank you so much for reading our stories; we hope you enjoyed them. And if you did, could we ask of you a very small favor?

Would you write a short review at the site where you purchased the book?

Reviews are make-or-break for authors. A book with no reviews is, simply put, a book with no future sales. This is because a review is more than just a message to other potential buyers: it's also a key factor driving the book's visibility in the first place. More reviews (and more positive reviews) make a book more likely to be featured in bookseller lists (such as Amazon's "also viewed" and "also bought" lists) and more likely to be featured in bookseller promotions. Reviews don't need to be long or eloquent; a single sentence is all it takes. In today's publishing world, the success (or failure) of a book is truly in the reader's hands.

So please, write a review. Tell a friend. Share us on Facebook. Maybe even write a Tweet (140 characters is all we ask). You'd be doing these authors a great service.

In fact, go ahead and do it now.

There is, after all, no time like the present.

Made in United States
Orlando, FL
31 August 2022

21792797R00253